The Ma

To Bookstore Barley

Edmund Kman

The Magdalene Code

Edmund Kwaw

Copyright © 2007 Edmund Kwaw
All rights reserved.
ISBN: 1-4196-6008-X
ISBN-13: 978-1419660085

Visit www.booksurge.com to order additional copies.

The Magdalene Code

PROLOGUE

Jerusalem AD 32

"This is heresy," Jakob fumed, leaping to his feet. "Why should we believe that the Master would not come directly to us with his request! Why would he entrust his teachings to a woman? He spat out the last words as if they tasted badly. "If," he snorted, "the teachings she claims to possess are even his." He slammed a closed fist on the table causing the crude wooden structure to shudder. "We should not permit this—we cannot permit it!" The burly Jakob, panting from the exertion of his outburst, dropped heavily back into this seat.

Raucous voices of accord and dissension erupted in the secret cave's inner chamber and echoed through its dark passages. Seldom had the elderly leaders of the Silent Brotherhood raised their voices, much less expressed such deep emotions. With the cowls of their dark robes pushed back on their shoulders, the seven exposed faces grew animated in the amber glow of the candles.

The air in the cave was damp, sweetened by the mixture of moss, burning herbs and candles burning in crude wooden sconces. Uncertain shadows flickered against the soft sandstone walls; the floor, enveloped in darkness, was cool under their sandaled feet, a contrast to the desert landscape without.

Miriam, hands trembling under the folds of her coarse hand-woven robe, stood motionless before the vigorous debate. Only hours earlier she had been blindfolded and escorted in silence to the inner sanctum of the cave, which, until this moment, she hadn't known existed.

Rising from his place of authority at the centre of the table, Eli, senior member of the Silent Brotherhood, the Grand Master of the lodge, raised his hand. Instantly, the chamber hushed against the distant echoes. Eli cleared his throat and looked at the woman, "Miriam," he asked gently, "how do we know that what you say is true?"

She stared at the row of elders, hoping to conceal her nervousness as she searched for the right words, the most appropriate response to Eli's challenge. Seconds seemed to stretch into hours, but the men, mostly out of respect for Eli, extended a modicum courtesy as they patiently awaited her response. Jakob, still red-faced from his protestations, shifted restlessly in his seat as he stared intently at Miriam as whispers rustled around him.

Miriam lowered her head, inhaled deeply, and then exhaled slowly as she reminded herself that she was the initiate of the Master. The Master had taught her well; she had nothing to fear. A calm assuredness washed over her frail body as she raised her head, gazed from one face to another, commanding their attention.

"You do not know that what I say is true," she began carefully. Seven pairs of eyes gleamed in the dark, ebony pinpoints riveted to her face. "You also do not know that what I say is false." She paused, allowing her words to finish the brief echo in the stone chamber. "But what reason do you have to doubt the truth of what I say? For, if it was not the Master who sent me—how would I have known of your existence?"

A murmuring crescendo filled the cold stone room as the seven old men discussed the merits of her response. Then Joshua, the Warden of the secret lodge, rose from his seat, one place to the right of Eli, and turned to Miriam.

"Miriam, " he paused with disdain, and inhaled deeply. "Why can you not disclose to us the contents of the Scroll that you say the Master has authored? Why would the Master now prevent us from learning his teachings if the Scroll contains his true teachings?"

Nods and murmurs of approval accompanied the statement and the men stared expectantly in the direction of Miriam.

Angry, Miriam clenched her fists under the folds of her handwoven robe. She felt like storming out of the room, rejecting these frail old men, pathetic figures engaged in a way of life the Master had rejected. They did not deserve to be the custodians of the wisdom of the Master. She reassured herself that their petty questioning was part of the Master's design, exhaled slowly and turned and calmly faced Joshua. "I cannot disclose the contents of the Scroll because that is the dictate of the Master." She paused and turned toward Eli. "The Master said that the teachings are for the sons and daughters of another age. They are not for the sons and daughters of this age. It is not for me to understand why the Master requested that it be so, but only to follow his precepts."

"That is not acceptable," Jakob bellowed from where he sat

"Miriam," said another man who sat at the left end of the table. "My brothers Eli, Jakob and Joshua have spoken well. What they say comes from a fear that we all share—that the contents of the Scroll may not be what you say it is. Tell me this, why would the Master entrust you and not us with such a Scroll?"

Miriam looked around at the old men. "How dare they challenge the judgement of the Master," she mused. She lowered her head for a few seconds to calm herself. "Did the Master not always seek to teach us lessons? Perhaps in entrusting me with the Scroll the Master sought to teach us another lesson. In truth, I, like you, cannot explain why the Master entrusted his writings to me." Miriam looked doubtfully at the men.

"This age that you speak of, how will the sons and daughters of this age know when it is upon them?" The man called Joshua said.

"There will be a sign in the heavens, and those who see it shall know that the age is upon them," said Miriam.

"I have heard enough." Eli rose from where he sat and stared intently at Miriam. "I do believe that Miriam speaks the truth and that the Scroll contains the Master's teachings." He paused, faced the men, turning first to those on his right and then on his left. "It is worthy that we give her the assistance she requests for it is the assistance sought by the Master."

The members of the Silent Brotherhood rose as one and without a word, followed Eli and Miriam along several dark tunnels to the gloomy depths of a smaller cave. The echoes of their sandaled footsteps merged with the sounds of trickling water, creating a rhythmic pattern, a prelude to a chant.

Joshua walked to a far end of the cave and pushed a wooden lever. With a grating sound, a small stone partition gave way, revealing a small cavern hewn in the cave's wall. He lit large candles perched on two natural sconces carved into the raw stone. They all turned and looked expectantly at Miriam. Only the sound of dripping water punctuated the cave's tomb-like ambiance.

From the folds of her robe Miriam retrieved a soft leather satchel bound with a leather string. Twenty-four by twelve inches, still warm from her body, it fit easily in her hands. Gingerly cradling it, she raised her eyes and slowly walked towards the cavern, oblivious to the faces that scanned her own. She focused on the small cavern that had been created many decades ago by the Brotherhood.

Reaching the cavern's lip, Joshua pointed to an unadorned earthenware jar on the ground. Miriam knelt down and dropped the leather satchel into the jar, secured the lid, then lifted the damp vessel into the shadows. Standing, she took one last glimpse of the jar, and then moved to the side. Joshua pushed the wooden lever once more, and the stone cover ground into place over the opening. He picked up a rock from the floor of the cave and struck the wooden lever until it broke. The cavern with its contents was forever sealed.

Two members of the brotherhood retrieved large wooden bowls containing a mixture of dry clay, gravel and hay to which they added water, stirring and kneading until it thickened to mortar consistency. Then they applied the thick paste to the rock surfaces, obliterating the opening. Finished, they retreated to their places, followed by Miriam. The assembly of the Silent Brotherhood sat in meditation for over an hour while the clay mixture hardened.

After the meditation, Joshua walked up to the sealed wall, inspected it, and nodded his approval to the others. As a single unit, the Members rose and walked in single file out of the cave, taking another route from the one that brought them to the inner cavern. Reaching the outside, the men placed rocks over the cave's entrance until it was blocked, and then sealed it with a mixture of red clay, stones and dried grass, camouflaging it to blend into the arid landscape. Satisfied with their work, the hooded figures threaded their way down the rocky hill, each wondering what secrets rested inside the Scroll, secrets of the Master, secrets for another age. No one looked back at the cavern. None of them would ever return to the site.

※

Haw River, North Carolina, May 7, 1972

Shrill voices, punctuated by the rumble of running feet, erupted into the sunny silence of the playground as the children exploded out of the doors of the Agnes Mildred Elementary School.

Six-year old Marianne Waters skipped hand-in-hand with her best friend, Megan Fellows, to a sand box about ten feet away from the swings. Sitting on the warm dry surface, they plunged tiny shovels beneath the surface into the moist sand below and started filling tiny buckets. They always built sand castles, just like they did at the beach. They liked to pretend that they were at the beach.

Marianne scooped a mound of sand, placed it in her bright red bucket, compacted the sand, then flopped it over and slowly removed the bucket to leave a perfectly moulded sand tower. She began making another mound when she heard someone call her name. "Marianne."

"Just a minute, I'm coming," she said, not looking up, still focusing on filling her bucket.

"Who are you talking to?" Megan asked, a confused look wrinkling her little face

"You said my name," Marianne retorted.

"No I didn't."

"Did too!"

"*Did not!*"

Marianne patted the side of the second mound she had made and raised her head to confront Megan. Before she could utter a word, she felt a tingling sensation run up her back. As if compelled, Marianne swung her head around to face a tree a short distance away from the playground. She saw the woman—stunningly beautiful with long dark hair that framed her pale face and flowed past her shoulders. She wore a long white gown that reminded Marianne of the dress one of her teachers had worn in the school's Christmas play.

The woman pointed to Megan, then raised a finger to her lips; with her other hand, she beckoned to Marianne.

Entranced, Marianne stood, filled with a mixture of fear and wonderment. She felt her little hands go clammy and she dropped the sand bucket. The woman waved to Marianne. Almost involuntarily, she waved back.

"Who are you waving to?" Megan demanded. She rose from the sand box and stood beside Marianne, peering into the trees.

"The lady over there, silly," she said without removing her eyes from the woman

"Where? What lady?".

"Over there, by the tree," Marianne pointed in the direction of the tree.

"I don't see any lady, Marianne! I don't like this game! Stop it or I'm telling," Megan shouted in her tiny voice, frightened and exasperated at the same time.

Marianne felt confused; her head felt a little dizzy. She looked at the woman and then at Megan. Why couldn't Megan see the woman?

The woman looked at Marianne, once again raised her finger to her lips and beckoned to Marianne.

Marianne remembered that she had been warned never to talk to strangers, but she felt oddly drawn to the woman in a way she could not explain. She stepped out of the sand box and started walking towards the woman.

"Where are you going Marianne?" Megan chimed.

"I'm coming," Marianne said.

"Where are you going, Marianne?" Megan pleaded.

"I'm coming," she called to the woman, and then over her shoulder to Megan, she said, "I'm just going to see the woman."

"What woman? I'll tell teacher that you were talking to a stranger, Marianne," Megan whined, petulantly stamping her foot.

Marianne whirled around, stuck a tongue out at Megan, turned toward the woman, and dreamily walked towards the tree. If Marianne had been paying attention, she would have noticed as the sounds of the children gradually faded into a distant vortex. She glanced over her shoulder to Megan running toward the school and the other children playing, but she could hear no sounds. It was as if she had stepped out of one world into another. Marianne began to feel frightened, but a controlling force seemed to drive her little legs forward. When she reached the woman, the shade of the tree seemed to envelop them; the air around them was still. Silence fell like a blanket around their shoulders.

"Hello, Marianne," said the woman, her voice kind and soft.

"Hello," Marianne said hesitantly. She was standing about three feet away from the woman. "Who are you?"

"I'm a friend." The woman held out her hand to Marianne. "Come, Marianne, I will not hurt you."

"What's your name?" Marianne's voice trembled with a strange mixture of excitement and apprehension. She kept her hands by her side.

"Same as yours—Marianne," said the woman.

"Really?"

"Really."

"Who are you?" Marianne asked again.

"I'm your friend. You're not afraid of me, are you, Marianne?"

Marianne shook her head, reached for the woman's hand and stepped closer until she could reach out and touch the glowing white garment.

"Do you like my dress?"

Marianne's eyes darted to the woman's face; she nodded.

"Come, let's sit and talk for a bit. Here, sit by the tree." The woman sat down against the tree trunk, gracefully folding the white garment around her slender frame. Marianne sat down beside her.

"Teacher will be angry," Marianne said quietly, as if imparting a secret. "I'm not supposed to talk to strangers."

"Don't worry, Marianne. You'll be fine. You are the only one who can see me. No one else can—not even teacher."

"Really?" Marianne chimed in wonderment.

"Really."

Marianne giggled and the woman smiled as she put an arm around Marianne's shoulder, gently pulling the child closer to her

"How did you know my name? Did teacher tell you?"

"No. But I know a lot about you, Marianne. Do you want to know why I called you?"

"Uh-huh," Marianne nodded. Though she felt unsure of herself, she felt calm in the woman's embrace.

"I came to tell you that you have a special gift. You will do something very important when you grow up," the woman intoned. "Do you believe me?"

"Yes. What will I do?"

"When the time comes, you will know, Marianne."

Marianne remained silent.

"Are you afraid, Marianne?" The beautiful woman raised her brows; a small smile crossing her lips widened.

Marianne nodded. A feeling of dread filled her as a whimper involuntarily escaped her throat. She understood what the woman was telling her, but she could not explain what it was, or how she understood.

"You will not see me again for a long time," the woman said softly, "but I will see you again when you grow up."

"Where will I see you?"

"Right here. We'll meet here when you grow up. She unclasped a silver pendant from around her neck, held it in her hand in front of the child. Marianne stared in awe at it until the woman's long pale fingers curled over it's gleaming surface. "Lets bury this pendant right here to mark the spot."

The woman easily scooped out a small hole in the earth beside the tree and placed the pendant in it. Together, Marianne and the woman covered the hole.

"Will you come tomorrow?" Marianne said.

"No, Marianne. I'll come back when you grow up. You'll know when to come and see me, OK?"

Marianne nodded solemnly, no longer afraid, but shivering a little with excitement.

"Can you keep a secret, Marianne?" The woman's face looked deeply into the child's, an eyebrow arched to punctuate the query.

"Yes, yes I can."

"Everything that I've told you is our little secret—just between you and me. We mustn't tell anyone about the pendant, OK?"

"OK," Marianne nodded.

"Friends?" The woman held out a curved little finger. Marianne, grinning, extended her little finger and curved it around the woman's.

"You've got to go now, Marianne. Your teacher is coming. Bye."

"Bye," Marianne said.

Marianne rose from where she sat beside the tree and swiftly walked towards the school.

"Marianne! Marianne Waters!" Mrs. Delisle, Marianne's teacher, Megan in tow, marched across the playground. The child ran to her teacher.

"Where have you been, Marianne Waters?"

Marianne didn't like it when her teacher called her by her full name; it meant trouble.

"She said she was going to talk to a stranger," Megan prattled. "She was talking to a stranger."

"I was...I was...."

Marianne cast one last look at the woman. The woman winked to her as she placed her finger over her lips. Marianne smiled and winked.

"Sorry, Mrs. Deslisle. I was just playing by the tree."

"She's lying. She said she was going to talk to a *stranger*. That's what she said," Megan protested, glaring at Marianne.

Mrs. Deslisle cast her eyes around the playground, then reined in the child clinging to her skirts. "Shush, Megan Fellows. You shouldn't tell lies. Look—there's no one here." Megan looked crushed. She glanced pleadingly to Marianne then to Mrs. Deslisle. The teacher whirled on her heels and started back to the building. "Come on you two, play time is over."

Marianne flicked out her tongue out at Megan as she merrily skipped after Mrs. Deslisle. Just before she passed through the school doors, Marianne glanced over her shoulder. The beautiful mysterious woman was gone.

CHAPTER 1

Hebron, Israel, December 15, 1997

The midday sun relentlessly scorched the Hebron Valley. Rivulets of sweat poured from under Ben Rabin's cap down his large face streaking the dust on his shirtless pot-bellied torso. Silently he cursed the heat as he deftly shifted the bulldozer's gears and skilfully manoeuvred the large machine through the dry valley. Shifting mounds of sand and rock to carefully designated areas of the site, Rabin's work was to make way for the construction of new Jewish settlements.

The machine's arm rose with protesting squeals as it lifted load after load from the pit. The air was motionless, but the sand created a little dust storm around the intruding machine. Rabin wiped the sweat pouring into his eyes with the back of his hand and felt the grit scratch his skin. He pushed another lever to move the arm back into the pit when he noticed a dark object on the sand pile.

The sight of a foreign object was not unusual—excavators like Rabin often came across odd shaped rocks, even animal bones, and most times he only gave the objects a passing glance. This, however, was different: the dark object looked like a clay jar. He felt a ripple of excitement. He knew ancient clay jars fetched a good price in the antiquities markets.

Rabin cleared his throat loudly, spewed out a ball of sandy phlegm over his shoulder, and jumped out of the bulldozer. Heart beating in anticipation, he scrambled up the mound, grasping at protruding grass tufts and stones to keep his balance and prevent himself from sliding. Near the top, he lunged and grabbed the jar, lost his balance, and slid to the base of the rocky pile. Capturing his treasure, he was oblivious to the muddy scratches on his belly.

Sitting in the shade of the bulldozer, its diesel idling noisily behind him, he scraped the jar's encrusted surface. Rotating it in his hands, he saw that the mouth of the jar had been plugged with a lump of hardened clay. He peered through a crack in the side of the jar and saw a pale withered roll inside. He shook the jar and the thing within rattled hollowly. He licked his crusty lips; the saliva dried instantly, leaving his tongue dry. He swallowed. The clay at the jar's mouth had hardened so much that it had become integral to the vessel; even water would no longer budge it. He debated whether he should break the jar to release the contents or keep it as he'd found it. Hastily reasoning that what was inside the jar was probably more valuable than the jar itself, he rose to his feet, took a few steps and smashed it against a rock. A cylindrical object fell at his feet; bronzed, the same colour as the dusty landscape, it appeared to be stiffened leather rolled around an inner core and secured in the middle with corded leather draw-strings.

With some trepidation, he glanced around to see if he was being observed. As he retrieved the brittle container at his feet, he squeezed it cautiously. Nothing happened. He held the roll to one eye and tried to peer into the tightly wrapped bundle, but he could not see inside. Rabin shifted the roll to his nose and sniffed. A faint stale smell tickled his crinkled nose, but he couldn't tell what it was. Probably some preservative, he reasoned.

Rabin hesitated, suddenly aware of a whispering hot breeze caressing the wet rivulets on his upper body. He wiped greasy sweaty palms on his dirty jeans, sat down again in the shade, and loosened the strings. The cylinder of leather groaned in protest as it reluctantly unfurled to reveal a tightly rolled parchment two feet wide and unlike any material that he had seen before. He blew at the particles of sand that clung to it and stuck the nail of his little finger underneath one edge. He could not open the rolled parchment leaves and only succeeded in ripping a little piece of fiber from the matted pages. Entirely freeing the curled parchment from the protective leather cover, he again raised the paper to his eyes and tried to peer into its hollow end. He could make out some writing.

Rabin was disappointed. The leather and the parchment probably weren't very valuable, but perhaps he could sell them separately and increase his profit. He replaced the bundle in its leather cocoon, and looped the ends of the brittle leather strings around the casing. Panting profusely, he pulled himself up into the driver's carriage, stashed the bundle in a dirty towel, tossed it into an Adidas bag under the seat, then shoved the big machine into gear.

⁂

"How much?" Rabin wore the pained expression of someone who'd swallowed a bitter pill and was trying to decide whether he should take a second one.

"Not very much—sorry," the man across the counter shrugged without making eye contact with the sweaty hulk before him.

The two men stood under a narrow awning in Jaffa's open market, shielded from the sun, but not escaping the breathless heat.

"How much?" Rabin hissed. He'd pressed the man for a price five times in the last fifteen minutes.

"What is this anyway?" The man gently picked up the roll of parchment, squinted as he sniffed at it. He placed it back on the counter, grimaced as he thoughtfully tugged at his long beard.

Rabin grew frustrated. "How should *I* know what it is—you're the expert. You're supposed to know about these things."

"Well," the merchant shrugged, "that's why I can't give you much for it." He pinched a corner of the bundle, lifted it disdainfully a quarter inch, and sniffed, "Look. The whole thing's stuck together—may never know what's written on it. Could just be a common inventory of goods. It may be worthless."

"You know it's not worthless, you cunning jackal," Rabin exploded. "It not worthless if it's been..." he broke off in mid shout, suddenly self-conscious. The artifact police could be listening. "Buried," he hissed, finishing the thought with a glare. He gritted his teeth and leaned forward, nearly touching the merchant's nose. "And it could be priceless. Look at it. Have you ever seen anything like this paper before?" Clearly, Rabin's patience was beginning to wane; he stepped back, arm extended, ready to pluck the bundle from the counter.

"Tell you what I'll do for you. Leave it with me and let me find out what it is then I'll know better."

"Ira. You insult me. I wasn't born yesterday! What do you take me for? A fool? So. I leave it with you and you find out that it is priceless, you'll tell me it's no good." Rabin gestured wildly with his arms; time to close the deal. "You don't want to pay me now? Give it to me and I'll find another dealer." He reached for the parchment, knowing that Ira Grossman, a prominent antiquities dealer would never let him take it away. They both knew that there was a market for these rarities.

This scenario wasn't new to the two men; they'd done business before. This practiced dance of greed became a mere prelude to the inevitable exchange of money—each believing he'd given too much and received too little.

"No need to be hasty, Rabin. I was only trying to protect myself. If I buy it from you, I take a big risk that it is worthless." Ira pleaded.

"And if it is valuable, you'll make a killing," Rabin said, keeping to the well-worn script. How often had they reached this impasse before?

This wasn't the first time the excavating contractor had brought antiquities to the dealer.

"Five hundred shekels. That's my last price." Ira lifted one shoulder to his ear and glanced away from Rabin.

"Add another five hundred and I'll not bother you again." Rabin moved his hand away from the bundle.

"Three hundred," came the quick retort.

"Two hundred."

"Done."

The two men quickly shook hands. Sighing, Ira counted seven hundred shekels and handed the money to Rabin, who licked his lips as he quickly pocketed the bills.

"Thanks. Always nice doing business with you, Ira." Rabin sauntered away, softly whistling to himself.

Ira Grossman replaced the roll of parchment in the dirty leather cocoon. He had no idea what he had, but he had a feeling that it was valuable. He had a nose for valuable things—and he could smell value in the parchment. Smiling to himself, he secreted the leather tube into an empty clay jar and slid the lid into place. He lifted the innocuous jar to a shelf behind the counter; he would keep it there until he found the right buyer. It wouldn't, he smiled to himself, take long.

CHAPTER 2

Hebron, Israel, September 30, 1998

Michael Bailey strolled through the Jaffa market. At five foot eight with short dark hair, he didn't stand out from the crowd, but blended into the hustle of determined local shoppers. A collector, he'd developed an intuition for rare and valuable artifacts and had come to Israel looking for something unique. Bypassing the usual tourist crap, he sauntered along an alley known for its rare offerings. He'd been here many times before, done business with some of the merchants, but knew enough to keep his expectations and his interest at a minimum. If the truth were known, Michael didn't know exactly what it was he was looking for—only that he would know when he found it.

Since his arrival in Israel a week ago, he'd visited to several locations—markets at Bezalel, Carmel and Nachlat Binyamin—but nothing had attracted his attention. Relentlessly, he'd scoured every antiquities stall, engaged several of his contacts in conversation, but whatever it was that compelled his search, it was not to be found. He moved on to Tel Aviv.

As his eyes swept over the numerous stalls crowding the Jaffa market, he recognized an antiques dealer nearly hidden among the general merchants. The sign on the awning announced the establishment's wares in both Hebrew and English. Michael strode purposefully towards the stall and within a few strides of reaching the counter, a man who had been sitting at the back moved forward to meet him.

"Can I help you, sir?"

"Hi. Michael Bailey." Michael stretched out his hand; the other man grasped it and shook. "Just looking to see what you have."

The man removed his hand and touched it to his chest. "Ira Grossman," he nodded, completing the introduction. "You're American, yes?"

Michael nodded as his eyes swept the shelves behind the shop's owner.

"What exactly are you looking for?"

Michael leveled his eyes to Ira's, looked directly into his face and smiled wanly. "Would you believe me if I told you that I don't know, but that I will know when I see it?" he said charmingly.

"I would. I would, indeed, sir. You are like me, you have the nose for quality antiques." Grossman grinned as he tapped the side of his nose to emphasize the point. "Well, look at some of my treasures in this case and on the counter. I'm sure you will find something you like," he demurred.

Michael walked slowly along the length of the glass case, closely examining the crush of items; he raised his head and scanned the items stacked precariously on the shelf behind the counter. To the unpracticed eye, it was a collection of the mundane, but Michael knew that this was where the precious could be openly concealed. His eyes quickly passed over religious minutiae, old dolls, statues of the Blessed Virgin, and an old turntable. Ira focused on every movement of his customer's eyes until he registered an almost imperceptible flicker as Michael's gaze swept the earthen jar.

"Ah. Let me show you something that might interest you." Grossman said. A smile spread thinly across his lips.

Grossman walked to the back of the stall and disappeared. Michael could hear the entrepreneur rummaging in boxes, and shortly, the man returned with a chunk of firewood.

"Perhaps this is what you are looking for?"

"Looks like a piece of wood to me."

"Are you a Christian, Mr. Bailey?" Grossman pretended to be taken aback, a disarming tactic.

"Why do you ask?"

"Well, if you are this may mean something to you." He leaned forward, proffering the firewood as if it were sheathed in gold.

Bailey glanced at it. He wasn't going to bite; it was an old trick. He didn't know what Grossman was up to, but he'd only play for a short time longer.

"Sorry. I don't get it. Maybe its because I'm not that religious."

"Not to worry. This has been with me for a long time." Grossman gazed lovingly at the chunk of wood. "There are many stories surrounding it." Grossman's eyes gleamed like those of a child. "One of the stories is that it is part of the stump to which Christ was tied when he was flogged." Still gazing at the piece of worthless wood, he continued. "There are those who say it is part of the Cross. But," he shrugged, "what do I know." Another self-depreciating shrug. "It was given to my Grandfather, who gave it to my Father, who gave it to me…"

Michael cut him off. Enough was enough; this guy was wasting his time. "Not interested." Bailey shook his head at Grossman, clearly intending to move on.

With one hand Grossman dropped the log in a basket behind the counter and with the other reached for Michael's sleeve. "Wait, I think I have something else you may like." Grossman searched behind the counter and selected an earthenware jar. Removing the lid, he slid his slender fingers into the opening and tenderly retrieved a fragile leather tube. It emerged from the jar trailing brittle leather strings. The object seemed to glow in Grossman's gentle embrace.

Michael checked himself. He was too much of a pro to reveal how attracted he was to the mysterious pouch, but a small shiver ran up his spine. "So, what have you there?"

"Wait and see." Grossman placed the pouch delicately on the counter, untied the strings and opened the wallet to reveal the roll of parchment. Michael watched as Grossman used his fingertips to slowly peel the edge of the parchment; he secured the free end with paperweights before gently unfurling the rest of the scroll so that the entire page lay flat on the counter. Bailey estimated that the whole parchment was three feet long by about a foot wide.

"So, what do you think?" Grossman, gestured with two upturned palms, barely able to contain his excitement,

"What is it?" Michael said blandly.

Grossman dodged the question with a shrug then elaborated, "A construction worker in the Hebron Valley brought to me—his machine dug it up. When I got it, it was all stuck together, but I kept it in the jar, and see? Maybe the air dried it, made it loose. So? What do you think, my friend?" Grossman grinned and leaned closer to Michael. "Looks valuable does it not?" he whispered.

Bailey peered closely at the parchment, heart beating so loudly in his ears that he feared the merchant could hear it. "Can't say. Can you read it?"

"No." Grossman shook his head. "But surely, it must be some ancient language." He emphasized the word *ancient*.

"How much?"

"Three thousand US." Grossman tilted his head sideways and looked at Bailey as ingenuously as possible.

"Three thousand? US? Jeez. That's too much. Especially since you can't read what it says."

"Ah, but *someone* will be able to read it. I just have not bothered to take it to the University to have it interpreted. I'm a very busy businessman." Grossman slowly shook his head as if to underline the sacrifice he was making. "Looks like Hebrew, maybe *very* ancient Hebrew." He knew that this hook would be successful; a secret smile slipped across his lips as he licked them.

"Look, I'll give you two thousand US for it. I think that's a fair price."

"Make it two thousand five and you can have it...even though I know it's worth more."

"OK two thousand five."

New York, February 27, 1999
Congested with boxes of all shapes and sizes, the small suburban basement that doubled as Michael's workplace and storage space was furnished with tables and shelves filled with artifacts. In the centre of this controlled chaos was a small desk illuminated by a reading lamp.

Michael tugged at the door of a small wall safe and removed the leather bound parchment. Gently, he placed the fragile package on the desk that was covered with acid-free linen. He'd been back from Israel almost a week, but this was the first he'd had time to examine it.

He spread the leather tube until it released the parchment. Donning white cotton gloves, he carefully lifted the parchment from the leather and placed it on a glass tray. Taking a pair of small soft plastic tweezers, he slowly peeled back both corners at the end of the scroll and then gently glued them to the glass tray with a special biodegradable, reversible adhesive. Then he slowly and carefully unrolled the rest of the scroll. He tilted the work lamp so that the beam of light fell directly on the parchment and adjusted the arm of the magnifying glass to focus on the text.

As he slowly moved the lense across the parchment, he made notes. The writing, as he had presumed, had Semitic characters, but most of them he couldn't recognize. The composition of the parchment material also eluded him; he hadn't seen anything like it before. He prepared a tiny fragment and dropped it into a glass tube with a screw cap; he'd send it to the lab for analysis and dating. Michael rose from the desk and returned with a Polaroid camera. After angling the light away from its surface, he photographed different sections of the parchment. When he'd finished, he released the parchment, allowed it to return to it's natural rolled shape, and placed it in the protective leather case. He returned it to the wall safe and locked the vault's door.

Michael paused in front of the safe, sensing as he had in the Jaffa market, that this scroll was meant to be in his hands. He had found what he'd been looking for—without knowing exactly what he had. The same shiver that travelled up his spine whenever he held the scroll returned. He extinguished the lights and walked up the stairs.

CHAPTER 3

New York City, March 11, 1999
    Three o'clock in the morning. The downtown was as gloomy as it was deserted. Traffic lights winked reflections on the wet pavement. As forecast, the rain had begun an hour earlier and swept through the city in fine sheets. Striking the warm pavement, the rain gave rise to a dense mist that whirled along the city streets. With the exception of the few stray dogs skittering along the sidewalks searching for love or sustenance, the streets were deserted. Another movement animated the street. A pale panel van, headlights dimly piercing the wet night, crept along the streets, pausing at intervals, as if lost. Pausing cautiously at each red light and stop sign, the driver took particular care not to be noticed.
    "See anyone?" the driver asked his single passenger.
    "Nope. Look, let's get on with it. There! Let's make the drop over there." The man leaned forward, pointed to the approaching side street.
    "Sure. Looks good. Never made a drop here, have we?"
    "Nope."
    "Okay. Get ready to unload the cargo," the driver said, smirking at his own joke.
    At a stop sign the van slowed, then made a swift right into a side street. The passenger, caught off guard by the sudden turn, nearly lost his balance. Steadying himself, he slipped out of his seatbelt and moved into the rear of the van.
    "Here looks good." The driver slowed to a stop, glanced over his shoulder. The street was deserted. A rat ambled along the wet gutter and disappeared down a drain. Rain drumming on the roof of the van was the only sound.
    "Steady there, man." The passenger moved a large bundle wrapped in a dirty tarpaulin next to the side doors.
    The van slowly accelerated along the side street until it came to

an alley opening behind a small family restaurant. A cluster of garbage containers crowded the building's service entrance.

"Get ready," the driver hissed. "Now!"

The van slammed to a stop, the driver jumped out and ran around to the side doors in time to help unload the bulky tarp-covered bundle. It took both of them to carry it a short distance to one of the garbage bins; grunting, they heaved the awkward package over the lip. It landed with a muffled thud on the layers of garbage. Swiftly, the men returned to the van, casually slid into the seats, and quietly melted into the shadows.

New York City, March 12, 1999

The garbage truck slowly backed into position, the beeping reverse alarm blending eerily with the shrieking cries from the gulls circling the site. The driver checked his side mirrors and punched a button on the instrument panel. The truck jerked slightly as the gears of the hydraulic mechanism locked. There was a grunting sound and the rear of the truck began to rise with slow shuddering movements. The driver's eyes darted to his side mirrors until he was satisfied that the rear of the truck had reached the desired elevation; he punched another button. There was another jolt of gears as the compressed garbage tumbled from the truck's open box.

The driver grabbed his lunch box, slid down from the truck's massive cab. The mid-morning sun glinted off the sweat covering his bulging tattooed arms and illuminated complementary designs inscribed on his baldpate. Shirtless, his torso barely covered by a stained quilted vest, he wiped his face with a damp bandana retrieved from his battered jeans. He opened his lunch box, took out an apple and viciously bit into it while waving away the swarm of flies that circled his sweaty head. Out of habit, he walked to his usual vantage point at the rear of the truck and scanned the garbage disgorging from the truck. This wasn't an idle exercise: he was looking for treasure. More than once he'd scavenged discarded electronics he could sell to a scrap dealer. It was true what they said, he chuckled to himself: "One man's garbage is another man's gold."

Again, he wiped beads of sweat from his brow, took a last bite out of the apple and flung the core into the pile of garbage at his feet. At that moment, he saw the large object tumble out of the truck. Startled, he raced to the front of the truck, leaned into the passenger side and hit a button on the control panel to stop the hydraulic mechanism.

Quickly, he returned to the rear of the truck and cast his eyes over the small mountain of garbage that had already formed. He couldn't see the large object any more. Gingerly stepping forward, he began kicking at the refuse with the toe of his boot. Soon, his foot hit something pliable but firm. More curious than cautious, he bent down and slowly began pushing aside the garbage with his dirty-gloved hands.

Suddenly, he jerked his hands away from the piles as if they'd been scalded. A shudder visibly travelled through his entire body as he stared at a pallid, limp arm protruding from beneath bulging and exploding plastic garbage bags. Instinctively shifting into rescue mode, he dropped the gloves and frantically tossed aside the garbage; perhaps the person was still alive. He pulled on the hand and it easily dislodged from the froth of discarded papers and food—unfortunately, the arm emerged alone, unattached to any body. With a silent scream, the driver lost his balance, fell back on his butt, the macabre handshake still in his grasp. His boots scattered more rubbish, revealing a sickening collection of pale mangled body parts with whitish skin; ragged scarlet cuts neatly edged the ends of each severed piece.

The putrid stench of decomposition, initially indistinguishable from the stench of rotting vegetable and animal matter, suddenly engulfed him. Gasping for breath, he released his grip on the dismembered arm. The arm, with its fringe of blue fingers, fell back on the garbage with a sickening thud. Shaking uncontrollably, the driver stumbled away from the body, unable to escape the suffocating sweet smell assaulting his nostrils. When he reached the truck he doubled over and vomited on his lunch box.

New York, March 13, 1999

Lieutenant James Jackson stood at the edge of the humid garbage dump holding a hand over his nose in a feeble attempt to keep out the putrid stench radiating from piles of rotting garbage. He was tall—six foot four in his bare feet—with a dark bushy beard that covered a substantial part of his lower face. He watched the members of the forensic team with renewed respect as they uncovered and documented the dismembered body parts. Yellow police tape marking the crime scene stretched in an irregular rectangle around the dump truck and its most recent deposit. Nearby, a huge pale man crouched beside an emergency vehicle; attendants were administering oxygen. Jackson noticed that the numerous tattoos on the man's arms and skull contrasted starkly with his pale skin. Gulls, disturbed by the intruders, shrieked in annoyance.

They rose and circled close to the ground, only to alight a short distance from where they had taken flight. They repeated their frenetic dance, eager to browse the new pickings.

"Don't know how you guys do it," said Jackson to the head of the forensic team. "So what've we got?"

"Some poor bugger. Male is all we know now. We'll have more when we put him back together in the lab. Lucky we got to what's left of him before the gulls did." The crime scene investigator waved at the screaming birds. As if on cue, they swirled into another version of their voracious dance.

"Any idea what killed him?"

"Difficult to say. Looks like he's been dead for a few days, judging from the state of decomp. May have been in the dumpster for some time before the truck picked it up. But," he paused and sighed, "we may never know what killed him."

"I take it you don't think it was the dumpster that did him in?"

"Nope. Not unless dumpsters come with dissecting blades."

"And I suppose you can't perform an autopsy?"

"We could, but it could be misleading. He's been dead too long and the truck crushed most of the body parts when it compressed the garbage."

"Bummer."

"But there's something you should see," the man turned around and beckoned to some of the other members of the team. They picked up a body bag and brought it to the two men. Jackson and the investigator squatted beside it. "Better cover your nose," he warned pulling back the zipper. The ashen face of the corpse stared at them with sightless eyes. "See the forehead?"

Jackson bent down and peered closely. "Yeah, looks like he's got a gash on his forehead—lots of blood." Jackson turned to look at the investigator, a quizzical expression shifting his face. "What's the significance?"

"Look once more—closely."

Jackson covered his nose with a handkerchief and leaned over the severed head. "Sorry, still looks like gash to me."

"Yeah, it's a gash all right, but let me show you something. See the outline of the wound?" Jackson followed his gesture. "See how the gash, as you call it, appears to be very neatly drawn, very regular?" Jackson followed the investigator's finger as he traced the outline of the wound; he saw what he'd missed.

"Looks like some kind of deliberate pattern—a shape maybe," Jackson said.

"Precisely," said the investigator, a gleam of satisfaction in his eye. "It's not just one random gash. There are several cuts made on our victim's forehead; the presence of this much blood tells us someone cut into the poor guy's forehead before they killed him."

Jackson grimaced. "Looks like someone wanted to send a message to who ever found the vic," he said rising.

"Could be, but we'll know better when we have a clearer idea about what the pattern is. Maybe it's a symbol of some kind."

"Could we get a picture of it?"

"Already ordered it. Will have it ready for you first thing tomorrow."

"Thanks." Jackson turned around and walked to his car. He felt queasy. His gut told him that too many bodies were suddenly turning up in the city—too many mysterious and gristly deaths. The crime lab better start coming up with some answers. So far, he was striking zero. Intuitively he knew that there were connections to be made in the recent rash of murder victims, but he didn't know why or who was responsible. Was it a series of coincidences or was there a serial killer on the loose?

CHAPTER 4

New York City, March 31, 1999

Eyes shut, her long elegant legs folded in the lotus position, the slender dark-haired woman sat alone, naked. The spacious room, unfurnished and darkened, was illuminated by five candles, one placed at each point of the pentagram painted on the dark hardwood floor. Sitting motionless in the center of the star, she slowly lifted her lids to reveal startling green eyes that blazed like emerald chips in the candle glow.

She exhaled deeply and stretched. She felt focused, energized and excited.

The vision she'd just received had momentous ramifications for the return of the Master. She had always known that at the end of the Age of Pisces, the advent of the Age of Aquarius would bring with it new opportunities for the return of her Master and she had waited patiently for the right moment. Now the time had come—the opportunity for which she had been waiting was at hand.

Part of the vision had bothered her, especially the images of a number of faces—the opposing force. Two faces, that of an old man and a boy, she subconsciously recognized. The time would arrive when she would be compelled to eliminate the opposing force before they could interfere with her plans. She smiled to herself. The old man and the boy would have to die. She inhaled and exhaled deeply, uncurled her long legs, and in one graceful movement rose from the center of the pentagram.

She was tall, close to six feet. Stretching her arms over her head, she executed a lingering stretch before walking out of the room. Locking the door behind her, she walked with slow, cat-like steps along a dimly lit corridor past many rooms. The massive house was secluded in one of New York's most prestigious, exclusive communities.

Her movements had the fluid grace of a well-toned athlete, a sleek and dangerous predator. Reaching a door at the end of the corridor, she paused to open a concealed closet, removed a full-length black silk robe and slipped it over her head. She glanced at a mirror in the closet and straightened the shoulder seams of the robe. Feeling satisfied, she reached into the closet and brought out a ram's head mask and she slipped it over her head. Gazing at her transformed reflection through the elaborately carved eyeholes, she liked what she saw: the Chosen One. The one who had been given the responsibility of paving the way for his return. She was The Messenger.

The Messenger reached for the door, turned the doorknob and walked into a large boardroom illumined by strategically placed candles. A gong sounded as she strode into the room and the gathering of people rose and bowed their heads.

The Messenger gazed in silence at the three men and two women around a massive table: her inner circle. As they raised their heads in homage to her, she saw the look of expectancy in their eyes; she felt glad. From the multitude of people who followed her Master, she'd selected them to be her immediate associates to prepare the way for the Master's return.

Unlike The Messenger, none of these people wore any disguises, though they covered their nakedness with black silk robes identical to her own. She preferred it that way. She knew each one intimately: their professions, who the members of their families were, their talents and strengths, their vices and weaknesses. Even if they had worn disguises, they could not have prevented her from knowing them as she did, for she possessed the power to pierce the veil of minds and read their very thoughts and emotions. Her guests knew little about her and she intended to maintain the status quo.

Regally she turned to her left to look at the man known by the code name, *Wolf*, her first assistant and one of the most powerful men in the United States. In his public life, this man sat on the boards of a substantial number of Fortune 500 companies. Extremely wealthy and authoritative in his own right, his primary function was supervising the management of the Brotherhood's considerable investments both locally and abroad.

Beside Wolf, sat another man, *Jaguar*, a distinguished prelate of one of the established religious denominations. Publicly, his massive ego was hidden by a much-admired pious humility. His primary responsibility was to win Christian souls for their Master. He was her second assistant.

The Messenger looked to her right at a woman in her late forties known as *Hyena*. She was one of the most dominant persons in the fashion industry—reputedly the wealthiest woman in the world. Like the animal that inspired her code name, she was a cunning competitor particularly ruthless at taking advantage of the weaknesses of those who opposed her. Hyena was her third assistant.

Next to Wolf sat the woman known as *Fox*. The youngest member of The Messenger's inner circle, she was in her early thirties. The Messenger smiled when she glanced at Fox. Like the animal after which she was named, her beauty concealed a quick, shrewd and calculating mind. The Messenger considered Fox to be her protégé, the one who in the course of time, would be initiated into the mysteries of the Master. Despite her age, she was considered to be one of the most influential lobbyists in Washington. Fox was her fourth assistant and held the primary responsibility for public relations.

Alongside Hyena lounged another man, *Lion*, the oldest of those gathered in the room. One of the most respected jurists in the country, this venerable gentleman sat on the Supreme Court of the United States. His responsibility was legal relations — ensuring, at all costs, that there were no legal impediments to the task at hand. He was her fifth assistant.

These five persons constituted The Messenger's inner circle, and under her supervision, co-ordinated the work required by her worldwide cadre of disciples in preparation for the return of their Master. Despite their wealth and influence, these five individuals knew that they owed their positions of advantage and power to her and ultimately to the Master. They also knew that just as she had bestowed such wealth and power on each of them, she could also break them in the blink of an eye.

There was a sixth seat, apparently unoccupied, that symbolized the presence of their Master at their meeting. This seat was opposite The Messenger. She regarded it affectionately.

The Messenger dipped her head slightly, ceremonially acknowledging their homage and walked slowly to the head of the table. As she sat down, she gestured for them to be seated. Following protocol, before taking their seats, the five persons bowed in the direction of the empty seat.

"My brethren," she said, glancing at each face before continuing. "It is time. Our disciples all over the world must be notified. We must begin the search."

CHAPTER 5

New York, April 5, 1999

As Marianne Waters slammed the door of her minivan and ran up the radio station steps, her shoulder-length auburn hair swirled around her collar. A lean five foot-eleven, Marianne looked like a model, younger than her thirty-five years. As she jogged down the station's halls, she tilted her left arm and glanced at her watch—only fifteen minutes to air time. She'd been lucky to snag the last parking space on the street and now there was just enough time to grab a quick cup of coffee. Shedding her coat, she quickly walked toward the canteen.

Coffee would do her some good—help the fatigue. Lately, since the nightmares started, Marianne woke up in the mornings feeling extremely achy and lethargic. Her nightmares always followed the same script: she would find herself standing in the middle of nowhere, staring at a naked and lifeless body. The only difference between these terrifying episodes was that the face of the corpse would change. Then, predictably, as she stood staring at the body, she would be filled with a deep foreboding. In her dream, fear filling her every pore, she would begin running, afraid to look back, dreading who or what might be following her.

Every night it was the same, and then she would wake up with a jolt, out of breath. Her husband Peter would reach for her, worry etched on his face. Drenched in sweat, she would mumble something incoherent. He'd hold her then, and the two of them would eventually fall asleep in each other's arms. Lately, Peter would fall asleep before she did; sometimes she couldn't get back to sleep. Last night was like that.

Marianne sighed as she walked into the canteen. Lazily stretching to the overhead cabinet, she removed a mug and poured herself a coffee. She shut her eyes as she gulped the warm fluid. It didn't matter that it was bitter; it was sweet and hot on her scratchy throat. The brew would go a long way in restoring her energy and her voice. A few seconds later, feeling revived, she headed back along the corridor to the broadcast room. She knew that Sarah Cummings, her production manager, would already be there.

Marianne waved to Sarah as she walked into the cubicle. She cleared a space on the desk for her mug, put on the earphones, and sat. She glanced at Sarah through the glass that separated them and winked in response to Sarah's questioning frown. Sarah smiled back.

Sarah Cummings was in her late thirties but looked a decade younger. Tall, with brunette locks clipped close to her head, Sarah's genius was working the phones, screening the show's call-ins with a polite, but no-nonsense spirit.

"Don't know how you do it, Sarah," Marianne said into her microphone.

"Yeah?" Sarah's voice sounded distant over the intercom.

"Always here, bright and shiny, like a new penny."

"Right. And how are we this morning?" Sarah laughed at her own affectation.

"Shitty," said Marianne.

"More nightmares? Same thing?" Sara couldn't keep the concern out of her voice.

"Yep." Marianne shuffled her papers, organizing herself for the show. "We ready?"

"All set. Five minutes to air," Sarah said. "You know, you should see someone about those nightmares."

"Like who?"

"I don't know, someone who knows dreams."

"Like a shrink?"

"Never said that, Marianne."

"I know, just me being ratty."

"How is Peter taking it?"

"Not good. He doesn't make a big deal of it, but I know how he's feeling. I am not sure why he hasn't walked out on me. I would have walked a long time ago."

"He's a keeper that one. And, of course, he's in love with you."

"Yeah, I know, but I'm worried that this mess will get too much for him." A pain shot across her eyes; she shut them tightly to block its raging through her cranium. "Mmmm. "Give me three minutes to focus."

Marianne rolled her shoulders, placed her hands on her lap and shut her eyes. She took a few deep breaths then began the usual process of centering herself by systematically relaxing her muscles. A short while later she opened her eyes and gave Sarah a thumbs-up.

Sarah returned the gesture and pushed a button on her side of the glass partition. A green light flashed in Marianne's booth, and she responded by activating the transmit button on her console. As the intro theme to her show subsided, she leaned into the microphone.

"Good morning, New York and welcome to KRCP Radio and another edition of Psychic Connections. I'm Marianne Waters and I'll try to do my best to help any of you with your spiritual life. Always remember, though, that you have complete control over your life and what we tell you here is only a guide. You have complete free will to either accept or reject what we say. We're here to inspire and encourage." She paused, now that the required disclaimers were out of the way, she was ready to get down to business.

"Who do we have on the line, Sarah?"

"The first caller is Joanne," Sarah said.

"Hello, Joanne."

"Hello." Marianne barely heard the weak voice through her earphones; she turned up the volume.

"What question do you have for me this morning Joanne?"

"Its about my relationship."

"Okay. First give me your date of birth," Marianne said.

"April 8, 1954."

Marianne jotted down a note on her note pad. "Your question is about your relationship to...?"

"My boyfriend."

"What's his name?"

"Jim,"

"His second name?"

"Stokes."

"Stokes as in S-T-O-K-E-S?"

"Yes, that's right."

Marianne shut her eyes. Listeners could hear the woman's nervous breathing on the other end of the line. It was part of the show; Sarah didn't mute the sound.

"I don't see anything wrong with your relationship, Joanne. If anything, I sense that you worry too much. You are worried that he's not being faithful to you, correct?"

"Yes," the caller whispered into the phone.

"There's nothing to worry about, Joanne. I sense that this man is a man of integrity. He loves you very much. But I do see that he has a presence, an attractive personality that draws people to him—including many women. Is that right?"

"That's true. I guess that's why I'm worried."

"Well, let your heart be at peace, Joanne. This man is very faithful to you."

"Thank you, Marianne." Listeners could hear the sincere relief and admiration in her voice.

"You're welcome, Joanne."

"Well, looks like were nearing that time when we have to go for a commercial break. When we return who's on the line, Sarah?"

"The next person after the break is Margaret," Sarah said.

Marianne took off the earphones, placed them beside the console and then executed a long and lingering stretch.

"So what are you going to do about the nightmares?" Sarah's voice boomed over the intercom.

"Don't know. I have a feeling that I'm soon going to find out what these the nightmares all about." And to herself, Marianne thought, "And I'm not sure I'm looking forward to that." She gulped more coffee and two aspirin; the pain behind her eyes was dull.

"Well, we're back and we have Margaret on the line. Margaret how can I help you?" Marianne shut her eyes and pressed the earphones closed to her ears as if the additional pressure would assist her in focusing in on Margaret's voice and vanquish the headache.

"Hi Marianne," Margaret said.

"Hello Margaret. How can I help you?"

"Well, I'm just calling to find out what's in store for me."

"In terms of your career? A relationship? What specifically?"

"Just generally for my life. Is that possible?"

"Sure, Margaret. Just give me a minute here as I shuffle the cards. As you may know, Margaret, to help my listeners I combine the Tarot cards with my gift of intuition or third sight. I'm already picking up something strong. Something significant is going to happen in your life."

"To me?" Margaret said.

"No. I'm not getting that. It won't directly affect you. The cards indicate that it will concern someone close to you."

Marianne felt a twinge in the pit of her stomach as she laid out the cards. Aspirin and coffee, she thought, but then what she saw before her in the cards rattled her. Something churned inside her, something she couldn't explain.

"There is a dark cloud over you, Margaret." Marianne said quietly; she almost choked on the words and quickly tried to regain her focus. The air between her and the caller seemed dead, suspended. Finally the woman's tiny voice broke the silence.

"What does that mean?"

Marianne cleared her throat; she had to get out of this without harming her caller. "It could mean any number of things." She squeezed her eyes shut again, trying to focus. Suddenly, a searing pain ripped across her temples; a bright white light seemed to pierce her head. Marianne got a fleeting glimpse of a face—then a naked and mutilated body. Involuntarily her head jerked back with such force that she fell backwards off her seat.

"Hello? Marianne, Marianne? What's happening?" the caller said. The crash to the floor was audible to the listening audience. Marianne was out cold.

As soon as Sarah saw Marianne fall, she slid a pre-recorded cassette into the playback slot, pushed the transmit button and rushed out of her cubicle.

"Are you okay?" Sarah leaned over Marianne's crumpled body. She was beginning to stir.

"Yes." Marianne looked up into her technician's worried face; she reached out, grabbed Sarah's hand and allowed herself to be helped off the floor.

"What happened?"

"I don't know, Sarah. One minute I'm listening to that woman, Margaret, and the next minute I feel a searing pain in my head and see a bright a light, then everything went dark. I guess that's when I fell."

"You need to rest, Marianne."

"Yeah, but first, what happened to that woman we had on line?"

"Don't know. We just went to our contingency plan—a musical interlude."

"But we have about twenty more minutes left." Marianne turned her wrist to peer at her watch.

"I know. Look, I'm going to ask Jack to take over. We'll just announce that you were called away on an emergency and that Jack's astrology show will continue from where you left off."

Marianne nodded. "Do you have the name and number of that woman?" she asked anxiously.

"Yes, what for?"

"Just thought I'd give her a call."

"You know that's against the rules, Marianne."

"I know, but it's something I need to do. I feel I should apologize to her for cutting her reading short."

"That's not necessary Marianne."

"I know it isn't, but I think it is the right thing to do. Moreover I didn't complete her reading. She could be really scared. I'd like the opportunity to finish the reading—reassure her. Come to think of it, it will be good for our ratings."

"Okay. I'll get you her name and number, but on one condition."

"What?"

"That you tell me what happened after you've spoken to her."

"Sure, Sarah. I'll fill you in as soon as I talk to her."

Marianne gathered up her folder and headed for the door, grateful that Sarah couldn't see her worried frown. She didn't like lying to Sarah, but she couldn't tell her about the vision that accompanied the jolting pain in her head. If she did, then she'd also have to explain that what she'd read in the tarot cards that had shocked her. In all her years as a psychic, she'd had never come across a similar situation. She needed time to find out what it all meant, and until she did, she couldn't tell Sarah anything. At least...not yet.

CHAPTER 6

New York, April 5, 1999
    Gerald Woodward shut the door and, as was his practice, walked briskly into his office. He burped loudly as he brushed away the remains of a sandwich that clung to his mousy brown sweater. Dropping into his chair, he sighed deeply, as if the effort of lowering his five-foot-eight frame was a strain. The march across campus had winded him. Though only in his early forties, Gerald knew he was woefully out of shape. He kept promising himself that he was going to do something about that, but the timing never seemed right. He swiped the thinning curly dark curly hair from his damp forehead with the back of his hand and reached for his mail in his IN-tray.
    Sorting the bills from the rest of the mail, he came across a hand-addressed envelope with no return address. He gazed at the familiar handwriting for a few seconds, but he couldn't remember whose it was. Gerald stuck his index finger under the corner of the flap and ripped open the seal. From the ragged envelope, two Polaroid photographs fell on his desk. He picked them up and squinted at them; they appeared to be photos of a yellowed manuscript with dark writing, but he couldn't make out specific characters. Though not badly out of focus, the images were too small to read. He dropped the pictures on the desk and reached into the envelope for the hand-written note.
    Glancing quickly to the bottom of the page, he smiled when he saw the signature. He hadn't seen or spoken Michael Bailey for quite a while. They'd been in school together and sporadically kept in touch over the years. He returned to the letter; Michael was writing to ask him to identify the origin and possible dates for the text fragments pictured in the Polaroids. Gerald wondered what Michael was up to this time—for as long as they'd known each other, Michael had been the adventurous one, always up to some scheme or other, always searching for God-knew-what in the marketplaces of the world. Gerald had sometimes vicariously lived Michael's adventures, offering his academic expertise as an archaeological linguist whenever he could.

Gerald picked up the pictures, squinted at them again and decided he'd be better off using a light table and magnifying glasses in the faculty lab—which would give him a good excuse to get over to the department. Lately, it didn't take much to get him to walk those five blocks downtown. Smiling, Gerald stapled the photographs to the letter and then dropped them back into his IN-tray. Tomorrow would do.

※

New York City, April 6, 1999
After classes, Gerald walked into the Linguistics Department of New York State University and made his way towards the lab.

"Hi Gerald." A slim woman with shoulder-length blonde hair working at one of the tables looked up as Gerald walked in. Her pouting lips spread slightly in a glossy smile. He hadn't expected to see anyone in the lab after hours, though if he had to meet anyone, he'd secretly hoped it would be her.

"Good evening, Jenny." Gerald let his eyes rove appraisingly over her athletic body; he paused his gaze on the flattering tight skirt that ended a few inches beneath the curve of her buttocks. Dr. Jenny Cameron, Assistant Professor in the Department, scandalized her female colleagues by her provocative "out there" garb—which secretly delighted the rest of the male faculty. No one dared criticize her openly, however, because few of them could match her impressive publishing record. She was an up and coming star in the department with three books on Indo-European languages under her belt. Gerald walked towards the table where she was examining an archival document. As he approached, she purposefully bent over the document, exposing more thigh. Jenny knew exactly what she was doing, and it had nothing to do with the paper on the table before her.

"Working hard I see, Jenny," Gerald said cheerfully.

"Yes, Gerald. I've got to finish this before tomorrow. Had to have another look at this document to correct a footnote." She straightened to look at him, rubbing together her white-gloved hands.

"For a class?" He tried to sound interested.

"No I have a paper to present to the Faculty tomorrow. Just polishing it—you know, last minute stuff."

"I see. Well, don't let me stop you," Gerald glanced at her bosom, lifted his eyes to meet hers, smiled, and started walking away. He'd been impressed with Jenny before he'd laid eyes on her. As a member of the hiring committee he'd reviewed her curriculum vitae; her credentials as a linguist had been impeccable, her publishing record enviable. So what, he thought to himself, if she provided a little eye-candy for the department. They could all use it.

"Haven't seen you in a while, Gerald—what've you been up to?" Jenny sweetly called after him, shifting her weight from one booted foot to another.

Gerald hesitated, catching the nuance in her voice. He had hoped she'd say something to him, open a door. Their last meeting had held a lot of promise.

"Nothing much."

"Busy now?"

"Not really." He held the letter aloft. "A friend of mine wants me to check on something for him and I need the light table to do that."

"Free for a drink?" Jenny slowly stepped towards him, stopping only when her breasts separated them from touching.

Involuntarily, he flushed, hoping desperately that she could neither see nor feel the heat beginning to surge through his body. "Sure. Why don't you come to my office later and we'll go somewhere for a coffee or something. I'll be working late tonight."

"Mmmm, me too," she said, not taking her eyes from his. Then, with a flip of her glorious blond mane, she turned on her heel and started back to her table. "Sounds fine. See you then."

The effect of her sculpted buttocks moving under the tight skirt wasn't lost on Gerald. He felt the slight hardening in his trousers, smiled to himself and walked to the back of the language lab.

Gerald stared at the magnified images in the photographs, his heart pounding his chest with excitement. He had never seen anything like it since the discovery of the Dead Sea Scrolls. The text was distinctly Semitic and he knew it had to come from a very ancient dialect. The dates could be early first century, really early—maybe AD 20 to 30. He recognized some of the characters, could make out some of the words. What thrilled him was that the text was distinctly religious.

Michael had only sent him fragments of the text, but Gerald read each word over and over again. There were gaps—the camera had been aimed at the center of the text, cutting off the margins so he couldn't read entire lines. But what he saw made him tremble. Barely able to contain himself, Gerald rose from the stool, snapped off the light table, and strode briskly out of the lab without so much as a glance at Jenny. She watched him leave; clearly he'd found something important in his friend's photos. She decided to keep the invitation to go for a coffee...or something.

Bursting into his office, Gerald reached for the phone as he simultaneously flipped through the Rolodex searching for Michael's phone number; he punched in the numbers. A voice mail indicated Michael was away, and he debated whether to leave a message or wait for his friend's return. Impulsively, he began to speak into the phone.

"Hi, Michael, this is Gerald. I've got the answer that you wanted. The text is certainly Semitic, probably dates around the first century. I'm really excited about what you've found!" Realizing he'd been holding his breath, he paused and then continued. "Look, I'll tell you more later, so call me when you get back."

Gerald depressed the release button to end the call and rapidly dialled another set of numbers.

"Hi, it's Gerald."

"Gerald...hello." The voice on the other end of the line sounded groggy. "Do you know what time it is Gerald?" said the man on the other end.

"I know it's late, but this couldn't wait."

"It must be pretty amazing for you to wake me up in the middle of the night."

"It's only ten o'clock for crying out loud."

"And all sane people are asleep at this hour. What is it?"

"I can't tell you over the phone, I'm coming over tomorrow. When can I see you?"

"Damn! Why did you have to wake me up if you are not going to tell me?"

"Because I want to make sure that you're home tomorrow, and by the way, I thought people in your position aren't supposed to swear."

"I didn't swear, I said damn."

"Same thing. I'll be there tomorrow afternoon—two sharp. Make sure you're there."

☙

At the sound of footsteps, Gerald whirled around, realizing in his haste that he'd left the hall door unlocked. He quickly replaced the phone as a tentative knock came to his door.

"Come in," Gerald said, tossing Michael's letter and photos on the desk and moving to the chair behind it. The door slowly opened; it was Jenny. He was momentarily confused until he remembered their earlier meeting in the lab and his invitation. She stood in the doorway, deliciously leaning into his office so that the edge of the door wedged between her breasts.

"Am I disturbing you, Gerald?" It was a loaded question, not lost on either party.

"No, um, ah...." Damn, he thought, he was stumbling. "Come in. I asked you to drop by didn't I?"

As she slipped into the office, she noticed Gerald's eyes never left her body. She deliberately closed the door, turned and sauntered toward him. She slipped into the chair across from his and crossed her legs.

"Actually, you're just in time to help me celebrate," he said, still more excited by what he'd discovered than by his seductively attractive guest.

"Really. What are you celebrating?" she said, forcing him to maintain eye contact.

"Probably the most important discovery since the discovery of the Dead Sea Scrolls," he confided, lowering his voice.

"Really?" She leaned forward, hand under her chin, elbow on her knee. Her arm pressed against her right breast, deepening the cleavage in the scoop neckline of her angora sweater. It was a practiced move.

"I think so."

"What exactly is it?" She arched an eyebrow. Gerald felt strangely quiet and excited all at the same time.

"A religious text. From a scroll."

"What kind of religious text?"

"I'm not exactly sure — too early to tell."

"Now, I'm really confused. I thought you said you'd discovered a religious text."

"I said I was celebrating the discovery of a religious text," he said. "I only have a portion of it. Here, look." Gerald reached for the photographs and handed them to her.

She held them side-by-side in front of herself, purposely not obstructing the professor's view of her breasts. "What does it say?"

"Not much, but enough to make me know that it is from a very old religious text." Gerald was aware that he was beginning to breathe hard again.

"Do you have the original? Can I see it?" Her tiny pink tongue flicked at her upper lip. The gesture was too obvious, even for Gerald. He gently removed the photos from her hands and sat back in his desk chair.

"Now, now, now. You don't think I'm going to let you in on all my secrets are you?" he teased. He tossed the photos on the desk.

"Oh, come on, Gerald. You've told me about this religious text and now that I'm all excited you don't want to show it to me."

"Well, I can't just show it to you. If I did, I'd have no secrets left," he chuckled.

"Spoil sport." She pretended to pout, then laughed. He loved the way she laughed; it made him feel warm, worthwhile. Suddenly, he wished he did have the scroll, but at the same time he was glad for the ambiguity of its whereabouts.

"I'll make a deal with you. As soon as I determine exactly what it all means, I'll let you see it. In the meantime I'd like to keep this whole thing under wraps. OK, Jenny?"

"OK, Gerald." She smiled.

"So," he rubbed his hands together, "how about we go out for a drink and celebrate?"

She let the question hang in the air for a moment too long. "Do we have to go out?" she whispered.

Gerald swallowed hard. "Well, what would you suggest?"

"We could celebrate your discovery...here...couldn't we, Gerald?" She rose from her chair, stepped close to him and sat on the desk directly in front of his chair.

༺

Jenny Cameron smoothed her skirt and jacket as she walked out of the Linguistics Department. Smiling, she recalled the escalating frenzy that had scattered papers and clothes during the desktop tryst with Gerald only moments ago. She'd left the poor man still breathing heavily, but obliviously happy.

She was also delighted. Slipping her hand into her jacket pocket, she felt for the Polaroid photograph she had picked up from the floor when she retrieved her bra and sweater. Gerald had been too tired after their copulation to notice a thing.

She wiped the little beads of sweat from her brow and tried to contain her exhilaration. Some time ago the word had gone out for all members to be on the lookout for any information concerning a religious text. She had never in her life dreamed that the information that her master sought would be dumped, literally, into her lap. The Messenger would be pleased.

Jenny reached her car, got in, locked the doors and placed her head on the headrest; she shut her eyes. She had to calm herself before she called her contact. She would certainly be rewarded if the text Gerald had found turned out to the one that The Messenger wanted. She relished the thought as she stilled her body.

She removed the phone from her purse, punched in the unlisted number and held the tiny instrument to her ear. She counted three rings, then terminated the call. Beginning to tremble again in anticipation, Jenny placed the phone in her lap and sat waiting. The return call came almost immediately, startling her; she picked up.

"You called, Dr. Cameron?" said a deep voice.

"Yes. I may have some information regarding a religious text. It comes from a scroll."

"What is the nature of this information?"

"I believe that a professor in my department may know something about the whereabouts of this text."

"Does this person have the scroll?"

"Possibly." Jenny Cameron paused, waiting for the follow up question; realizing that it wasn't forthcoming she continued.

"He has Polaroid photographs of portions of this religious text."

"What makes you believe the pictures are of the text we seek?"

"He described it as the most important discovery since the Dead Sea Scrolls."

"I see."

"Can you get a copy of the photographs?"

"I already have one," Jenny said triumphantly.

"You have done well." Though congratulatory, the monotone voice lacked emotion. "Send it by courier to this address." The mysterious deep voice dictated an address, asked Jenny to read it back, and then ended the call.

Jenny flicked the car's ignition and her BMW roared to life. Still aroused, she slipped it into gear and disappeared into evening traffic

꿎

New York City, April 7, 1999

Holding the Polaroid photograph that had been delivered that afternoon, The Messenger sat in the center of the star. Joy filled her body; she had no doubt that it depicted part of the scroll that she and her members had been searching for all these years. It had arrived; it was close. She shut her eyes, oblivious to the hard cold floor beneath her nakedness, the spitting candle flames and the elongated shadows dancing on the walls.

Slowly she went into her mind's eye, allowing her spirit to follow the energy path left by the photograph. It led to the man who had been in possession of the picture: a tall dark sweaty man with short curly hair. Her nose wrinkled involuntarily. She could not tell if this man possessed the scroll—that insight eluded her.

The Messenger opened her eyes and stared at the photograph, almost willing it to speak and give up its secrets. Frustrated because of this limitation in her power, anger coursed through body. She involuntarily clenched her fist; the photo crumpled in her hand. Unconcerned, she returned to her thought path. She had to find out if the man who had the picture also had the scroll itself. If he did—she smiled—she would remove it from him. She alone would do this. Pleasure rippled through her muscles at the thought. Time, of course, was of the essence: there were only a few more months until the cusp of the millennium.

CHAPTER 7

New York City, April 7, 1999

Shivering, Marianne pulled the windbreaker tightly around her body as she walked up the steps to Woodward's front door. She paused for a moment on the doorstep, uncertain about her mission and about herself. Her earlier compulsion to see Margaret Woodward, the woman who had called the station the day before, had been replaced by a feeling of awkwardness and unease. Marianne thought about dashing back to her car, but a nagging intuition that this woman could somehow shed light on the nightmares kept her from fleeing.

She sucked in a deep breath, exhaled slowly, and then pushed the doorbell. It seemed like an eternity before a woman appeared at the door.

"Yes?" said the slender brunette. Strands of silver highlighted her hair, giving her a distinguished appearance. She was elegantly, though simply attired in a turtleneck and skirt.

"Good morning. I'm Marianne Waters. I'm here to see Margaret Woodward."

The woman responded with an instant smile of recognition. "Oh! Why, hello. I'm Margaret. Come in." Opening the door wide, she led Marianne into a stylish living room. "Can I get you something?"

"Coffee?"

"Oh dear. I'm so sorry, we just ran out of coffee this morning. Gerald, my brother, just went to the store. He'll be home any minute It's just two blocks away, if you don't mind waiting. Could I offer you something instead? Tea or orange juice or a cola?"

Marianne felt comforted by the woman's genuine warmth and hospitality. "Orange juice will be fine," she smiled.

"Great. Just be a moment." Margaret soon returned with a tray laden with juice, some cookies and two glasses. She poured a glass of golden liquid and handed the glass to Marianne.

"I was really surprised when you called," she gushed. "Marianne, I'm one of your biggest fans—you've made my day. I'm thrilled you could visit!"

"Well, I thought I'd come and give you a second reading since your first one was interrupted."

"That was really nice of you."

"Was yesterday the first time you've called the station?" Marianne inquired as she reached into her purse to remove a pack of Tarot cards.

"Yes—though I've had readings done before," Margaret enthused.

"How did you find the readings?" Marianne started shuffling the cards.

"Okay, I suppose." She shrugged and took a long drink of juice. Marianne noticed she was sitting on the edge of her seat, anticipation clearly written on her face.

"You don't sound like a real believer," Marianne said gently with a smile.

Margaret shrugged, sat back on the couch. "I suppose I've been a skeptic for sometime," she shyly admitted.

"That's normal, Margaret. Until you've had more experience with the Tarot it may not connect for you."

She leaned forward again; a frown creased her brow. "Marianne, the other day when you did my reading, you said that there was a black cloud over me, what did you mean?"

"We'll, that's why I'm here. I'm not sure what exactly I was seeing, so we'll redo the cards and see in just a moment." She continued to shuffle the cards. Margaret nodded, eyes fixed on the flow of cards in Marianne's hands. There was a sound at the front door.

"Oh, I hear Gerald at the door." Margaret rose and moved toward the foyer. "Yes that's him."

"I'll wait," Marianne said. "We don't want to be interrupted."

"Sure." Margaret reached the vestibule. Marianne could hear a murmur of voices, then Margaret returned with her brother who was carrying two bags of groceries.

Marianne rose as they entered to the living room.

"Hello, I'm Gerald," he said as he placed the parcels on a table and walked towards Marianne, his hand outstretched.

Marianne gazed at his face, stunned. Instantly her blood turned to ice. An overwhelming nausea rose in the back of her throat as Gerald Woodward drew closer Marianne could feel panic shuddering through her body. His smile quickly dissolved into puzzled concern. Though she was sure she'd never met this man, she was positive she'd seen his face somewhere before.

Filled with a foreboding sense of doom, Marianne instinctively knew she'd made a terrible mistake in coming. As if in slow motion, Gerald's hand connected with her own. Suddenly she was overcome with fear. At that very moment Marianne suddenly remembered where she had seen Gerald Woodward, and her only thought was to bolt from the house.

Without a word, Marianne disengaged her hand from Gerald's, snatched her purse from the couch and ran past him to the front door. She paused for a brief second, whirled around and looked at the astonished faces of Woodward and Margaret.

"I'm sorry," she cried. "I thought I could do this—but I can't. Please forgive me." She turned to leave, then looked over her shoulder. In a voice hoarse with emotion, she whispered, "Take care of yourself Mr. Woodward." Tears of embarrassment flowed down her face as she slammed the door and rushed down the steps to her car.

*

"Hello, Peter. What's up? I came as soon as I got your message," Sarah said breezing past a dejected-looking Peter Cannon. As she took off her coat she tried to make eye contact, but Peter kept his head down, obviously upset.

Softly closing the door, Peter paused and swallowed hard. Sarah had never seen Peter in such an emotional state. Normally the six-foot-four businessman, with his impressive cobalt eyes and full beard was the epitome of confidence and strength.

"I don't know what's happening, Sarah." He paused and continued resignedly, "Marianne came home bawling her eyes out and asked me to call you." He looked at Sarah, helpless. "I tried to get her to tell me what was wrong but she wouldn't. Maybe you can find out what's going on. I'm at my wits end."

Peter Cannon led Sarah into the living room where Marianne, wearing a soft blue bathrobe, was curled up on a loveseat, her face buried in her hands. Sarah sat close to Marianne as Peter sat in a chair across from them. She'd never seen her friends in such distress.

"Marianne what's wrong? You look sick. Another of those nightmares?"

Marianne lifted a tear-streaked face, eyes red and puffy. "Thanks for coming Sarah. I really need to talk to someone." Distanced from the women, Peter looked pained

"What's up?"

"I went to see Margaret Woodward."

"And?"

"It's her brother."

"What do you mean, 'It's her brother?' You're not making any sense Marianne."

Peter sat forward in his seat and asked. "Who is this Margaret Woodward?"

Ignoring Peter, Marianne wailed, "I've seen him before, Sarah?"

"I don't understand, Marianne." Sarah placed a comforting hand on Marianne's shoulder; she realized her friend was trembling.

"Who is Margaret Woodward?" Peter asked again, the strain showing in his voice.

Marianne pulled her bathrobe tightly about herself and peered intently at Sarah. "I've seen him before—in my dreams."

"Will someone please tell me what is going on?" Peter pleaded.

Sarah turned to him and hastily recounted the story. "Marianne had a vision when she was doing a reading for a woman—Margaret Woodward—during her show. She collapsed when she had the vision. When she came to, we'd already moved to the next show, but first thing Marianne said was that she wanted to see this woman in person."

"Geez!" Peter hissed at his distraught wife. "Why on earth would you want to do something like that? Why would you want to go chasing after a stranger you'd seen in your dreams? Aren't the nightmares enough?"

Marianne turned to Peter as if she was seeing him for the first time. "Please try to understand Peter. I felt something during the reading that I thought was connected with these awful nightmares, and afterwards I sensed meeting the woman would help me understand them. I didn't know why, at first, but when I got there I understood—after she introduced me to her brother. He was the man I've seen before in a nightmare."

Peter, clearly frustrated, retorted, "I have tried to understand, Marianne, but you never tell me what is really going on!"

"You're not making sense, Marianne," Sarah chimed in. "What was this man doing in your dreams?"

"I haven't told either of you everything about those nightmares. I get glimpses, visions of people—and they are all dead. Their bodies are mutilated." She began to sob again.

"They're what!" Incredulous, Peter threw his hands in the air.

Sarah glared at Peter; he shut up. She turned back to Marianne, trying to keep her voice calm. "So how does this woman's brother fit in?"

"I saw him when I had that attack at the station. It was his sister who called. When I was doing the reading for her, I got a vision of him. He was dead, you guys—dead. I know he's going to die and there's nothing that I can do about it!" Marianne dissolved again into uncontrollable tears.

You mean you went to see someone for whom you had done a reading? Isn't that dangerous? And why on earth would you want to do that?" Peter was beginning to lose his cool again.

Sarah interjected. "There's nothing you can do about it, Marianne. You only had a dream and for all you know, maybe nothing is going to happen. Now. Just think for a minute about all the other people that you've seen in the nightmares, do you know if they're dead?"

"I don't know."

"Well, it may all be your imagination getting into overdrive, "Peter said. Those people may not even be dead. You're just upset because you saw a man who looked like the corpse in your nightmare. It's awful and disturbing, but it's not real."

"That's not the upsetting part about the dreams, Peter."

"I don't understand."

"I don't just think those persons I've seen are dead. I think they were murdered."

"Murdered? Why would you think that?" Peter was beginning to sound frustrated.

"I don't know. Just a hunch, I'm a psychic, remember?"

"Oh, right." Peter couldn't keep the sarcasm out of his voice and he hated himself for it. He'd always supported his wife, but this was beginning to scare him.

"I've never felt so useless in my life," she wailed.

"It's not your fault Marianne, get over it."

"I don't think I can, at least not yet. You see that's not all that's been happening to me."

"What do you mean?" Sarah asked. Peter was shaking his head.

Sarah looked pleadingly from Sarah to her husband. "Recently I've become very forgetful. There are times when it just seems like I've lost my memory. I've no idea what I've been doing for long periods of time. It seems like I just black out and come to much later. But because I can't remember I don't know if I blacked out."

"I'm sure there's a perfectly simple explanation for what's happening to you." Peter was trying hard not to be judgmental and to remove the edge from his voice.

"It's easy for you to say. But what if I'm the one who's...doing it?"

"Meaning?"

"What if I'm the one who's killing all the people I've been seeing in the nightmares."

"Come off it, Marianne," Sarah interjected, "There's no proof that those people are dead, remember?"

"I know, I know. But what if they *are* dead and the nightmares that I've been having are just some subconscious recollection of the killings—or maybe I'm visualizing what I may be about to do..."

Peter raised both hands in despair and rose from the chair. "I'm sorry," he said, "I can't handle this now. I need some air." He strode towards the kitchen. His footsteps faded; the back door slamming shattered the silence trailing his exit. Marianne dropped her head in her hands and wept.

Sarah turned to her friend, placing a consoling arm around her shoulders. "Why didn't you say something about all this before, and more importantly, why did you keep the whole story from Peter?" Sarah looked toward the garden. "No wonder he's upset."

"I know I should have told him all the details," Marianne sobbed, "but I thought these nightmares would go away. I figured it was just stress and I didn't want anyone, especially Peter, to think that I was going crazy or something."

"Stop it, Marianne. Now you're being really silly."

"You don't understand..."

"Of course I do. You're upset because you can't explain the visions you're having and you can't stop the carnage that you see in your nightmares."

"Its more than just worrying about the nightmares, Sarah. I also feel connected to the murders. That's what scares me and makes me think that I'm responsible in some way. Its just like you've done something and you relive the event all over again."

"I don't believe for one moment that you've killed anyone, Marianne. I've known you for a long time and you're just not that kind of person."

"I hope that you're right." Marianne stared into the distance, no longer weeping, but clearly still distraught.

Both women remained silent for a brief period until Sarah blurted out, "Did you tell him?"

"Who?"

"The brother. Margaret Woodward's brother. Did you tell him about the dream?"

"How could I?"

"So what did you do?"

"Nothing. When I saw him and realized that I'd seen him in the vision, I just freaked out and fled."

"You just ran away?"

"What did you expect me to do, tell him that I'd seen him in a vision lying dead and that he's going to be murdered?"

"I guess not."

"So what do I do now?"

"I don't know. Go to the police?"

"I'm not sure they'll even talk to me, but it's worth a shot. After all, it's become accepted police practice to use psychics, hasn't it?"

"Yes and the NYPD probably do. And, just as you said, lots of police departments do. First, though you need to tell Peter everything that you've shared with me."

⁂

Marianne opened the French doors to the back deck. Peter reclined on the lounge, eyes shut. Marianne sat on the cushion beside his knees. "Hi," she barely whispered, the remorse in her voice tinged with anticipation.

"Oh, hi," Peter said, opening his eyes and gazing into her face. "I didn't hear you coming."

"Can I join you?" She looked miserable; his heart went out to her.

"Oh, sure. Sorry," He lifted his arm and shifted to make room for Marianne to squeeze into the small space beside him. He closed his arms around her as she stretched her full length next to his body and rested her head on his chest.

"Are you angry with me?"

"No," he paused, "just disappointed." He gently lifted her chin and looked into her still swollen, red-rimmed eyes. "I don't know why you couldn't trust me, Marianne," he said softly, "I am your husband after all. Your 'best bud', remember?"

"I know I should have trusted you, and I'm sorry I didn't. Its just that I was afraid of what you might think if I described all the details and..." Her voice trailed off as she felt tears sting her eyelids

"Well, you could have trusted me enough to find out what my reaction would be."

"I know. I'm sorry."

Peter tightened his arms around her, felt the tension in her body melt as she curled into his embrace. "Don't shut me out, Marianne."

"I promise I won't."

CHAPTER 8

New York City, April 8, 1999

"Can I help you?" From behind the counter the burly desk sergeant glanced from Marianne to Sarah and then to Peter. He had an unnerving way of moving his eyeballs from side to side without any movement of his head.

"Yes. We need to speak to someone," Sarah said.

"About what?"

"We need to speak to someone who knows something about psychics—I mean the paranormal," Sarah said.

There was a moment of silence as the sergeant, confused, shifted his eyeballs questioningly from one woman to the next.

"What exactly do you need to talk about, m'am?" He fixed his eyes on Sarah.

Sarah glanced at Marianne and they both stared at the policeman for what seemed like an eternity.

Finally Peter spoke up." Look, do you use psychics in your work?"

"Yeah. I think in the past we have," the sergeant sounded cagy.

"Well, we'd like to speak to the officers who worked with psychics."

"We don't work that way, sir," the policeman paused condescendingly, "You have to tell me what your problem is and then I can direct you to the correct department. Like I said, sometimes we use psychics in our investigations—but I have to know what exactly your problem is before..."

"I think—I believe someone is going to be murdered," Marianne blurted out before he could finish his sentence.

"Excuse me?" The officer frowned and craned his head slightly in Marianne's direction.

Sarah stepped forward, redirecting his attention. "Sir, we'd really like to speak to someone who knows something about working with psychics. I think it would be much easier to explain the situation to them—don't you agree?" Sarah said.

He looked at the trio, dropped his pencil next to his logbook and uttered a sound that appeared to be a mixture a sigh and a huff. "Right," he said obviously irritated, "take a seat and I'll be back with someone," he said. He turned on his heel and disappeared into an adjoining office. A short while later he returned with a harried-looking man in a dark crumpled suit. The man came around the sergeant's desk and extended a hand to Sarah.

"Morning. Lieutenant James Jackson. I'm the commanding officer of this precinct. Sergeant Hoaken says that you have some information about a possible homicide. If you'll come with me, we'll be able to speak more freely." Jackson led the trio into an interview room and gestured for them to sit at the room's sole table.

"Can I get you something—coffee, water?"

"I'll have coffee, black," Marianne said.

"Coffee, two sugars, no cream," Sarah said. Peter gestured that he didn't need anything.

Jackson briefly left the room and returned with two steaming Styrofoam cups. He placed the cups on the table, pulled up a chair and sat down directly across from the two women. Quickly surmising that Peter was obviously there for support, Jackson didn't bother to address him.

"So, what's the story? Sergeant Hoaken mentioned something about psychics. Maybe you should tell me what brings you here."

Marianne held her cup in both hands as if it could prevent the tremors that involuntarily coursed through her body. She looked directly into Jackson's eyes. "Lieutenant Jackson, my name is Marianne Waters. I am a psychic. I have a weekly program Psychic Connections on KRCP."

"Isn't that the show where people call up to get a reading or something?"

"Yes, one of the many services our station provides. As I…"

"Well, what do you know," Jackson said. A boyish smile creased his face as he stretched out his hand to Marianne. "So, you are the Marianne my wife keeps talking about. Wait till I tell her that I met you." The smile vanished after they shook hands; Jackson became all business. "So, what can I do for you Ms. Waters?"

Marianne hesitated, and then launched into her story. "Last week I got a call from a woman named Margaret Woodward."

"Is she the one who's going to be murdered?"

"No, it's her brother, Gerald Woodward," Marianne said.

"I see. What makes you believe he's going to be murdered?"

"I had a vision of him lying dead."

"Where?"

"I don't know where, just somewhere. He'd been stripped naked and was just lying there."

"Just a moment. Did you know this Woodward guy and his sister before the woman called the station?"

"No."

"Then how did you know he was the one you saw in your vision?"

Marianne looked at Sarah and Peter and then at Jackson. "I went to see Margaret Woodward after she called the station."

"I see. He was alive when you went there?"

"Yes."

"Can I ask you why you went to see her if you'd never met her before?"

"It's rather personal, but I suppose you should know. Lately, I've been having nightmares—horrible visions—of people who've been murdered. I don't know who these people are. When Margaret Woodward called the station, I got another of these visions, but this time it was her brother I saw." Jackson's face shifted; Marianne hastened to add, "Of course, I didn't know it was her brother at that time." Marianne could hear herself getting flustered; she was afraid she was losing her nerve. "You see, I thought going to see her would help me understand the visions that I'd been having."

"I see." Jackson leaned backwards into his chair and placed the pen with which he had been making notes on the table. It seemed to be a gesture of closure.

"So what are you going to do—I mean what're the police going to do?" Sarah asked.

"That's difficult to say, miss. With the exception of Ms. Waters' statement that this man, Gerald Woodward, is going to be murdered there's nothing concrete to go on. We can't just devote resources on the basis of mere suspicions."

"But the man could be killed!" Marianne faltered.

"Maybe. And maybe not,"

"Geez!" Peter interjected, stepping into the confusion at the table. "I thought you guys are always asking for tips on possible crimes. What's the name of that project..." Peter began tapping the table with his forefinger in an effort to recall the program's title.

"You mean Crime Stoppers?" Sarah asked.

"Yeah, that's it, Crime Stoppers. What's the use of telling people they can call a number to report a crime or a possible crime, then tell them that you can't do anything about it." Peter said.

Jackson decided to be patient. "Sir, let me clarify that. With Crime Stoppers we can only act if an actual crime has been committed or is in the process of being committed. We can't act on potential crimes."

"But Lieutenant, I believe that a crime is about to be committed," Marianne pleaded. "I saw it in my vision and I'm not usually wrong..."

"That may be," Jackson paused, placed his arms on the table and leaned forward, "but we have our procedures. Let me ask you this: those other people in your visions—have you any idea who they are, where they live, any information at all?"

"No," she said sheepishly, beginning to feel the situation was hopeless and that she'd been foolish to come to the police. She felt like the village explainer. Her story was beginning to ring hollow even in her own ears.

"Well, if you did, we could check to see if we have files on them. Then there would be some basis for doing something for this Woodward guy."

"I see." Marianne said. eyes lowered. Beginning to feel defeated, she slouched in her chair.

Peter, desperate, leaned across the table. "Well, I don't get it. You have a name, an address, and information about a possible murder. What more do you need?"

"As I said, it's not as simple that, sir."

"Lieutenant Jackson," Peter paused and pulled his chair closer to the table, "if I came to you and told you that I knew of a plot to murder a public figure, you would take it seriously wouldn't you," he said earnestly.

"I probably would, but only because you had provided me with concrete evidence: facts. Ms. Waters hasn't got any facts, just a vision—a belief—that someone is going to be murdered. The best I can do is to send someone over to the Woodward home to see that everything is okay, but I can't assign officers to protect this guy twenty-four hours a day in the based on a hunch that something could happen to him."

"We get your point. I suppose that'll have to do," Sarah said dismally.

"Yes. Well, thank you for your help," Marianne said. "Here's my card. The Woodward's address is on the back."

"Yeah, thanks," Peter waved a hand, rose from his seat and followed Marianne and Sarah to the door.

"We'll certainly contact you if something happens." Jackson called after them.

Marianne whirled on her heel and stared at Jackson, "It'll be too late then," she said.

Outside the interview room, Jackson followed them through the station towards the exit. Passing a cluttered desk, Marianne caught sight of a poster with photographs. She paused, then picked it up. The six portraits, some in black in white, some in colour, depicted both men and women. The quality of each varied; some were obviously taken from family shots, while others appeared to be driver's license photos. Collectively the faces stared at her; she stared back, searching each face the way a reader studies an obituary page. The faces all looked familiar to her—too familiar. Suddenly weak-kneed, she staggered. Peter caught hold of her arm and held her firmly to his side.

"Marianne, what's the matter?" Sarah said.

"Who are these people?" Marianne held out the poster to Jackson. The sheet trembled in her hand.

"Missing persons. We usually put together pictures like these and send them out nation-wide. Why? You recognize any of these people?"

Marianne's shoulders began to shake as hot tears poured down her pale face. "They're the faces I've seen in my dreams! They're not missing. They're dead."

CHAPTER 9

New York City, April 8, 1999

In his haste Gerald Woodward nearly tripped over the seat belt as he bolted from his car and raced up the walk of the impressive brownstone. He pushed the doorbell, cast a quick glance at his watch and stood staring at the entry as if the intensity of his stare would open it.

A short while later a somber Jeffrey McCarthy, Bishop of New York City, opened the door. Short, slightly overweight, the bespectacled man with thinning gray hair looked dignified in clerical collar, pale gray shirt and black cardigan.

"Hello, Gerald," said McCarthy in a tone that was neither warm nor alienating.

"Hi," Gerald said, pushing unceremoniously past the bishop. "Sorry to bother you, but I'm sure you'll be interested in what I have to show you."

Rolling his eyes, the bishop said, "Come in, come in," more to himself than to the man disappearing down the hall. "This better be good," he said under his breath as he followed his guest at a much slower pace.

Gerald dropped into one of the overstuffed living room sofas and removed a Polaroid picture from his pocket. When the bishop came into the room, he stretched out his arm and handed it to him. The clergyman cocked an eyebrow and said, "What's this?"

"You tell me," Gerald said, barely able to hide his glee.

"I can hardly see it—the Polaroid's not very sharp."

"Sorry, I forgot." Gerald delved into his pocket and brought out a magnifying glass. "Here, use this," he said handing it to the older man.

McCarthy sat down beside Gerald and focused the lens of the magnifying glass over the image.

McCarthy shrugged. "Looks like some sort of writing." He offered it back to Gerald.

"I know what it looks like, I'm not stupid. You know what I'm after—tell me the genus of the language?" Gerald snapped, leaving the photo in the Bishop's hand.

The bishop peered again at the photograph. "Can't be sure, but it looks Semitic. Like I said, some of the characters are not that clear."

"Right, right. You're on the right track. Just so you know, a friend of mine who deals in antiques took these pictures and wrote to me asking me to date the language. From my examination of the characters, I'm pretty sure this dialect dates as far back as AD 30 or 40."

"That far back?" The bishop glanced at Gerald over the top of his reading glasses.

"Yes."

"What language is it?"

"I'm pretty certain the language is Aramaic, and I think it is from another Scroll."

"Interesting."

"Isn't it?" Gerald Woodward stared at the bishop for a brief moment, unmistakable expectancy in his eyes. He waited for Bishop McCarthy to grasp the significance of what he'd just said.

The bishop, aware of Gerald's expectations, refused to allow a modicum of interest to enter his voice. "So, is this why you woke me last night and why you've come all this way?" he asked drolly. "Just because of some text?"

"I knew you'd say that. " Gerald sounded a little testy. "Look. This is not just any text. Don't you think that the language has any significance? Another scroll in Aramaic?"

The bishop shrugged. "Not really. Aramaic was a language that was spoken around the time of Jesus, but so were other languages." He handed the photo back to Gerald.

"You don't think the fact that Aramaic is the language that Christ and his disciples spoke has any significance?"

"Really, Gerald—not particularly. Aramaic is still spoken by the inhabitants of a small village in the Middle East." Then, in an effort to sound pastoral, he quickly added, "Maybe I don't see the significance because I can't read Aramaic as well as you can and, in any event, you've only shown me a picture of what may be a whole text." He held out his hands, palms up, inviting Gerald to respond.

"True. I grant you that. So I'll tell you what the writing says." Gerald sounded eager to please, which was exactly where McCarthy wanted him.

"So what does it say?" McCarthy said innocently.

"Remember, I don't have the whole text." Gerald's eyes flickered with excitement; he licked his lips.

"So? What does this fragment say?"

"Keep your hat on." Gerald carefully removed a small sheet of paper from his pocket and placed it beside the Polaroid on the table.

"From my analysis," Gerald cleared his throat as he picked up the sheet of paper, but didn't continue his thought. Reflexively he cleared his throat again. "I was able to make out a number of references to 'the Christ.' There are also a number of references to 'new age.' In one phrase those expressions appear together with the expression 'shall reappear.' There are other words I could not recognize, but it's not a stretch to think that whole sentence has something to do with the reappearance of the Christ in the new age."

When Gerald finished reading, both men remained silent. He glanced at Bishop McCarthy who broke the silence.

"Is that an accurate translation, Gerald?" he gently queried.

"Yes it is," Gerald tried not to sound annoyed. "Remember? I am the expert in ancient languages,"

"Of course, I know you are," the bishop tried to sound conciliatory, "but, I guess what I'm really asking is...do you realize what that could mean?"

"Why do you think I came to see you?"

"Could it mean what I think it means?" The bishop looked away in an effort to conceal his true feelings from the eager academic beside him.

"It could."

"Do you have the text?"

"That depends."

The bishop whirled to look him in the eye. His face momentarily contorted as he spat, "Cut the crap, Gerald. What's all this *it depends* crap? You either have it or you don't."

Gerald, stunned by the bishop's sudden aggressiveness, mumbled contritely, "Okay, okay. I don't have the scroll." A thin film of sweat glistened on his face; he felt his heart rate increase; the pulse in his neck moved against the finger as he pulled the collar away from his neck.

Bishop McCarthy stared hard at Gerald. "Who has it?" he said evenly.

Gerald, recomposed, snapped back, "Now, you didn't think I'd tell you *that* did you? At least not now." He swiftly pocketed the photograph and the sheet of paper.

"Do you know how important that document is?" the Bishop said softly, trying to restore the man's confidence. "I mean, think of the consequences for humankind if it fell into the wrong hands."

"And your hands are the right ones?" Gerald said tersely.

Immediately sensing a shift in intonation, the Bishop assumed to a gentler tone. "I never said that, Gerald, but we could prevent it from falling into the wrong hands..."

"It could also make whoever possessed it famous and wealthy. Well, I'm not at liberty to tell you who has the original text. Not now anyway. But, I have a proposal for you."

Bishop McCarthy, sat back in the couch, hands on his knees. He sighed audibly, a rather saintly touch he thought to himself. "Here comes the real reason why you're here. What do you want, Gerald? Money?"

"To join forces."

"To do what?" His bushy eyebrows rose high over his gold-rimmed spectacles.

"Join forces," Gerald repeated, "You know—collaborate."

"I know what join forces means, I mean what are we going to do as, ahem, a joint force?"

"Well, I know who has the text. I also know that if I tell him what it really says, I'm never going to get my hands on it."

"So what do you want me to do? Steal it?"

"I didn't say that."

"Well, what do you want from me?"

"Look, my friend, you have connections, resources," Gerald paused and looked meaningfully at the bishop. "Maybe you could make him an offer, a generous offer, and tell him how important the document may be—etcetera, etcetera. And then, you can allow me to undertake the only authorized translation of the text. Come on. Do we have a deal?"

"I'll think about it. So who has the document?"

"Let me know what you're thinking and maybe I'll tell you." Gerald stood and made for the door. "Later, padre, I've got to go now."

With his back to the bishop, Gerald couldn't see the dangerous set of the man's mouth and the eyes burning into his back.

༄

Bishop McCarthy sat in his office in apparent contemplation, hands pressed against one another with fingertips touching his lips. Eyes lowered, sitting motionless for over thirty minutes after Gerald left the room, anyone looking in would have thought the man was deep in prayer. The bishop was indeed submerged in reflection, but not the meditative kind. His mind raced, analyzing the implications of Gerald's disclosure. Was the text really another Scroll? The first set of Scrolls, the Dead Sea Scrolls, had raised issues about the origins of Christianity and the Church that had not as yet been resolved. If what Gerald had shown him was authentic—and they both thought it was—then the implications were thrilling. Without a doubt its contents would be of staggering significance to the whole of the Christian world, at the center of which was the Church.

Thus even before Gerald had departed, McCarthy had made up his mind that the text was paramount for the Church's very existence. His mission was clear and compelling: he must do everything in his power to secure it for the Church.

Bishop McCarthy rose from his seat, and glanced at his watch. It was already noon. Walking to his desk at the far end of the room, he reached for the phone and pushed a button.

"Maggie, book me on the next flight to Rome." He ended the call and punched another series of numbers.

"Hello, this is Bishop McCarthy, something's come up. I need to go to Rome. We need to meet upon my return." Quickly replacing the receiver, he walked purposefully out of the room.

CHAPTER 10

Rome, April 8, 1999
Bishop McCarthy deplaned at the Alitalia gate and walked briskly ahead of the other passengers into the terminal. Thanks to the amenities of first class, the flight from New York to Rome had not been stressful. Nonetheless he'd spent a sleepless night over the Atlantic thinking about the implications of Woodward's revelation. He glanced at his watch: 1:00 PM Rome time. He'd need to get some sleep before his 9:00 AM meeting at the Vatican tomorrow.

McCarthy made it to the baggage claim section in ten minutes, retrieved his overnight bag and walked quickly in the direction of customs and immigration. The woman at the immigration counter took one look at his clerical collar and large crucifix and waved him through the turnstiles. He caught the first taxi in the rank and headed for the hotel.

The Vatican, April 9, 1999
The Vatican, since time immemorial, has been an independent state in the heart of Italy. The affairs of the Vatican are managed by a body known as the Curia which is made up of nine sacred congregations. Perhaps the most well known of these is The Congregation for the Doctrine of the Faith or CDF. The CDF is the Catholic Church's watchdog on all matters concerning its teachings or doctrine in the faith of the world's Catholics. Until 1965, the CDF was known as The Congregation for the Holy Inquisition of Heretical Error. It is the most powerful body within the Catholic Church and its head, with the exception of the Holy Father, is the Church's highest-ranking spiritual authority.

The CDF has a wide range of responsibilities, including investigating all reports of miracles, appointing priests and bishops, disciplining the clergy, and investigating all findings of sacred objects including sacred texts. It is in connection with this latter function that

Bishop Jeffrey McCarthy scheduled an urgent meeting with Cardinal Marcello Lombardi, head of the CDF.

The Palace of the Holy Office housing the offices of the CDF is situated on the south side of St. Peter's Square, outside the walls of the Vatican City. The bishop, refreshed from his travels, arrived half an hour early for his appointment. He was greeted with polite but disinterested courtesy after offering his identification papers and instructed to wait in the lobby. At exactly 9:00 AM the bishop was ushered into the offices of Cardinal Lombardi.

The cardinal, an imposing figure at six foot four, gracefully elevated his trim 200-pound figure from an antique gilt chair as Bishop McCarthy passed through the carved doors. The heavy fine cloth of his dark vestments rustled as he extended his hand. The bishop felt a twinge of envy as he noticed the mauve trim on the cardinal's vestments, a visual symbol of rank and power.

"Good morning, Jeffrey." The Cardinal spoke without a trace of an Italian accent. "Hope your flight was uneventful."

"It was. Thank you, Your Eminence."

"Let's dispense with the formality, shall we. We've known each other too long. Marcello is fine."

"Sure." McCarthy couldn't bring himself to use the cardinal's first name.

"You've met my assistant, Father Nicholas Fraccaro?"

"No I haven't." McCarthy reached out and shook the hand of a dark thin man.

"Before we begin, would you like a cup of coffee?" Lombardi said.

"Yes, thank you." McCarthy nodded, familiarizing himself once again with the simple yet opulent furnishings of the Cardinal's chambers. He'd been there before, but this time he was not too overwhelmed to appreciate the subtle touches of executive privilege.

"Nicholas, could you ask Michel to bring us some coffee." The priest nodded and walked out of the office.

"Come, Jeffrey, sit down. So, how are you?"

"Somewhat jet-lagged, but I'll survive."

"And the city that never sleeps?"

"Still the same."

As the two men exchanged small talk, a diminutive man, dressed in a spotless white coat buttoned to the throat, walked softly into the office carrying a tray with an elegant coffee service. Father Fraccaro supervised the placing of the tray from a distance. The man poured and then left as silently as he had entered.

"So," the cardinal said casually, as he ushered Bishop McCarthy to a pair of leather chairs surrounding the coffee service, "tell me about this text that has been found."

"Well, to be honest, Your Eminence, I don't know much. Professor Gerald Woodward, my cousin actually, claims to know who has the text. He didn't want to tell me much more about its origins."

"How do you know this text exists?"

"Gerald showed me a Polaroid depicting a portion of the text and asked me to date the script."

"I see. And you think we should be concerned about this text?"

"I can't say for certain if we should be concerned, but I think we should show some interest. It's in very good shape, written in Aramaic—clearly first century. In the fragment in the photograph I could make out these words." He handed a sheet of paper to the cardinal that bore notations in the bishop's careful hand.

The cardinal's eyes revealed nothing as he scanned the phrases on the paper. He sipped thoughtfully on his coffee, taking time to compose his thoughts before replying.

"Why don't you find out as much as you can about this text, and if we determine that it gives some cause for concern, we shall act. Any action at this moment would be premature, would it not?"

Bishop McCarthy squirmed in his seat, then reached for the sugar. With silver tongs he deposited two cubes into the fragrant brew. He tried to match the cardinal's cadence and measured words. He didn't want to give away the anxiety that was gnawing at his heart. Surely the cardinal already knew the urgency of this situation or he wouldn't have agreed to meet face-to-face in Rome.

"I agree," he said, slowly stirring the contents of the demitasse. "But wouldn't waiting for it to surface only ensure that it falls into...ah," he paused, searching for the right words, "let us say, the wrong hands?"

"What do you propose?"

"I propose that we open our own investigation—discrete of course—to find out who has the Scroll. Once we find out where it is, we can determine the exact nature of its contents and then act at that time."

"Sounds appropriate. Start the investigation, and yes, make it discrete. Keep me informed." He folded the paper containing the bishop's notes and slipped it into a pocket.

Without breaking eye contact, the Cardinal Lombardi rose from his seat, a signal that the meeting had ended. Hurriedly, the bishop removed the cup from his lips, nested it back on the saucer, and placed them on the table. His hurried, awkward movements contrasted with the cardinal's gracefulness; a calculated gesture on the cardinal's part, McCarthy thought with annoyance. The bishop quickly grasped the cardinal's hand and pressed his lips on the proffered ring.

"Thank you for coming, Jeffrey. Have a safe flight back." Cardinal Lombardi ushered McCarthy to the door that was promptly opened by the obsequious Father Fraccaro who followed the bishop out of the room.

After McCarthy's departure, Cardinal Lombardi began pacing his office, brow furrowed in thought. The information he had just been given could have momentous consequences for the Church. They had to first find and then obtain the Scroll. It must be obtained at all costs. He strode to his desk, called reception and asked for an external line.

❦

Father Nicholas Fraccaro quickly crossed the Vatican garden and walked down the hill toward the cluster of buildings that housed the Vatican Museum and the papal palace. A tiny tic under his left eye began a rhythmic twitch as the priest excitedly pushed forward across the cobblestones. Bypassing the preliminaries reserved for guests, he was immediately ushered into the office of Cardinal Vitorrio Folino.

The cardinal, a corpulent man with a pudgy head to match, hid much of his bulk behind a huge oak desk. Raising his eyes as Fr. Fraccaro walked in, he sighed and then lowered them again to continue scrawling his signature at the bottom of a letter.

"Good morning, Your Eminence," Fraccaro said.

"Good morning, father. What brings you here?" The cardinal shifted pages and continued pushing his pen across paper.

"Cardinal Lombardi just had a meeting with Bishop Jeffrey McCarthy of New York." The tic around his eye increased in tempo.

"What was it about?"

"Apparently, a text has been found—could be another Scroll."

"Really." Cardinal Folino ceased writing and raised his head. His eyes glistened darkly behind swollen lids. "Where was this found?" The restraint in his voice barely concealed the contempt he had for the sweaty little rat-faced man before him.

"I don't know. It appears that someone with photographs of the text showed it to the bishop." Fraccaro's breath quickened, drying his already constricted throat.

"I see. Thank you very much Nicholas, this is very valuable information. Keep me informed," the cardinal intoned as he dismissed the priest with a backhanded wave.

"Thank you, Your Eminence."

Nicholas Fraccaro's face flushed as he scurried from the office into the courtyard. He felt pleased that the Cardinal liked the information. The Cardinal had even called him by his first name. He'd never done that before. If it continued this way he would soon be elevated. The twitch below his left eye vibrated down his cheek to the corner of his mouth, animating the thin rodent lips.

Cardinal Folino rose from the imposing oak desk. Clasping his hands behind him, the cardinal's red-sashed belly protruded into the room, advancing ahead of his tiny feet as he began to pace the office. He needed to think.

As the head of the Vatican's Finance Office, he oversaw and managed the funding of all the Church's ventures all over the world. He enjoyed the power to withhold money from those who did not do his bidding or disagreed with him in any way. Despite this, he had long come to realize that however much power this office afforded him, he could never trump the head of the Congregation of the Doctrine of the Faith, Cardinal Marcello Lombadi. All cardinals knew the Holy Father's policy: in the event of any conflict between the doctrine of the church and issues relating to faith and all other matters, church doctrine and faith issues held sway.

This policy annoyed him daily. For as long as he had worked at the Vatican, he had coveted the office of Cardinal Lombardi. As far as Cardinal Folino was concerned, his colleague, a moderate on issues of doctrine, was nothing more than a traitor to the principles and doctrines of Catholicism and was not worthy of the office of the head of the CDF. That position rightfully belonged to him. Folino fumed silently. He had to get rid of Lombardi.

Today's new development seemed a barb in his flesh. A scroll had surfaced? Angrily he clenched his fists; his long manicured nails dug in to the soft flesh of his palms. He squeezed harder, imagining Lombardi's face, his triumphant face. Why had Lombardi received the news before he did? Fraccaro should've controlled the situation more—the smarmy priest would pay for that. The visitor should have been redirected to his office. Cardinal Folino released his fists, stared at his hands, and licked the little drops of blood that had appeared at the places where his nails had pierced the flesh.

Almost as quickly as it flamed, his anger dissipated. A smile wrinkled across the obese face as he gently reproved himself for feeling impatient. His plan, after all, was working; it was only a matter of time before he would topple Cardinal Lombardi. He'd succeeded in not only getting the innocuous Father Fraccaro into Lombardi's office, but also placed him in the trusted assistant's position. Perhaps the time had come, Cardinal Folino mused. The discovery of the text might just be the opportunity for which he had been waiting. If he played his cards right, he could soon be the new head of the CDF. Cardinal Folino ceased pacing and walked briskly out of the office.

❦

"Hello Mr. J., this is the Cardinal."

"Good morning, Your Eminence." The jarring ring had jolted the man into full alert. Wide-awake, he leaned over to peer at the glowing numerals on his bedside clock: 6:00 AM—11:00 PM in Rome, he thought to himself. The last thing he expected was to get a call from the cardinal.

"Are you still in bed?"

"Oh, no I'm awake! Ah, that is, I am in bed, but I'm awake. I've been reading." The man lied. He switched the phone from his left to his right hand and sat upright, careful not to rustle the sheets. "How can I be of assistance, Your Eminence?"

"There is something that needs to be done to further the work of Opus Dei."

"Anything for the cause, Your Eminence."

"Bishop McCarthy was in the Vatican this morning. It would appear that a Scroll has surfaced."

"Really!" The man reached for his cigarettes, slipped one between his lips and quickly lit it.

"Yes. Apparently the Bishop's cousin, someone called Gerald Woodward, has photographs of the text and knows the person who possesses the Scroll. I would like you to determine the whereabouts of this person and also keep a close eye on Bishop McCarthy. I'd like to know everything that goes on concerning this Scroll."

"It shall be done Your Eminence."

"This is of paramount importance. Do you understand?"

The man took a long pull on his cigarette and exhaled. "Yes I do. It shall be done, Your Eminence."

The line went dead.

Mr. J. rose from the bed and headed for the bathroom, the cigarette still dangling from his lips. Positioned before the toilet bowl, he felt elated. They were beginning to trust him.

He flashed back to the time when as a teen he'd been approached to join Opus Dei, an ultra right wing organization in the Catholic Church. He'd filled out a series of complicated forms, and a few months later he received a membership card together with an invitation to join a select group of members specially selected by the heads of the Opus Dei. This group, a little known faction of the Opus Dei, comprised of people who would do anything to protect the Church and its teachings. Upon joining he was told that he would be contacted, anonymously, whenever there was the need for any work to be done. The phone call he had just received was the second assignment he had been given by his contact, the man who called himself The Cardinal. Mr. J found himself wondering about the cardinal's identity. Was he really a prelate of the Church or was this merely a code name? If he was a real cardinal, which one was he? Apparently this assignment was an important one, and that meant that the leaders of the select group were beginning to trust him.

Flicking his cigarette into the toilet as he flushed, he turned to face the mirror. Inspecting his dark-whiskered chin, he toyed with the idea of advancing to the leadership of the select group. He glanced at the clock: 6:15 glowed from beside his bed. If he had a quick shower, he could get to Bishop McCarthy's office and plant the bugs before the staff came to the office. He couldn't afford to waste time; the cause was important. Instead, he returned to the bedroom and pulled on his pants. The shower could wait.

CHAPTER 11

New York, April 11, 1999

"Good morning, all," Bishop McCarthy greeted the two men seated in his office.

With some effort, Martin Case, Bishop of New Jersey, pulled his two hundred and fifty pounds out of the chair. Though he was five foot seven, most of his weight settled around his girth. By contrast, Reverend Father James Boyle, the head pastor and parish priest of the Diocese of Manhattan gracefully rose to his full height, just slightly taller than his colleague; his dark clerical suit draped nicely on his slender frame.

"Good morning," the men chimed.

"I hope this won't take long, Jeffrey, I have to attend a parish barbecue," chuckled Bishop Case. He patted his stomach for emphasis.

"What I have to tell you *is* important." McCarthy said, his smile vanishing. "I've just returned from Rome and a meeting with Cardinal Lombardi,"

"I see," said Case, a frown creasing his forehead.

"Let me get right to the point." McCarthy looked at both men, and then sat. With uncertainty filling the air, the priests exchanged solemn glances and in unison sank into their chairs. "My meeting with the Cardinal concerned the discovery of what I believe to be another scroll."

"A scroll?" said Boyle.

"Yes, a scroll."

"You mean...like the Dead Sea Scrolls?" said Boyle, leaning forward in his chair.

"Yes. And possibly just as significant," the bishop said, eyes peering over his gold reading glasses.

"What do you mean you believe it is *another* scroll?" said Case fingering the crucifix that balanced on his rotund belly.

"Let me fill you in. A few days ago, my cousin the professor paid me a visit and showed me a photograph of portions of a text that, according to him, may have been written as far back as 30 AD. He doesn't have the scroll, though he knows who does. The owner sent photographs of text fragments and asked him to date them. He realized they revealed some important sacred ideas and came to see me."

"Who has this scroll?"

"I don't know, he wouldn't tell me. But I'm sure I'll be able to get him to divulge that detail later. In any event, Cardinal Lombardi's opinion is that we should investigate the matter, discretely of course, and when we know all the facts take the appropriate action. That's why I've called you here today."

"What would you like us to do?" said Boyle.

"Just keep your ears and eyes open; notify me immediately if you learn anything from within your parishes."

"Do we know what this scroll contains?" Case said.

"No. At least not much. It's a religious text, vital to the church, I believe. The photographs contained very little text, but it was enough for me to see that it is potentially very significant. The Cardinal wants to know more, which means that he's taking this seriously. That means the Vatican is taking this seriously, and you can be certain the Holy Father will have heard about it. I have reason to believe that the whereabouts of this scroll could come to your attention—it's somewhere close to this city, and it may be known in one of your congregations." McCarthy paused and looked at both men. They nodded. He continued so softly that both priests leaned toward him. "When something this important surfaces, someone is bound to know something and start talking. Be alert!"

The bishop leaned back in his chair and looked directly at the priests. "Any questions?" he barked. The men met his forceful gaze, then nodded in assent. McCarthy slapped the arms of his chair and rose smartly to his feet.

"Well, that's it then, thank you both for coming."

⁂

The man known as Mr. J. walked out of the building and into the parking lot. When he got into his car, he placed a call.

"Hello, Max?"

"Yes," said the voice on the other end.

"There's something I need you to do for me. Meet me at our usual place at 2:00 PM tomorrow," said the man. "I'll be waiting in the parking lot."

⁂

New York, April 12, 1999

Max Jeremy Silvers, a thin wiry man with a bushy mustache too big for his face, darted between the cars in the parking lot until he came to a dark gray sedan with tinted windows waiting at the far end of the park, its engine running.

Panting from the slight exertion, he tapped on the passenger side window of the sedan. He made a mental note to try again to quit smoking. The door swung open and he got in beside the driver.

"Hello Max," said the man.

"Hey, what's up."

"There's something important I need you to do for me."

"Yeah?" said Max."

The man slipped a photograph of Gerald Woodward across the leather seat. "I want you to watch this man, find out everywhere he goes and whomever he sees or talks to. His name and address are on the back."

Max stared at the photograph for a few seconds, flipped it and memorized the data before handing it back to the man.

"I take it you don't want me to call you?" Max said.

"No, I'll call you."

"That's it?"

"That's it."

Max opened the door, stepped into the warm sunshine and squinted as he watched the smoky sedan pull away. Closing his eyes, he could see the image of Gerald Woodward etched on his eyelids.

CHAPTER 12

New York, April 15, 1999

The Messenger could see Woodward about three car lengths away. She sat in silence in the warmth of her darkened vehicle. Concealed in the shadow of the alley, she watched his every move. So predictable, she thought to herself. Nightly, his appetite brought him back to the strip, crawling slowly in his car, scanning the women who postured as they peered through the windshield. He would drive to the end of the street, execute a three-point turn and then cruise back for a second look. Inevitably he'd stop close to one of the women, open the door and the chosen one would slide in, pulling the door quickly behind her. His car would then speed away. Oblivious to all but his prey, he never deviated from the pattern.

The Messenger watched his car hurry by the alley entrance. She shut her eyes for a brief moment and reviewed her plan. She knew failure was out of the question. Opening her eyes, she reached for the keys. The engine roared to life as she slipped it into gear and exited the alley. This night she would not follow them. Having followed the man for about a week, the Messenger knew his destination. No, tonight was not the night.

Max hid in the shadows across the street from where the Messenger had been observing Woodward. He'd watched Woodward for the last three days; the guy seemed to be a regular on the strip. He withdrew further into the shadows as the car carrying Woodward and the woman accelerated past his hiding place. He waited for a few seconds, ready to follow, and opened his window to toss his cigarette butt. The sound of another car ignition and the flash of headlights in the alley across from his car caught his attention. He delayed for a moment, observing a sleek black sedan emerge from the inky depths of the alley. As the vehicle passed his hiding place, he glimpsed the silhouette of a woman.

"So *that's* where you disappeared to," he mused under his breath.

If Woodward had been married, he would have assumed that the woman was a private investigator trying to get some dirt on the old boy for a pissed-off spouse. But Woodward wasn't married. So then who was this woman following Woodward? He was baffled.

He fired up the small, dark compact he'd rented, quickly deciding that he wouldn't follow Woodward and the hooker. He knew where they were going. Instead, he'd follow this new broad who'd been casing Woodward. Surely, his client would be interested. Max slowly turned onto the main drag, keeping his eyes glued to the faint taillights of the black sedan. He followed at a safe distance, dialling with his free hand.

"Hello, Mr. J., this is Max." An awkward silence followed.

"Your instructions were not to call me," the voice said evenly. A hint of a threat lingered in renewed silence.

"Yeah, I know, but I thought you'd like to know—I got like a new development."

"What is it?"

"There's someone else interested in Gerald Woodward."

"What do you mean?"

"Well, I waited for him at his house. Only this time, there was another person waiting for him too."

"How do you know this person is interested in him; he could just have been waiting there for someone."

"Well, that is what I also thought until this person, who is a *she* by the way, started up her car and started following him just ahead of me."

"Did you say *she*?"

"Yep. Some broad. Couldn't get close enough to tell you what she looks like though. She followed him all the way from his home. I lost her, and then I spotted her again hiding in the alley. She left after he headed back with the hooker."

"Who is she?"

"Like I said, Mr. J., I didn't really see her face and I lost her before I could make out the plates. But when Woodward left the strip, she pops up again—only she's headed in the opposite direction. I followed her to an expensive part of town. Couldn't get close to the place because there was a gate and a wall around the premises."

"Did you get the address?"

"Sure."

"Give it to me."

"Forty-seven Dovecourt Avenue."

"Find out who lives there; let me know."

"Yeah. Later, Mr. J." Max, instantly aware he'd lapsed into familiarity, quickly added, "Ah...shall I phone you?"

The line went dead, a dial tone the only response to his question. A cold sweat broke out on Max's upper lip.

CHAPTER 13

New York, April 14, 1999

"Good morning." The police officer touched the bill of his cap as he stepped in front of Marianne, staring intently as she made her way toward the studio building. The morning light bathed the sidewalk golden as rush hour traffic crowded the street.

From behind her, a second officer said, "Ms. Waters?"

"Yes." She swung to face him, concern beginning to creep into her voice. Keep calm she told herself. "What can I do for you? I'm just about to go on air."

"We'd like you to come with us to the station, Ms Waters. Lieutenant Jackson asked us to escort you," said the first officer.

"Can it wait until I've done the show?"

"I'm afraid not ma'am. Our orders are that we are to take you down to the police station—Lieutenant's got some questions."

"You mean you're taking me in for questioning? Concerning what, exactly?"

"Just following orders Ms. Waters. You'll have to speak to the Lieutenant about that." The second cop moved closer, ready to take her arm. Instinctively Marianne moved back a step. As she did so, Sarah emerged from the building.

"What's going on Marianne? We only have five minutes before the show starts."

"They're here to take me down to the station for questioning."

"What for?" Sarah said, becoming alarmed. " Is something wrong?"

"These gentlemen aren't saying just yet, but they're pretty insistent, so I guess I'd better go and find out what they want with me."

"Hold on." Sarah stretched out her hand to the trio. "I'm coming with you." She flashed a look of defiance at the two officers. "Just wait and let me tell Bob to take over."

"Could you tell him to call Peter and let him know what is happening? He can meet us at the station."

Sarah quickly returned and jumped into the back seat of the police cruiser with Marianne. Within seconds they found themselves heading for headquarters. Sarah, agitated, chatted incessantly during the whole trip. Marianne stared out the window in silence and in pain. "The lieutenant," she said to herself, "must have found something." Involuntarily, she shivered.

❧

"The reason I've asked you here is that we've found a couple of bodies, Ms. Waters," Lieutenant Jackson said grimly, searching Marianne's face for a reaction. The woman's features remained immobile. "Just so happens," he continued somberly, "that the deceased are two of the missing persons whose pictures you saw the last time you were here. Remember those? You had a pretty strong feeling when you saw the photos." Jackson looked from Marianne to Sarah and then to Peter who had just joined them. A uniformed officer stood at the back of the room, adding a degree of formality that began to spook Marianne.

"Yes of course I remember, Lieutenant," she responded abruptly. "Are you surprised? I did tell you that they were dead, didn't I? That was why I reacted so powerfully to their pictures."

"That's true. You did."

"Then, what's the problem?" Marianne said, leveling her eyes to meet his.

"I'm not sure I really believe in psychic powers," Jackson said with a tilt of his head. "And, at the time, you neglected to mention how you knew these folks were dead."

"So what are you saying, Lieutenant?" Peter asked, staring fixedly at the lieutenant.

"Look! What is going on?" Sarah fired back at Jackson before he could answer Peter. "Just what do you mean by bringing her down to the station—like, was this *necessary*?" Sarah glanced at Marianne and then at Jackson, lips pursed and arms folded across her chest."

"He thinks I killed them." Marianne said quietly without taking her eyes off Jackson's face; her hands remained flat and still on the tabletop. She glanced at Sarah, then back at Jackson. "I'm right, am I not, Lieutenant? You think I killed them."

"That's bullshit!" Peter shouted angrily. "My wife's a psychic, a well-known psychic. People trust her. She came to you to tell you that she believes that some missing persons are actually dead and you suspect *her* of murdering these people? What kind of crap is that?" Peter sounded exasperated. "If my wife killed those people, do you think she'd be stupid enough to come and tell you?"

"We can't rule anyone out," Jackson said to him, then turned to Marianne. "Ms. Waters we need to be able to eliminate you from our lists of suspects."

"That's nonsense and you know it!" Sarah exploded defensively. "Why are you harassing this woman? She's above reproach—a national radio celebrity. We only came in before because she had some valuable information to share with you, and whatever you believe..."

"Let me put it this way." Jackson interrupted the rant and waved Sarah into silence. He leaned on the table bringing his face within a foot of Marianne's. She kept staring into his eyes. "I *believe*, Ms. Waters, that you're not telling me everything. I believe that you know more about how those poor people got murdered—maybe even know the identity of the likely suspect."

"Do you have any suspects?" Peter demanded.

Jackson drew back from Marianne to address him. "No we don't."

"So Marianne is your sole suspect?" Sarah charged.

"I'm not saying that—not yet anyway."

"What are you going to do with me?" Marianne asked meekly. She was beginning to tire. Pain shot through her temples.

"Nothing at the moment."

"What about Gerald Woodward?" Marianne said anxiously, leaning forward.

"We checked on him—he's fine." Jackson returned her intent gaze. "You're free to go now, but don't leave town, Ms. Waters, just in case we need to contact you."

Peter's jaw dropped; Marianne slumped in her chair and quietly began to sob. The lieutenant briskly left the room. Sarah glowered at his retreating figure as she slipped an arm over Marianne's heaving shoulders.

CHAPTER 14

New York, May 1, 1999

Woodward down-shifted into first and slowly cruised the walk. His eyes darted over the scantily clad women; their flesh glowed eerily in the lamplight. They stared back at him and struck a variety of provocative poses as he drove by, vying for the attention of this well-known, well-paying customer. He had no idea that behind his back they laughed at him, exposing his sexual foibles and ineptitudes over late night dinners in Chinatown.

He moved quickly down the block, licking his dry lips, feeling the ache in his groin. He knew from experience how to discern the particular sexual fetishes and appetites of the women by their displays. Though he knew many of the girls, Woodward never made up his mind about who to select until he got to the stroll. It was only after cruising, inspecting, that a particular urge determined the woman he would select for the evening. Tonight, he noticed, the menu was more varied than usual. As always, he was slow to choose; some of them were waving at him, urging him make up his mind. Then he saw her.

The woman was standing some distance away from the others, sufficiently close to a street lamp to ensure high visibility. She was blonde. Woodward noticed that her outfit, although suggestive, was quietly elegant.

Woodward drove slowly past her to the end of the street, turned and made his way back. He stopped a few feet away, lowered the power window on the passenger side, and leaned over the seat so that he could appraise this new one.

The woman peered back at him, slightly inclining her head. She spoke clearly, but softly; he could barely hear her.

"Hi there. Looking for company tonight?"

Woodward swallowed. "Yes. Come on in." He leaned over and opened the door.

She walked slowly and gracefully to the car and got in, lifting her stiletto-heeled legs one after the other with unhurried elegance. She pulled the door closed.

"Haven't seen you around here before—new to the area, are you?"

"You could say that."

She smiled. Woodward hit the accelerator.

⚜

Well-groomed lawns surrounded his two-storey house. He parked, got out, walked over to the passenger side and opened the door. This marked a change; he almost never opened the door for the women he brought home. Somehow, though, this one was different.

The woman shifted in her seat, lifted her long legs out of the car, and deliberately placed her feet on the ground. Woodward stepped to the side and cast a quick glance up the woman's thigh. She strategically paused to reveal a tantalizing bit of black lace at the top of one leg. She stood beside him and Woodward noticed immediately that she was taller than he was and had the well-toned body of an athlete.

Woodward shut the car door and pushed the button on his anti-theft device. The car beeped once. He turned to the woman, placed his hand in the small of her back and ushered her up the driveway to the house. As they moved in unison to the front door, he slipped his fingers over her silky buttocks.

"Patience." The woman whispered. Excited, he dropped his hand and shuffled his keys to open the front door.

Woodward's attention was so focused on the woman that he failed see they had been followed by another car now parked a block away. The driver waited, watched the couple enter the house, then stealthily slipped behind a row of bushes near the entrance, careful to get into position below a window before the security lights extinguished. When they snapped off, he raised his head and peered into the house.

He watched Woodward lock the front door from the inside, pocket the keys and then escort the woman to the living room. He motioned for her to make herself comfortable on the sofa as he dimmed the lights.

"Why don't you wait here. I'll fix us a drink. What'll you have?" Woodward said.

"Gin and tonic."

"Back in a jiffy." Woodward disappeared into another part of the house. When he returned, clad only in a bathrobe, he carried two ice-filled glasses in one hand and two bottles in the other.

"My, my, eager aren't we." The woman smiled, arching an eyebrow. He liked her tone; she seemed more educated than the rest. He liked that.

"Just thought I'd get comfy." Woodward set the bottles and glasses on a side table and, after mixing the drinks, handed a glass to the woman.

With a slow deliberate motion, she uncrossed her long legs and spread them a little. The silk skirt rustled, again revealing a bit of lace as she reached across her body for the glass. The scarf that had been thrown loosely around her neck slipped as she moved, revealing the rounded mounds of her breasts.

Woodward slid down onto the couch beside the woman, took a sip of his drink. Awkwardly and too quickly, he put his arm around her shoulders leaned over and kissed her fully on the lips. Her mouth was hot, wet. She kissed him back, arousing him even more. Then she stopped.

"Have any music?" she asked.

"Sure." Woodward reached for the remote control and pushed a button. There was a soft whirring sound and a wall of the panelling slid to the side, revealing an entertainment centre containing an impressive array of electronics and an enviable music collection.

The woman rose from her seat, sauntered over to scan the CD titles in his collection, selected one and pushed the play button. She felt his eyes on her body. Soft music filled the room. She turned, and with practiced fluid movements, slowly and seductively danced to the music's tantalizing rhythm.

She stopped a short distance away from where Woodward sat and began to sway. His throat went dry; he felt his body began to stiffen and burn. As she moved, she closed her eyes and slowly caressed her body, moving her hands from her breasts down over her abdomen and then across her thighs and up her rotating hips. The silk of her garment seemed to glisten and flow around her. Woodward felt the warmth of the gin in his belly and began nodding his head to the music, mesmerized. Slowly, rhythmically, she peeled away the filmy dress; it rippled and floated down to her feet. She was naked except for black lace-topped stockings, which clung to her thighs.

The woman opened her eyes and looked at Woodward. He sat enthralled by the sensuous display, held captive by the intensity in the woman's eyes. It was an intensity he'd never experienced before.

The woman moved gracefully toward Woodward, paused for a moment before him, swiftly untied his bathrobe, and then straddled him.

They embraced. As her tongue darted around his mouth, Woodward was euphoric—he had the intoxicating feeling of being possessed. He felt powerless to resist; in fact, he felt suddenly helpless, and at the same time, he'd never experienced such a massive erection.

She stopped kissing him. She raised her head above his and peered into his face. Her fingers dug into his back, pulling his chest forward. Feeling her hot moist breath sweep over his shoulders, he raised his head to look at her. What he saw at first excited him, then frightened him to the very core of his being.

The woman's facial features distorted; the intensity in her eyes that he witnessed earlier was replaced by something terrifyingly different. He felt as if he was being swallowed into the very depths of a fiery cave. Woodward's heart pounded. He tried to move from underneath her, but her thighs clamped on either side of his and her fingers dug deeply into his shoulders preventing any movement. He gasped as incredible sexual excitement gave way to absolute fear.

Woodward began to struggle violently, trying hard to free himself from the woman's grasp. But the more he struggled, the stronger she became and the weaker he felt. His limbs seemed to wither, their ability to move drained. His breath came in short gasps and he could feel himself beginning to choke. Wondering if she'd drugged him, he struggled to maintain consciousness. Terror rippled though his body, leaving him at once feeble and rigid. Beseechingly he raised his head to look at the woman.

"Where is the Scroll?" the woman hissed, her voice metallic and harsh.

"The...the what?" gasped Woodward.

"The Scroll! I know you have it—where is it?" she screamed. Her voice took on a reptilian quality and seemed to echo in the room.

"I-I don't have it." Woodward stuttered, blackness closing in like dark velvet on his peripheral vision. "Was this how it was going to end?" he wondered. Was this the stroke, the heart attack, the aneurism he'd always feared? He struggled to focus, struggled for his life.

"Dunno...where...it...is." The words came in raspy whimpers between gasps. Who...who are y-you?" Someone was beginning to dim the lights in the room.

Woodward never got the answer to his question.

In a startling moment of clarity, he watched the woman raise her right arm above her head. He opened his mouth to scream, but no sound would come.

"Don't you die on me, you son-of-a-bitch," she bellowed in a strangely male voice that seemed to come from a place far removed from his consciousness.

Slipping into convulsions, he noticed that her fingers had become massive elongated claws as they plunged downwards into his chest, sending shards of pain through his entire body. Woodward's bizarre last thought was that he had seen the woman before, but he couldn't remember where. He saw his own blood spatter the walls as the air from his torn lungs exploded below his chin. His head flopped forward on her breasts, which he saw in that final moment of abject terror, were covered with iridescent scales.

༄

Max saw the woman—at least, he thought it was a woman—murder Woodward. It wasn't the violence that chilled his blood; it was the ungodly scream that emitted from the house. For a brief moment he was petrified, unable to move. Then he saw the naked woman rise from the sofa and he shuddered, involuntarily taking a step backwards. The security lights blazed; he froze in his tracks. He hoped the woman hadn't noticed the sudden glare outside the window.

With his heart pounding against his ribs, he shoved himself against the building and glanced into the room just as the woman whirled toward the window. She'd reacted to the security lights suddenly flooding the lawn. Her eyes narrowed, focused, and Max knew he was in trouble.

As he bolted from the window, Max saw her out of the corner of his eye. Instantly she raised her arms and extended them in his direction. Almost immediately, Max felt as if his eyes had been wrapped in barbed wire and that he'd swallowed razor blades. The pain was excruciating, but he forced his legs to continue pounding the ground. Gripping his head with both hands, he knew that he had stayed a moment too late and that he may just pay for that mistake with his life.

Panicked and with rivulets of sweat pouring down his face, he ran in the direction of his parked car, when suddenly, he realized that everything had gone very dark. He slowed down and stared about him. It was pitch black; he couldn't see anything. What had happened to the streetlights? The house lights? Rational thought began to wane. Overcome by a surge of paralytic fear, he knew that he was running for his life.

Within seconds, he crashed violently against a tree in his path and fell heavily to the ground. Scrambling to his feet, his fear compounded. Wildly, he looked around, searching for a pinpoint of light—*any* light.

The black enveloped him. Shaken, in pain, he rubbed his eyes, but to no avail. He was so dazed that he barely noticed that he couldn't even see his hands. Had the woman thrown something into his eyes? That wasn't possible, he thought—she'd been inside the house. Maybe his collision with the tree had rendered him temporarily blind? He had no answers.

With hands stretched out before him, Max decided to walk rather than run in the direction of his car. His feet seemed to be on solid ground, either on concrete or asphalt. In desperation, he hoped that someone, anyone—a pedestrian, passer-by in a car, or a kid on a paper route—someone would see him. But he could hear no one. Not a sound guided his feet. He knew, however, he had to keep moving.

Then he heard the sound of an oncoming car. "Where were the headlights," he thought to himself. A momentary euphoria swept over him, as he raised his hands and waved. "Help me," he cried out.

No sound emitted from his mouth. Extremely agitated, silent tears poured down his face, as he realized that his voice was gone as well.

With the bone crushing impact, he felt an odd sense of relief as his body sailed through the air. In that instant, the pain dissipated from his head and the inky night wrapped him gently in her arms. Max slipped into unconsciousness before his head struck something hard on his way down. Blissful silence concealed the sound of his broken limbs tumbling through the underbrush.

˞

Max raised his hand to his head. It ached terribly. He felt a deep gash on the side of his head and a sticky wetness on his fingers. Blood. He couldn't tell how much he'd lost, but he felt weak, as if he'd lost quite a bit. Gingerly he shifted his body. The slightest movement sent hot shooting pains through his side and down his spine. Nothing broken, he decided in amazement.

Disoriented, he struggled to remember how he'd gotten in this place. He breathed in the cool night air, forcing himself to remain calm. Images flooded his consciousness. A woman's bare arms, long claws. Velvet blackness. No light anywhere. He remembered the sensations. There was the rough bark of a tree, falling on cold wet grass, a car. God! The car hit him! That was the last thing he remembered. There appeared to be something in his eyes. He rubbed his eyes but they didn't clear. The awful truth hit him: he was blind.

He could hear cars passing above him some distance away, but he had no idea what time it was, or how long he'd lain there. The shrill chirping of the crickets told him it was still dark. He needed to get to a phone, to contact Mr. J.

Slowly, he rose to his feet and stood still, listening again for the sound of the cars. They were to his left. He guessed that the road ran parallel to where he stood. He reasoned that there were two options open to him. He could scale the ravine, hail a car and then ask to be taken to his home or to a hospital. That didn't make sense. Woodward's murder meant that the area would probably be crawling with cops, so climbing the ravine was not a good idea. The second option was to try to distance himself from the scene, then get help.

He dropped to his hands and knees, searched around until his right hand touched a substantial stick. He picked it up, ran his hand along it. Straight and about four feet long, it was sturdy enough to do the job. He pulled himself upright. Holding the stick like a blind man's cane and extending his other hand, he started walking slowly away from the area. He didn't know where he was going or what was going to happen to him. Primal instincts replaced thought: get as far away as fast as you can.

CHAPTER 15

New York, May 1, 1999

The cop vomited profusely into the bushes. As the lieutenant walked up the steps, the young officer raised his sleeve to wipe his lips, gestured to the front door, and then turned to heave again.

"Poor bugger," Jackson thought to himself. "Shouldn't take rookies to the bad ones." He steeled himself and stood inside the entryway. The flash from the crime scene investigator's camera created a strobe light effect as it bounced off the walls of the home. Sunrise began to pale the sky to a dull gray; it was raining.

Jackson moved to the door of the living room and surveyed the crime scene. He stood there for a few minutes, motionless. This was how he liked to operate in a murder investigation. He closed his mind to all sound, all stimuli, as he systematically dissected the scene. The deceased became secondary as Jackson's eyes traveled over every surface, took in every detail, and sought the anomalies in the room.

He started the inventory of what he did know. There was nothing extraordinary about the room. Upper middle-class house. Moderately affluent neighborhood. Lots of university folk lived in this subdivision. Owned by a professor who lived with his sister. She'd called it in, he remembered. The name had instantly caught his attention: Woodward.

With the exception of the body of Woodward lying face-up, eyes wide, spread-eagled and naked on the couch. Blood from the massive wound in his chest had sprayed the wall, soaked the couch and pooled on the hardwood floor. Yet everything seemed to be in its place; it was all too tidy. This bothered Jackson. The room revealed little about a possible motive for the murder. This was an act of powerful rage, committed with explosive violence.

In a murder with this magnitude of brutality, he would have expected to see something obvious left behind by the killer or killers. Here, there was nothing. No bloody footprints, no messages, no weapons, nothing. He sighed. It was going to be one of those investigations.

He spotted the two glasses; both still contained clear liquid. Woodward obviously had a visitor; was this person the murderer? As to whether the visitor had been a man or a woman, they would know soon enough. Given the fact that the vic was completely naked, Jackson presumed that the meeting had been sexual.

"Lieutenant?"

Jackson turned around and saw the young policeman standing at the entrance to the hallway.

"Yeah, Stevens," Jackson said.

"You may want to have a look at this, sir, in the study," said the sergeant.

Jackson followed him down a short hallway and turned right. The uniform stood just before the doorway, standing aside for his superior.

"Somebody must've been looking for something."

Jackson stepped carefully into the room's entrance and emitted a low whistle. "Yeah," he said, "And I wonder if they found what they were looking for."

Unlike the living room and the other parts of the house, the study was reduced to chaos. Drawers had been pulled out of desks, file cabinets lay on the floor, the bookshelves had been emptied—books and papers were strewn everywhere.

"Get forensic in here. Pronto. And don't let another soul in here until they've finished." Jackson backed out of the room.

"Where's the sister, Stevens?"

"Who?"

"The woman who discovered the body."

"Outside in one of the cruisers. We called the paramedics. She's shook up pretty bad, but she's still coherent. We're taking a statement now."

"Bring her to the station when you're done. I'm headed there now." Jackson continued down the hallway and entered the living room. He glanced at the body now being photographed and walked towards the door.

"What about the other guy?" the policeman said.

"What other guy?" said Jackson.

"The one who says he hit a man with his car and called the police."

"Right. That call came in a few hours before this one did, right? You searched the area?"

"Yes sir. Came up with nothing. No body. Car's pretty banged up, though. He hit something. We're waiting for light to search the area. The rain doesn't help."

"Must have been some animal."

"Probably. But the guy's pretty shook up. Says he's positive he hit a man and knocked him through the air. Just wondering, lieutenant, these incidents being so close—could the person, this guy who was hit be the murderer? I mean, sir, presuming it was a person he hit and not an animal."

"Don't know. We'll have to see what forensics comes up with. Right now—gut feeling—I don't think there's a connection. But bring the driver to the station, take his statement and then let him go."

Jackson headed for the door. He had no answers for the murder. He only had a lot of questions. Most of the questions were for Marianne Waters. She predicted Woodward's death, but he remained skeptical that she'd seen it all in a dream. If she had, it was a very bad dream.

⁂

"Good Morning, Miss Woodward. I'm sorry for your loss."

Margaret Woodward raised her red-eyed, puffy face and nodded. Her skin was deathly pale and her clothes hung limply on her body. Shock was setting in and Jackson knew he had to get to work.

"Anything I can get you? Coffee, tea?"

"Coffee, please." Margaret Woodward's voice shook.

Jackson signaled to the policeman who stood at the door and turned his attention again to the distraught woman.

"Miss Woodward, is there anything, anything at all that you could tell us that would help us in our investigation?"

"I don't know. I don't know where to start." She looked pleadingly at the lieutenant, bruised by grief.

"Did your brother have any enemies?"

"Not that I am aware of."

"Did he talk about people who may have had something against him?"

"No. Everyone liked him—at least I think so. He was a Casanova, I do know that, but that's about it."

"When you say he was a Casanova, you mean he was a womanizer."

"Yes."

"Are you aware if he was bi-sexual?"

Margaret Woodward's eyes flashed affrontingly, then began to fill with tears.

"I don't mean to be disrespectful by that question, Miss Woodward. We have to examine every possibility."

"I don't think so. I don't know, I never considered such a thing."

"Was there any change in his attitude recently, anything that might have seemed unusual or out of character to you?"

"I'm sorry. I can't think of anything—no, wait. After Marianne Waters came to see me and I told him why she'd come, he became very withdrawn for sometime."

"Is this the same Marianne Waters who has a psychic radio show?"

"Yes, do you know her?"

"My wife listens to the program. Why did she come to see you?" Jackson said.

"I called her radio show for a reading. When she was doing the reading over the radio, something happened. It got interrupted. At first I thought something had happened to Marianne Waters."

"Why do you say that?"

"Because of the way it happened. She started by telling me that there was a dark cloud over me. She was about to explain what she meant. Then I heard a loud noise, sort of a crash, then there were voices calling her name, and then the phone was disconnected. I switched the radio back on to see what happened, but another program suddenly replaced her show."

"Is that what upset your brother?"

"Oh no. It was what she said after that—later."

"What did she say?"

"She said something was going the happen to someone close to me." Margaret Woodward's voice trailed off as the implication of what she said suddenly dawned on her. Her eyes grew large and she looked into Jackson's face, eyes wide, frightened.

"Oh my God—she predicted it!" Margaret Woodward broke down and wept.

"I'm sorry Miss Woodward." Jackson reached for the tissues and handed the box to her.

Margaret Woodward dabbed her eyes and wiped her nose.

"I apologize. It's just that I just realized that she'd predicted it all along. If only she'd not run out, if she'd explained what she meant... given us some details...maybe Gerald would be alive."

"When you say if she hadn't run out, what do you mean?"

"Marianne Waters came to my place to do a second reading. She said she felt bad about my reading having been interrupted so she wanted to do a second one. She started shuffling the cards, and I asked her what she meant when she'd said there was a dark cloud over me. She said she couldn't tell exactly. Gerald came in, she looked at him like she knew him, and then she just...ran out of the house."

"She ran out? How? I'm still not getting this, Ms. Woodward."

"She just apologized and bolted. I remember thinking that she looked like she'd seen a ghost when Gerald came into the room."

"Did she give you any reason why she had to leave so quickly?"

"No, she only said something about not being able to do *it*?"

"Do what?"

"I don't know, the reading I suppose."

"And this was what upset your brother?"

"No. He became withdrawn when I told him what Marianne had said. I guess he was worried."

"I see."

"He seemed happy. I mean recently. Something about his work."

"Do you know what this was about?"

"Not really, we rarely had conversations about his work. He kept it all pretty hush hush. But he said it was something that would make him very famous."

"I see. What exactly did he do?"

"He was a professor of ancient languages at the university and an expert paleographer."

"Pardon my ignorance, when you say he was a paleographer, what is that?"

"He was an expert in dating ancient documents by analyzing their languages. It wasn't unusual for him to get a text or a manuscript of some kind that he'd been asked to date. He's made some very important discoveries..." Her voice trailed off and a wave of grief swept her entire body.

"I see."

She brightened suddenly. "You may want to speak to Jeff—Jeff McCarthy. The Bishop. They're cousins."

"Bishop McCarthy, the bishop of New York? Why would I want to speak to him?"

"It's just that he probably knows more about Gerald's work than I do. You see Gerald visited him recently. Sometimes he consulted my brother when religious manuscripts needed some work." Her voice trailed off. "I guess I better call Jeff, he can help me with the... arrangements..."

Jackson knew he was losing her to fatigue and grief and to that terrible preoccupation that hangs like a shadow over a victim's families as they face the imminent funeral. "I appreciate your assistance, Miss Woodward. I just have one more question. Did your brother have any steady girl friend or any other, ah, romantic interests we should know about?"

"I know he was very attracted to a professor at his faculty, but I never got to meet her. Last week he talked about how she was 'very hot.' It was crude, I know," she sniffed, embarrassed. She fumbled with a tissue, wiped her nose. "I guess it's the way some men talk about women these days."

"Do you know the name of this professor?"

"I know he called her Jenny, I don't know her family name." Her voice trailed and fresh tears steamed down her face. There was nothing more that this witness could tell him.

"Thank you, Ms. Woodward, for enduring my questions at this difficult time. You've been very helpful. Again, I'm sorry for your loss. The officer will take you to a friend's house or to a hotel. Our special victims' unit will notify you when you may return to your home. I'll be in touch."

Jackson rose and extended his hand to Margaret Woodward. She grasped it weakly and hobbled from the room, a confused and broken woman.

Jackson reached for the phone. "Get me Edwards as soon as he comes in the building."

CHAPTER 16

New York City, May 2, 1999

"You in Lieutenant?" Francis Edwards poked his head around the door.

"Hey Frankie, come on in," Jackson said.

Edwards, a forensic pathologist in the New York Police Department, ambled into the office and dropped his six-foot frame into the couch with a grunt. With smudged horn-rimmed glasses, a developing paunch that appeared to be making an attempt to escape the restriction of a tightly buckled belt, and unruly curled hair graying at the temples, he lacked the Hollywood panache of television crime scene investigators.

"You look like you've been put through the wringer, Frank."

"Yeah. Got the case load from hell."

"So, got anything for me?"

"For you, I got something special." Grunting, Edwards pushed his glasses up on his bulbous nose and looked into the steaming surface of his coffee cup.

"Don't keep me waiting, Frank. What've you found?"

"Not found, learned. You guys find the body and I gather the evidence. My job it to use science interpret the evidence—the evidence speaks to me."

"Hold the lecture, Frank."

"OK, OK don't get your knickers in a knot. First, you were right about the possibility of sexual activity having occurred. We found traces of vaginal fluids. I'm running a DNA profile."

"Good. What else?"

"Well, as you saw, the vic had a gaping wound in his chest cavity. But the COD was an aneurism?"

"An aneurism? What?"

"Yep. Probably brought on by shock. That's why when the guy's heart was being ripped out of his chest, there wasn't a massive amount of blood..."

"His what? Hold up, what are you saying?" Jackson, incredulous, leaned forward in his chair and peered at Edwards who was immersed in his notes.

"Sorry?" Edwards raised his head and stared at Jackson, a mild confusion on his face.

"The vic's heart's been removed from his chest?"

"Yeah. I said that he suffered an aneurism before the heart was extracted from his body." Edwards, characteristically bland, peered over his glasses to an incredulous Jackson.

"You mean the someone removed his heart?"

"Yanked it out to be exact."

"Jesus! What kind of woman would so something like that?"

"I never said it was a woman."

"What about the vaginal fluids?"

"Well, it does indicate sexual activity with a female but the evidence can't prove that the same woman killed him—that's up to you to find out."

Edwards flipped the note pad on the couch beside him and leaned forward in his seat.

"I said yanked it out because the edges of the wound would have been clean and neat if a knife or some sharp object had been used. The edges of Woodward's wound looked more like lacerations by a clawed animal—ragged and torn. Never seen anything like it." Edwards paused, and wrinkled his nose, eyes squinting through the thick lenses. "Except," he began slowly, mouth skewed as if tasting something bitter, "When I was a teenager I went camping with some friends and we came across an animal mauled by a grizzly. The edges of Woodward's wound looked like that."

"Jeeze. What kind of weapon could have done that?"

"Don't know. Must be something that looks like a claw. There's no weapon, and no remnants or residues in the wound that I can connect with a weapon. Nothing to identify what caused the gashes. Autopsy explains why the blood spatter is inconsistent with this wounding being the cause of death. A person—or persons—extracted the heart *after* the guy suffered a fatal aneurism. That's why there's not a huge amount of blood spray." Edwards smiled thinly as he looked at the shocked look on his colleague's face.

"Can't tell you how the heart was ripped out or why. Again, that's your job. You never know what some psycho can dream up. Do know one thing though—whoever did it would have to be extraordinarily strong. To rip a person's heart out like that, the blow would have to slice tissue, penetrate fairly dense muscle, and crush bone. This guy's ribs were splintered like he'd been hit been hit by a grenade. Almost like he'd swallowed a grenade if you ask me. I've never seen damage like this. Then, of course, the organ's missing, along with some substantial lung tissue."

Edwards rose from the couch and stretched. On the way to the door he dropped an envelope on the desk in front of Jackson.

"Here're my preliminaries," Edwards said, voice totally devoid of emotion. "When the rest of the tests come back, I'll let you know what's up."

"Thanks, Frank."

"No problem."

Edwards paused, then turned to look at Jackson. "Know something?"

"What?"

"In all my years as a forensic pathologist, I've seen some real psycho killings, but this one's unique. There's a lot of missing data here. I have a feeling you'll need lots of luck on this one."

"Thanks a lot."

"By the way, I nearly forgot."

Edwards reached into his lab coat's pocket and extracted a transparent plastic bag and tossed it to Jackson. "The finger print guys asked me to give this to you when I told them that I was coming this way."

Jackson caught the plastic bag and examined it. "Where'd this come from?"

"Our guys found them on the grounds of the Woodward house, close to a fresh set of footprints. Looks like a wallet and some other stuff that probably fell out of it. And guess what."

"What?"

"The wallet belongs to our pal Max Silvers."

"Slick Max?"

"The one and only. The guys also found a car hidden in some bushes about fifty feet from the Woodward house. The car's registered to Max. Looks like Slick was on the premises that night," Edwards said.

"Wonder what was he doing there?"

"Guess you'll be asking him that pretty soon."

"Looks like it." He watched as Edwards slipped out of the office. "Thanks Frank," he called reaching for the phone.

"Anytime," came the muffled reply.

Jackson barely heard. His mind was racing as he jabbed at numbers on the phone pad. As he waited for a connection, Jackson emptied the bag's contents onto his desk with his free hand; the wallet tumbled to the blotter along with a piece of paper scribbled with numbers. They looked like lottery numbers. Jackson put the paper aside and began to sort through the wallet's contents.

There were a few dollar bills, the usual credit cards, business cards and a New York driver's license. Turning it in his hands, Jackson peered at the familiar face and read the name: Maxwell Jeremy Silvers. Jackson chuckled at the thought that Slick Max who projected a tough-guy image had Jeremy as a middle name.

Jackson sorted through the business cards. Most were trades or commercial business cards but one stopped him short: the one bearing the name Jeffrey McCarthy, Bishop of New York. Jackson slammed down the receiver. Woodward's sister had mentioned that Woodward and Bishop McCarthy were cousins.

Jackson rose from his desk and began to pace his office. He liked to pace when he was thinking; it focused his attention, helped him think clearly.

So far the Woodward murder baffled him. There appeared to be no motive for the murder. He was certain that someone had been looking for something that Gerald Woodward owned. But what? He had no idea why the man had died, if he'd in fact been murdered, or why his body had been so hideously mutilated. Very little made sense to him.

To make matters more confusing, it seemed as if the incident that he had initially dismissed as being unrelated to the Woodward murder, was connected to it. Finding Slick's wallet indicated that not only had Max been on the scene that night, but it was also likely that there *had* been a man hit by a car—and that man was Max. Still, there were so many unanswered questions. If it was Max who'd been hit by the car, where was he? It stood to reason that he was alive; otherwise his body would've turned up by now. If Max had gone to the trouble of hiding the car, it figured that he'd also concealed himself near Woodward's house. Why, then, if he was alive, had Max left his car in the bushes? Why hadn't he recovered his car instead of leaving it for the police to find?

"Where are you, Slick?" Jackson said to himself.

He suddenly stopped in mid-stride and pushed a button on the intercom to summon his assistant.

"Rob?"

"Yeah boss."

"Get the paperwork started to exhume those bodies from those recent cold case files."

"You mean the ones that were originally on our missing persons list?"

"Yeah, those are the ones. Then get hold of Edwards and tell him that we want a re-examination of those corpses. Tell him to keep in mind the way Woodward died. I want to know if there's any connection."

"Right. The doc's gonna be thrilled by that I bet."

Jackson hit the off button, grabbed his coat and headed for the door. Slick Max and Bishop Jeffrey McCarthy were both due a visit.

CHAPTER 17

New York City, May 2, 1999

"Bishop Jeffrey McCarthy, please," Jackson said. The elderly woman at the reception desk looked at him with the pained expression of one suffering an extreme case of constipation. Her glasses perched on a wrinkled nose as she peered over them at the lieutenant as if she'd encountered a foul odor.

"Do you have an appointment?"

"Unfortunately not, but I'm sure..."

"Sorry. His Grace is very busy. You'll have to make an appointment." The woman gave Jackson a stern look. The creases in her nose transferred to her puckered mouth.

Jackson removed a business card from his pocket and handed it to the woman. "Please give the Bishop this card and tell him that I'd like to speak to him. This is a homicide investigation. I'm sure he'll want to make time for me."

Jackson turned on his heel and walked to a seating area where he flopped into a deep leather sofa. He glanced back at the woman and noticed that she was speaking in low tones into an intercom as she examined his card. Jackson reached for a magazine and began to flip through it.

The magazine pages blurred as Jackson's mind went over the visit he'd just made to Max's apartment. Max hadn't been there. A woman, probably a girlfriend, obviously very worried, informed him that Max hadn't been home for a week now, and much to her distress, he hadn't called either. That meant one of two things. Either Max was implicated in the Woodward case or he'd witnessed the event and, being afraid for his life, had gone into hiding. Jackson wasn't sure which of the two scenarios was the most probable.

The lieutenant flipped through the remaining pages of the magazine and returned it to the table. Just as he reached for another magazine, a man entered the room and stood a short distance from him.

"Lieutenant Jackson?"

Jackson looked up at the man; neither smiled. "Yes."

"Please come this way, the Bishop will see you now."

Jackson rose and followed the man through several corridors until he stopped in front of a door and knocked on it.

"Come in," came the curt reply. The man turned the knob and slowly pushed open the door.

"Your Grace, this is Lieutenant Jackson." The man stood to the side, waited for Jackson to walk into the office and then he left, shutting the door silently.

Bishop Jeffrey McCarthy, dressed informally in a dark suit and shirt with a clerical collar, rose from behind a huge oak desk and walked towards Jackson, extending his hand. "Lieutenant Jackson, please come in."

Jackson, confused as to how to address the Bishop, stood still for a moment. Making up his mind to simply address the man as Bishop McCarthy, he walked forward and shook hands.

"Please come and sit down. May I offer you something to drink—coffee?" McCarthy said as he ushered Jackson to a seating area furnished with a leather couch and two wing chairs.

"Water's just fine," Jackson said.

"No drinking on duty?" The Bishop smiled at his own joke.

"No sir."

The Bishop opened a cabinet, took out a small bottle of spring water and a glass and placed them in front of Jackson, then sat facing him.

"So what brings you here? Something about a homicide?"

"Look, Sir, let's not play games. Surely you must have anticipated this visit, Bishop McCarthy. We're investigating the suspicious death of Gerald Woodward. You knew each other well, did you not?" Jackson looked into the bishop's face; it remained passive, expressionless.

"Yes. Moreover we are, or shall I say, we *were* cousins. Very sad, his death. His sister contacted me this morning. Do you have any idea how he died? Are you looking for suspects?"

"That's what we were hoping you'd be able to help us with."

"Me?" McCarthy looked surprised. "I'll give you all the help I can, but I can't see how I'll be very useful to your investigation."

"When was the last time you saw your cousin?"

"Maybe a month ago."

"Did you speak with him?"

"Yes, I did."

"Do you remember what you talked about?"

"Nothing special if that's what you mean. I can't remember exactly what we talked about."

"Did he ever discuss his work with you?"

"Sometimes. There were times when he was working on translating a document and he would call me and ask me for my religious perspective on his translation."

"Did he discuss any such translation the last time you saw him?"

"Yes he did."

"What was the nature of the discussion?"

"He was dating a text and he wanted my opinion about his findings."

"What were his findings?"

"Well, I only saw a fragment of it in a photograph, so I don't know much. He did say that he believed that the text was a sacred text of some kind that had been authored around the time of Jesus."

"How important is this text?"

"That depends."

"On what?"

"On its contents, what it says. You see, lieutenant, there are lots of texts dating from our Lord's time. Not all are significant. Why do you ask?"

"Well, Woodward's library was ransacked. It appears that whoever killed him was looking for something. Now, if this text he was dating is valuable and someone knew its value, that person or persons also knew that he was working on it and they may have killed him to get their hands on it."

"I see."

"So let's say this is an important document. How valuable would it be?"

"Well, potentially—and this is very hypothetical—it could have considerable value. For example, if it was something approaching the significance of the Dead Sea Scrolls, the text would hold more than monetary value. Of course," he chuckled, "it could also be a shipping manifest, in which case, we're talking about something considerably less important."

"Dead Sea Scrolls?"

"Yes, these were the Scrolls that were discovered many years ago. They cast doubts about the origins of Christianity."

"I see." Jackson grew pensive. "Did your cousin ever express any fears that his life might be in danger?"

"No. That was the last thing I'd expect to hear from him. He was an academic leading a pretty uneventful life, lieutenant. Remember, he lived with his sister. That must tell you something," the Bishop said, barely masking his condescension.

"Do you know anyone by the name of Max Silver?"

McCarthy tilted his head upwards and frowned in thought for a brief moment. "No, it doesn't ring a bell. Why?"

"The police found your business card in a wallet that belonged to a man called Max Silver. The wallet was found on the premises of Gerald Woodward's house the day after the your cousin died."

McCarthy grew still. Jackson noticed the bishop's lips compress and his eyes harden. He'd struck a nerve.

"Would you know how he came to have your card?"

"Couldn't say, but it wouldn't be unusual for him to have my card."

"Really? Why's that?" He was getting stonewalled, he knew, but he pushed forward.

"You sound as if I'm under investigation, Lieutenant," he said tersely, and then seemed to consciously modify his tone. "I frequently pass out my card to members of my parish. The cards change hands. As to how this person, Max Silver, came into possession of my card, I haven't a clue. I may have given it to him, or he may have obtained it from a member of my parish."

"I see. Well, thank you, Bishop McCarthy—here's my card." Jackson rose and shook hands with the Bishop. "If there's anything you think of that might help our investigation, please don't hesitate to contact me."

"Yes, I will be happy to Lieutenant. But, before you go...may I ask a favor?"

"Certainly."

"My cousin, Gerald and I, were very close. His death came as a shock to me and to the members of our family. I'd like to help in anyway that I can to shed some light on this. If possible, I'd like to be informed of the progress of your investigation—if that's appropriate, of course." The condescension had returned to the cleric's voice.

Jackson hid his annoyance. "I'll see what I can do."

"One more thing. This thing about my business card being found in the wallet of a man who could be the murderer is very troubling and could create problems for me, personally, as well as for the Church. The press would have a field day with that information if they got whiff of it. May I request that this piece information remain confidential until it needs to be disclosed?"

"First of all, Bishop McCarthy, no one's saying Silver's a suspect. He's merely a person of interest at the moment. As for keeping your name out of the press, I'll do my best, but I can't promise anything, you understand."

"Yes, of course," the bishop demurred, suddenly assuming an attitude of humility. "Thank you." He raised his eyes, made contact with Jackson, and said purposefully. "Nonetheless, I appreciate you keeping me informed."

Jackson simply nodded and walked towards the door, unsatisfied with the interview. He had a gut feeling that the Bishop knew more than he was letting on.

※

Worry clouded the aftershock of his cousin's death, and McCarthy figured Jackson was probably well aware of his discomfort. The interview, he knew, hadn't gone as smoothly as he'd planned. He had lots to worry about. Gerald was the only one who knew the person who had the sacred text in his or her possession. With Gerald's death, the bishop had now lost his only direct link to that person.

There was also the more pressing concern—who killed Gerald and why? Jackson mentioned that someone had been searching for something at the house. Though the lieutenant hadn't said so explicitly, Gerald had been murdered. Had the killer been looking for the Scroll? If this was the case, there was a whole new dimension to the quest because now the Church was competing with a person or persons unknown to obtain the Scroll, a clear indication that the Scroll was more important than originally thought. He must inform the Vatican about this new development as soon as possible.

Something stirred in his gut. The fact that his business card had been found and was a second link to Gerald's death was a disturbing detail, one that could mean potential problems.

McCarthy returned to his desk and dropped into the chair. He massaged his temples and squeezed his eyes shut. Suddenly he felt very tired.

※

Mr. J. sat at his desk staring at the recorder before him, a stunned expression on his face. He replayed the conversation between the cop and McCarthy. This had been the first he'd heard about Woodward's death.

Questions flooded his head. "Obviously the professor had been murdered? Had he been killed because of the Scroll? The fact that the police had paid McCarthy a visit suggested that they believed he was involved. Where was Max Silver?" He turned and stared at the phone, a distant expression on his face.

"Why hasn't he called?" he wondered out loud.

It was unusual for Max not to return his call. Max was usually very reliable in providing him with progress reports on his assignments. Frustration washed over him; he pushed out of his chair and began pacing the room.

A frown creased his brow. He wasn't so concerned about the apparent disappearance of Max Silver, as he felt powerless over the man's whereabouts. Suddenly he'd lost control over the situation.

"Damn!" he said to himself, "There has to be a way! There has to be a way!" he muttered to himself as he repeatedly pounded his right fist into his palm.

Interrupting his pacing, he glanced at the desk. Motionless, he stared at the phone and then suddenly rushed to open the top drawer and frantically began rummaging inside. Quickly he found what he was looking for—a slip of paper on which he had written the address of the woman who'd been following Woodward the night Silver had called him.

He stared at the paper. "47 Dovercourt Avenue," he said out loud. He had no idea who lived at that address, but he had a feeling that this woman was also interested in the Scroll. This could be the key. He felt certain that learning more about this woman would reveal the whereabouts of the Scroll and the people who were after it.

Grabbing his keys, he rushed from his office by the rear entrance and walked a short distance to a payphone. Glancing around to make sure he wasn't being observed, he dialed a private number. After a few rings, the call was answered.

"Hello, Mr. Bellamy?"

"Yes," said the voice at the other end.

"This is Mr. J. I need you to find out all you can about the person or persons residing at 47 Dovercourt Avenue."

"Must be a wealthy person," said the voice on the other end of the phone.

"Why do you say that?"

"It's an exclusive area—very expensive. You live there, you gotta be loaded, When do you need this?"

"As soon as you can?"

"You also want an internal investigation?"

"What do you mean?"

"Well, we could simply find out who lives there and tell you, but we could also get someone to go in, take photographs of the grounds and maybe the inside of the house. Of course, that'll cost more."

"Spare no expense. I need to know everything about who lives there."

"Hey, it's your buck. Will do."

"Our usual arrangements apply of course."

"Right. I don't call you; you call me. Later we arrange a place to exchange information for payment."

"That's correct."

Mr. J. replaced the receiver. His hands were damp and a cold sweat glistened no his upper lip.

CHAPTER 18

The Vatican, May 4, 1999
Cardinal Lombardi stared pensively at the wall, elbows resting on the desk. His hands formed a triangle so that only the tips of the fingers of both hands touched.

The call he had just received from Jeffrey McCarthy left him feeling unsettled and unsure of what to do next. He resisted the urge to read too much into the death of Gerald Woodward.

Perhaps McCarthy was right. The person who had killed the man had been looking for the Scroll. That would indeed suggest that the Scroll was valuable. His eyebrows arched. And *that* meant the Scroll was of utmost importance to the preservation of the doctrine of faith of the Church, which would justify a full-scale investigation with all the financial muscle of the Church being brought to bear. He squeezed his eyes shut. No, that wouldn't work. He didn't want to start a full-scale investigation because that would mean disclosing the existence of the Scroll before its importance could be ascertained.

He sighed, leaned back in his chair and clasped his fingers behind his head.

"May I be excused, Your Eminence?"

Cardinal Lombardi looked up. He had forgotten that his assistant, Nicholas Fraccaro, was standing close to his desk.

"Sorry, Nicholas. Yes, that's fine. I need some time to think."

"I shall return in an hour, Your Eminence."

"That will be fine."

Nicholas Fraccaro left the office and headed for the offices of Cardinal Folino. The muscles around his eyes began twitching uncontrollably.

CHAPTER 19

New York City, May 3, 1999

Michael Scott and his wife, Jamie jogged every evening with Shane, their German Shepherd. Usually they traveled along the trail that led from the rear of their house, through a ravine, and emerged onto the park behind the local high school.

Today, as they took the turn up the ravine Shane bolted. Michael ran after him, finally catching up to the dog who had halted and was frantically barking.

"Here, boy." Michael Scott pulled the leash from his pocket and leaned forward to attach it to his pet's collar. He'd never seen Shane behave so erratically or seen him so distressed. The hair on the dog's back was standing on end.

"What is it, boy?" Michael Scott stared at the bushes in front of them.

Jamie jogged to a halt beside him. Breathlessly she said, "Probably a squirrel or something."

"No, I don't think so. He's not usually this excited unless something is wrong. Here, let's go and see."

Michael let the dog drag him into the bushes. He recoiled when he saw a man lying on the ground with congealed blood covering his face. Adrenaline pumping, he crouched beside the moaning man and called out to Jamie.

"Call 9-1-1—there's a badly injured man back here! He's hurt bad, but he's still alive." Shane began whimpering pitifully and lay at Michael's feet, eyes darting uncertainly from his master to the prone man.

CHAPTER 20

New York City, May 6, 1999

"Edwards here. So, OK, I'm eatin' a little crow here, lieutenant."

Jackson shifted the telephone to his other hand, walked around his desk and sat down.

"Hey, Francis. What's up?"

"Your hunch was right. We exhumed all the bodies of those missing persons. I had a closer look at them—this time taking into account the advanced state of decay—and there were similarities. Couldn't say for certain that they're all missing hearts, but some of them could have the same trauma to the chest judging by the pattern of shattered rib cages. Not sure if the tissue, where it's even present, can be compared to the wounds on Woodward. But I found a few with remnants of skin and tissue that look like they are."

"Thanks, Francis."

"Sorry I didn't notice a pattern earlier."

"No problem. We weren't looking for connections when those vics came in. Who knew?"

"Still. Pisses me off that I missed it. The families are really upset with the exhumations and we'll be running more tests, so they won't be returned any time soon. Got some real heat here, but we can't avoid it." He sounded resigned, but Jackson knew Edwards was unstoppable when there was work to be done. He was one of the finest forensic docs on the eastern seaboard.

"Looks like we're dealing with the same guy—a serial killer."

"Looks like. How about the DNA profiling? Any positive results?"

"None. We ran every shred of DNA evidence through our databases—no matches, no common factor. All the victims were unrelated and bore no evidence of any other DNA. Remember, I'm dealing with pretty advanced decomp and lots of partials here."

"Right." Jackson returned the phone to its cradle and left his office. The hunch had been right, but he still had no clue to the murderer's identity. The only DNA not belonging to the victims was the vaginal fluids sample found on Woodward's body—and that was inconclusive. What Jackson did know was that whoever it was was out there, ready to kill again. Frustrated, he headed for his car. So far, the only leads, if he could call them leads, were Marianne Waters, and a woman at the university he'd identified as Professor Jenny Cameron.

One day at a time, he told himself as he headed for the parking lot—and one more pain in the ass if this lead went bust as well.

❧

New York City, May 7, 1999

"I'm looking for Professor Cameron," Jackson said as he knocked on the open door. "Professor Jenny Cameron?"

What he thought was a student sat at the only desk in the room. Jackson figured grad students were really coming up in the world; this one was stunning. He wondered where the prof was; he readied himself for a stout woman in sensible shoes, hair done up in a silver bun with a pencil stuck through it, and dressed in mouse-hair garments.

"Yes?" Jenny Cameron, whose head had been buried in a book, raised her head and stared blankly at Jackson as she re-crossed her long bare legs. Her leather mini skirt inched up her thighs ever so slightly. It was all he could do to contain a double take and resist the urge to release a silent whistle. "Woodward, you lucky bastard," he said under his breath.

"Yes?" she repeated, this time with more authority and a slight show of impatience.

"Ah...Lieutenant Jackson, NYPD. The department secretary said I could come up." He stumbled, looked at her as he thumbed over his shoulder. The awkwardness of his gesture left him feeling slightly foolish. "I'd, um, like to ask you a few questions."

"Concerning?" Jenny Cameron lowered the book she had been reading and she rose from her desk. She leaned forward on her fists, a calculated move which compressed her ample breasts, and stared into Jackson's eyes.

"May I come in? It's about Gerald Woodward."

"Oh? Professor Woodward. Yes, come in."

Jackson moved into the office, sat in the chair across from hers, all the while not taking his eyes off the comely shape of Jenny Cameron as she strode to the door, shut it and returned to her desk. She enjoyed his gaze as she lifted her arms to arrange her hair behind her shoulders.

"You said you want to know something about Gerald."

"Yes. How long have you known him?"

"About a year. He hired me; we're colleagues. Why, has he done something wrong?" He noticed a smile flicker across her lips as she folded her arms under her breasts and leaned forward on the desk.

"When was the last time you heard from him?" asked Jackson, determined to ignore the obvious.

"I don't know, maybe two weeks ago, perhaps a little more. Of course, we bump into each other in the department and in the lab. Why the interest, Lieutenant Jackson? Gerald forget to pay some parking tickets?"

"Professor Cameron, Gerald Woodward was found dead, murdered, in his house a few days ago."

"Oh my God!" Jenny Cameron's hand flew to her mouth. Jackson had shocked the woman; the flirtation was clearly over. This was the first genuine reaction he'd gotten from her.

"Are you serious? How did this happen?" Jenny Cameron's lips trembled and her eyes grew wide.

"We don't know, Professor Cameron, we were hoping you'd be able to help us. Was he depressed or anxious lately? Did he talk to you about anything that was troubling him or mention that he was fearful of something or someone?"

"Like what?"

"Well, like enemies for instance. Did he have any enemies to your knowledge?"

"No."

"Did he possess any valuables that he discussed with you?"

"Like what?"

"I don't know. His study was ransacked, so we figure whoever killed him many have been looking for something of value." Jackson was beginning to feel impatient with her obvious deflections. Clearly she was shocked, but she was also scrambling for time.

"I don't know. I mean, we never discussed any valuables—never anything personal about his home or anything like that." Jackson could see that she was becoming emotional. Her face grew flushed and he saw that she'd been taken completely off guard. He could also see that her head was swimming with ideas and he intended to get at more of those before he left.

Jenny Cameron pulled a tissue from a box on her desk, dubbed at her eyes and stammered. "He lived with a sister, I know, but…"

"Did you work together?"

She looked at him blankly. "Like I said, we were colleagues, if that's what you mean?"

"I mean did you work on the same projects?"

"No, we're in the same department, and of course we share interests in linguistics...but I really don't..."

Jackson quickly fired another question to keep her responses candid. "So you wouldn't know anything about what he was working on."

"I'd probably have an idea about some of the things he was working on if he discussed it with me. But apart from that I'd know very little about his current projects."

"We spoke to his sister and she mentioned that he'd told her that he was working on something that he said would make him famous. He wasn't very specific. Would you have any idea about what this project concerned?"

"No."

"Just a few more questions Miss Cameron. I apologize if you find this question sensitive, but I need to ask it. Was your relationship sexual?"

Jenny Cameron raised her head and looked at Jackson, confusion passed like a wave across her face and was quickly replaced with defiance.

"I don't think that's your business, Lieutenant."

"We need to know Miss Cameron?" Jackson watched her become flustered, then pause; he chose to wait out her silence.

"Why is that important?" she said softly, eyes lowered.

"We have evidence of sexual activity before he was killed."

"I see. And you suspect me in his murder?"

"That's jumping way ahead of where we're at for the moment, Professor. We need to eliminate as many people as possible from Woodward's circle of friends and acquaintances. Normal procedure, as I'm sure you understand."

Jenny Cameron, eyes still lowered, worked her lips wordlessly. Raising her head, she said hoarsely, "Yes, our relationship was sexual."

"When was the last time you met with him socially."

"Definitely not yesterday or the day before if that's what you're getting at." Jackson detected fear tinged with anger. More defiance. "About a couple of weeks ago," she shrugged.

He watched as she began fingering papers on her desk, eyes averted. "She's definitely working something in her head," he thought. "Wonder what lie's coming next."

"Would you be willing to provide us with a sample of DNA?"

"Sure—but I didn't kill him," she protested meekly.

"Thank you Professor Cameron. I'll have a lab assistant call by the office this afternoon to take a sample."

Jackson rose, headed for the door then stopped, turned and looked at Jenny Cameron. "By the way, do you know someone by the name of Max Silver?"

"No. Should I?"

"Just thought I'd ask. Did the name ever come up in your conversations with Professor Woodward."

"No." She sighed, swivelled her chair away from him and looked out the window, clearly dismissing him.

"Well, I'll be leaving now. If you think of anything at all that might help us, don't hesitate to contact me." Jackson reached into his pocket. "Here's my card." She ignored him; he flipped the card on the desk.

"Just one more question, Professor." He stretched out the word *professor*. She swung her gaze back to his face. He caught a look of cold contempt. "You wouldn't know if Gerald Woodward was a member of a cult or anything like that would you?"

Her face remained motionless, unreadable. "No. Why?"

"Oh, because of the way he was killed. Just thought I'd ask. Thank you Professor Cameron."

Jackson saw the colour drain from her face as he turned on his heel and hurried out of the office. A chill ran down his spine. She was lying, he was sure of that, but as to how or why, he couldn't figure. More questions—fewer answers; damn.

☙

Jenny Cameron dried her eyes, dropped the tissue into the garbage container beside her desk. The tears surprised her, even more so that she'd cried for almost twenty minutes after the lieutenant had left. She reached for another tissue, punched a series of numbers on her phone to redirect all calls to her voice mail, rose and walked quickly out of the office. She felt confused. Gerald? Murdered? Tears burned again in her eyes, but she realized that this was not the time. She had to inform her contact that the police had been asking questions. It was important that nothing expose the existence of the Brotherhood. Moreover, it would not be good if her contact sensed that she was emotional: it would be a sign of weakness.

She crossed the street to the parking lot. In her car, she dialled, listened for the required number of rings, ended the call and waited.

A short while later her cell rang.

"You called?"

"Yes. I just got a visit from a Lieutenant Jackson from the NYPD."

"What did he want?" The voice was neutral—bland.

"Gerald Woodward, the one who had the photographs, has been murdered. The Lieutenant came to ask me questions about him. I thought you should know. Of course, I couldn't tell him much. I didn't mention the photographs."

"You've done well. What did he want to know?"

"He wanted to know whether Gerald Woodward had any enemies, whether we had ever discussed valuables, and he wanted to know about his work."

"And you didn't tell him anything about the photos or what the professor was working on last week?"

"No."

"You've done well. Thank you. We shall deal with it. But you are to keep your knowledge of the work and the photographs secret. That is what the Master commands."

"No one shall know. The policeman also asked me other questions and I don't know what to make of them. He wanted to know if the name Max Silver had ever come up in my conversations with Gerald Woodward."

"Why did he ask you those questions?"

"I have no idea. I've never heard that name." Her last remark was met with stony silence. She felt her heartbeat quicken and her throat grew tight.

"OK, we'll deal with it."

The phone went dead.

Immediately after his call from Jenny Cameron the man redialled and raised the receiver slowly to his ear. He closed his eyes as he waited.

"Yes," said the Messenger.

"It is I, Master. We may have a problem. Nothing serious at the moment, but it could become a problem."

"What is it?" The Master's voice sounded impatient. The man hurried to explain.

"Jenny Cameron was contacted by the police about Gerald Woodward, the professor who had the photos. So far, he claims his visit is just part of a routine homicide investigation.

"Did she say anything to draw attention to us?"

"She said she did not."

"What do you think?"

"I can't say that I am a hundred percent sure…"

"How reliable is she?" the Messenger snapped.

"Reasonably reliable, but it is difficult to tell what she'll do. She had a sexual relationship with him." The man elongated the vowels in the word *sexual*.

"I see. We don't want any problems. Not at this time. Deal with it. Do not draw any attention to us. The words were delivered with staccato precision."

"I understand, Master. There is also one other thing. She also said that the police asked her questions about someone called Max Silver. I'm not sure what that means."

"Find out all that you can," said the woman before the line went dead.

Hands trembling with excitement, Mr. B. returned the receiver to its cradle.

CHAPTER 21

New York City, May 9, 1999

Jenny Cameron parked in the lot farthest away from her department so she could take a long walk; the exercise, she thought, would help clear her mind. Gerald's murder had come as a nasty shock, not because she'd been attached to him, but because she'd come to some very uncomfortable conclusions about her part in the matter. She still couldn't believe he was dead.

Swiftly, she turned up a lane that led directly to the faculty's back entrance. She slowed her pace when she came to the newspaper boxes; the headlines seemed to shout at her.

Macabre Murder in New York
NYC Serial Killer?
Police Review Suspicious Deaths
Prof's Murder Linked to City Deaths

Jenny rummaged through her purse, clumsily pushed coins into a box and grabbed a newspaper. The door slammed as she eagerly scanned the lead article. Her hands began to shake uncontrollably as her eyes raced down the column. Fighting tears, she scurried into the building, praying all the while that she wouldn't run into anyone. Stoically she walked through the department's office, keenly aware that all eyes were on her. No one dared say a word as she shot past the secretaries, eyes level, and darted into her office. Closing the door behind her, she crumpled into her chair and wept bitterly, the newspaper creased in her hands.

The article said that Woodward had been found dead with a massive hole in his chest cavity. The police spokesperson gave little details, but an unidentified source suggested that the victim's heart had been extracted and that linked his murder to several other corpses recently uncovered in the New York area. The article went on to list other unexplained deaths and speculated on the possibility of a serial killer at work.

Jenny Cameron knew that this could only mean one thing; someone from the Brotherhood had murdered Woodward. Guilt and shame swept over her; she felt betrayed by the Brotherhood and responsible for Woodward's death. She'd been the one to alert the Brotherhood about the pictures, and the next thing she knew, Woodward was dead. He'd been murdered for the text—there was no other reasonable explanation. She never imagined that providing the Brotherhood with the information would result in the man's murder.

"Why did they have to kill him?" she asked, shaking her head.

Jenny's despair soon gave way to a determination to put things right. She reached for Lieutenant Jackson's business card, and quickly dialled the number.

"Jackson."

"Lieutenant, this is Jenny Cameron."

"Professor Cameron. What can I do for you?"

"I know who killed Gerald." After this outburst, she broke down and sobbed.

There was silence at the other end of the phone.

"It only dawned on me this morning after I read the morning paper. It's someone from the Brotherhood."

"Steady there, Professor Cameron. What is this Brotherhood?"

"Its sort of like a religion. They were looking for a text and I told them I'd seen pictures of the text in Gerald's office. I think they killed him to get the text." The words tumbled from her lips.

"Where are you now?"

"At the university."

"Can you come down to my office?"

"I was supposed to do two lectures, one in a few minutes, but I don't think I can teach my grad class this afternoon. I'm too upset. I'm going to cancel." She dabbed her nose with a tissue.

"Can you get here sometime in the afternoon, say around two?"

"Yes, I think so."

"I'll be waiting."

"Lieutenant Jackson?"

"Yes."

"I'm really frightened. I don't know what they might do to me if they find out that I called you."

"Our meeting will be confidential, Professor Cameron."

"Right. I'll see you this afternoon."

Jenny hung up and felt relieved, convinced she'd done the right thing. It would not bring Gerald back, but at least it would help put the killer behind bars and stop this insanity. In that instant, she decided to cancel her membership in the Brotherhood. Why, she wondered, had she ever joined such madness?

Filled with renewed determination, she wiped her eyes, notified the administrative assistant to cancel her afternoon class, snatched the briefcase from the floor, and headed for her first lecture.

ॐ

The man who'd been listening to the conversation between Lieutenant Jackson and Jenny waited until the extension light for Jackson's line extinguished, and then gently replaced the phone on its cradle.

Nonchalantly, without betraying the excitement surging through his body, he rose from his seat, purposefully walked to the coat rack, and retrieved his jacket.

"Hey, Joe. Going for some smokes. You need anything?" he said to the other cop sitting at a desk.

"No thanks, Mike,"

"OK man, cover for me. I won't be long." Mike said as he headed for the exit.

ॐ

The Messenger sat in the center of the Pentacle, eyes shut. Little beads of sweat sparkled on her brow. Alerted to the Cameron woman's betrayal, she resolved to take action, this time without any help. Mentally migrating into her inner being, she summoned the powers at her disposal. Soon she felt herself being transformed, her shape shifting. Her body doubled over. She experienced the sensation of falling through space, and in her mind's eye, she saw herself exit her physical body and soar upwards as a bird of prey. She felt the cold damp air, heard the wind beneath massive wings as she ascended above the city. Banking on wind currents and swells, she pushed against the air and enjoyed the sensation of complete control. How clearly her eyes worked! She marveled at their acuity as she gracefully flew toward the university. A high-pitched scream emitted triumphantly from her feathered throat.

ॐ

Jenny checked her watch. It was 1:30 in the afternoon. That gave her only thirty minutes until her appointment with Lieutenant Jackson, but she could make it if there was very little traffic.

She got into her car, threw her purse onto the passenger seat and slammed the door. She lay her head against the headrest and shut her eyes for a few seconds. She sighed, opened her eyes, and glancing over her shoulder for oncoming traffic, she inserted the key into the ignition and turned it. There was a whirring sound followed by a sustained coughing. She swore to herself, turned the key again as she simultaneously pumped the gas pedal. This time the engine caught and the car surged forward away from the curb. She made a mental note to call her mechanic.

Glancing at the clock on her dashboard, she still had enough time to make it to the police station. She swung the car onto the university boulevard. Good, she thought, no traffic. She accelerated in an effort to recover lost minutes.

Drawing close to the main entrance, she suddenly glanced up to see a remarkably large bird sitting on top of one of the pillars supporting the gates. She marveled at the bird's size and beauty. What a rare sight to see a raptor in this city, she thought fleetingly. Again, her eyes were drawn upward when the bird abruptly took flight and disappeared from view.

In the next instant, the bird hurtled down in front of her windshield, its huge talons bared and coming directly at her head. Instinctively she raised both hands to protect her face. Simultaneously she slammed on the brakes. The car flew into a sideways skid, and propelled by centrifugal forces, spun out of its lane towards the stone and iron gates.

Panic-stricken, she grabbed for the steering wheel and spun it forcefully, but she knew that it was too late. The car headed directly for a stone pillar. Jenny Cameron never saw the impending crash, instead she found herself locked in a stare with the giant bird. Its remarkable emerald eyes glowed into her very soul. As the car slammed into the monolithic column, the force of the impact pulled her out of her seat, through the windshield headfirst into the gate. The scream never left her severed throat.

CHAPTER 22

New York City, May 21, 1999

"It is I, Master. I have the information that you requested," said the squat little man.

"What information do you have for me, Mr. B.?" the Messenger said.

"The police found a business card belonging to the bishop in a wallet that belonged to the man called Max Silver. They found it at Gerald Woodward's house. They also found footprints in the garden behind the house and they believe that this man Silver was on the premises the night that Woodward was murdered."

"Who is this Max Silver?"

"From what I've been able to determine, it seems that he's a mercenary of some sort. He hires himself out for a price."

"I see. Where is this man?"

"He's nowhere to be found."

The Messenger rose from behind her desk and began to pace the darkened room. She stroked a large feather across her cheek, down her throat and across her breasts. At the other end of the phone line, the man waited patiently in silence.

Anger burned inside The Messenger. She knew that Silver was the person who'd been watching at the window on the night that she'd dispatched Woodward. She didn't know how much the man had seen, but she knew he'd never identify her because not only had she worn a disguise, she'd rendered him blind and mute. Still, she felt uneasy. Not finishing off Max Silver when she had the chance seemed a minor error at the time, but she would never forgive herself if it cost her the ultimate prize. She was so close to their goal, she could not afford to fail. As long as Max Silver remained alive there was always a risk, however small. Her identity must remain a secret if she was to achieve her goal.

She walked back to the desk and stood close to the phone.

"Mr. B?"

"I await your command Master."

"Max Silver must be found. We cannot afford to fail this time, do you understand."

"Yes, Master."

"When he's found, eliminate him."

"Yes, Master."

"Does the Bishop know who this man is?"

"From what he told the police, I think not. He claims that he frequently hands out his business cards to the members of his parish and that's how Silver may have come into possession of the card."

"Keep me informed," she concluded. The Messenger ended the call, walked around the desk and flopped into a chair.

Brow furrowed, she pursed her lips. How exactly did Max Silver fit into the picture? Was he just been a peeping Tom? A burglar? Or had he been there for something else? From the information she'd been given, it seemed likely that he'd been hired to follow Woodward. But, by whom? There could be only one reason to hire him: the Scroll. Whoever hired Max Silver knew about the Scroll. The crease between her brows deepened.

The Messenger knew she had to find out who her competitors were. So far her sources hadn't even hinted that anyone else was aware of the Scroll or its significance. If she was indeed in a race to obtain the Scroll—it was a race she was determined to win.

She laid the long beautiful feather on a platter on her desk; immediately it burst into flames.

CHAPTER 23

New York City, June 3, 1999

Rudolfo Bellamy, Rudy to his friends, walked down the steps of the city's Property Registry offices. Hitting the sidewalk, he ran his fingers though thick curly hair and swaggered towards his car. He looked more awkward than suave in an ill-fitting suit that unevenly draped his five foot-six frame. Barrel-chested, with a small paunch that spilled over narrow hips, Rudy was almost a caricature of himself. He spat on the sidewalk, then shoved dark aviators on his oily round face.

Rudy had been looking into the property title of 47 Dovercourt Avenue. He hadn't expected much at the registry office because years of experience had taught him that most people who owned valuable property in New York's upscale neighbourhoods preferred, for tax purposes, not to have the property listed in their own names. Almost invariably, the property was registered under a corporate name. This meant that anyone who wanted to know the real owners of the property had to go to another registry for information about the incorporators or the shareholders.

As Rudy had anticipated, 47 Dovercourt Avenue was owned and registered by a corporation, Tricom Limited. He also knew that finding out who owned Tricom Limited wouldn't be easy. Further complicating the matter was the fact that Tricom Limited was an offshore corporation, registered in Guernsey, and unlike United States corporations, their documents weren't easily located in the corporate registry.

"Where the fuck is Guernsey anyway?" Rudy said to himself.

He tossed the bundle of photocopied documents concerning Tricom Limited onto the passenger seat of his convertible, shifted, and then shot away from the curb. Instantly, he hit the brakes, as a skateboarder careened in front of his car. The teen stumbled off his skateboard, hurled loud curses in Rudy's direction, snatched up his board and ran quickly to the sidewalk. Ignoring the boy, Rudy sped noisily away, oblivious to the grit that his squealing wheels churned in his wake.

Rudy didn't know where Guernsey was, but he knew that any corporation that did business in the United States but was registered offshore usually intended to keep their affairs secret. In other words, he knew he was headed for some big time trouble if he continued working on Mr. J's assignment. As he reviewed what he had so far, an uneasiness stirred in his gut, the kind he usually got when he was about to get in over his head.

Rudy debated whether he should call Mr. J. and tell him to forget this assignment, but he convinced himself that it was too early to back out. Besides, the money was good—very good—and Rudy needed the cash.

Reaching for his car phone, he pushed the pre-programmed number that connected him directly to his office.

"Hey Nancy."

"Hi Rudy."

"Look up a place called Guernsey—it's an island somewhere."

The woman at the other end giggled.

"What's so funny, Nancy?"

"You said Guernsey's an island *somewhere*."

"O.K. So tell me *somewhere*." Rudy was used to Nancy's dumb humour, but he persevered because the broad was actually smarter than she looked and she often saved him a lot of time.

"Guernsey's an island off the coast of France. It's really a British territory."

"Well, I'll be a horse's arse. Get a map anyway and stick something on it so that I'll know where it is. Leave it on my desk."

"Sure. Anything else?"

"Yeah. Call Craig at the New York IRS and let him know that I need a favour—tell him I'm on my way. And Nancy, don't go anywhere until you speak to him *personally*."

"The things I do for you Rudy..."

"Yeah, yeah, yeah," he cut her off and replaced the phone as he came to a squealing stop at a red light.

⁂

"Hey, Craig. Got my message?" Rudy strode into the paper-strewn office.

"You bet I did." Craig Emond peered over round rimless glasses that gave him a professorial appearance. He was dwarfed in the clutter of books and journals lining his office. He managed to look as annoyed as he sounded; Rudy ignored the look.

"I told my secretary that I didn't want to be disturbed, but your Nancy managed to convince her that she had to speak to me because it was a matter of life and death. You teach her to do that?"

"Not exactly. I just told her to make sure that you got the message."

"So, what can I do for you?" Craig sighed, eyes returning to the papers on his desk.

"I need to find out the owners of certain city property. Just so happens that the property is registered in the name of a corporation."

"So go to the corporate registry. Why do you need me?"

"Because the corporation is registered offshore—Guernsey."

"Bummer. You need a flight to Guernsey, maybe?"

"Don't be a smart ass. I figured that if the corporation owns property here, then it pays property taxes here. So someone writes the checks for the taxes, and if you could check the records, there may be a contact person."

"Not necessarily. I don't think I'll be able to give you much help."

"Why?"

"Well, if my hunch is right, there'll be no contact person—no identifiable individual who writes the cheques for a corporation like that."

"Why? Don't they pay their taxes?"

"They sure do. I'll show you. By the way, buddy, you know I could get fired for telling you all this stuff and showing you the records."

"So what's your point?" Rudy flashed a lopsided grin and shrugged his shoulders.

"You owe me one," Emond sneered as he swivelled in his seat to face the computer. He keyed in his password and as the screen lit up, he turned to face Rudy. "What's the name of the property?"

"47 Dovercourt Avenue."

"Hmmm, expensive area." Emond typed, waited a few seconds and the monitor filled up with data. "Just as I thought. Look." He pointed to a section of the screen. "All property taxes have been paid, but there's no person who paid it."

"Then how did it get paid?"

"EFT."

"EFT?"

"*Electronic Funds Transfer*. The payments were wired to Uncle Sam. The government likes people who pay their taxes either by automatic debit from their accounts or by wire transfers from another account. Less work for them."

"So where was the money wired from? Shouldn't be difficult to contact the bank and speak to a manager."

Emond smiled without taking his eyes off the screen. "Not unless you'd like to travel to Switzerland."

"What d'you mean?"

"The payments were wired from a Swiss bank."

"So there's no paper trail whatsoever?"

"Hold on a minute." Emond scrolled through several screens, typed some more, and stopped.

"There's something else," he said, squinting at the monitor.

"Looks like Tricom Limited also operates a charity—says here *The Brotherhood of the Ram*. Ever heard of it?"

"Nope. Anything else?"

"No."

"What happens when Uncle Sam wants to investigate the corporation?"

"Well, that's easy. The government sends a request to the country's police authorities requesting assistance in producing documents for an investigation. If those authorities consent, the documents are sent to the FBI or whoever's conducting the investigation. But almost invariably, when it comes to finding the owners of an offshore corporation that wants to keep its affairs secret, there's not much that Uncle Sam can do. What an investigator may find is that the accounts are registered in the name of some little old lady, somewhere in Europe, who recalls being asked to sign some documents a long time ago. In most cases the old lady has no idea of what she signed."

Rudy's face registered disappointment. Mr. J. wasn't going to be pleased. Shit. He hoped it wouldn't affect that fat retainer.

"Sorry I wasn't of much use to you, Rudy."

"Thanks anyway. At least I know what I'm up against."

Emond swung around in his chair and looked at Rudy. "We still on for next weekend?"

"Sure." Rudy said absentmindedly. He brightened. "Say, can I get a print of the tax records?"

"You know I can't do that, Rudy."

"Come on. It is not as if I am a criminal or something. No one will know."

Emond sucked in some air, squeezed his lips, then whispered tersely, "OK, but anyone finds out that I did this, I'm toast."

"No one will find out—promise," said Rudy. He tried to sound earnest.

Emond hit a button on his keyboard and a few seconds later the printer spewed sheets of paper. When the printer finished, he gathered them up, quickly placed them in a plain envelope and handed it to Rudy.

"I owe you," said Rudy.

"You owe me *big* time," said Emond as he turned to his books, a pained look on his face.

Rudy walked out of the office. In the hallway outside, a man with an IRS identity tag clipped to his jacket stood at the water fountain engrossed in a file. He glanced up and smiled as Rudy walked by. Rudy nodded in response and hurried down the hall, so preoccupied that he failed to notice the man's gaze followed him. After Rudy turned a corner, the man strode behind him to the elevators. As Rudy pushed the elevator button the man raised his left hand and, pretending to rub the back of his neck, spoke into the transmitter in his wrist watch.

"He's getting onto the second elevator, don't miss him. He's wearing a dark blazer over a brown sweater," said the man.

The man returned to his office and pulled out an electronic device connected to his computer terminal. The device sent an alert anytime anyone working at a computer in the New York City Internal Revenue offices referenced any data concerning 47 Dovercourt Avenue or Tricom Limited.

Typically, the light came on a few times a year. When it did, it only took a few seconds to trace the computer terminal uploading the data and verify the nature of the inquiry. Most reports were routine.

When an IRS employee worked on a file, the computer requested that person's password as well as task codes specifying the particular reason for uploading the file. It was the IRS' method of ensuring confidentiality of tax documents. Thus, by accessing the password as well as the task codes, it was possible to trace any interest in a particular file.

That afternoon the man's system signalled that a staff member, Craig Edmond, had accessed Tricom's file. As was his practice, the man checked the input sequences to determine whether the information was being uploaded in the ordinary course of business. The input sequences indicated that though the file uploaded for a tax assessment of the property, a tax assessment of the property had been done six months ago and another wasn't due for a year. This was the kind of red flag that the spy-ware was designed to detect.

The man had been given strict orders to report any unusual interest in 47 Dovercourt Avenue. Duly alerted, he'd walked to Craig Emond's office, and pretending to examine a file, listened surreptitiously to the conversation behind the closed door. He heard Emond discussing the file with another man, someone who was definitely not an IRS employee. Suspicions confirmed, the man decided to stay in the corridor to see who Emond's visitor was. As he waited, he quickly called another member of the organization to be on standby in the lobby to follow whoever came out of Craig Emond's office.

The man felt pleased with himself. He knew that he'd done something important, though he couldn't be sure how important. It didn't matter really. He knew that the Master would be pleased.

Rudy parked his car in its usual slot in the underground garage of his office tower. Disconnecting his car phone, he slipped it into his jacket pocket, reached over to the passenger seat, picked up the documents concerning Tricom Limited, and headed for the elevator that would take him to the lobby.

As Rudy stepped into the elevator, he was so preoccupied with his own thoughts that he didn't see the car that had followed him pull into the parking spot across from his. When the elevator's doors closed, the driver left his car and walked over to Rudy's convertible, leaned into the car and tried to open the glove compartment. Finding it locked, the man glanced around to make sure he was alone, then reached into his pocket and took out a small wallet. He selected a small screwdriver, inserted the flat edge in the glove compartment lock and jacked open the door with one smooth movement. He rummaged through the compartment until he found the insurance card and copied down Rudy's personal information.

New York, June 6, 1999

Wearing the same jogging pants and undershirt he'd slept in, Rudy lounged in front of his television, slightly hung over, watching the Saturday football game, beer in hand. The doorbell sounded.

Grumbling under his breath, he hauled himself out of his chair and lumbered to the bay window. Through the sheer curtains he could see a dark maroon car parked in his driveway. Shifting his gaze to the front step, he saw the back of a man in a black suit standing on his doorstep holding a black briefcase.

"Aw, not a frigging Jehovah's Witness at this time of the morning," he despaired.

Rudy ambled to the door, prepared to summarily dismiss the man. He opened the door and his mouth opened, but before he could utter a word, the man whirled on him. Rudy felt a heavy blow to his temple. Clutching his head, he sank to his knees; then everything went black.

Rudy came to on his couch trussed up like a turkey. The television blared, sound coming in chunks of noise as the man in front of it channel surfed. Rudy managed a grunt, born more of pain and confusion than rage. The man slowly turned to face him.

"Ah, there you are—awake at last. I was beginning to wonder if you were ever going to wake up."

A thin smile played on the man's pockmarked face. He flipped the remote control onto a side table, rose from the chair and sat beside Rudy on the couch.

Rudy blinked; pain shot across his eyes with every tiny movement. The man simply watched him for a moment. Squinting, Rudy looked at his uninvited guest. Broad shouldered, about six-feet tall, he guessed, trying at the same time to clear his head. Rudy noticed the man's large, meaty hands—like those belonging to a basketball player or a prizefighter.

"Who are you? What do you want?" Rudy's tongue felt thick in his mouth. He squeezed his eyes shut, then open. The pain was excruciating. He swallowed hard.

"That's a funny question. I should be asking you the same questions. Not the first one though, I know who you are. You've been doing some snooping, Rudy, and my clients don't like it." His voice was calm and velvety smooth, but his eyes glittered with points of excitement.

"Don't know what you're talking about."

"Now that's very cliché don't you think? People always say that, especially in the movies."

The man paused, rose from the couch and looked about the room. "You got anything to drink? I'm thirsty and if that's the way you're going to answer my questions, we'll be here for a very long time, so I might as well have some refreshments."

When Rudy didn't respond, the man disappeared into the kitchen. Rudy heard the refrigerator door open and shut, then he recognized the sound of a pop can being opened. The man reappeared carrying a cola. He sat beside Rudy.

"So. Where did we leave off? Oh, yeah. I wanted to know why you were asking questions about my clients. What d'you say Rudy?"

"Still don't know what you're talking about."

"Sure you do, Rudy—47 Dovercourt Avenue, and Tricom Limited. Those two names ring a bell?" The man glanced sideways at Rudy.

"Ah, I see you've made the connection. Look. Let's save ourselves some grief—why don't you tell me why you've been asking questions." The man gently shook the can of cola. Rudy noticed the erupting fizz, noticed the man didn't drink.

"I...I was asked to find out who lived at 47 Dovercourt," stammered Rudy. Suddenly, he felt fear, a fear in his core that he'd never experienced before. He watched the man's hands, unable to concentrate on much else.

"Ah yes," the man intoned quietly, gently. "You're a private investigator. I nearly forgot. Who hired you to make these inquiries?"

"I...I...I don't know."

With frightening speed, the man's open palm violently pushed Rudy's head against the back of the couch. Rudy's eyes flew open in pain. Slowly, the man's thumb and index finger pulled apart the lower and upper eyelids of Rudy's right eye so that the eyeball protruded from its socket. With his other hand, the man slowly raised the cola until it was level with Rudy's eye.

"Do you know what happens when a can of soda is emptied into an eye, Rudy?" The voice had a surreal calmness.

The pressure of the man's fingers around his eye increased until Rudy thought that his orbital bones were being crushed.

"It feels like it's going to fucking explode, Rudy," he whispered into his ear. "And the pain—its terrible. Now, let's get back on topic. Who asked you to do the snooping?"

"I'm telling you the truth," Rudy pleaded, his voice a high-pitched whine. "I don't know his name. I only know him as Mr. J."

"Mr. J.? How romantic. So, where do you meet this Mr. J.?"

"I've never met him. He calls me, gives me my assignment and then when I'm done he pays me."

"How does he pay you?"

"Cash. He calls me and lets me know where he's dropped off the money. Gives me a different drop off place every time."

"What happens when you have to deliver something to him?"

The pressure on Rudy's eye remained constant. He could feel little droplets of pop fizz on his cheek; hear the exploding bubbles. He stared at the ceiling. The parched surface of his eye began to burn; though tears streamed down his face, his lids, pried back, could not deliver the moisture to his eyeball.

"I mail it to a postal box or I drop it off at a place he selects. I've never met him in person before." The words tumbled from his mouth; he couldn't speak fast enough.

"How convenient." The man paused; Rudy waited for a lessening of the pressure on his eye that didn't come. "Tell you something, Rudy. We're gonna make a deal with you."

"What deal?" His breath came in short bursts; he could feel his heart pounding in his chest.

"You help us reach this Mr. J."

"And what do I get?"

The man chuckled under his breath, which blew hot and sour on Rudy's cheek. "You, Rudy? How about we let you live?" The man grinned. He had surgically enhanced teeth.

"But...but, I don't know who he is."

"Hmmm. Yeah. I'm coming to that. You been paid for this gig yet?"

"No."

"So he's going to call you soon, right?"

"Maybe."

"What do you mean maybe? He pays you for work you do, right?"

"Yes, but I've already sent him some documents. I don't know when he's going to call."

"OK. So, when he calls, you tell him you got more information. It's a package of documents, see, and you need to drop it off. When he selects the drop-off point, you let me know. We'll give you a package—you drop it off. See? And then you leave the rest to us. Kapische?"

"Yes, but..."

"But what?" The gentle voice disappeared; the pressure around his eye increased.

"He may not believe me," Rudy wailed. "I...I've already sent him all the documents that I had."

"Well, it's up to you to make him believe you. If he doesn't," the man's fingers seemed to sink into Rudy's eye socket. Rudy yelped. "You're toast," the man finished.

With a final vicious push around Rudy's face, the man released his hold and rose from the couch. Rudy's head launched forward as if on a spring, eyelids blinking furiously.

The man stepped back and tossed a card onto the couch. "Here's a number where you can reach me when he calls you."

"By the way, if you're thinking of doing something stupid like being a hero or getting greedy, don't even think about it. We'll be watching you. Make one slip and we'll be all over you like a duck on a June bug. Understand?"

Rudy nodded. His eyelids barely contained his swollen eyeball. Through watery eyes, he peered at the man's back as he headed for the front door.

"Be hearin' from ya Rudy. Don't be a stranger, OK buddy? I'm sure you won't find it too difficult to get out of those ropes." He chuckled again and disappeared. A few seconds later, Rudy heard the car's engine fire then fade as it backed out of the driveway.

The ropes loosened more quickly than Rudy anticipated. He threw his hands to his face and stumbled into the kitchen to get ice for his aching eye. There on the counter, next to the pop cans, was an open bottle of drain cleaner. With shaking hands, Rudy reached for the refrigerator door.

CHAPTER 24

New York City, June 7, 1999

"Ms. Waters, may I come in?" Jackson stood on the doorstep, feeling slightly contrite after their last meeting. He wasn't used to feeling this way, but gut instincts told him that she could help with the Woodward case. Nothing had moved in that file for over a month and he feared the case was going cold.

"You're not coming to place me under arrest are you?" Marianne smiled; she was, however, only half joking.

"No. I just need a little help, that's all."

Marianne Waters stood aside to let him in and then followed him into her living room.

"You've already met Sarah Cummings." Marianne gestured in the direction of her friend who sat on a couch. Her husband rose from his chair when Jackson entered the room and nodded curtly. The remains of dinner for three were still on the dining room table.

"Yes. Good evening, Miss Cummings."

"Good evening Lieutenant. What a surprise." Sarah looked uncertain.

"And you know Peter, my husband." Jackson nodded in Peter's direction, ignoring the man's obvious hostility.

"Can I get you anything?"

"No, I'm fine. I won't be long." Jackson sat opposite the trio and cleared his throat. "First, I'd like to apologize for the way I acted the other day. I guess I was desperate for answers."

"I'll say you were," Peter interjected acidly.

"To what do we owe the pleasure of this visit, lieutenant?" Marianne queried.

"I need your help, Ms. Waters, or whatever insights you care to share."

"Is she still a suspect?" Peter demanded, unable to mask his disdain.

"It's OK. Peter."

"No its *not* OK!" snapped Peter. "The guy was a jerk to you. If I were you, I wouldn't give him the time of day."

Marianne turned to Jackson and sighed. "I'm sorry. I don't know if I can be of any more help than I've already been, Lieutenant."

"What I need to know, Ms. Waters, is this: is there anything else you can recall about the dreams and the visions that you had just before you came to my office?"

"Like what?"

"Well, did you get a vision of the person who was committing the crime and could you identify where these people were killed? I'm not sure of what I'm after. I guess I'd just like you to elaborate on what you've already told me."

"I can't think of anything more, lieutenant. The last vision that I had was of Gerald Woodward. I haven't had any more visions since then."

"Maybe the killer has stopped," Sarah said. "I've heard that serial killers sometimes do that. They go on a killing spree and then they stop for a while...maybe forever."

"I don't think the killer has quit. Gerald Woodward was found dead a few weeks ago."

"Oh my God," Sarah exclaimed.

Marianne seemed to shrink in her chair. She lowered her head into her hands. "If only you'd believed me he'd be alive."

"Maybe—maybe not," Jackson said.

"What do mean *maybe*?" she wailed. "I *told* you he was going to be killed. All you had to do was to provide him with some protection. If you'd only listened, he'd have been safe—alive!"

"See what I mean, this guy still doesn't believe you." Peter said impatiently, his eyes burning into Jackson's.

The lieutenant ignored him. "That's not what I meant. Given the circumstances surrounding his death, I don't think police protection would've prevented this from happening."

"Why is that?" Sarah looked confused.

"Well, his study was ransacked—it was a total mess when we found him. Looks like whoever killed him was looking for something. From what we have gathered, this person or persons would have stopped at nothing to get it."

"What were they looking for?" she asked.

"I have no idea. There's a suggestion that he was working on some valuable document, so the murderer may have been looking for it. That's another thing I was hoping you could help me with."

"What about the other murders? Did those people also have something the killer was looking for?" Sarah interrupted.

"Its hard to say, Miss Cummings. The bodies of the other people were all found outdoors, in various locations around the city. We've exhumed and re-examined the remains. The only similarity connecting them is a massive wounding in the chest cavity."

"What?" Marianne said.

"All the bodies had wounds in their chests. According to our forensic pathologists, there is some evidence that their hearts were ripped out of their chest cavities."

"Oh my God!" Sarah raised her hand to her mouth. Her face had gone ashen and her body began to shake uncontrollably.

"Are you all right, Miss Cummings?"

"Sarah! What's going on?" Marianne moved to sit beside her friend. She glared accusingly at Jackson. "I think you've upset her. Did you have to be so graphic? I think you've given her a terrible shock!"

"I'm sorry if I upset your friend. Look. I think you've given me all you can. Coming here was a long shot. I'll be going now, Ms. Waters, but if you think of anything, please let me know."

As Jackson rose, Sarah outstretched her hand and pleaded, "Please don't go. I'll be fine. Please stay. There's something all of you should know."

"What is it Sarah? I've never seen you like this before?" Marianne became increasingly alarmed.

"Can you get me a glass of water?" Sarah whispered, then sank back in the couch.

"I'll get it," Peter rushed to the kitchen and quickly returned. Sarah's hands trembled as she took the glass of water.

"Are you going to be OK?" Marianne asked, obviously deeply concerned for her friend.

"Give me a second, I'll be fine."

Jackson sat down again. "Is there something that you know about the murders, Miss Cummings?"

"Yes. Yes, I think I do." Sarah broke into sobs again. "They're back..."

"*Who's* back?" Marianne demanded.

"The ones responsible for these murders. I know who they are. Oh God, I can't believe that they're back!"

Peter moved forward and gently removed the glass from Sarah's hands. "Let me put this down for you. You could hurt yourself."

"Thanks Peter."

Jackson sat on the edge of his seat. "Can you be more specific, Miss Cummings?"

"About what?" Sarah gave him a confused look.

"About the people responsible. I need names and places—that sort of thing."

"I can't give you that because I don't know who they are." Sarah shuddered.

"I'm not sure I understand you Miss Cummings."

"God, Sarah! I've never seen you this way before. You're trembling all over. Who are these people?" Marianne repeated.

"I don't know their exact identities. They're called *The Watchers*—someone called a *Watcher* leads them. I only made the connection that they were the ones responsible for these deaths when you said that the bodies had their hearts ripped out."

"Who are the Watchers?" Jackson questioned. He felt excited, but years of interrogations had taught him to be patient.

"They're a satanic cult."

"So that's what she meant," Jackson said thinking out loud. He paused to digest the information. "She was telling the truth after all," Jackson said to himself.

"*Who* was telling the truth?" Marianne asked, exasperated.

"About a month ago, I got a call from a woman, a Professor Jenny Cameron up at NYU. She and Gerald Woodward had been in an intimate relationship. She told me that the members of some brotherhood had killed Woodward. I didn't take her very seriously at the time, mostly because I had no idea what she was talking about. But what you just said fits somehow with what she said she wanted to share with me."

Marianne looked at Sarah. "How do you know these people?"

"Its a long story. I had the unfortunate experience of coming into contact with them some years ago."

Peter jumped in. "Look Lieutenant Jackson, seems like this woman, this Professor Cameron, could lead you to the killers. Why don't you contact her? Why are you here bothering us, upsetting Sarah?"

"I can't—she died in a freak accident on her way to see me. Her car spun out of control and she ran into a concrete pillar. You know—those gates at the university. Died instantly."

"That was no freak accident," Sarah softly interjected. She looked directly at Jackson. "They killed her to silence her," she said solemnly. She looked around the room at the stunned faces of her friends and the lieutenant.

"I need to take you to see someone who can better explain who these people are. He may be the only one who can help you, Lieutenant Jackson. The only one who can help us—other than God, that is."

"Who is this person?" Jackson said.

"He's a priest."

CHAPTER 25

New York, June 9, 1999

An elderly aide ushered Sarah, Peter, Marianne, and Lieutenant Jackson into Monsignor Josephs' small but elegant office. The Monsignor sat in front of a hearth, his sightless eyes staring into the fire as his fingers moved quickly over the Braille book in his lap. Hearing their entry, the Monsignor set the book aside and rose from his chair. Jackson appreciated that though the priest was in his early seventies, he was fit and agile. Tall and slender, his thinning silver hair seemed to float above a prominent forehead and angular features.

"Sarah?" he said as he proffered a hand.

"Yes, Monsignor, it's me. How are you?" Sarah walked over to the priest, touched his fingertips and then affectionately embraced him.

"As well as can be expected, my child. How have you been doing?"

"Fine—until now that is." Her voice cracked.

"Everything is *going* to be fine, Sarah." He held her gently and with fatherly assurances, comforted the petite woman.

"But, Monsignor, they're back—*they're back*." Tears burned in her throat.

"I know, my dear, I know." Monsignor Josephs cradled Sarah's head on his shoulder. "But we'll defeat them just as we did the last time. Now Sarah, you must introduce me to your friends." Monsignor stared in the direction of Lieutenant Jackson, eyes opaque pale blue circles in his face.

"Excuse my manners. Monsignor. Meet Lieutenant James Jackson, NYPD, Marianne Waters and Peter Cannon. Peter is Marianne's husband. Lieutenant Jackson, Marianne, Peter—Monsignor Josephs."

The Monsignor extended his hand. The trio, exchanging glances, each shook his hand.

"Please sit down. I suspect Sarah forgot to mention that I'm blind." There was an awkward silence. "You don't have to feel uncomfortable in my presence. May I offer you some refreshments? Coffee? Tea?"

Monsignor Josephs pushed a bell beside his chair and waited. A few seconds later, a young priest arrived.

"Would you please bring us some coffee, Father Paul?"

After the priest left the room, he turned to Sarah. "So the Watchers are back."

"We, I mean *I* think so, Monsignor. I..."

"Pardon me, but I still don't get it. Just exactly who are the Watchers?" Jackson interrupted.

"Before I explain that, perhaps we should tell the Monsignor why we're here." Sarah turned to Marianne. "Do you want to start?"

"Sure. Well, Monsignor, I've been having strange dreams for some time now. In those dreams I have a vision of people who've been murdered. They were pretty graphic and personally horrifying. A few weeks ago, I was doing a radio show and a woman called. She wanted a reading done."

"Yes, Sarah's told me about your program. You are psychic then?" said the Monsignor.

"Yes. I have that gift, Monsignor. Anyway, while I was doing her reading, I got a vision of a man who'd been brutally murdered. This vision impacted me so strongly that I literally fell out of my chair, unconscious. We went off air before I could finish the reading. When I came too, I was so disturbed that I thought that if I visited this woman in person I'd be able to get some answers about what I'd seen in my vision."

The young priest returned with a tray of refreshments while Marianne was speaking. She paused for a moment as he set down a tray and waited until he left the room.

"Well, when I went to see this woman I found out that the man in the vision was her brother. I was terribly shocked—I just panicked and ran out of their home. That's where Lieutenant Jackson comes in," Marianne said, nodding to him. Jackson took the cue to continue;

"They, I mean Miss Cummings and Miss Waters, came to my office and told me that they had reason to believe that that this man, Gerald Woodward, was going to be murdered. Then, just as they were leaving, Miss Waters spotted a poster with pictures of a number of missing persons. She claimed they were all deceased, murdered based on visions she'd had of them. I have to be honest, Father, I was a little skeptical. I don't much believe in psychics. But then we found the bodies of these missing people in various parts of the city. Within days, we also found the body of Gerald Woodward in his home."

"Gerald Woodward died in his home?" The Monsignor sounded stunned.

"Yes," said Jackson.

"That's very brazen." The Monsignor, grew pensive, lowered his head, his sightless eyes rapidly moving back and forth across the floor. For a few minutes, no one spoke.

"Why's that, if I may ask?" Jackson said.

The Monsignor's blank eyes found Jackson's face. "The Watchers do not typically go after people in their homes. If they choose to kill, typically it's a ritualistic act and the bodies are abandoned, discarded like the ones you found. It makes me wonder…" The Monsignor suddenly grew silent and again lowered his head.

"Wonder about what?" Sarah said, leaning forward in her chair.

"Well, it may be that there was a particular reason for murdering Gerald Woodward. Either he was a member who strayed—or he had something they wanted. Was an autopsy performed on Gerald Woodward?" the Monsignor asked.

"Yes."

"Did they find any strange marks on his body?" said the Monsignor.

"Such as?" Jackson said cautiously.

"Any unnatural markings on the corpse—for example, did it look like he'd been branded or ritually cut?"

"No. I'm sure if there'd been something, the forensic pathologist would have noted it. One significant thing he did mention, however, Woodward had a massive hole in his chest. And, I should mention that some of the other corpses might have had the same chest trauma. Come to think of it, a few that were not too badly decomposed had evidence of symbols carved into their foreheads."

"I see." The Monsignor nodded thoughtfully. "So, we can conclude that the murderer was most likely looking for something they thought Gerald Woodward had in his possession."

"Something? Like what?" Sarah said.

"Could be anything, anything at all. Anything that would benefit to them in achieving the ultimate purpose for their existence."

"What's their ultimate purpose?" Marianne said.

"Bringing back their Master," said the Monsignor.

"You mean *the devil?*" Marianne said.

"Yes."

"I thought all that stuff about the devil was a myth," Jackson said incredulously.

"I'm afraid it isn't. Maybe it's time I answered your first question, lieutenant." The Monsignor shifted in his seat and settled into the chair. His sightless orbs, the color of glacial ice, stared ahead at something the others could not see.

"Most of us who believe in the reality of evil and the devil do not believe in the physical presence of Lucifer and his angels, or in the physical manifestation of evil. We're taught to have a holy fear of God and a fear of doing what is evil. However, the fallen angels do exist and they can indeed be physically present in our lives at one time or another."

"You mean there are devils walking among us?" Peter said.

"Is that so hard to believe?" the Monsignor asked. "Look at all the evil in the world and even right here in the City."

Peter gave a little shudder. "Yeah, well, I never thought of it in quite that way. Scary when you think of it in those terms,"

"It certainly is," Jackson said, a trace of skepticism in his voice.

"You will not find these demons walking among us with horns and pitchforks, but, believe me, they are here. The Watchers have existed for as long as I can remember. If you go and check any old newspapers for reports of strange murders—usually unsolved ones—you'll find the odd cases were the victims reportedly had their hearts removed. There have always been periods, after the defeat of the leader, when there are no murders. Then later, a new leader is chosen or ordained, if I could use that term, and sent to continue the work. Then the bizarre murders resume."

"So it is the leader—the Watcher—who does the killings?" Marianne said.

"Most of the time. The killings are part of ritual and are connected to the belief that the more blood the Watcher has on his or her hands, their power is increased. Some years ago, Sarah and her friends had the unfortunate task of finding and defeating the Watchers."

"What? Sarah! What is that about?" Marianne interjected. "You never mentioned any of this to me!"

"It's not something I like to discuss," Sarah said softly, eyes downcast. "At that time the Watchers were after Andrew."

"Andrew—*Andy*? Your son? Why?"

"Well, Andy was born under a particular astrological configuration and because of that, he was born with certain gifts or powers that the Watchers desired. He was also the only one who could recognize the Watcher." Sarah fell silent; tears coursed down her cheeks.

"I'm sorry. I had to ask, Sarah. This is all so new, so shocking. It's beginning to make a little more sense though." Marianne gently touched her friend's shoulder.

Sarah wiped tears from the corners of her eyes. "That's OK"

"Good ultimately triumphs, Sarah, never forget that," said the Monsignor.

"So the Watchers are something like a satanic cult?" Jackson said.

"They're more than a satanic cult. The human followers may belong to a satanic cult, but the leaders are a group of satanists who revere an order of fallen angels called the Watchers."

"So if they're all satanists, what's the difference between the satanic cult and the Watchers?" Jackson said.

"The Watchers, according to the ancient book of Enoch, are said to have been an order of angels that was supposed to keep an eye on the affairs of humanity. In the course of their duties, they became corrupted and bore children with humans. These children turned out not to be human, but demons who wreaked havoc on the rest of humanity.

"It is said that God destroyed these demons. He appointed Michael the Archangel to round up the Watchers and imprison them in the valleys of the earth until such time as they could be hurled into the everlasting fire. According to the book of Enoch, these fallen angels, the Watchers, now comprise Lucifer's immediate army on earth."

The Monsignor paused, leaned forward for his coffee and slowly raised the cup to his lips. He took a sip and continued.

"The human members of the satanic cult are just that—human—mere members, while the Watchers are fallen angels and high satanists in the sense that they possess powers bestowed on them by their master that the humans do not have."

"So these Watchers are back and you believe they have something to do with Gerald Woodward's death and the other deaths as well," Marianne concluded.

"Yes, it would seem so," the Monsignor said.

"So why are they back, what do they want?" Peter paused, a worried look etched on his face. "Why has Marianne been having these nightmares? Do these horrific dreams have anything to do with these Watchers?"

"I am not sure what the link is between Marianne's nightmares and the Watchers," the Monsignor paused and his voice became soft and reassuring. "It could well be that like many psychics she has a gift for prophetic visions."

"A little while ago, Monsignor, you told me that since their exile from heaven the Watchers live for one thing—to prepare the way for the return of their Master," Sarah said.

"Exactly. In the same way that Christians believe in the second coming of Christ, the followers of Satan believe in the return of Lucifer. In the same way that the Guardian Angels assist humanity in many ways, the Watchers help the followers of Satan to bring about the return of Lucifer. The followers of Satan believe that the coming of the millennium will see the return of Lucifer."

"You mean they want to bring back the devil?" Jackson asked, obviously unconvinced.

"Yes." The Monsignor said with certainty and authority.

"Holy smokes—I mean—ah, sorry Monsignor," Peter raised his hand to his mouth.

"Oh my God," Marianne whispered.

"The only question is how do they intend to accomplish this, this time?" The Monsignor paused and turned in Jackson's direction. "When you found the body of Gerald Woodward, what else did you find?"

"Nothing much," Jackson said.

"I thought you said the library had been trashed," Sarah said.

"The library?" the Monsignor said.

"Yeah, that's right. The study had been ransacked. Whoever killed him was looking for something in that library."

"Who was Gerald Woodward? What was his occupation? It may be important," asked the Monsignor.

"He was a professor at NYU. Professor of ancient languages—a paleographer, according to his sister."

The room fell silent for a moment, then Jackson added excitedly, "Wait, I think I know what they were looking for! I got a call from a professor at the university, Jenny Cameron. She was in the same department as Gerald Woodward and I guess they were, ah, romantically involved. Earlier, in the early stages of my investigation, I spoke to her about Woodward's death and basically she stonewalled me. Later, she called me—did a one-eighty—said that she knew who murdered Woodward. She claimed he'd been killed by something called the Brotherhood. She said the members of this organization were looking for a religious text and she told them that Woodward had pictures of it. I guess she blamed herself for his death."

"A religious text? Did she give you details?" The Monsignor gestured animatedly.

"No. But she asked me to speak to the Bishop of New York, so I did. The Bishop told me that Gerald Woodward had been to see him about a text of some kind. He couldn't tell me much about it because he hadn't seen the whole document. He mentioned that it was a Scroll."

"Did you say the Bishop?"

"Yeah, Bishop Jeffrey McCarthy. The Bishop and Woodward were cousins."

"We've got to speak to that woman as soon as possible and get more details," declared the Monsignor.

"Can't. I'm afraid she's dead—car accident. Happened a month ago today in fact," Jackson said.

"They got to her before she could get to you," said the Monsignor sadly.

"Did you find any religious text in Woodward's house?" Sarah asked Jackson.

"No, we weren't looking for one, but if there'd been one the killer or killers probably took it," he replied.

"What exactly did the Bishop say about this Scroll?" the Monsignor inquired.

"Well, when I asked him how valuable this text was, he said he couldn't say exactly, but he said it could be as important as some other Scrolls...."

"Like the Dead Sea Scrolls?" Peter asked leaning forward in his seat.

"That's it," said Jackson.

The trio fell into an uneasy silence. The Monsignor appeared deep in thought. After several minutes, he slowly raised his head; his sightless eyes stared hard into space. "Saint Michael protect us," he whispered, "they're searching for the Scroll of Miriam!"

"The Scroll of what?" Jackson asked, beginning to feel out of his depth.

"Not what, my dear friend, but who. The Scroll of Miriam—Miriam of Magdala—also known as Mary Magdalene." The Monsignor turned towards the others. He inhaled and spoke with a new assertiveness. "The Scroll must not fall into their hands."

"Tell us more about this Scroll, Monsignor," Sarah said.

The Monsignor sat back in his chair. He signed heavily. Fatigue seemed to come over him like a shadow.

"It is said that Miriam of Magdala was the first confidant and initiate and, maybe, the only confidant and initiate of Jesus. Esoteric theologians believe that before his death, Jesus taught her many lessons and revealed holy secrets to her. They believe that Christ instructed Miriam to record all he'd taught her and to keep this knowledge a secret until the sons and daughters of the coming age found it in the course of time. Mary Magdalene did as our Savior commanded and, with the help of a mysterious sect called the Silent Brotherhood, hid the document."

"So has this document been found?" Sarah said.

"It could be. I know of no other religious document or Scroll that would interest the Watchers at this time."

"I've heard of the Scroll, but I always thought its existence was a myth," Marianne said, "you know like the stories of the holy grail."

"There is a lot more truth to myths than you think. But think about it—given what we know, there is no other explanation. Gerald Woodward was a professor of ancient languages and a paleographer. The lieutenant just told us that the Bishop has confirmed that he was dating a Scroll which would have been written in an ancient language from Biblical times, possibly Aramaic. Woodward told his girlfriend about the work, she told the Watchers. Woodward's library is ransacked and he ends up dead."

"So that's what she meant when she said he was working on something that was hush hush," said Jackson under his breath. More pieces were beginning to fall into place.

"What's that?" said the Monsignor.

"Oh. Gerald Woodward's sister. When I interviewed her she told me that her brother was working on something that he said was highly confidential."

"The Scroll must be found," the Monsignor declared. "We must find who has it before the Watchers do. Do you know where the pictures are? You mentioned something about pictures of the text. There may be a note or something that will lead us to the person who has the Scroll."

"I don't know. We'll have to get a warrant to search his house again," said Jackson.

"What about his office at the University. The pictures may be there," Marianne suggested.

"That's true. I'd forgotten about his university office," Jackson said.

"But how do you know that the Watchers don't already have the Scroll?" Sarah said.

"If they did, it would not have been necessary to kill the other professor, Jenny Cameron. She had to be eliminated to prevent her from disclosing too much before the Scroll was located. Police scrutiny would have hampered their efforts," the Monsignor said.

"I think the Monsignor's probably right," Jackson said. "After all, the accident—if it was an accident—happened on her way to see me."

"I hope you're not thinking what I think you are, Monsignor," said Sarah.

"I think you know, my dear. It's part of destiny. You are all a part of this now," the Monsignor said.

"What's he talking about?" Jackson said.

"Its up to us to recover the Scroll," Sarah said softly, not taking her eyes from the Monsignor. The Monsignor nodded.

"Like I said I don't think the Watchers have the Scroll. Someone sent Gerald Woodward pictures of the Scroll. We have to find this person before the Watchers do," he said. "It's no coincidence that you have all been brought together. You have been chosen. But you cannot do this alone. You'll need some assistance from Sarah's friends. They've been in this situation before."

"Excuse me, Monsignor. I don't get it. I see that the Scroll and the death of Woodward appear to be connected, but I don't think the recovery of the Scroll has anything to do with me. My job is to find the bad guys—the murderer or murderers," Jackson said. "Moreover, I'm not sure I completely believe this thing about the Watchers. I'm not saying it's not true, just that I can't believe it all quite yet."

"That's perfectly all right. We cannot compel you to believe anything. You must act in accordance with your own conscience. I will say this, however, you are more connected with this whole thing than you realize. It may not seem clear at this time, but it will become clear to you very soon. I hope that we can rely on you for assistance when we need it?" The Monsignor stared in the direction in which Jackson sat.

Jackson shrugged. "We'll see."

"I'm still not exactly sure about the significance of all this. Monsignor, please tell us more. Why is the Scroll so important?" Marianne said.

"Nobody knows exactly what is in the Scroll. But many esoteric theologians believe that many secrets are revealed in the Scroll, including the precise time of the return of the Christ. It is also said to contain the secrets of the resurrection and ascension," said the Monsignor.

"The secrets of the power over life and death," Marianne said in a hushed voice.

"Exactly."

"Okay," said Jackson. "That makes more sense. I can understand why some people wouldn't mind getting their hands on that kind of information."

"Precisely," said the Monsignor. "Sarah, you must contact Stephen and the others. Where is Andrew?" the Monsignor said.

"In Scotland, on holiday," Sarah said.

"He'll have to be contacted; you know we need him. Let him know that it is time again. When you contact him, let me know the date and time of his arrival," said the Monsignor.

"I'll take you to the airport to meet him, Monsignor," said Sarah.

"That is not the reason why I need the date and time of his arrival," said the Monsignor. "I need to protect him," said the Monsignor.

"Do you think he'll be in danger?"

"He may well be. We *all* may well be. We must be prepared. And, my friends, the Scroll must be found before the cusp of the Millennium," said the Monsignor.

"Why?" Marianne asked.

"Nobody knows what is in the Scroll, but if the legend is true, that is the time when the Christ will return to walk the face of the earth. If my guess is correct, the Watchers intend to prevent this from happening."

"No shit," said Jackson under his breath.

Sarah counted on her fingers. "We have less than five months to find this person."

"One person out of a whole country," Marianne said.

"One person in the *whole world*," chimed Peter.

"Time is of the essence, my children, and we have precious little of it left."

CHAPTER 26

New York City, June 17, 1999
"Yes, James. What's up?"

"Lieutenant?" the young officer stood at the door of Jackson's office.

"Just reviewing the weekly hospital reports and I came across one that I thought you might want to see."

"Yeah?"

"Got a John Doe being admitted to the General. A couple who were jogging found him. Ambulance brought him in."

"So?"

"Well, the paramedics picked him up in a ravine in the same part of the city as the Woodward house. I was thinking about that guy who said he hit someone around the area the same night the prof was killed. I figured that this John Doe could be the man that the driver thought he smacked with his car."

"No shit!" Jackson moved to the edge of his seat. "How long ago was this? When was he admitted?"

The young officer glanced at the sheet of paper. "Just over a month ago, the second of May. That's about the time our friend Slick Max disappeared..."

"Shit. Why can't these damn reports circulate to us sooner?" Jackson shot out of his desk chair. "Could be our boy—or not. Better get over there, pronto! Know if our John Doe has been discharged?"

"Nope, not unless they did it in the last twenty minutes."

"Great. Let's check it out. Even if he's been discharged the hospital should have an address—unless he's homeless." Jackson raced around his desk, grabbed his jacket and walked briskly towards the exit. "Let's move, James."

ॐ

Within five minutes after they left the office, Mike rose from his seat outside the squad room and stretched.

"Gonna stretch my legs a little—maybe grab a sandwich. Want something from the store?"

"Sure Mike. Sandwich'll be fine. Want some cash?" said John.

"Don't worry about it. Cover for me. Back soon."

Mike quickly left the office and headed to a nearby café. He stopped short and ducked into a phone booth.

"Hey, it's me. Just called to let you know that the guy who was on the premises of the Woodward house has turned up in the hospital. A John Doe."

"Which hospital?" queried the man with the deep voice.

"The General. Jackson and another officer are on their way to see him."

"Thank you. The Master will be pleased with your assistance." The line went dead.

Mike hung up the phone and continued on his way to the café, whistling off-tune as he walked. He felt pleased. Once again he'd provided the Messenger, with invaluable assistance. He licked his lips; he had no doubt that he would be amply rewarded.

<hr />

"Holy Shit James! Look who we have here."

"Isn't that...?"

"You're damn right it is—Max Silver, Slick himself." From the doorway Jackson stared at the sleeping man. "Looks a little worse for wear, but I sure want to hear what he has to say."

"Gentlemen. Did I hear that you know this man?" They turned to face a doctor standing in the hall. She'd been attracted by Jackson's outburst.

"Yeah, we know him, Doc." He flashed his badge. "Lieutenant Jackson, NYPD. Sergeant James," he said, gesturing with his thumb. Your patient's Max Silver—we've been looking for him. Had no idea we'd find him here though. How is he? Can we speak to him?"

"When he wakes up, sure. It's nice to put a name to the face. We thought he was an amnesiac, but I guess if he's known to the police, he may have opted to remain anonymous. He was in pretty bad shape when they brought him in. He'd lost a lot of blood and was unconscious. No ID on him—no one knew who he was. He's much better now and due to be discharged in another week. Guess he'll be pretty surprised to see you guys. By the way, speaking to him is fine, but he's pretty slow with answers," said the doctor.

"Why's that?" Jackson was puzzled.

"I thought you said you knew him?" The doctor looked at both men obviously confused.

"I don't understand," Jackson said

"He's mute. But you must know that."

"He's what?"

"Mute, meaning he is incapable of speaking." said the doctor impatiently as she examined his chart and jotted notes.

"I know what mute means, but are you sure?"

"Yes, officer," said the doctor. "I examined him myself when he first came in. He has massive scarring on his vocal cords...like we see on some burn victims, though there's no sign of burn injuries. Quite the conundrum." Her brow furrowed. She stopped writing on the chart and looked quizzically at Jackson and Sergeant James. "But...do I understand you correctly? Are you saying he wasn't mute when you knew him?"

"That's right. In fact, we used to call him 'Slick Max' because he was quite the talker—always giving us elaborate stories whenever he got jammed up."

"Well he *is* mute now. I wonder what a blind man was doing in a ravine—but I guess that's your job to find that out." The doctor shrugged her shoulders and started for the door.

Jackson put his hand on her sleeve, stopping her. "Did you say *blind?*"

"Yes, this man's blind—his retinas are destroyed. We don't know if this happened when he was injured or if it was a previous incident. If he was sighted, then something pretty violent happened to cause this level of trauma to his eyes."

The doctor's pager suddenly sounded. "Oh, that's me," she said. "I have to go. Take as much time as you like with Mr. Silver. His hearing's just fine, by the way, and you can use that notebook next to his bed. He communicates by writing. Stop by the desk on the way out, won't you. We'll need some more information.

Jackson stood staring at the sleeping form of Slick Max. He hardly believed it. Slick Max, blind and a mute. How could that have happened? People just didn't get that way overnight. He knew that he'd have to wait for Max to wake up to get answers to his questions. Instinctively he knew that he couldn't afford to leave the man alone—he could almost smell the threat—but from where and from whom? He had no idea.

Jackson turned to his sergeant, "Call the desk. We need twenty-four seven surveillance on this guy. Get a uniform down here, pronto!"

"Hey Slick, can you hear me?" Jackson and Sergeant James had been waiting next to Silver's bed for three hours, watching him sleep. There had been a delay in getting an officer to cover the door, so the lieutenant had decided to wait it out in the room.

Groggy, Max turned his head Jackson's direction, opened his eyes. The orbs were completely white, covered in a thick milky tissue. Jackson winced.

"Hey Max. How ya doin' buddy? Jackson here. Doc says you can't see me or talk, but you can hear me. You got yourself in quite a jam, looks like."

A low guttural sound issued from the prone man's throat; weakly he raised his hand, pointed to his mouth and his forehead and shook his head.

"Yeah. I understand. Can you write?"

Max nodded.

Jackson reached for the pen and pad and handed them to him. "Can you tell me happened?"

Max groped for on the pad, scribbled, and turned it so that Jackson could read what he'd written. The scrawled note was terse. "Don't know. Think it was the woman."

"What woman?" Jackson said.

Max scrawled, "Woman at the house."

"The Woodward house?"

Max nodded.

"What were you doing at Woodward's house? You know him?"

Max scratched on the pad and handed it to Jackson. "Woodward asked me to meet him."

"Why?"

He shrugged. Jackson knew he was holding something back, but decided to pursue a different tack.

"Did you see what happened to him?"

Max nodded and wrote frantically. When he'd finished, he shoved the pad toward Jackson. "Got there early, saw him and woman, making out. Then the woman stabbed him. She heard me. Think she threw something in my eyes."

"Can you describe this woman?"

Max nodded and jotted more words on the pad. "Beautiful, very tall, leggy blonde—long hair. Saw her on the strip before."

"Did you see her face?"

Max tipped his open hand in short sideways movements, indicating that he didn't get a good look her face. "Just one of the girls; pretty. Tired now. Need sleep." He handed the pad back to Jackson.

"Thanks, Max. We've got a man outside your room. Your lady friend won't be visiting you in here. I'll be in touch again later." Jackson walked out of the room with the pages Max had written. His mind was racing.

"What're you thinking, boss?" asked the sergeant.

"Just about what Slick Max just told us."

"Think that psychic woman did it?"

"Don't know, James. Some of the stuff Slick told us seems pretty vague—it's all pretty subjective. I don't know. We've got only circumstances, nothing concrete. Max said it was a woman who did the guy. The forensic evidence confirms a woman had contact with Woodward just before he died. Max said it was a beautiful woman with long legs, but he claimed it was one of the girls from the strip. Said he'd seen her before. With the exception of the blonde hair, that description fits Ms. Waters—she's got real nice long legs," said Jackson, "but so do a lot of those girls."

"So, maybe she could have been wearing a wig"

"That's true."

"Who knows? Can't think of any reason why Max Silver would make up a story," said James. "If I were a betting man, I'd put everything on the psychic."

"Yeah. My gut tells me the same thing, James. But, we got nothin'. This whole psychic thing seems spooky, and it's beginning to sound like a lot a mumbo-jumbo. Looking at opportunity, I can place her there—but motive? Can't figure that yet. Her husband seems like a straight-up guy, but I don't think he knows shit."

"Yeah, boss," James shot him a look as the elevator doors closed, "we're always the last to know."

⚜

Max Silver had the pad ready in his hand when the duty nurse walked into his room.

"Good afternoon, Mr. Silver. It is nice to be able to put a name to your face now. I see we have a policeman outside your door. We don't often see that on our ward. I understand it's for your protection. Just want to let you know that we'll be looking out for you too. No need to worry; just get better. Ready for your medication?"

Silver nodded, he wished she'd quit the bull. When he felt the nearness of the woman, he reached out touched her and handed her the pad.

She read what he'd scrawled across it.

"Sure, Mr. Silver, I'll make the call for you. Don't you worry one bit. Now here's your medication." She watched as Max took his medication and removed the tray from the nightstand when he was done. "I'll make that call now, Mr. Silver."

The nurse left the room, walked to the nurse's station and reached for the phone. Quickly punching in the numbers written on the pad, she followed his instructions.

"Hello, this is Nurse Robbins at the General Hospital. I'm calling on behalf of one of our patients here, Mr. Max Silver. He was involved in an accident and lost his sight as well as his speech, and so he asked me to call this number to let someone know that he's been admitted here."

"Thank you nurse Robbins," said the voice on the other end. "Which room is he in?"

"Room 748, seventh floor in the West Wing of the hospital...."

"Thank you very much, Ms. Robbins." The voice cut her off before she could finish her cheerful banter.

∽

Mr. J leaned back in his chair. He realized that he was faced with a dilemma. With Gerald Woodward's murder, the surfacing of Max Silver could pose problems not only for him, but also for the cause. It was imperative that there be no connection between him and Max Silver. There was only one way to ensure that.

Mr. J. walked to a framed painting on the wall and removed it to reveal a small wall safe. Rapidly spinning the combination dial in both directions, he heard the tumblers click. He opened the safe, reached into it and removed a small leather wallet. He opened it, checked the contents and slipped it into his breast pocket.

He then reached into the safe for a small rectangular wooden box and placed it on a table and opened it. There was a mirror on the inside of the lid. The box contained nested trays of various neatly arranged facial disguise accessories. He selected a mustache from the collection, applied a thin layer of organic adhesive, and positioned it on his face. He smoothed and pressed the mustache into place with his fingers. Next he covered his eyebrows with false ones to match his mustache. Finally, he selected pair of dark rimmed rectangular glasses and surveyed his appearance. Satisfied, he placed the box back in the safe, replaced the painting and hurriedly left the room.

⁂

"Good evening, I'm here to see someone on the seventh floor, West Wing. Could you tell me how to get there?"

"Certainly. Go to the end of the hall way, take your first left, and you'll see the arrows that point you to our various hospital wings. Follow the overhead arrows until you get to the West Wing elevator bank, then just take one to the seventh floor."

"Thank You."

Mr. J. ran a finger over his mustache and followed the directions until he came to the elevators of the West Wing. He stepped aside for an elderly couple to get in and he followed.

"Which floor?" Mr. J. asked.

"Fifth please," said the old man.

Mr. J. pushed the fifth and sixth buttons and the doors to the elevators shut. When the elevator reached the fifth floor and the elderly couple stepped out, the doors closed and he pushed the button for the seventh floor.

When he reached his destination, he followed the numbers on the doors until he came to room 748. As he approached the room, he hesitated. Down the hall, a policeman stood outside the door. Mr. J. slowed his pace and turned as if he were going to the nurse's station. The cop looked uneasily from side to side then darted for the men's room.

He made his move and slipped into room 748. Max Silver was sleeping.

"Hello Max." A gentle nudge on his shoulder brought Max awake with a start. He consciously made his voice soft, non-threatening, broaching sympathetic. "It's OK Max; it's just me. The nurse called and told me you were here."

Max uttered a guttural sound, raised his hand and pointed to his mouth and then groped for the pad and pen on the nightstand. He scribbled a note and handed it to the man.

The note said, "No voice. Blind."

"Don't worry about it. What happened to you?" said the man.

Max scribbled another note and handed it to the man. The note said, "Long story. Followed Woodward with the woman to his house. The woman killed him. I think she threw something into my eyes. Police were here today."

"What did you tell them? Did you tell them who sent you?" His voice remained sedate, disguising the sense of urgency and apprehension he felt.

Max shook his head, wrote on the pad and handed it to the man. "Told them that Woodward asked me to meet him."

"Good. Not to worry. I'll look after you, Max. You see that you get well, and when you get out of here your payment will be waiting. Now you get some rest." He patted Max's shoulder reassuringly.

Max felt a flush of relief. Mr. J. sounded satisfied. Still medicated, Max relaxed; sleep again overcame him.

Mr. J. furtively reached into his breast pocket and removed the leather wallet, opened it and removed a hypodermic syringe. Then with one swift movement, he slipped the needle into the IV tube connected to Max's arm. "I'm sorry I have to do this, Max, but I can't take any chances," he whispered.

Max Silver's sightless eyes flew open, he gasped, stiffened and then lay still. Very still. Mr. J. waited for a few seconds and then peered into the corridor. The cop hadn't returned. The whole encounter had taken less than five minutes.

Mr. J. pocketed the syringe and Max's note pad and silently slipped away to the nearest exit. He knew that there was no need for him to hang around. Max wouldn't be resuscitated. The drug he had administered was almost instantaneously fatal.

Mr. J. was so preoccupied with his speedy exit that he didn't notice the tall muscular orderly. The man saw him enter Max's room, then watched his covert retreat as hospital staff raced into the room with a defibrillator. The orderly picked up a pail and followed him.

CHAPTER 27

New York City, July 30, 1999

Michael Bailey stepped out of the taxi and stretched. It had been a long flight, after a very nice holiday, but he was glad to be back in the good old USA.

Bailey got out his wallet, removed a few notes and handed them to the driver and then picked up his bags and bounded up the stairs to his front door. He set the luggage down in the hallway and walked directly into his living room. First things first, he thought and headed for the answering machine. The indicator flashed rapidly. He sat beside the phone and pushed play back. He skipped a number of messages and listened to others. Eventually, he heard an excited Gerald Woodward asking him to return his call as soon as possible. Michael debated whether to call him back immediately.

Deciding that Woodward sounded like he probably had a lot to say, he opted to call his friend after he'd returned from grocery shopping. Maybe he could invite the professor over for dinner and they could discuss whatever it was that seemed to have lit a fire under the old boy. Bailey was ready for some good academic conversation, eager to get back to work. He hurried to the kitchen, picked up the small-wheeled shopping cart and left the house.

Bailey walked out of the corner store with nearly a full load. The excitement in Woodward's voice still in his head, he decided not to wait and headed for a pay phone. Better to contact the guy as soon as possible and invite him to dinner that very night.

He dialled Gerald's university number and shortly the Department of Languages receptionist came on the line.

"Hello, Professor Gerald Woodward, please."

"*Who* are you looking for sir?" the woman queried. She sounded astonished.

"Woodward," Bailey repeated.

"Professor Woodward?" the woman asked again.

"That's what I said. Is there a problem?" said Bailey impatiently.

"Are you a relative or a friend?" the woman asked.

"I'm a friend. Look, what's going on?" said Bailey.

"I'm sorry, sir. I thought you knew. Professor Woodward is dead. He was found murdered in his home about two months ago." She heard a gasp on the other end of the line. "Hello? Sir? Sir?"

"Yes, I'm...I'm here...just stunned." Bailey leaned against the phone booth and gasped for air.

"I'm sorry sir. Were you a close friend of...?"

The line went dead.

⁂

Some distance from the University, the woman assigned to monitor calls to the Department of Languages for inquiries about Gerald Woodward stared at her computer screen. Just as the call ended, the computer beeped and flashed the originating call's location. The woman quickly wrote down the address, spun on her swivel chair as she reached for the phone. Hastily she dialled.

"Hello, I have a location of a caller for Gerald Woodward."

"Excellent. Give it to me," said a male voice at the other end.

"It came from Albany—78 Ravine Side Drive."

"Good work. Thank you."

The man at the other end of the line quickly hung up. Hands shaking, he placed a call to an unlisted number in Albany.

"Hello, its me. We have a location, 78 Ravine Side Drive in Albany. Get some men there—fast."

Within minutes, four men piled into a car and headed for the place where Michael Bailey had placed the call. Shortly after that they arrived at the grocery store.

A man left the passenger side of the car and walked around the area; he placed a call on his cell phone.

"Hello, this is Joseph. We're here. It's a mom'n'pop grocery store. He called from a pay phone outside."

"Anyone there?" asked an authoritative voice.

"There are three people—three phones; two men and one woman using them. What does our guy look like?" said Joseph.

"I have no idea. Follow the males, get some identification, find out where they live, and report back to me."

"Sure."

Five minutes later, two of the hired men picked the pockets of the men who'd been speaking on the pay phones, relieving them of their wallets. Meanwhile, their other two partners followed the unsuspecting victims.

Neither of the men they followed was Michael Bailey.

CHAPTER 28

New York City, August 4, 1999

Monsignor Josephs opened the door to the office. The sound of voices grew silent as he walked in.

"Good morning everyone...sorry I'm a little late. These old bones of mine are not what they used to be," the Monsignor said.

"If you ask' me, you don't look your age Monsignor."

"Thank you Sarah, you're too kind," the Monsignor chuckled. As the Monsignor made his way into the office, he stopped before a young man.

"Hello, Andy, my son, how are you?" said the Monsignor, extending his hands in greeting. "Recovered from the long flight? You seemed a little tired at the airport last night."

The young man rose and embraced the Monsignor. "Still a little jet-lagged, but fine otherwise. How are you today, Monsignor?"

"How did he know it was Andrew sitting in that seat?" Marianne whispered to Sarah. She cast an inquiring look around the room.

"The Monsignor always knows, Marianne. You'll come to appreciate that very soon," said Sarah with a knowing smile.

"Andy and I share a strong bond," said the Monsignor as he sat down on the couch beside the young man. Gazing around the room with opaque eyes, he added, "Well, it's quite a gathering we have here, I'll do the introductions for the benefit of Marianne who is the only new person here." The Monsignor named the people in the room and continued. "The only other member of the group who is not here is Melanie."

"Melanie is in Malaysia, Monsignor. She's in the middle of finishing up research for her doctoral thesis, so she couldn't make it," said Stephen.

"That's fine," he said, and then by way of explanation turned in Marianne's direction and added, "Melanie is Stephen's fiancée, Marianne. You'll meet her some day. Andy, of course you know, is Sarah's son, and Stephen is a freelance journalist who likes to dabble in astrology,

"As I mentioned in our earlier meeting, Sarah, Andy, and Stephen all share the unenviable history of battling, if I could use that expression, the Watchers. Sarah briefly told you about the first encounter with the Watchers which came about because the Watchers sought to harness the powers that Andy possesses due to the particular circumstances of his birth."

"What do you mean by *particular circumstances* of his birth?"

"According to an old prophesy, a child would be born under a particular astrological configuration, and possess certain gifts. This child would be the only one who at a particular time could recognize the Watcher for who he really is—a demon. Andy is that child. As well, Andy has certain gifts that the Watchers desire to harness in order to bring about the return of their Master. According to the prophecy, there was only one person whose destiny was to protect Andy.

"The task that Stephen and the others faced the last time, was first to find this person who could protect Andy before the Watchers got to him, and also find Sarah and Andy before he could be captured by the Watchers."

"We very nearly didn't make it," Stephen interjected.

"And here we are again," Sarah sighed.

"This time, the task is to find the Scroll before the Watchers do," the Monsignor said. "We all have to work together in the same way that we did the last time."

༺༻

The Monsignor knew that although he physically could not protect his friends from things that could happen to them, he could protect them from any spiritual and psychic attacks by the Watchers. Their meeting lasted several hours. He bid his friends good-bye, then thought about what he needed to do next.

His white cane tapping the way, the Monsignor walked briskly along the corridor that led from his room to the small chapel. When his cane touched the heavy oak door, he paused for a moment, folded it, and touched the door, running his hands over its carved surface. His lingering fingers reminded him that the carving depicted the chapter in the Book of Revelations where Saint Michael the Archangel stands over the dragon with a raised lance. He smiled.

The Monsignor pushed the heavy door and moved into the chapel. Turning right, he walked a calculated number of steps up the side aisle. At the end of the aisle, he turned left to make his way towards the center of the chapel, slowing to ascend two steps. He genuflected in front of the altar.

His fingers traced along the altar surface until he found the box of matches that was always kept there. The Monsignor walked around the altar and feeling for the protruding end of the wick of each candle, he lit all four candles.

Drawing himself to his full height, the Monsignor stood at the center of the altar, crossed himself, and began intoning the ancient ritual that would invoke the protection of the Archangel over his friends.

*

New York City, August 4, 1999

The Messenger opened her eyes. Her eyes blazed in the light of the five candles surrounding her. She fumed with a mixture of fear and anger. She'd had another vision of the old man—that infernal priest—and his friends. This time the vision had been vivid and she knew why. They had come together again to thwart her.

It was not only this collective opposing force that frightened the Messenger. She'd also sensed an unseen presence, something, or someone she could not as yet see or understand. The Messenger knew that this presence had something to do with her but she could not explain how, or why, nor did she understand what it was. It seemed as if there was a part of her that was out of her control, rebelling against her. Her inability to understand what was happening irritated her. She leaned forward from the lotus position in the center of the pentacle and slammed her fists into the floor in frustration and annoyance. The power of the blow, driven by the intensity of her anger, dented the hardwood.

Reminding herself that she needed to focus, she shut her eyes, inhaled deeply and exhaled slowly. She calmed herself. Soon, an idea began forming in her mind. She would eliminate them *all*, starting with the boy and his mother. She would do so in the same way that she'd eliminated the Cameron woman. A satisfied smile played on her lips.

The Messenger shut her eyes. She focused all her energy on changing her form. Her shape began shifting. Soon she became one with a four-legged creature of the night. When twilight dissolved into inky darkness, the creature slipped out of the dwelling and, impelled by an instinctual force it did not understand, started racing through the city's alleys and streets towards a prey it had never before stalked. A short while later the creature arrived at a house. Lurking in the bushes, it caught sight of the woman and her son through the softly glowing windows. The creature did not know why, but they were familiar. They were the prey. As it watched, it saw the boy disappear from view and then reappear at the front door. The creature, driven by a compelling force, crept closer to the edge of the bushes, poised on powerful haunches, ready for the kill.

※

Andy tied the garbage bag and walked to the front door, unlatched it and moved outside. The night was eerily quiet and unusually cold. He strode quickly down the driveway. As he reached the curb, he heard an unearthly snarl and saw a terrifying creature hurdle across the street towards him, fangs bared. A scream froze in his throat. Paralyzed, he stared in impotent fear at his attacker. Just as the creature lunged at him, there was a loud thunderous crack, and the animal collapsed in mid-air as if it had hit a glass wall. The force of the impact hurled the creature back onto the opposite curb. As Andy fled into the house, he could hear the thud of the animal's body hitting the pavement, hear the explosion of breath, a raspy scream of rage and the scraping of claws. He slammed the door, locked it, and raced for Sarah.

※

Violently crashing into an invisible wall, the Messenger was wrenched from the creature and slammed into her own body. She fell backwards in the centre of the pentacle, banging her head against the bare floor. The Messenger opened her eyes, stunned and rageful. A growl lingered in her throat. Slowly she rose to a sitting position; she glanced at the wall of mirrors. Dripping with perspiration, she saw her eyes were bloodshot and narrowed in anger. This had been totally unexpected.

"Damn them," she murmured. It was obvious that her adversaries were well protected. She must find another way of defeating them. She rubbed the back of her head, rose from the center of the pentacle and walked slowly towards the door. Her muscles ached from the impact.

CHAPTER 29

New York City, August 7, 1999

Marianne walked out of the kitchen and into the living room with a freshly made mug of camomile. Wrapping her robe around herself, she dropped into an easy chair and sipped the tea. She didn't know why, but she felt restless. Reaching for the remote, she channel-surfed for a few minutes and, not finding anything interesting, turned off the television.

"Are you coming to bed?" Peter called from their upstairs bedroom.

"In a minute." She pointed the remote control at the lower part of the entertainment centre and flicked another button. Soft classical music filled the room. She turned down the volume and let the tea warm her. She felt sleepy. Peter was snoring softly upstairs, and she told herself that she would rest her eyes a little and then join him. Slowly, she felt herself irresistibly drifting off; her eyelids involuntarily closed, heavy with sleep.

⁂

She wore a long flowing gown; a generous hood covered her head and draped her shoulders. Moving forward, she felt her thighs rubbing against each other and realized that she was naked underneath the silky garment. Pausing, she sensed a tremendous amount of energy flowing around and through her.

Suddenly, before her on a raised stone slab covered with a dark material, lay a man. Naked from head to toe, his arms and legs had been bound to the sides of the platform. Entranced by the pale light that turned his smooth skin translucent, she moved toward him.

Raising her head, she stared at the full moon, rotund and near in the velvet sky. She knew that in a few seconds the time would be ripe. She looked around her; the expectant faces of her followers were shadowed in the hoods of their cloaks. She smiled. A warmth surged through her body and she felt her nipples harden against the smooth sensuous silk of her gown. Then, as if signalled by an unseen presence, she watched her index finger reach out and trace a symbol across the chest of the man who lay on the slab. Her nail, with the bevelled sharpness of a scalpel, sliced shallowly and neatly into the naked flesh, marking her movements with little beads of blood as she drew a symbol of the zodiac. The man's breathing increased, rapidly raising and lowering his chest; she felt him shiver under her touch. His mouth opened in terror, but no sound escaped his throat. She gazed in wonder and delight at her handiwork. Locking her eyes on his, she felt pleased to see his terror. His lips parted, but again there was no sound. Softly, she touched his mouth with her finger, leaving behind a scarlet drop on his lower lip. She took one step back.

She saw herself raising both arms over her head as the low thrumming of a monotonous chant rose from those gathered around her. Though the words escaped her, she knew the chant praised her. When her hands reached their full height, nearly scraping the moon, a hush fell over the gathered assembly.

Then, without the least hesitation, her hands descended with a force she did not know she possessed and plunged into the torso of the man. Her fingers slipped into his chest as if she were diving into still water. Slipping through muscle and forcing apart ribs, her fingers touched the pulsating heart. It felt like a small animal in her grasp, wiggling to be free. She smiled, paused for a moment and let her fingers caress the outline of the man's heart. So soft, yet firm, pulsating with life against her palms.

Then without warning, her fingers choked the heart, and with a rib-shattering twist of her wrists, she wrenched it out of the man's chest. Triumphantly, she held the still throbbing organ aloft. A loud roar of approval rose from the gathering followed by a chant of adoration for their leader. As warm blood streamed down her arms, into her sleeves and under her breasts, she felt an intoxicating surge of power unlike any she'd ever felt before.

Marianne woke with a jolt, shivering but feeling strangely energized. Her mouth was dry and her throat ached, but she kept her eyes closed. Another nightmare—and this one more vivid than anything she'd ever experienced. She rubbed her eyes, releasing moisture from them, leaving her cheeks wet. She lay motionless, eyes still closed as she wondered why the night sounds seemed so loud inside the house. Slowly, she opened her eyes.

To her complete astonishment, she was not lying in her easy chair but on her backyard lawn. The full moon rose directly over her head. A sudden breeze swept over her body and she shuddered. She was stark naked.

Instinctively, though not fully awake, she covered herself and stumbled to her feet. "Oh my God," she said, and then cursed softly to herself. Walking in her sleep had happened before, but why on earth had she taken off her clothes this time! Hugging her body, she bolted into the house and turned on the kitchen lights. The door slammed behind her. She felt ashamed, confused. What was going on?

"Honey? Is that you?" Peter called from the upstairs.

"Yes, I'll be there in a minute," she shouted back. Her clothes must be in the living room. She reached to turn off the light switch and saw the blood, first on the switch and then on her hands. Her heart started racing; her mind sped for logical explanations. Her period wasn't due for another two weeks—had she bled prematurely? She raised bloodstained hands in front of her face. Fearing the worst, but not sure what the worst could be, she looked down at her inner thighs, but there was no blood on them. Instead, blood ran in streams from her arms, dripped off her fingertips, and streaked her torso around her breasts.

Suddenly, images from the nightmare flooded into consciousness. Riveted to the spot in shock, she began to shake uncontrollably. Forgetting her nakedness, she began to wail as she collapsed in a heap on the floor. Blood seemed to be everywhere, warm and sticky to the touch. She caught sight of her reflection in the French doors. Blood stained the hollows of her eyes and outlined her shaking body in crimson rivulets.

Peter, alarmed by her animal-like screams, charged into the kitchen. Naked except for his boxer shorts, he came to a screeching halt and stood staring in disbelief. "O my God! What happened Marianne? *What have you done?*"

"Oh God, no...no! Oh God—it can't be," Marianne repeated over and over as she sat on the blood-smeared floor, knees pulled tightly to her chest, sobbing and rocking herself.

CHAPTER 30

New York City, August 15, 1999

From deep within the stillness of the house, Sarah heard the doorbell chime. She waited for a few minutes, but there wasn't a sound beyond the door. She pressed the button again, this time leaving her finger on it for a few seconds. Nothing.

Something was definitely wrong. Sarah had called, left messages, but she hadn't heard from either Marianne or Peter for about a week. Marianne always made it a point to tell Sarah if she would be away and where she was going. Marianne simply hadn't shown up for work and hadn't left any messages. The station was in an uproar over her disappearance; loyal listeners had been calling, demanding to know why the program wasn't on air. Sarah was beyond worry—she was alarmed.

Sarah stepped into the front flowerbed and pressed her face close to the living room window, peering between slits in the drawn curtains. The interior was cloaked in shadow; neither sunshine nor lamp glow penetrated the gloom.

She scurried along the side of the house to the backyard gate, unlatched it and walked into the garden. The coverings in all the windows had been drawn. Sarah knocked on the French doors, but only silence greeted her. The wind played a lonely riff in the backyard trees and despite its warmth, Sarah shivered.

"Something's happened to Marianne and Peter," she thought, trying to suppress panic as she headed for her car. "Time to pay the lieutenant a visit—he needs to know about this."

❧

"Have you heard from Marianne?" Sarah blurted out as she burst into Lieutenant Jackson's office. Her heart pounded in her throat.

"Whoa there, Ms. Cummings. Is your friend missing? I haven't heard from her since our visit to the Monsignor. If anyone knows where our psychic is, I figured it should be you. You work with her, don't you?"

"Yes, yes. Of course. You know I do. But, lieutenant, what I'm trying to tell you is that she hasn't reported for work in about a week—none of us have seen her since we last saw you."

"You've visited her home?"

"I just came from there!"

"And?"

"Nothing, the whole place is locked up. Looks like she's gone on a holiday or something—only, she hasn't gone on vacation or we'd know at work. Believe me, nothing like this has ever happened before!"

Jackson grew pensive. "I don't like this."

"I don't like it either. I have a feeling that she's in some kind of trouble."

"She's in trouble all right, but not the kind you're thinking about."

"What do you mean?" Sarah looked thoroughly confused. She sank into the chair opposite the lieutenant.

Jackson reached for the phone and pushed the button for the direct line to desk sergeant.

"Put out an APB on a Marianne Waters and her husband, Peter Cannon. Check with my assistant. He has the file with her last known address." Jackson let the phone drop. He stood, returning Sarah's astonished stare.

"I don't understand," she said. "Just what's happening lieutenant? Did I just hear you say something about an APB on Marianne and Peter?"

"Yes, you did. I'll level with you, Ms. Cummings. I've never bought all that stuff your priest said about demons and all that satanic cult nonsense. We've long suspected that your friend Marianne is more involved in these murders than she's telling either of us."

"But, I thought you said you no longer suspected her," Sarah said quietly, fighting to remain calm.

"Well, I've changed my mind," said the lieutenant with a dismissive flourish of his hand. "Look, Ms. Cummings, there was someone at the house on the night Woodward was murdered who saw the whole thing. Apparently the professor asked this man to meet him there. He arrived just in time to witness a woman killing Woodward. Unfortunately, she saw him as well. She threw something in his eyes. Now he's blind—he's also mute. But he can write and his description sounds like your friend. I'll grant you, it's a pretty vague description, and initially I had some doubts, but now your friend appears to have bolted. Sounds pretty guilty to me. My gut instinct tells me she's still our prime suspect."

"I didn't say that she'd *bolted*," Sarah protested.

"What would you call leaving town in a hurry and not telling anyone when you are a suspect in a homicide investigation?" the lieutenant challenged.

"But how can you explain Peter's disappearance?"

"He's her husband, isn't he? He could be an accessory. If he knows something, then logically he'd also drop out of sight with her."

"Marianne didn't kill Woodward," Sarah said firmly. "I think your witness has made a mistake. Don't you see, he said the woman threw something in his eyes and now he's blind. *But* you also said he's now mute. How'd that happen? It wasn't Marianne. That was something no human could do. Don't you get it lieutenant? That's what these people do. The Watchers have the power to do things like that. Supernatural powers." Sarah was beginning to feel exasperated. "Besides, Lieutenant Jackson, I've known Marianne for a long time—she's *not* a murderer."

"Look. I don't know who or what these Watchers are—or if they even exist outside of your little group's imagination. What I do know is that Marianne Waters is real and the evidence always seems to point to her. Is she the murderer? I can't prove that yet. I'm certainly not as confident as you are that she's innocent. But in this business it's evidence and not confidence that matters, and right now the evidence points to your friend."

"OK," she said emphatically, "Where is this man who says he saw Marianne?"

"Had a heart attack in the hospital. I'm afraid he's dead."

Sarah threw her hands in the air. "Don't you see what's happening? This is all being done to frame Marianne. Don't you find it strange that the only person who says he saw Marianne suddenly dies of a heart attack?"

"Come on, Ms. Cummings. Are you saying that these Watchers also killed our witness?"

"I don't know..." Sara said, her voice trailing off despondently. She looked pleadingly into Jackson's eyes, "But is that so difficult to believe?"

"It is for me," Jackson said flatly.

"Oh fuck!" Sarah snapped, as she stormed out of his office.

Jackson dropped into his chair, suddenly exhausted. He picked up a pen and started twirling it between his fingers as he went over the evidence in his mind.

Intuitively, he was quite certain that Marianne Waters had killed Gerald Woodward. True, the evidence was still a little sketchy, but her sudden disappearance was incriminating. If Sarah and the others believed that the so-called Watcher had murdered the professor, then in his books, Marianne Waters *was* the Watcher.

Still, Jackson felt uneasy. What Sarah had said about Max Silver's sudden blindness and speech loss—and then the heart attack—challenged him. Still, something wasn't quite right. He had to admit that it did seem strange and more than coincidental that Max, who had been there on the night of Woodward's murder, would turn up blind *and* mute. The doc didn't have a good explanation for how he got in such sorry shape, but she'd also said that they were planning to release him soon. No mention of any other ailments. Apparently no one thought that Max would die of a heart attack the very day they discovered him in hospital. If Marianne Waters had murdered Woodward, and knew Max witnessed the whole thing, then why wait so long to off him too? The whole thing was beginning to stink.

If Max hadn't died of a heart attack as a result of injuries sustained in the accident, who would want to murder him? It seemed unlikely that the members of the cult that Sarah and her friends believed in could be responsible. Had they bothered with such finesse in the past? Why wouldn't they just kill him outright; why bother with making the guy blind and mute? If Max Silver's death was a homicide, and it wasn't the cult members, then who killed him? If it was a cover up, who was doing the covering—and why? Waters' disappearance was suspicious and he couldn't rule her out. But, it could be that there was a new player on the scene—one who would kill to keep his or her identity a secret. Jackson didn't like this scenario.

He dropped the pen and rubbed his temples with his fingers. There could be only one reason this new player had entered the picture—the text that Woodward was working on when he died. It dawned on him that the recovery of the text was more connected to his investigation than he'd initially believed or, he reminded himself, had wanted to believe. The first thing he had to do was get Max Silver's autopsy results.

❧

"Are you sure you want to do this?" said Stephen.

Stephen, Andy and Sarah stood on Marianne's doorstep.

"Yes. What else can we do?"

"We could wait a bit, Mom," said Andy. "Leave a note or something. Maybe give her a few more days to contact us. What if she comes back tomorrow and finds that we've broken her door? She's not exactly going to be thrilled."

"Yeah. I agree with Andy, Sarah. I mean, how well do you know Marianne? What if she is the Watcher. Jackson told you a man at the scene identified her as the person with Woodward that night."

"Like I told the lieutenant," Sarah retorted, impatient with her young companions' questions, "I think the man who identified the woman as Marianne made a mistake. As for the door, I'll just apologize to her and get it fixed. At least it can be fixed. I'll never forgive myself if there's something wrong with her, or if she's inside and hurt, and I could have done something about it. I just want to make sure that everything is all right,"

"OK it's your call," said Stephen.

Sarah moved away while Stephen and Andy examined the door.

"Is there another entrance to the house—at the back maybe?" Stephen said. "This lock looks solid. We'd have to break it and we'll end up doing quite extensive damage to both the door and the frame. Besides, I don't like the idea of breaking the front door and leaving the house unprotected for any length of time."

"You've got a point there. There is another entrance in the back." Sarah led Stephen and Andy into the backyard.

The trio walked up the steps of the deck in front of the French doors. Stephen bent to examine the lock.

"It's a dead bolt. Easiest way to get in is to break the glass. Makes repair a lot easier too. Does she have an alarm?" Stephen said.

"Yes, but I know the code," Sarah said. "Lets get on with it!"

Stephen looked around and not finding a suitable implement, turned his side to the French doors, and swiftly hit a pane with his elbow, instantly shattering the glass. The sound of the alarm filled the yard and the house. Stephen carefully reached through the opening in the door, turned the dead bolt and opened the door.

Sarah pushed aside the curtains and ran to turn off the alarm. A few seconds later, an eerie silence enshrouded them.

Cautiously, Andy and Stephen walked into the living room. The curtains on all the windows were closely drawn. The house was dark and a musty odour filled the air. Sarah flicked the switch on a living room lamp.

"Well, no one's at home. Looks like no one's been here for a while," said Andy.

"Where do you suppose they've gone?" Stephen said, peering into the dining room.

"I have no idea. It is not like them to vanish without telling anyone. I only hope nothing has happened to her."

"Well, let's look around. We may find something to clue us into where she's gone or what may have happened to her," Stephen said. "Why don't you look down here while I check upstairs. Andy, you get the basement."

Stephen took the stairs two steps at a time. Shortly he returned.

"Anything?" Sarah gave Stephen an inquiring look.

"No everything looks normal to me. Bed's unmade, that's all."

Andy called to them from the bottom of the basement stairs. "Was Marianne religious?" he inquired.

"Not particularly. Why do you ask?" said Sarah.

"Come and see."

They stopped at the bottom of the stairs. Andy pointed to a large circle with a five-pointed star in its center. A pentagram had been drawn in chalk on the bare concrete floor. Small brass saucers containing the residue of melted candles rested at each point of the star.

"Oh my God!" Sarah stood riveted to the bottom of the stairs. "This wasn't here before."

"What do you think it means?" Andy said.

"I don't know," Sarah whispered.

The trio stood in silence, minds racing, searching for answers to the puzzle. Before they could absorb the images before them, they were startled by footsteps on the stairs behind them. Whirling in unison, mouths open, they saw Peter descend the basement stairs. He gaped at the Pentacle.

"God, what now?"

❦

"Sorry we busted your French doors, Peter, but we were worried about you and Marianne." Sarah paused. The four of them sat on the stairs. She looked inquiringly at a very distracted Peter and asked softly, "Where is Marianne?"

"I don't know. I expected her to be here. We had a huge argument after the blood incident. I told her I couldn't take it any more; I needed some space. That night I just left. I went to stay with friends in New Jersey."

"Blood incident?" Sarah asked.

Peter turned to look her full in the face. She noticed he was trembling, distraught. His reply came in short bursts of raw emotion.

"I don't know how to explain it. Last week. I woke up to find that she wasn't in bed. Then I heard the kitchen door opening. I heard her crying. I ran down into the kitchen and there she was—naked, on the floor, covered in dirt…and…and there was blood all over her face, her hands, all over her body!"

"What?"

"She was stark naked. Apparently she had spent the night outside, like that." Peter paused; he stared into space as if trying to make sense of remembered images. "I tried to help her, but she was hysterical. She pushed me away and ran up to our bathroom and showered. By the time I cleaned up the mess in the kitchen, she came down. She wasn't too coherent. That's when we argued. I told her I'd had enough. I had to leave. I went to the basement to get a bag." He stopped and looked at each of them and then pointed to the basement. "*That* wasn't there when I left," he said bitterly.

"Did she explain where all the blood came from?" Sarah asked.

"She wouldn't tell me. I only know that it wasn't her blood; she wasn't injured." Peter said softly. He looked pleadingly at Sarah. "Do you think she killed someone? God! It was everywhere!"

Sarah shook her head. They sat in silence, each feeling a loss for words to either explain or to comfort.

"I don't know what to do anymore, Sarah." Peter's voice caught in his throat. Head down, wringing his hands, he began to shake. "God knows I love my wife very much, but I have no idea what's happening to her—or to us. I don't know where she is or how that got down there, or what it all means." His voice trailed off as his hands covered his face.

The sounds of his sobbing created little echoes in the eerie silence that filled the house. A terrible sense of foreboding blanketed the room. The red pentagram burned in their minds.

Below them in the basement, the mythic symbol glowed on the floor. One by one, each of the five candles spontaneously burst into flames.

CHAPTER 31

New York City, August 18, 1999
"May I come in?"
Jackson raised his eyes and saw Edwards peering at him from the doorway.
"Sure, Frank, come in."
Edwards headed directly for the couch in Jackson's office and unceremoniously flopped down with a huge sigh.
"So? What's up?" Jackson said.
"Good news I hope."
Edwards adjusted himself in the couch like an old dog searching for optimum comfort. Sinking into his habitual seat, he placed his hands behind his head and leaned back.
"Yeah?" Jackson said.
"Finished the autopsy on that guy who died at the hospital," said Edwards.
"And?"
"Your hunch was right."
"He was murdered?"
"Certainly wasn't natural causes."
"How?"
"Someone took him out with potassium—lethal injection—about 100 mil-equivalents in his system."
"Potassium? Any idea where that came from?"
"Well, generally potassium can be found in emerge or on wards— could've been a hospital worker or else stolen from pharmacy."
"And the stuff's lethal? Fill me in, doc, I don't get it."
"Potassium chloride's a common drug in emergency rooms. Usually it's administered in cases when dehydration is a problem—and used in much smaller doses. Your friend Max Silver had an IV in his arm. Someone just slipped a needle into the tube and the potassium went directly into the blood stream. Resulted in an almost instant heart attack. Would've burned like hell on the way to his heart, but then...

bang! Old Max would've never known what hit him. Gives heartburn a whole new meaning.

"Geez. That's harsh. So, doc, someone had this planned?"

"Yep. Your guy had no chance. Instantaneously fatal. Probably wouldn't have found it if we didn't do a tox scan. There it was—a massive dose. Thank heavens we did it quickly. Good call on ordering a complete autopsy."

"Thanks Frank. It was just too suspicious. Now my job is to find out who did it—and how the murderer got by our cop outside Max's door. Can't say this is welcome news."

"Can't always bring you good news you know."

Jackson scowled as he reached for the phone; Edwards grunted, hauled his considerable bulk out of the cushions and ambled out of the office.

⁂

New York City, August 30, 1999

"Lieutenant Jackson? This is Jeffrey McCarthy. *Bishop* McCarthy."

"Good morning, Bishop, what can I do for you?"

"I'm just calling to find out how your investigation into the murder of my cousin is progressing," said McCarthy. The Bishop could feel his heart pounding in his chest, but he erased the disquiet from his voice with studied precision.

"I'm afraid it's all ongoing, Bishop. We haven't apprehended anyone if that's what you're asking. We questioned a man who was on the premises the night your cousin was murdered..."

"Is this the man who had my business card?" the Bishop interrupted, instantly wishing he didn't sound so anxious.

"Yeah. Apparently this man was supposed to meet your cousin that evening. He saw your cousin with a woman. He claimed this woman killed your cousin."

"Good Heavens! Do you know who she is?"

"Well, we have a suspect in mind, but she's left her residence and we haven't found her yet. We will though. It's only a matter of time."

There was an awkward silence at the other end of the line. The Bishop closed his eyes and pinched the bridge of his nose. "At least," he intoned, "the family will be pleased to know that things are progressing. Perhaps soon we'll have some closure in Gerald's murder.

"Hopefully."

"I'm curious lieutenant, this man—did he tell you how he came into possession of my business card?"

"No. Quite frankly, we didn't ask. After what he told us, that detail seemed irrelevant. You were probably right—there's any number of ways he could've had that card. Just a coincidence more than likely."

"Yes, I agree." McCarthy paused again. "One other question, lieutenant. If it was a woman who murdered my cousin, any clues as to why she did it?"

"Nothing at the moment. But remember we discussed the manuscript your cousin was working on? Could be that she was interested in that."

"Really? That's pretty extreme don't you think? Why wouldn't she just steal the document?"

"I agree it seems desperate—people don't usually kill for something like that, but then again, I've seen people killed for less. Perhaps his murder is an indication of the importance of the text.

"Let me run something by you, Your Holiness. I've interviewed some people—one of whom is a priest incidentally—who seem to believe that the document has some religious importance for a cult of devil worshippers. These people suggested that the murderer, who they believe is some kind of demon, is the leader of this cult."

"Demon?"

"Yeah. Sounds pretty far fetched doesn't it. What d'you make of it, I mean, from your professional viewpoint, shall we say?"

"Rather incredible."

"True. It also seemed rather incredible to me—at first."

"Lieutenant, you sound as if you're giving this some credence."

"Yeah, well, let's say I'm not sure. If the text is as significant and important as these folks claim it is, then I can appreciate why someone would kill for it. So, Bishop, I'm keeping an open mind—for now."

"You said 'if the text is as significant as they say it is.' Do your informants know what the manuscript is about?"

"No. But they believe it is a Scroll; they claim that it may have been written by a female follower of Jesus."

"Really? Did they say who she was?"

"Yeah. Miriam something. I've forgotten. This priest can give you more information. Then maybe you could explain it to me."

"Certainly, what's his name?"

"Josephs, Monsignor Josephs."

There was a momentary silence at the end of the line. Jackson didn't miss it. He waited.

"Thank you lieutenant," said the Bishop abruptly. "You've been most helpful. Will you continue to keep me current on the investigation so that I may keep the family informed?"

"I will. And, get back to me, will you, if you talk to Monsignor Josephs."

McCarthy ended the call and pushed another set of numbers.

"Hello, James?"

"Yes?"

"McCarthy here. Is there a Monsignor in your parish by the name of Josephs?"

"Yes, he's a visiting lecturer at the seminary. Why do you ask?"

"James, we may have a dilemma. It would appear that the Monsignor and some of his friends are also searching for the Scroll. Apparently the Monsignor knows more about the Scroll than we do."

"I see," came the priest's quiet response. "What shall we do, Bishop?"

"I'd like to convene a meeting and invite him to attend."

"Consider it done, Bishop."

CHAPTER 32

New York City, September 1, 1999

Monsignor Josephs gently but firmly grasped the elbow of the young priest. He caught the odor of garlic and stale beer coming from the young priest's cassock and smiled, remembering his own youthful seminary days, debating fine points in theology over pints in the campus pub. The young priest knocked at the door, and without waiting for a response, guided the blind man over the threshold. Monsignor Josephs stiffened slightly. He sensed that there was more than one person in the room, possibly three or four. He knew he was being summoned, but the reverend hadn't mentioned other people joining them.

He heard them rise to their feet. "Ah," he said to himself, "there are three," His cane brushed against a carpet on the hardwood; imperceptibly, he adjusted his gait as he released his escort's elbow and stepped forward.

"Good morning, Monsignor, please come in." Father Boyle moved to his side and led him into the group.

"Monsignor, I have with me Bishops McCarthy and Case with whom you are acquainted, I expect."

"Just by name," said the Monsignor. He extended his hand in the direction of the two men. The two prelates each in turn leaned forward and nervously shook the Monsignor's hand. Josephs smiled inwardly; why is it, he wondered, that sighted people always get a little nervous touching a blind person?

"Good morning all," said the Monsignor.

Boyle led him to a chair.

McCarthy spoke first. His voice was all business and filled with the authority of his rank. "Thank you for coming, Monsignor. I'm sure you will be able to help us in this matter."

"I hope I can, although I'm uncertain why you've asked me to come here."

"Yes, of course. Let me fill you in," Bishop McCarthy's rush of words flooded the room. "A few weeks ago, my cousin, Gerald Woodward, a paleographer at the university, came to see me with pictures of what he believed to be a sacred text of some sort. He received photographs of parts of the text with a request to date it. He came to me with the photos, quite excited because he thought it was an important find—comparable to the Dead Sea Scrolls, or so he claimed. He'd ascertained that the text was Aramaic. Naturally I was interested, but my cousin played his cards pretty close to his chest, if you get my drift. Later, I met with Cardinal Lombardi in Rome and he authorized me to discretely investigate this find. Though we started looking into the matter immediately, we weren't fast enough. My cousin was murdered just a couple of weeks ago."

McCarthy paused for effect. Bishop Case murmured something sympathetic and crossed himself as his colleague pushed on with the story.

"When Lieutenant Jackson from the homicide division came to interview me about my cousin, he mentioned that you and some friends are also searching for this Scroll. That is why I asked the Reverend to bring you here today. I must ask: can you enlighten us about your involvement?"

No one spoke. The three men stared anxiously at the blind cleric. The office echoed with traffic noises, heightening the silence in the room for what seemed like an eternity.

Bishop Case could no longer stand the suspense. "What do you know about this text, Monsignor?"

The Monsignor drew in a deep breath. "The text to which you refer, is the sacred Scroll of Miriam of Magdala, or perhaps more accurately, I *believe* it is this scroll."

"Miriam of Magdala! She wrote a Scroll?" Bishop Case's incredulity was blatant.

The blind priest ignored the Bishop's remark and continued. "It is attributed to her because she revealed its existence after the death of Christ," said the Monsignor. "Whether she wrote it herself is still a subject of debate."

"I see," said McCarthy softly. He leaned forward in his chair. Bishop Case looked from one man to the other and kept his mouth shut. Clearly, there was some credibility to what was unfolding before him and McCarthy was taking this all very seriously.

"The esoteric theological literature suggests that after the death of Christ, Miriam of Magdala hid this Scroll with the assistance of the members of a secret society called the Silent Brotherhood. According to the legend, it was to remain hidden from the world until the appointed time."

"And this is the Scroll which Professor Woodward was dating?" McCarthy said.

"I believe it is..."

Case interrupted impatiently, "What is the basis for your belief? Could it not be some other Scroll?"

The Monsignor turned his opaque pale orbs toward Case. "Yes, of course, you are right. It could be some other Scroll, however, I am certain it is the Scroll of Miriam of Magdala—primarily because of the other people who are searching for it."

"You mean the cult?" McCarthy interjected. "Lieutenant Jackson mentioned that you believe that a cult of some kind is involved."

"Yes" he replied simply. "A cult of satanic worshippers is interested in this Scroll."

"Why would they be interested in this *particular* Scroll?" Boyle sounded confused.

"Because of what they believe the Scroll contains," said the Monsignor.

"I don't understand, Monsignor," Case said. McCarthy, he noticed, remained silent.

"No one knows precisely what is contained in the Scroll of Miriam of Magdala. Remember, it was hidden and was not supposed to be revealed until the appointed time. It is said, however, that the Scroll illuminates secrets of the resurrection, the ascension and the re-appearance of Christ."

A pervasive silence again filled the office with as the four men stared at each other. Of all of them, only the Monsignor prayed to himself as he fingered the rosary in his pocket.

❦

Rome, September 2, 1999

After the call, Cardinal Lombardi's hand remained motionless on the handset. He couldn't believe what he'd just heard from Bishop McCarthy. Could it be the Scroll of Miriam of Magdala? Was it the ancient document that would reveal earth-shattering secrets about Jesus Christ and His return to earth? Had it really been found?

Cardinal Lombardi removed his hand from the phone; his fingers were numb. Despite the air conditioning, he noticed that his palms were clammy. He wiped them on his cassock, removed his crimson skullcap, and wiped his nearly balding head with a handkerchief. He rose from his seat feeling burdened not only by the weight of his position, but also by the decision that he would have to make. He had already assumed that the Scroll was of some importance, but the news that the scroll could be the legendary one authored by Mary Magdalene had massive implications for the Holy Mother, the Church. Once the scroll's code had been deciphered, its secrets revealed, of what use would the world's millions of Catholics have for the Church, her priests and faith-based teachings? Everything could be determined from the Scroll. The Church and its doctrines would be rendered obsolete, a historical relic.

As a servant of the Church, he could not sit by and let that happen. He would have to locate the Scroll, and then suppress it.

Yet, Cardinal Lombardi was a man of conscience as well as a theologian. He realized that if the Scroll indeed contained what it was reputed to, then it would be a revelation of the Holy Spirit that would herald the coming of the New Jerusalem. If so, then not even the Church had the right to suppress it. Cardinal Lombardi was conflicted: torn between his honesty and his love for the Church for which he had given his whole life. Of one thing he was certain—the Church's interests of must be preserved.

Lombardi decided that he needed a walk; he needed to think very carefully about his next move. Whatever he decided could make or break him—and the Church. There was no middle ground. Replacing his skullcap, he strode purposefully from his office. Had anyone seen him leave, they would have noticed the deep furrows etching his brow.

"Your Eminence, I have some more information," said Mr. J.

"Yes?" said the man who called himself the Cardinal.

"It would appear that the Scroll is more important than we ever imagined. Its authorship may be attributed to Miriam of Magdala."

"The Scroll of Miriam of Magdala?" The Cardinal was stunned.

"Yes, Your Eminence. It is said that Miriam…"

"I *know* what the Scroll of Miriam of Magdala is!" the Cardinal snapped. "Where did you get this information?"

"A Monsignor in New York City—he's also searching for the Scroll."

"How certain is he that it *is* the Scroll of Miriam of Magdala."

"He appears very certain, Your Eminence."

"Right. Then you must do all you can to obtain it. It's very important, do you understand?"

"Yes, Your Eminence."

"Spare no expense and leave no stone unturned. Our Holy Mother the Church deserves to be protected. We *must* have the Scroll, do you understand?" the Cardinal hissed into the phone.

"I do, Your Eminence. I shall find it and get it for you."

CHAPTER 33

New York City, September 3, 1999

Oblivious to the insidious smell of urine and semen, Marianne sat huddled in a corner all but concealed by discarded clothing, ragged plastic bags, empty bottles and assorted debris left by the homeless who sheltered in the abandoned warehouse. She was unrecognizable as Marianne Waters. Dark circles lined her eyes and her hair was a tangled mess, encrusted with bits of vegetation and dirt. Her clothes were dirty and torn in several places and her nails were soiled with a mixture of concealed blood and mud.

Fatigue pulled at her body. Awake for close to forty-eight hours, she felt like sleeping but fought the urge, afraid the nightmares would return. Several times when she'd fallen asleep one of the vivid nightmares had occurred and she'd awakened to find herself in a new location, with blood on her soiled hands, and with no memory of how she'd strayed from where she'd fallen asleep or where she'd been.

Questions flooded her mind as she crouched in the rags. Where did she go after she fell asleep? Why could she remember the violent events that took place during the nightmares, yet she couldn't remember how she got to the sites? She didn't fully understand what was happening to her, but steadily she became convinced that her experiences were connected to the deaths of the people in her dreams. The awful truth frightened her. She'd frequently awakened to find blood on her hands. Who were the victims? What was their relationship to her? Had she murdered all these people?

The specter of insanity lurked close to her consciousness. Marianne pushed the thought away. She didn't feel particularly crazy, but there was nothing rational to explain either the nightmares or the awful reality of her bloodied hands.

Marianne knew that until she found answers to her questions and discovered what was happening to her, she couldn't face Peter, her friends, or even the authorities. She groped for her purse under some of the rags, and relieved to find it intact, clutched it tightly against her bosom.

Her eyelids grew heavy and she felt herself dropping off. Her body demanded sleep. She told herself a quick nap would restore her energy and promised herself to wake when she felt dreams encroaching. As she dropped off, she realized that she desperately wanted to speak to someone. A sob vibrated through her body as sleep blanketed her in darkness.

New York City, September 3, 1999.

"Sarah?" Her own voice sounded strange in her ears—hollow and more raspy than she'd ever heard before.

"Hello, who's this?"

"It's me, Marianne."

"Marianne! Where are you? Are you OK? Where have you been? The office has been frantic—nobody knew where you'd gone. We went to your home, but of course, when you weren't there, we were so worried!" As her words tumbled out, Sarah tried to disguise her anxiety beneath a veneer of calmness and sympathy.

"You've given us quite a scare. You sound like you've been crying. More nightmares?"

"Yes—but it's more than that. Look," she pleaded with Sarah, "I'm sorry. I just had to disappear for a while. I couldn't stay at home any longer. I don't know what's happening to me, Sarah. It feels like I'm a completely different person. I wanted to talk to someone but I didn't know who to call. You're the only one who seems to understand…" Marianne's voice trembled and began to fade.

"Where are you? Did you make it back home?" Sarah knew she had to keep the line open.

"No. Central Park. The gazebo at the east end."

"Stay put," Sarah nearly shouted into the phone, then lowered her voice, "I'll be there in thirty minutes. Look, Marianne—can I at least tell Peter? He's terribly worried about you? The poor guy's a wreck."

"No! No, I can't face him just yet, not now. It'll only upset him more. Please come alone," Marianne pleaded. "If I see you with any one else, I'll have to leave."

"It's OK Marianne! I'll be alone." Adrenaline rushing through her body, Sarah rang off and grabbed her coat.

She arrived at Central Park exactly thirty-five minutes after Marianne's call. Shoving a few dollars at the cab driver, she walked briskly into the park. Turning off the path, she saw the gazebo and made out the silhouette of Marianne sitting inside. Bounding up the gazebo steps, she embraced her friend. The two women clung to each other until Sarah pulled away and held Marianne at arms length.

"Oh, Marianne. God, you look awful. What's wrong? Are you sick? Tell me what I can do! How can I help?"

"Oh, Sarah..." Marianne's voice trailed off into sobs. "I don't know what's happening to me. I'm really scared." She fell back into Sarah's arms and wept uncontrollably.

"You need sleep, Marianne, and a hot bath. We need to get you home."

"I can't go home, Sarah, not yet. Not until I know what's happening to me. And I'm afraid of falling asleep," she wailed.

"The nightmares? You said that they've come back?"

"Yes. That's why I'm afraid to sleep."

"I don't understand, Marianne. Before, when you had those nightmares, you weren't afraid to go to sleep. What's so different now?"

"The dreams are more vivid now, Sarah, more horrifying and more real. I think I do certain things when I sleep—bad things. I sleepwalk or something, and find myself in odd places. I have no idea how I got there."

"There's nothing wrong with sleepwalking, Marianne..."

"It's not *just* sleepwalking, Sarah!" Marianne practically shouted, fists clenched. "It's what I *do* when I sleepwalk." She grew silent, blew her nose and swallowed hard. "Sarah, I think I may have killed some people."

"You what?"

"I'm not sure, Sarah. When I fall asleep I have the most horrible nightmares. I dream I am that person—the Watcher—the one who's been killing people."

"Marianne," Sarah tried to sound consoling, but she was clearly shaken by her friend's declaration. "Look, I'm sure it is only your imagination playing tricks on you. You've been working so hard these past months, and you're stressed. Sure, you started having these nightmares, and of course, we've all been talking about the Watchers. It is quite natural that you'd incorporate all these bits and pieces into your dreams. Actually, it's a wonder that we've all not been having nightmares. Why I..."

Marianne turned on her heels and began pacing around the gazebo, shaking her head. "No, no, no! You don't understand! Sarah. Anytime I dream that I'm killing someone, I wake up—I'm outdoors—and I'm *naked*."

Sarah stepped closer to Marianne, interrupted her pacing, and held her close.

"Shu-sh-sh," she intoned, trying her best to calm the distraught woman. "Marianne," she said softly, "I'm sure there's a perfectly sound explanation. It's the stress, all those horrible headlines. You're..."

Marianne jerked out of her friend's embrace. "Listen to me!" Sarah grew alarmed at the level of agitation in her friend's voice. "The dreams and the sleepwalking—that's not all, Sarah! When I wake up, I have blood on my hands—sometimes I'm covered in blood! *Somebody else's blood!*"

"What?" Stunned, Sarah instinctively stepped back from Marianne.

"I don't know how," she said, holding her upturned palms toward Sarah, "or why, but when I wake up, I have blood on my hands."

The skin around Marianne's nails was clearly caked with the dark red ochre of dried blood. Sarah's eyes fell to the brown stains in the folds of Marianne's long tattered skirt.

"How...how does the blood get on your hands?" Sarah stammered, trembling.

"I don't know, Sarah. When I sleep, I dream. I dream awful, realistic dreams that I'm killing someone, and the next thing I know I'm awake, naked, and I have blood on my hands." Marianne paused and wiped her eyes with the back of her hands. "I just don't know anymore." She sank onto the gazebo bench and stared disconsolately at her feet.

"*Dreams* that you're killing people?" Sarah whispered as she sat beside Marianne. Confusion crept into her voice. What had happened to her friend? Did she really know who Marianne Waters was?

"Yes. I see myself pulling their hearts out—just like the police told us happened to those bodies."

"Marianne. Forgive me for asking. How could you be asleep during all this?" There was dread in her voice. She waited for the answer, not really wanting to hear it.

"I don't know Sarah. I am not sure about anything any more."

"Oh, God! You know what this could mean?" Sarah rose off the bench and began to walk around the gazebo. She clasped and unclasped her hands nervously.

"Yes, Sarah. The thought has crossed my mind, many times—maybe I *am* the person behind all these bizarre murders." Her eyes grew wild, then filled with tears. "But I'm so confused, I don't feel like a killer, honestly I don't." Marianne dabbed her eyes. "I can see that I've scared you, Sarah. I'm sorry."

"That's OK. I must confess I'm a little shaken right now."

"What do I do now, Sarah?"

"I don't know, Marianne. I'm sure there's a perfectly logical explanation for what's happening to you—logical or psychological—but I don't know what it is. Just come home with me and..."

"No! I can't do that! I can't face the others, Sarah. Not even Peter. That's one of the reasons why I ran away from home."

"You can't run away forever, Marianne, you'll have to get some help. I don't know what, though. Please! Why don't you come back with me? I'm sure between us we'll be able to figure a way out of this conundrum, a way to help you."

"I don't think that's a good idea, Sarah. I've thought about it several times, but it just won't work. I can't even go to a hospital or a clinic. Think about it. Even if the others believe that I'm not doing the killings—and I doubt that they will—the lieutenant sure isn't going to believe me. He'll most likely lock me up!"

"I know. That's true...but what are you going to do? You can't just live on the streets..."

"I don't know. I need more time to think about things, figure out what's happening to me." She looked pleadingly at Sarah. "If I find that there's no way out, I'll call you and turn myself in."

"Oh, Marianne," Sarah broke into tears and embraced her. The two women wept in each other's arms for sometime. Marianne pulled away first.

"I'm sorry to put you through this, Sarah, but I had to speak to someone. I have no explanation for what's happening. Maybe I am the Watcher. Maybe I become possessed at night and I kill people. I don't know, I just don't know..."

"You're sure you want to do this on your own—you don't want to come back with me?"

"I'm sure. I'm not ready. Not yet. I have a feeling there's something I must do. I don't know what that is, but I need time to find out. I'm sorry, Sarah. I've got to go now."

Before Sarah could say another word, Marianne ran down the steps of the gazebo and disappeared into the developing mist.

"God be with you, my friend." Sarah said softly. Helplessly she watched from the gazebo. "God be with you."

CHAPTER 34

New York City, September 4, 1999

Sarah and Peter stood before a seething Lieutenant Jackson. "You *what?*" he raged, glaring at them.

"Don't look at me; I wasn't there. I had nothing to do with it!" Peter raised both hands in resignation.

"Yes you did have something to do with it," Jackson snorted with disgust. "You saw her in your home with blood on her hands! You must have suspected that she was involved, yet you never reported it to the police. That's being an accessory in my books!" Jackson dropped into his chair and flicked the pen he was holding onto the table. He whirled on Sarah.

"And you're pushing being an accessory as well, Ms. Cummings!"

"What else could I have done?" Sarah pleaded.

"She confessed to you and you let her go?" Jackson rolled his eyes in disbelief. "What were you thinking? You could have called me and told me where you were meeting her! We would have picked her up. Now she's disappeared again—and God only knows where!"

"It wasn't exactly a confession, lieutenant. She said she didn't know what was happening to her. She's going to turn herself in if she can't discover what's happening to her."

"Yeah, yeah. That's just great. *Great!* And how many more murders will that take?" Jackson shouted, throwing his hands in the air. "Geez, I don't believe this."

"Lieutenant, I don't think she's the Watcher. I've known Marianne for many years. She would never kill anyone. She's kind and compassionate and she's always helping people and…"

"Right, right! Then how do you explain the blood on her hands? She told you that she has blood on her hands after she has a dream and that she thinks she's killed people." Jackson glared at Sarah; she nodded meekly.

"What more evidence do you need? An ad in the New York Times!" He was on his feet again, leaning across the desk.

"Lieutenant, Jackson," she began again, determination returning to her voice, "I came to you because I thought maybe your department could be on the look out for her, just to make sure she's safe. She's just asked for some time to figure this thing out—can't you back off a little until then? She did confide in me and I think she'll call me again. It's only a matter of time."

Jackson sank again into his chair, passed his hands through his hair and heaved a sigh.

"Look, this is what I'll do. We're going to try to find her, and I'll ask my men to hold off arresting her—for now. I'll give her forty-eight hours to turn herself in. If she doesn't, she'll be arrested on sight. If your friend does call again, tell her that. I don't care if she's figured it out or not. If she is the one responsible for these murders—and all the circumstances are pointing in that direction—then the city's other citizens deserve our protection and that means getting Ms. Waters off the streets and locked up."

"OK that's fair, I suppose, but I really don't think she's the murderer."

"Ms. Cummings, I've been in this business for more than fifteen years. Believe me, most serial killers claim they didn't do it. It's the first step towards pleading temporary insanity or multiple personalities or that their Aunt Peggy did it." Jackson snorted in derision.

"Thank you. Lieutenant." Sarah turned and headed for the door with an ashen Peter.

"One more thing—both of you," he snapped.

Sarah and Peter stopped in their tracks and faced him.

"The next time either of you pull something like this, I'll charge you with obstruction of justice."

Sarah and Peter left the station, each feeling more confused and worried than ever. Although a part of her could not bring itself to think of Marianne as a murderer, Sarah couldn't dispute the circumstantial evidence against her friend. Marianne, by her own admission, may have entered into some sort of altered state and killed several people. Her bloodied hands and clothing were indisputable proof that something was terribly wrong.

As Sarah slipped behind the wheel she knew she had to tell the others—fast. With their experience, they'd surely offer some insight into what was happening to Marianne. She turned to look at Peter. He'd laid his head back on the headrest; the ghostly pallor in his face hadn't disappeared. Despair etched his face.

Are you all right?" she asked softly, a look of concern on her face. Peter remained grimly silent.

※

"Where did you meet her?" Stephen said.

"Central Park."

"What was her mood? What was she like? Where's she been?" Andy rapidly fired questions at Sarah.

"Very frightened. Confused and disheveled. Said she hadn't slept in days—and she looked like it too. She couldn't explain what was happening to her."

"You say she told you that when she has a nightmare, she wakes up with blood on her hands?" Monsignor said.

"Yes. She's bloody and nude and in a strange place she can't remember going to or being in. She implied that she might be possessed or something. It was all pretty scattered—and scary. I saw the dried blood on her hands and on her skirt. What do you think Monsignor?"

"I'm not sure exactly. The only explanation I can think of is some sort of split personality. She may be two entities—neither one aware of the other. One part of her is good, the Marianne we all know and love, and the other is evil—the Watcher."

"Of course. Multiple personalities. I never thought of that. It's a form of schizophrenia, isn't it?" said Stephen.

"Yes, some people describe it that way. What Marianne may be experiencing is an extreme form." The Monsignor reached for a water glass and raised it slowly to his lips.

"But that can be cured, can't it?" Sarah said uneasily.

"Not really. It can be controlled, though. If Marianne is suffering from schizophrenia, she needs help—expert help—and fast."

"You don't sound too confident, Monsignor." said Andy.

"Schizophrenia is not diagnosed that easily, my friend. What she's experiencing may be this affliction or it could be something else." The Monsignor lowered his head.

"In other words, she may be the real thing." Andy said slowly.

"What do you mean?" Sarah said glancing anxiously at the three men.

"She may be the Watcher." Andy whispered.

"I'm not saying that she is. She may be. If she's the Watcher, then contacting you was just a ruse, part of her plan," the Monsignor said.

"In our quest for the Scroll, we have to be careful. We can't trust anyone outside our own circle. Don't forget—the evil one is a deceiver."

The Monsignor's words were met with silent assent from the three friends gathered in his office.

"By the way, Andy. How are you feeling today?" said the Monsignor.

"Much better today, thanks. I was quite shaken after that attack."

"If it's any reassurance, the Messenger now knows that you're protected, so there's no need for any of you to worry about similar attacks. You still have to be careful. There may be other attempts on your lives by the Messenger's agents. I suggest that you be each other's keeper. Always work in pairs."

"That's a good idea," said Stephen glancing at Sarah and Andy. They both nodded.

The Monsignor settled back into his chair. "So what do we know so far?"

"Not much, only that there are thousands of antique dealers and collectors in the city—and the state for that matter," said Stephen.

"It's also possible," said Andy with a sigh, "that the person who has the Scroll is not even in New York."

The Monsignor cast sightless eyes about the room. "You sound like you've given up hope."

"Well, you'll agree it's a pretty daunting task to find one person when you have no particular leads," Sarah said.

"Speaking of leads, has anyone heard from the lieutenant about the search of Woodward's office?" Stephen said.

"What he said is that they didn't find anything—*nada*." Andy sounded dejected.

"What about the second Polaroid?" the Monsignor inquired.

"It wasn't in the office," said Sarah.

"What about his house?"

"Humm. Come to think of it, I don't think the police searched the entire house," Stephen said. "They did secure the place as a crime scene, but I don't believe that they went back after the murder. At least not for the Polaroid."

"Would a search of Woodward's house be useful? I thought whoever killed him trashed the place. Wouldn't they have taken anything relating to the Scroll?" asked Andy.

"They may have," the Monsignor said thoughtfully, "but we don't know that. I believe that whoever killed Woodward was looking for the

Scroll itself. It's possible that something that could help us may still be in that home."

Sarah brightened. "Monsignor has a point."

"What if our search of the house doesn't reveal anything? We still need another strategy. Somehow," continued Stephen, "we need a way of narrowing down the list of collectors and antique dealers who may have contacted the professor."

"Any suggestions?" The Monsignor's question was met by a brief period of silence, broken by Stephen.

"OK, let's start with what we know. We believe that someone who has the Scroll sent pictures of it to Gerald Woodward. Now, I bet this person is a collector rather than an antiques dealer," Stephen said.

"Why do you say that?" asked Sarah.

"Just a hunch. I don't think a dealer would go to the extent of trying to have the document translated or dated." Stephen said.

"A serious dealer would. But, let's say we take your view. Let's say this person is a collector, where does that lead us?" The Monsignor asked.

"Well, let's say you are a collector with a document you think is valuable, but you can't read it to confirm your hunch. Whose help will you enlist to interpret the document—a friend or a stranger?" Stephen said.

"Most likely a friend or someone you already know, an acquaintance," Andy sat forward in his seat.

"What if you don't have a friend who's an expert in ancient languages like Woodward?" Sarah said.

Stephen shrugged. "Then you would send it to a stranger, I suppose. But that's quite risky. I thought it unlikely—especially since Woodward isn't the only expert in ancient languages. I checked. Whoever sent him the pictures must have known him and trusted him," said Stephen.

"So where does that leave us?" Andy frowned.

"Well, first, we try to match the names of Woodward's acquaintances with the names of collectors. We might come up lucky."

"That's a good idea," the Monsignor said. "At least, it's a start."

"So where do we start searching for Woodward's acquaintances and friends?" Andy said.

"Woodward had a sister. The lieutenant mentioned her. You could start there," said the Monsignor. "Surely, she'll have some information."

"That's right, I forgot about the sister. There'll also be school yearbooks and things like that in his home," Sarah said.

"Just before you leave, you should know that I met with Bishops McCarthy and Case in Reverend Boyle's office. He's the parish priest for Manhattan."

"Anything wrong?" Sarah said.

"Not exactly. Professor Woodward told Bishop McCarthy about the Scroll. The Bishop was checking it out with me."

"I remember Lieutenant Jackson mentioning that McCarthy and Woodward were cousins," interjected Sarah.

"Yes. I gather the Bishop reported the finding to the Vatican. Now they're also interested in locating the Scroll. The Bishop wanted to find out more about it and so they invited me to shed some light on their inquiries."

"How did they know that we were searching for the Scroll?" Sarah said.

"The lieutenant told Bishop McCarthy about our mission."

"Well, this time at least," said Stephen grimly, "it's not only the four of us against the Watchers."

CHAPTER 35

New York City, September 16, 1999

"Hello. It's Mr. J. here. Why are you calling? Is it about your fee?"

"Yeah, I've been waiting for you to return my call. Also got some more information for you. It's quite number of pages and bulky, so I'll need a place to drop it off."

"I thought you'd already sent me all the documents. What's in this package?" Mr. J. was clearly annoyed.

"Yeah, well the documents that I sent you didn't tell us about the people behind Tricom Limited—the owner of 47 Dovercourt Avenue—because it's an offshore corporation. I managed to get an affiliate in Guernsey, where they're registered, to provide a copy of Tricom's corporate registry records."

"I see. Splendid. Did you manage to get pictures of the grounds?"

"Nope, security was too tight."

"Right. This is how we'll make the exchange. Take the package to Union Station and place it in locker number 222 in the general waiting area. The key to that locker is in an envelope at the car rental office located at the end of that same floor. It's called Dominion Car Rental. Ask for the envelope for Mr. Williams."

"What about my payment?"

"It'll be waiting for you in the same locker. Be there at two tomorrow afternoon."

"Will do."

Rudy hung up, exhaled heavily and wiped the beads of sweat from his forehead.

New York City, September 17, 1999

"Hi. I'm here to pick up a letter for Mr. Williams." Rudy smiled nervously at the woman at Dominion's reception desk.

The woman slipped an envelope across the counter. "Here you are Mr. Williams." She smiled.

"Thank you." Rudy dropped a fiver on the desk, slid the envelope into his pocket, and hurried for the bank of lockers. Fleetingly he wondered whether the woman knew that Williams was not his real name. He didn't care. His heart thumped heavily against his chest as he dodged through the crowds.

Rudy reached the lockers in less than two minutes. A throng of people hovered around the lockers in the 200 numbers, either retrieving or stowing luggage. Just his luck, he thought nervously. He waited until a space cleared in front of locker 222 and quickly stepped forward. The key tumbled into his hands from the torn envelope. He held his breath as he shoved it into the slot; the key turned effortlessly.

Rudy sensed that his every move was being watched. He tried not to look too closely at anyone to avoid arousing any suspicions. Questions flooded his mind. Was the man called Mr. J. watching him? Where was he? *Who* was he? The other men were certainly there, but where were they?

Rudy was scared. Heart racing, he quickly opened the locker. A small thick envelope lay inside. He licked his lips, replaced it with a large padded envelope, and then slipped the envelope containing the money into his pocket. He locked the door and, without looking around, deliberately made his way to the nearest exit. Outside on the street, Rudy heaved a sigh of relief as he slipped into his car. With the door securely locked, he gingerly checked the envelope's contents. Ten thousand dollars in crisp hundred-dollar notes stared back at him. Instantly Rudy made two decisions. First, he decided that he didn't want to be around when Mr. J. learned the truth after he opened the package. Then he decided that he needed a holiday—a long, long holiday.

Reaching for his cell phone as he drove away, Rudy punched the speed dial for his office. His secretary came on the line.

"Nancy?"

"Hi Rudy."

"Listen very carefully, Nancy. I made copies of some documents some time ago."

"The Tricom file?"

"Yeah. There are duplicates of the copies I put in the file. Remove the duplicates and place them in my safety deposit box. Do it today, you hear. I'll be going away for a while—maybe a month or so. I'll be in touch to let you know. If you don't hear from me in about a month or if something unusual happens to me before then, take the documents to the police. You understand?"

"Sure, Rudy. Anything wrong? I've never heard you sound like this."

"I'm fine, Nancy. Just do as I say, OK?"

"Sure."

Rudy hung up, tossed the cell on the seat beside him as he looked over his shoulder for oncoming traffic. He waited for the car in the next lane to overtake him, and then, with a squeal of tires he changed lanes and headed for the airport.

In the international terminal, Rudy found the shortest line to the reservations desk for a flight that left in an hour. He fingered the passport that he always kept in his pocket. The wad of bills had been safely deposited at a banking machine into a series of accounts. Too risky to try to take that amount through customs. He was feeling better now. Only a few short minutes and he'd be heading for the gate and on his way overseas. He felt suddenly calm, pleased with his decisions and expeditious action.

Soon, a man with a slight limp carrying an overnight bag joined him in the line. The man bent to place his bag on the ground, and seemingly accidentally bumped the bag against Rudy's thigh. Rudy whirled around to see the diminutive man.

"Sorry, my good sir. I did not mean to stumble into you," said the man in a foreign accent.

"No problem, buddy, no harm done." Rudy smoothed a hand over his thigh and thought nothing more about the encounter. The reservations clerk summoned him to the desk and he easily booked a flight to Bermuda. After purchasing his ticket, he walked over to a phone.

"Craig. Rudy here."

"Hi Rudy, what's up?"

"Just listen, Craig. You remember that 47 Dovercourt Avenue file?"

"Sure I remember, what about it?"

"Its hot. I don't know how, but someone managed to find out that I had been asking questions about the property and the owner, Tricom Limited. They were not, shall we say, too pleased. I'm calling to give you a heads-up bro. You may have been compromised."

"Shit, Rudy! I knew helping you would be trouble."

"Sorry, Craig. I think things may be getting quite hot. You may need to get away for a while. I'll be lying low for a few days myself. I just thought I'd warn you. Hey! Gotta go now—they just called my flight."

"Thanks a bunch, Rudy, you..."

Rudy rang off before Craig could finish the expletive, checked his watch and the boarding pass. He still had thirty minutes before the flight would board. He inhaled deeply and exhaled slowly; he felt much better. He headed towards security.

Twelve feet in front of the security check, a sharp pain ricocheted through Rudy's chest. He clutched at his throat. Another sharp pain shocked through his sternum and Rudy felt his legs buckling. As he fell to the ground, fear washed over his prone body. Through a fog he saw people cluster around him. Somewhere far, far away, he heard a woman scream, or was it his own scream? The pain rocketed through his entire body as convulsions rippled his limbs. Then everything became very quiet and then very dark.

When the paramedics arrived, Rudy was pronounced dead, apparently from sudden cardiac arrest. As Rudy's body was covered and wheeled away, a man in the crowd, the same man who had followed Rudy to the airport and had queued behind him at the reservations desk, moved with a hint of a limp to a payphone and dialed.

"It's me. It is done." The man hung up and limped out of the terminal.

❦

Mr. J., wearing rectangular tinted glasses and a fedora, returned to his car in Union Station's parking lot. He'd just retrieved Rudy's package. He was in such a hurry that he didn't notice the large man, dressed like a tourist and carrying a video camera get into a car some distance away. Earlier, this same tourist had been taking pictures of Union Station. Mr. J had no idea that he'd been the main star of most of the shots. Neither was Mr. J. aware, as he pulled out of the parking lot, that the man was following him.

❦

New York City, September 18, 1999

The security guard walked to the elevators and pushed the button. When the door opened, he stepped confidently into the car, pushed a number on the panel, and watched the digital display change as the elevator rose.

Shortly, the car stopped. The man stepped out and looked about for a few seconds, turned left, then walked along the corridor until he came to a door. He removed the key cluster hanging on his belt, selected the appropriate one, and opened the door. Swiftly he entered, quietly shutting the door behind him.

Inside, he slipped on latex gloves, picked up the telephone and unscrewed the cover of the receiver. After inserting a small listening device in the phone, he replaced the cap. Next, he surveyed the office, then quickly climbed onto the desk and stuck another listening device to the top of a bookcase.

The man climbed off the desk, straightened it, and a short while later, walked out of Mr. J's office. Earlier that day, that same man had placed a number of listening devices in Mr. J's home.

In a room, far, far away, a red light blinked on a console. A tape machine began to hum.

"We're in."

CHAPTER 36

New York City, September 20, 1999
"Hello, Your Eminence?"
"Yes, Mr. J."
"I have the name of the organization also searching for the Scroll."
"What is it?" The prelate reached for a pen.
"It's an offshore corporation by the name of Tricom Limited, registered in Guernsey,"
"What is the nature of this corporation's business?"
"Can't really tell you. It doesn't say much in the documents."
"Do you have any idea why such a group would be interested in the Scroll of Miriam of Magdala?"
"Nothing definite—apart from the fact that it would be a valuable asset for anyone who got hold of it."
"Can you tell me if this organization's related to the satanic cult that is said to be interested in the Scroll?" said Folino.
"Can't say that either. What I can tell you is that this corporation's somehow connected to the woman I saw following Woodward just before his death. I had a man following Gerald Woodward; that's how we found out about the woman."
"I see. Any idea who this woman is?"
"No."
"Try and find out who she is. If she is connected to this corporation, it might be advantageous to join forces with her in our quest."
"I believe I know where she lives. My man followed her home."
"Good, then make contact and keep me informed."

༺༻

The Messenger smiled to herself as she listened to the tape-recorded conversation between the Vatican office and the man called Mr. J. It was clear from the conversation that the Vatican was also searching for the Scroll. Amused that the Vatican wanted to enlist her help in finding the

Scroll, she chuckled to herself. The Messenger was even more pleased by another fact. The Vatican was linked to Mr. J., the same man who had been seen by one of her men emerging from the hospital room of Max Silver shortly after his death. A plan formed in her mind.

※

The young woman, dressed in a janitorial staff blue overcoat, slowly pushed a trolley along the corridor. The cart rattled with the usual jumble of cleaners and detergents. As she ambled along, she stopped at waste bins, emptying them into a garbage bag.

The woman halted in front of a door at the end of the corridor, removed some keys from her pocket, rummaged through them and inserted one into the keyhole. She turned the key, but the lock didn't budge. She removed it and selected another. After two more tries, one turned easily. Letting herself in, she pushed her cart into the office and then locked the door behind her.

Inside, the woman slid the cart to a corner and launched into action, methodically searching the office. Swiftly, she sifted through all the papers piled on the desk, carefully putting everything back where she'd found it. Then she went through all the drawers. Completing her search of the desk, the woman surveyed the room. What had she missed? She bent down behind the desk and picked up the half-full waste paper bin.

Emptying the contents on some open floor space, she picked through the rubbish with painstaking diligence, returning most of the litter into the bin until the only items that remained were crumpled paper and opened envelopes. She unfolded each crumpled paper ball. None of them contained useful information and she balled them up again and tossed them.

Then she examined the envelopes; most she discarded. After this exercise, only two opened envelopes remained: one legal size envelope with a typed address, postmarked Florida, and a letter-sized, handwritten envelope postmarked Albany, New York. She pushed the two envelopes into her pocket, cast a final look around the office and pulled her cart back into the corridor, locking Gerald Woodward's office twenty minutes after she entered it.

※

New York City, September 30, 1999

"We have information which leads us to believe that the person who possesses the Scroll, lives in either Florida or here in New York."

"What is the nature of this information?" said the Messenger.

"First, we recovered two envelopes from waste paper in Woodward's office that are postmarked approximately two weeks before the Cameron woman notified us that Woodward had the pictures."

"Surely this basket would've been emptied before you found the envelopes?"

"We learned that shortly after news of his death, the University placed his office off limits until an investigation had been completed. So nothing in his office had been disturbed."

"Continue."

"One of the envelopes is postmarked Cocoa, Florida, the other, Albany, New York. Recently, one of our brethren who was monitoring all calls to the Department of Languages at the University traced a call from someone who wanted to speak to Gerald Woodward. The call was made from a payphone near a convenience store in Albany. I sent some men to the area and asked them to follow people they observed using the payphone. Although we couldn't connect anyone we followed to Gerald Woodward, we believe that the person who placed that call to the University is the person who might possess the Scroll."

"So the person lives in Albany?"

"We believe that is very likely, though, we're not ready to rule out Florida. Perhaps the person lived in Florida, but is now in New York and used the payphone to call Woodward."

"How do you propose to find this person?"

"Our best hunch is that he or she is a collector of artifacts and probably an acquaintance of Woodward. We intend to focus our search that way."

"You have done well. You will be amply rewarded if the Scroll is found. Continue; spare no expense," said the Messenger.

"The Scroll shall be found, Master. There's one more thing, Master."

"Yes?"

"The private investigator who had been asking questions about us has been eliminated, but not before he was able to provide his contact, a man called Mr. J., with information about 47 Dovercourt and Tricom Limited."

"So this man, Mr. J., has information about us."

"Yes, Master." There was a slight tremor in the speaker's voice.

"Then obviously, our Mr. J. will eventually have to be eliminated as well. For the moment, however, he may prove useful to our cause. When the time is right, I shall issue new directions."

The line went dead.

CHAPTER 37

New York City, October 5, 1999

As part of his evening routine, Mr. J. strolled through the park behind his home. Suddenly two men emerged from the bushes and approached him. The smaller of the two men faced Mr. J. as the second one with Neanderthal features fell into step behind him. Alarmed, he stopped in his tracks. The man in front of him smiled and extended his hand.

"Good evening, I don't believe we've met."

"Excuse me?" said Mr. J. glancing nervously over his shoulder.

"I said I don't believe we've met. My name is Smith, John Smith, and I think yours is Mr. J."

"You've got the wrong person, Mr. Smith," said Mr. J., sounding genuinely affronted, hoping to bluff his way out of the threatening situation.

"I don't think so. You see, we know a great deal about you, Mr. J. We know that you've been asking questions about us." He paused for effect; he watched Mr. J. swallow hard and continued with satisfaction. "I believe we may have a mutual interest."

"Sorry. You've got the wrong person." Mr. J. was adamant. He began to walk away but was restrained as the second man put a heavy hand on his right shoulder. He froze in his tracks, staring at Mr. Smith.

"Just hear me out, Mr. J. You'll soon realize that we do have the same interests." The small man signaled to his partner to release the man. "We know you are searching for a certain ancient document—so are we. My principals would like to meet with you to discuss our mutual quest."

"Who are you? Why do you think I am this person you call Mr. J.?" He could feel the adrenaline course through his body. He looked desperately from side to side, but the three men were apparently alone on the path. He quickly calculated that he was too far from houses or traffic to summon help. The rest of the pathways were vacant. He could feel rivulets of cold sweat run down the curve of his back.

"Well, in the course of our search we learned from one of our contacts—you may know him—a private investigator called Bellamy..." Mr. J. flinched, the man continued, "Ah, I see the look of surprise on your face. I assume that you didn't realize that Bellamy knew about you. Well, actually he didn't want to admit it, but we convinced him and he led us to you. He also advised us that you've been asking questions about us." The small man paused. "Shall I continue?" He sneered.

"Go on." Mr. J's face was expressionless. He struggled to remain calm and to modulate his breathing.

"Well, we assumed that your interest in us has something to do with the document. Now if this is true, then you also know the importance of this item. Seems obvious that with our mutual interest we should be able to work together."

Mr. J. stiffened. "Assuming that I am this Mr. J., what exactly is it that you want?"

"My principals simply want to meet with you. Why work against each other when we could combine our efforts and move more quickly toward a resolution?" The man's voice was thin but smooth and soft.

"Who are your principals?"

"Lets just say we are a group interested in recovering the document."

"When can I meet with them?"

"We'll collect you tomorrow morning at your home—eight o'clock."

Mr. Smith, also known to the Messenger as *Mr. B*, deftly pushed past Mr. J., and sauntered up the path, the Neanderthal in tow.

Shaken, but relieved, Mr. J resumed walking, though at an accelerated pace. He was breathing hard and it wasn't from the exercise. As he walked, he glanced frequently over his shoulder; Mr. Smith's receding figure suffused into the encroaching gloom. Fear tingled through his limbs. He hadn't expected this turn of events, but perhaps this was the opportunity he'd been waiting for: the chance to make some real money.

⁂

New York City, October 7, 1999

A black sedan with dark tinted windows stopped outside Mr. J.'s front door. No one got out. Mr. J. emerged from the house and walked briskly to the waiting car. Inside, Mr. Smith shook his hand and smiled. Neither man spoke. The car moved smoothly into traffic. About thirty minutes later the car stopped outside the large gates of a treed estate and paused as they slowly swung open. The car crept onto the grounds and stopped before an impressive home.

Smith led Mr. J. into the house, ushering him into a lavishly furnished living room.

"Please have a seat, someone will be with you shortly." The small man with deep-set eyes left the room. Mr. J. cast his eyes over the impressive furnishing. He felt uneasy and very aware that he was being watched. But by whom?

In a matter of moments a deep male voice from behind Mr. J. said, "Good morning, Mr. J.," He jerked to his feet, whirled to face a tall silver-haired man standing behind the chair, immaculately manicured hand outstretched.

"Good morning." He shook the proffered hand and noticed the man's flawless, almost effeminate skin and expensive suit.

"Please sit." The man walked around the chair and stood beside Mr. J. "Can I get you something to drink?"

"No, thanks. I'm fine." Mr. J. felt a sudden chill run down his spine as he looked up into the man's translucent turquoise eyes.

"Well then, shall we get right to business?" The man gracefully sank into a brocade-covered chair across from Mr. J.

"I believe my associate Mr. Smith has told you about our quest?"

"Not exactly. But, first, may I ask, who are you? You seem to know who I am..."

"You mean me personally or who are we?"

"Both."

"Forgive my manners; I should have introduced myself." Mr. J. wasn't sure if he was being mocked. The man smiled slyly; his language was slow and highly refined, calculated to punctuate Mr. J.'s discomfort.

"My name is Robert. I represent an international organization that collects ancient artifacts."

"What organization?"

"I'm afraid I cannot disclose more than what I've told you."

"What do you want with me?"

"Well, like I said, we collect ancient artifacts. We have been searching for an important piece called the Scroll of Miriam of Magdala. When we learned that you've been asking questions about us, we assumed that your interest had something to do with our search for the Scroll. That's why we contacted you." The man sat back in his chair and peered intently at Mr. J. "I assume that you do know of the Scroll—otherwise you would not have agreed to come here."

Mr. J. nodded. The tall man leaned forward in his seat, peering intently at his guest.

"Good. Well, here's our proposition, Mr. J. We'd like you to work with us, join our efforts towards what would appear to be our common goal."

"What makes you think that if, indeed, I am searching for this Scroll, I would need your assistance or find it advantageous to form some alliance with you?" He tried to sound confident, but it was a confidence he didn't feel.

"Let's just say you interest us. We are aware of your activities—*all* of your activities—seems that you have, shall we say, *invested* a great deal in recovering the Scroll."

"I'm not sure I understand." Mr. J. fidgeted.

"Your associate, Max Silver? I believe the police are investigating his murder. We know that you asked Mr. Silver to follow Gerald Woodward—perhaps to steal the Scroll from him. We also know that Mr. Silver was at Woodward's home the night Woodward died. You were also seen entering and leaving Max Silver's hospital room on the day that he was murdered. Indeed, you were the last person to see him alive—apart from the doctors and nurses who tried to revive him, of course. The police might be interested in your activities, don't you agree?"

"There's nothing incriminate me!"

"Come, come, and don't let's quibble over the obvious. Let me put it this way. All that it would take is an anonymous tip to the Police and the Press—with photos—and they'll be all over you. On the other hand, if you play your cards right and we find the Scroll together, it could be yours to do with as you please."

"Why would you give me the Scroll?" Mr. J. was genuinely confused.

"We have no interest in the actual artifact—we only want the information contained in it. The document itself is of little use to us."

"But I thought you said you collected artifacts."

"We do, in a manner of speaking. But in this case, we want the Scroll because of the ancient information that it contains. Once we have that, the actual Scroll as an artifact has no value to us. So you see, it would be advantageous to both of us to work together, agreed?"

"What do you want me to do?" Mr. J. said.

"Well, our investigation indicates that there is a third party interested in the Scroll; our mutual competitor, if you will. An ageing priest, a Monsignor Josephs, together with some of his friends, is also searching for the Scroll. They pose a threat to both our interests. We'd like you to find out what you can about their operation, the progress they are making in their search for the Scroll and any other relevant information. You'll report to Mr. Smith. He'll keep you advised about our ongoing search to maximize our efforts."

"That's it?"

"That's all that we require. Simple isn't it?" The man smiled thinly.

"And in exchange you will give me the Scroll after you've read it? And it will be intact?"

"You have my word." The tall man chuckled under his breath as if in response to a private joke and then rose abruptly from his chair. He strode toward the door without waiting for Mr. J. to comment further. Over his shoulder, he said dismissively, "That is all for today. Mr. Smith will escort you back to your residence."

As Smith moved into the room, the silver-haired man paused and turned. His eyes burned across the room. "One more thing, Mr. J."

"Yes?"

"Any breech of confidentiality about our arrangement will have severe consequences. We don't want any unpleasantness, now do we?" He wasn't smiling.

CHAPTER 38

New York City, October 12, 1999

"Hi. Miss Margaret Woodward?"

"Yes?" The woman looked slightly dazed as she stared at the couple on her doorstep. She peered through the crack in the door, the security chain still firmly attached.

"Mrs. Woodward, my name is Sarah Cummings, this is my son Andy. I know this is going to sound a little off the wall, but we're here because of your late brother. We've been working with Lieutenant Jackson, and we're aware that your brother died under suspicious circumstances. We believe, and I think the Lieutenant may have shared this with you as well, that your brother was killed because of an ancient scroll that he was working on. It's possible that you may be able to help us learn more about this document and contribute to the case. May we come in and talk to you? We promise not to be long."

Uncertainty crossed her brow, then she shrugged. "I guess so—if you think it will help." Margaret gently closed the door, undid the chain and then motioned them into the living room. Sarah noticed a mantle full of sympathy cards and a framed photograph of Gerald Woodward.

"Please sit down. May I offer you some coffee?"

"No thank you," Sarah said.

"You mentioned Lieutenant Jackson? Are you working for the police?"

"No, not exactly, but we keep in touch with Lieutenant Jackson regularly. He knows that my friends and I have an interest in the document your brother was helping to translate. We don't want it to fall into the wrong hands," Sarah said.

"There's no document here—the police searched," Margaret protested, shaking her head. She gazed from one to the other. Her eyes were still puffy; obviously, she'd recently been crying.

"Yes, we know your brother didn't have the document, but we're trying to locate the person who has it. We thought you might be able to help us," Andy said gently.

"Me? I have no idea about Gerald's work. We never specifically talked about it," Margaret said. Distress was creeping into her voice.

"We thought," Andy hastened to add, "that is, it would help if you could remember a few of his friends and acquaintances who are perhaps art dealers or antique collectors."

"I don't know. I could try, but I don't think I'll be of much help. I pretty much kept the household. Gerald mostly did his work at the university."

"We think a friend or former student or even a classmate might have sent him the document. For example, would your brother have kept any school yearbooks or anything like that around here?" Sarah said.

"If he did, they'd be in the study." Margaret waved vaguely in the direction of a hall.

"May we have a look?" Andy asked gently.

"I don't see why not. I haven't touched his room much since the police left. Just tidied a few things off the floor..." Her voice trailed off. With a sigh, Margaret Woodward lifted herself out of a chair and led them down the hall.

"I'll leave you to your search. How long do you think you'll be? I have to leave in an hour for an appointment."

"We'll leave whenever you're ready to," Sarah said smiling. "We don't want to impose."

Margaret nodded and left the study.

Sarah and Andy quickly and thoroughly looked through all the desk drawers and searched the library shelves for anything that would help them identify the person who possessed the Scroll. After about an hour they concluded that there was nothing to be found. Just as they were about to leave the room, Margaret returned.

"We're all done here, Mrs. Woodward," Sarah said.

"Find anything helpful?"

"Afraid not," Andy said.

Sarah brightened. "Do you know if he kept any address books or things like that?" she said.

"Not that I can remember."

"We forgot to ask—what schools did he attend?" Sarah said pulling a small pad from her purse.

"Washington Senior High School, then he did an arts degree at Jefferson College and from there he obtained other degrees at New York University."

"Thank you. That may help." Sarah replaced the small pad.

"I'm sorry I've not been of much help."

"Actually, you've been quite helpful. We'll keep in touch and let you know if we make any progress," said Andy.

❧

New York City, October 22, 1999

"So what do we do now?" said Andy.

Andy, Sarah and Stephen huddled in a downtown coffee shop.

"We have lists of arts and antique collectors and the lists of students who were in Woodward's classes and a list of his High School and College classmates." Andy motioned to a sheaf of stapled pages on the chair beside him.

"Seems obvious. We try to match them," said Stephen.

"Do you know how long it will take to match these names?" Andy said.

"Ages if we tried to do it manually," said Stephen. "It's a long shot, but it's all we've got."

"Do you have a more efficient way?" said Andy.

"I don't, personally, but if these lists are computerized, it may be possible to use a sorting program to process them," Stephen said.

"Right!" Sarah sat up in her chair. "That's what your girlfriend did last time isn't it?"

"Yeah, Melanie's a crackerjack when it comes to these things. She's quite a programmer," Stephen said.

"I don't get it," Andy said, "fill me in."

"Well, the last time we got involved with the Watchers we had to find the identity of the man who was born under a particular astrological configuration. Melanie used a statistical program to narrow the search. I'm sure she could do the same thing with this data."

"I'll see if all this information's digitized," Sarah offered.

"I'm sure it is—everything's computerized these days," Stephen said.

"It would be a lot easier if we had the Polaroid." Andy sounded dejected.

"That doesn't necessarily follow," Sarah said. "We'd still have to try to find the person who took the picture."

"Sure it does. Look, we might find that person if we had the batch number from the Polaroid."

"Yeah, right dear. It'd more helpful if we had a fingerprint or an address or…"

"Hold on Sarah. Andy may have a point there. Tell us more, son."

Andy leaned forward in his chair; excitement animated his voice. "Well, I was reading just the other day about how all films are manufactured with batch numbers. Unlike other films, when a Polaroid is used, a faint number appears on the picture's back. That's the batch number I was talking about. That number can be used to trace where the batch was shipped. If we know the shop where the batch was shipped, we'll know who bought that particular batch. That would narrow our search field."

"I'll say it would. And with any luck, we could even find out the buyer," Sarah said.

"Like I said, if only we had the Polaroid." Andy sank back in his chair, deflated.

"You're right. It may still be around, Andy. Now, think guys—if you had Polaroid snaps of a valuable document, where would you most likely keep them?" Sarah said.

"In a safe, or some other secure place."

"OK. Lets think like Professor Woodward. Put yourself in his shoes. You receive these Polaroids in the mail, look at them, read the accompanying letter, and then, maybe, decide that you'd work on the translation in the near future. Where would you put the letter and the snap?" Sarah said.

"Somewhere in the office,"

"Where else?"

"Probably in my pocket. I'd probably carry it on me.... My God, Sarah, he could've had it on him," Stephen shouted.

"Yeah—a Polaroid is small enough to fit into a pocket," Andy said, excited by the prospect.

"We've got to get back into Woodward's house," said Sarah, rising from her chair and already moving toward the door as the two men scrambled to gather their papers.

CHAPTER 39

New York City, November 2, 1999

"I found it!" Andy clutched a dark tweed jacket with leather elbow patches. Triumphantly, he held up a Polaroid snapshot.

"Well, I'll be damned," Stephen said, a grin spreading across his face.

Stephen, Sarah and Andy stood in Gerald Woodward's bedroom where they'd been searching through the dead man's clothes.

"Checked the back?" Stephen asked.

"Yeah. The number's faint, but you can make it out. It says, QR1-99. Here—have a look." Andy handed it to Stephen.

"Yeah, you're right. That's what I see too."

"To think that all the time we've been looking for this and it's been right under our noses," Sarah said.

"Well, it's true what they say. The most obvious spot makes the best hiding place." Andy said.

"So what do we do now?" Sarah said.

"Call the manufacturers and find out where this batch was shipped. I can handle that."

"OK. Why don't we meet at Monsignor Josephs' later this evening."

As the trio walked out of the bedroom, they met Margaret Woodward coming from kitchen.

"Any luck?"

"Actually, yes. We finally found the picture of the document your brother was working on in a jacket pocket."

Stephen showed it to Margaret. "May we keep it for now? We'll give it back as soon as possible."

She squinted at the image and shrugged her shoulders. "Sure, you can have it, but is that going to be helpful in finding out who killed him?"

"We hope so. We'll keep you informed. Promise." As they hurried down the hall, Sarah said over her shoulder, "Thank you for letting us impose the way we have, Margaret. We'll be in touch."

※

New York City, November 7, 1999

"I understand that you've found the photograph of the Scroll," the Monsignor said.

"Yes, it was in Woodward's jacket pocket all the time," Sarah said excitedly. "Stephen's contacted the manufacturer to find out more."

The Monsignor turned sightless eyes toward Stephen. "Have you been able to find out anything?"

"Yes, Monsignor, I have. I called Polaroid and gave them the batch number. I told them I wanted to find out where it was purchased. They were somewhat cagey at first—wanted know if it concerned a lawsuit. I told them that I had a photo and wanted to find the person who took it and figured that if I knew where it was sold, I'd be able to find the person. So they told me that the batch number was sent to a particular distributor and gave me the number. I called the distributor and they gave me the name of the store. And guess what? It's here—in New York!"

"So then, can we assume that the person who has the Scroll is in the city or in the state?" asked the Monsignor.

"Looks like it—Albany, to be exact." Stephen said. "A store called Photo Mart. There are a number of them around, but this particular batch was sent to a particular store in Albany."

"Albany?" said Andy.

"Most likely our collector lives there unless he was just passing through and only stopped to purchase the film." Stephen said. "I know," he said softly, "that's a pretty big supposition—and we could be way off base, but..."

"Even if this guy does live in Albany, we still have a pretty big problem, though. How do we find out who he is?" said Andy.

"What about phone calls?" Sarah said.

"I don't follow you. Phone calls?" said the Monsignor.

"Yes, you see it's likely that whoever gave the pictures to Woodward may also have called him, or Woodward could have called this person. If we can get the telephone records, let say, beginning a couple of months before he was killed, and we look at all the phone numbers incoming or outgoing to Albany, that might point us in the right direction and eventually, maybe even to the person," Sarah said, optimism coloring her voice.

"Great idea, Sarah," Stephen chimed, "but the real question is— how do we get Woodward's phone records?"

"Lieutenant Jackson," the Monsignor said. "He has the authority to provide us with the phone records."

"I'll ask him," Sarah said, "Right after I tell him what we've found!"

"Don't forget to ask for the records for Woodward's office as well," said the Monsignor.

"Right."

CHAPTER 40

New York City, November 15, 1999

"Good morning Ms...." The clean-shaven man hesitated as he glanced at the nameplate on the desk of the woman. "Capriotti, Ms. Capriotti." Flashing a near perfect smile, he straightened to his full six-foot height. His immaculate double-breasted suit fell handsomely about his mature frame, perfectly tailored to accommodate his broad shoulders and trim hips.

Immediately, the woman who had been concentrating on a computer monitor looked up and returned his smile.

"Can I help you, Mr....?"

"Richards, George Richards." The man reached into his inside pocket, removed a business card and handed it to the woman. "I have found the offices of the American Society of Art Collectors haven't I?"

"Yes, well, it's the New York chapter anyway. We only administer the New York branch of the Society, which, as you may know, is national. I see that you're a collector yourself." The woman glanced at the business card.

"Yes I am. Just moved to New York City from Toronto, Canada."

"Well, welcome to the city. How can I help you Mr. Richards?"

"I'd like to apply for a membership in the association. I assume I can obtain information about the membership directly from you, can't I."

"Yes you can," she said, a slight frown crossing her brow, "you can purchase a membership, but of course, we can't give out any information about our members."

"Of course, sorry to be ambiguous, I meant that I'd simply like to join the Society. Can you help me with that process?"

She beamed, relieved that she hadn't disappointed this handsome man. "If you'll have a seat, I'll have you see our manager, she handles all the new memberships." She gestured for him to sit in a plush leather chair as she scurried into an inner office. Minutes later, she returned with another woman.

"Mr. Richards, I'm Mary Humphreys, the Society administrator." She extended her hand.

He rose, reaching for the woman's hand. "*Carrie* Humphries?"

"Mary Humphreys" she gently corrected him.

As he shook hands, he gently brushed his other hand over his lapel and activated a miniature camera. The camera snapped five quick pictures of Mary Humphreys. An extra sensitive, voice-activated recorder concealed in his pocket, had already recorded her voice. The machine's sophisticated pickup head enabled it to recognize even the minutest modulations in voices and accents to produce a flawless copy of the sounds.

"Please follow me, Mr. Richards." She led the man to a small boardroom where the oval table held a number of documents. "Please have a seat. If you'll just complete these few forms, I'll issue your membership card. There is an annual fee of a hundred dollars, payable to the society upon application for the membership." She remained officious, but polite.

Mr. Richards, still smiling, sat down, removed a hundred dollar bill from his wallet and passed it to Mary Humphreys. He picked up the pen and began filling out the forms.

A mere ten minutes later, George Richards, clutching a number of papers and brochures, was ushered out of the boardroom into the reception area by Mary Humphreys. As she turned to shake his hand again, he clumsily dropped some of the documents and quickly bent down to retrieve them. She bent down at the same time. In the confusion, she didn't notice him deftly steal the security key card clipped to her jacket pocket. When he stood up, he smoothly pocketed the card, all smiles as he apologized for his ineptness. Charmed and slightly flustered, Mary Humphreys mumbled a good-bye as he walked out of the office.

Once outside the office, Richards made a mental note—no cameras in the corridors, no cameras in the office itself. As he left the building, he removed the security key card and glanced at the photograph above the name.

"Piece of cake," he said to himself.

꒜

At seven that evening, a woman, wearing slacks, a long-sleeved sweater, and bearing a striking resemblance to Mary Humphreys walked into the office tower housing the American Society of Art Collectors.

She walked up to the reception desk, smiled at the security guards and flashed her card.

"Left some things in my office," she said pleasantly.

"Go right on up, Ms. Humphreys," said one of the security guards.

"Thank you," said the woman.

Casually she walked towards the bank of elevators, pushed one of the buttons and waited, her back to the security desk. When the elevator door opened, she stepped in, held her card against the barcode reader, and when the light changed from red to green, pushed the button for the eighth floor.

Stepping out of the elevators, she turned right and made her way down the corridor until she came to the American Society for Art Collectors offices. She swiped her card through the reader. When signaled by the voice recognition prompt, she activated the tiny recorder.

"Mary Humphries."

The door lock sounded a small buzz, then clicked. Quickly, she pushed the heavy glass door and walked into the room. Snapping on the lights, she moved quickly. Sitting behind the desk in the reception area, she turned on the computer. Immediately, the screen demanded a password.

"Piece of cake," she said to herself.

She punched in a combination of letters and numbers. After about five tries, the computer accepted the proffered password. The screen reflected in her glasses as she scanned the database until she came to the file she wanted. She slipped in a disk and download it.

Five minutes later, she strode past the security desk, holding up her small brief case. "Got it," she said out loud as she waved. The security guards waved back.

About five hours later, a man left the offices of the Florida Chapter of the American Society of Art Collectors. He carried a similar disk in his breast pocket.

CHAPTER 41

New York City, November 15, 1999

Marianne sat upright on the park bench on which she'd been lying. Her eyes glowed with a new intensity.

She'd been wandering for several days, searching for answers to what she was experiencing. Suddenly, as she lay there, it had all come to her—she had the answers she was looking for. She scrambled off the bench and walked with renewed energy toward the nearest subway line. Her first task was to get to the main library and search their database. About forty-five minutes later she breezed through the door of the New York public library and walked up to the reception desk.

"Excuse me, how can I find a record of births in the State of New York for 1963?" Marianne said.

The woman at the information desk removed the rimless glasses perched at the end of her nose and, with the expression of someone who'd just found dog excrement on her shoe, reviewed the disheveled Marianne.

"I'm sorry, what did you say?" the woman asked, barely able to keep a civil tone.

"I'm looking for records of births in the State of New York for 1963." Marianne ignored the woman's look of distain.

"Those records will be on microfiche now." The woman's voice softened somewhat when she realized that Marianne was neither impaired nor crazy. Something about her earnestness made the librarian suddenly want to help this unfortunate street person. "You could also search the newspaper database for the births and deaths sections of the newspapers for that year. Though those newspapers will also be on microfiche."

"How do I get access to the microfiche?"

"They're kept on the second floor—the readers are on the same floor, but there's a fee of twenty dollars for an hour of use. You have to pay here." The woman gave Marianne a doubtful look accompanied by a slight sideways tilt of her head.

Marianne ignored the subtle gesture, opened her purse and handed the woman a crisp twenty-dollar bill.

Slightly surprised, the woman took the money and handed Marianne a receipt. "Give this to the microfiche attendant."

"Thanks." Marianne pocketed the slip of paper and walked towards the elevators. At the Microfiche counter, Marianne handed it to a short bespectacled man who gave her a vague look, walked to the back of the reception area and returned with two boxes of microfiche.

"The fiche readers are at the end of the hall," he intoned without looking at her and returned to his work.

Marianne hurried down the hall and sat down before a vacant reader. She scanned the dates on the boxes and opened one of them. It'd been years since she'd done this kind of research, but her fingers seemed to know exactly what to do. She flicked on the reader's light and placed the first microfiche in the magnification slot. Spinning the knob to bring the writing into focus, she scrolled to the end of the document.

Not finding what she was looking for, she removed the microfiche and replaced it with another until after about thirty minutes, she found the copy that she wanted. She scrolled the document until she came to the birth announcements and obituary sections. She scooted her chair closer to the machine as she scanned the list of children that had been born that week.

Then she found what she was looking for.

It was as she'd anticipated, but seeing it was no less staggering. She sat back and stared at the screen. Her hunch confirmed, she now knew that there was only one course of action open to her.

"This isn't going to be easy," she said to herself as she hurried down the stairs and flew out of the building.

CHAPTER 42

New York City, November 20, 1999

Half asleep, Marianne sat with her head resting against the bus window. As the bus wove in and out of traffic, her head occasionally bumped against the window, but she ignored the discomfort because the irregular jostling kept her awake. She was actually grateful for the otherwise annoying movement. At least this way, she thought, there was no chance of having another nightmare.

Marianne raised her arm and looked at her watch. The bus had left New York two hours ago. She had almost fourteen hours before the bus would reach Charlotte, North Carolina. From there, it would take her another half hour to get to her destination—the place where it had all started.

Thirty minutes after the bus reached Charlotte, a taxi dropped her off at what used to be the parking lot of the Agnes Mildred Pre-Elementary School in Haw River.

"You sure this is where ya'll wanna go?" the taxi driver drawled. "School's been closed near five years, I think. There's no one here, 'cept the caretaker, maybe."

"I'm sure, thank you." Marianne opened her purse, paid the driver and then she stepped out of the taxi into the pervasive silence of the empty lot. Weeds pushed their heads through cracks in the asphalt and faint traces of white painted lines hid below the brush.

Lost in childhood memories, Marianne surveyed the desolate surroundings of the dilapidated school buildings. When she turned around the taxi had vanished; she hadn't heard it leave. Suddenly she felt a deep loneliness. As she left the parking lot and headed for the playground, her head filled with the sounds of children at play—as if she'd traveled back in time—thirty years ago when it had all started.

In the playground, she walked towards the tree where she'd met a mysterious woman—the woman no one could see except her. She stopped a short distance from the tree, a little frightened. Questions flooded her consciousness. What would happen when she got to the tree? What if nothing happened? Where was the woman who had promised that she would come?

She inhaled deeply and walked the rest of the distance to the tree. Nothing happened, but intuitively she knew what to do. She looked around for a digging tool, something to scrape away the hardened red earth. She spotted a pointed stick a few feet away, picked it up and began digging. The earth was much harder that she'd expected and the stick splintered with the effort. Under her breath she chided herself for not bringing a trowel. Then she laughed; how could she have known she was going to be digging in the earth this day?

She looked around and saw a broken piece of pipe near the shambles that was playground equipment. Grabbing it, she returned to the tree and feverishly clawed at the ground. The tool easily accomplished the task and after ten minutes of scraping and digging, she saw a glint in the dirt. She dropped the tool and started brushing away the dirt with her hands until she saw the fine chain attached to a pendant. She sat back on her heels and surveyed her find. The pendant looked exactly as it had when they'd buried it thirty years ago.

A strange sense of unease coursed through her body as she pried the pendant out of the soil with her fingernails. Standing, she held it gingerly, fearful that it would crumble. She smoothed away the earth to reveal its untarnished surfaces. It seemed to glow in her hands as if it had an inner life of its own. Gently, she placed it in the palm of one hand and folded her long fingers over it. "What now," she thought.

A gentle hand on her shoulder startled her out of her musing. Whirling around, Marianne saw the woman standing there—the woman from thirty years ago. She looked exactly as Marianne had remembered her, unchanged, ageless.

"You came back," the woman said. Her voice was soft, nearly lost on the gentle breeze that wafted past Marianne. She felt the coolness of the moving air against her damp skin; a tendril of hair moved across her cheek. She felt unafraid, calm.

"I came back many times over the years, hoping that you'd be here, but you never were."

"Your time had not come. I knew that you'd come when the time was right."

"What do you mean?" Marianne said, unable to take her eyes off the woman's face, searching it, comparing it to the face etched in her memory from so long ago.

"You know what I mean or you would not be here today. I cannot reveal what you must discover for yourself. But I can tell you this, Marianne, the time is fast approaching when you'll have to make a choice."

"Is what I suspect true?"

"You are the only one who knows the truth, Marianne. Search your heart and soul, the answers are there."

"Is there any way you can guide me?"

"There's only one thing I can do."

"What's that?"

"Show you how to find the answers, but you alone must choose to find them. I will say this, if you decide that you want to find the answers, walk through the arch of the swings. If you choose not to know, just return to the parking lot. The taxi will be waiting. The choice is yours, Marianne." She pointed to the parking lot and Marianne followed her gaze. The breeze rustled in the weeds, then died.

"What will happen...?" Marianne said as she turned back, but the woman was no longer there.

Marianne stood by the tree, staring at the swings. She smiled at the irony. The swings so innocent looking and yet so daunting. A part of her sought to end it all. Wanted to just walk away from the playground. Yet there was also a part of her that demanded answers. She opened her fingers and stared at the pendant in her hand and then gazed at the swings. Her cheeks grew warm as tears flowed gently down her face and neck leaving wet tracks on her dusty skin.

She wiped her eyes with the back of her hand, slipped the pendant into the pocket of her skirt, and walked towards the swings. The heat from the bare earth rose to warm and dry her face; her hands hung limply from her side. She stopped about two feet from the swings and stared at the space between the arches. What would happen when she went through it? A mixture of fear and curiosity rippled through her core. She reached out and touched the space between the swings. Nothing happened. Mustering up her courage, she inhaled deeply and stepped into the arch.

Immediately a tremendous surge of energy swirled around her and, for what seemed like an eternity, she felt herself being lifted and carried through myriads of time, tossed through waves of history. Images, sounds, smells and ideas flooded her senses. She absorbed everything feeling neither fear nor wonder. Revelation. Illumination. It was what it was. Marianne was a witness, separate, yet present.

Then almost as quickly as she'd entered the arch, Marianne found herself on the other side. The woman stood waiting for her.

"Now do you understand, Marianne?" asked the woman, a gentle smile on her lips.

"Yes, I do," Marianne said simply.

"Go now. Time is of the essence."

CHAPTER 43

New York City, December 1, 1999

"I've found it, I've found it!" Stephen shouted as he jumped up from where he'd been pouring through the phone records they'd managed to obtain thanks to Lieutenant Jackson. Sarah came running into the dining room from the kitchen.

Stephen pointed excitedly to the scattered pages. "Look, Woodward made only one call to an Albany number from his office—April 6th—just before he was murdered!"

"Think that's the one?" Sarah said.

"Very likely."

"Did you find a name and address in the reverse directory? Should be there," Sarah said.

Stephen reached for the book, rapidly flipped through the pages, and ran his finger down the list as Sarah looked over this shoulder. Stephen's finger stopped and traced laterally across the page. "Yup. Here it is."

He read aloud. "Bailey, Michael—50 Ravine Drive." He and Sarah stared at each other.

○○○

"Hello, Mr. Bailey, my name is Stephen Da Costa. You don't know me but we have a mutual acquaintance, your friend Gerald Woodward, who, I'm sure you've heard, was murdered. We believe that your life may be in danger as well. It's difficult to explain over the phone. My friends and I are on our way to see you—please wait for us. This could be a matter of life or death."

"Answering machine?" said Sarah.

"Yeah. I hope that he listens to it when he gets home. Come on, let's go."

"Right. I'll leave a message for Andy, Maybe we should call the lieutenant just to keep him up to speed—maybe ask him to come as well. You never know what could happen," Sarah said.

"Good idea. We'd better call the Monsignor too." Stephen said as he punched in the lieutenant's number.

"Hello. Is the lieutenant in?"

"No. Should be back in about twenty minutes. You want to call back or leave a voice mail?"

"Could you just give him this message—it's urgent that he get it as soon as possible. Please tell him that Stephen Da Costa called. Tell him that we've found out the address and we're going there. We hope that he'll meet us there."

"Right—the address?"

"Its 50 Ravine Drive in Albany—home of a Mr. Michael Bailey."

"OK. Got it. I'll let him know."

Stephen rang off and quickly placed a call to Monsignor Joseph as Sarah scribbled a quick note to Andy.

"Left a message for the lieutenant—got through to the Monsignor. Says he'll ask the Bishop to meet us there. He believes that Michael Bailey may be more inclined to believe our story if the Bishop's with us," said Stephen.

"That's not a bad idea. Maybe I should ask Andy to call the lieutenant again after he gets here—let him know the Bishop's going too."

"Couldn't hurt. He may even get a ride with the lieutenant."

❦

"Hello. It's me."

"Yes, Mr. J.?"

"I have information. The Monsignor and his friends have identified the person who has the Scroll."

"Excellent. Who is this person?"

"We still have a deal? You promised that I could have the Scroll when you'd finished with it." Mr. J. tried to dampen the desperation in his voice.

"We have a deal," said the man at the other end dryly.

"OK. The name of the man is Michael Bailey. He's got a house on 50 Ravine Drive, Albany. I understand that the others are on their way there even as we speak."

"Thank you. You have done well and shall be rewarded."

"When will I get the Scroll?"

"We shall be in touch as soon as we review it." Before Mr. J. could protest the man abruptly ended the call and placed another.

"Get the chopper ready. We have a name and address."

CHAPTER 44

New York City, December 1, 1999

A distracted, somewhat disheveled man opened the door. His eyes darted quizzically from Stephen's face to Sarah's.

"Yes?"

"Good afternoon, we're looking for Mr. Michael Bailey," said Stephen.

"I'm Michael Bailey."

"Mr. Bailey, my name is Stephen Da Costa and this is Sarah Cummings. We left a message on your voice mail telling you that we'd be dropping by..."

"Just got in. I haven't had time to listen to my messages," Bailey said curtly. "What is it that you want to see me about?"

Sarah looked earnestly at the man. "It's about your friend Gerald Woodward." She watched a look of surprise cross Bailey's face. "Perhaps it would be better if we sat down and had a chat. May we?"

"Yeah. Yeah, come on in. I just found out about Gerald's death. I'd sure like to know more." Bailey opened the door wide for Stephen and Sarah to enter and then led them into the living room. His suitcases stood just inside the foyer, numerous airport tags sprouting from their handles like small flags.

"Please sit down. Coffee?" said Bailey.

"Thanks, Mr. Bailey, but we don't have time for the niceties," said Stephen. "You see, we believe your life may be in danger even as we speak, so let's get straight to the point."

"What?!" Bailey sounded dubious; he wasn't smiling as he sank in a chair opposite the couch where Sarah and Stephan perched. "Look, I—", he began to protest.

"Mr. Bailey," Sarah interrupted, "Did you send a picture of a document to Professor Woodward?" Sarah said.

"Why yes. Just before I went on vacation. I called the University a few weeks ago after I returned home and that's when I learned that Gerald was dead—murdered, actually—at least that's what the receptionist said."

"That's true, I'm afraid," she said. "We believe that whoever killed him either thought he had the document or that he knew its whereabouts. He died before they could get the document, but we believe it's still in the owner's hands."

"What's so important about this document? What do you know about it?" Michael Bailey said cautiously. He looked hard at both of them as he sank into his chair, curled fingers covering his mouth, bright blue eyes narrowed as he waited for their explanation. He felt his pulse quicken as a sense of immanent danger filled his skull.

"We believe that the document is your possession. You may or may not know that what you have is the Scroll of Miriam of Magdala." Bailey's eyebrows shot up, but otherwise he remained motionless. Stephen hurried ahead. "It's supposed to have been authored by Miriam of Magdala either based on her own experience or with Jesus Christ's instructions."

Stephen's words seemed to echo in the small living room. A silence fell around the trio as they waited for Bailey to react. Slowly he leaned forward, elbows on his knees, hands clasped.

"Geez! I had no idea the artifact was so significant—I mean, I had a hunch it was more than a simple scroll—there was just something about it..." His voice trailed off and silence again blanketed the room. Thoughts seemed to race through Bailey's brain. He frowned as he pondered. Suddenly he murmured just loud enough for them to hear, "That's probably why he left me that message."

"What message?" Sarah said, leaning forward.

Michael Bailey looked at them earnestly. "I sent a picture of part of the Scroll to Gerald so that he could date it. I didn't send him the whole thing because I wanted to be sure of its value first. Well, he called me afterwards, while I was away, and left me a message saying that he wanted to speak to me about something. He sounded very excited." Bailey's frown returned. "But why would anyone kill him? They could have just asked to buy it from him—if he had it that is—or he could've just told them I had it."

"We don't have an answer for that just now," said Stephen. "But, there may be a simple reason. The Scroll may be the most important document of all time. Priceless really. A lot of people would dearly love to get their hands on the information that it contains. You see, this Scroll is said to contain the mysteries of the resurrection and the ascension. But more importantly, there's some speculation that it contains clues regarding the time of the re-appearance or return of the Christ."

Bailey looked stunned. "I had no idea..." he started lamely.

"No one knows for certain the exact content, but discussions about this particular Scroll have been raised through the ages by theologians and historians discussing what they call the *Magdalene Code*. You can only imagine that if what they think is contained in that Scroll is true, then the world will be a very different place."

Sarah interjected. "So you see, Mr. Bailey, there are those who will kill to possess such information. We believe that Gerald Woodward was killed by a group of satanists who want the Scroll. Our group wants to prevent the Scroll from falling into their hands."

"Oh my God," Bailey said softly as the full impact of what Stephen and Sarah said began to sink in, heightening his fear and his suspicions.

"Even as we speak, they are searching for you—the present owner of the Scroll—and they won't hesitate to murder again to possess it," Sarah said simply.

"So what do I do?" Bailey said, helplessness creeping into his voice.

"Come with us and bring the document with you. You and the scroll will be safe with us," said Stephen.

Bailey recoiled slightly at the suggestion. Caution darkened his eyes. Suddenly he blurted, "How do I know that *you're* who you say *you* are?"

"Well, you don't exactly. We hoped Bishop Jeffrey McCarthy, the Bishop of New York City, would meet us here so that he could support our story, but obviously, he's not here yet. But logically, you've got to believe us, because if we were only after the Scroll, we could have killed you the minute we got here and seized it ourselves," Stephen said plainly.

"Mr. Bailey, our only interest is to ensure that the document does not fall into the hands of the satanists," Sarah pleaded.

"What happens after I come with you? What happens next? Won't those satanists still be looking for me?"

"Not if we expose them first, which is what we're aiming to do as soon as we get you and the scroll to safety," Sarah replied.

Bailey rose and paced the room. After a few seconds, he turned around and looked at them.

"OK. I don't know why exactly, but I believe you. Wait here. I'll go and get the Scroll and then we can leave."

Bailey disappeared into his basement; in a few minutes he returned with a thick cardboard tube capped at both ends with aluminum screw tops. "Right. I'm ready," he said.

"Lets go," Stephen said.

"Hold on a second. Before we leave, I'd like to know where it is we're going. And I want to make a phone call," Bailey declared, pulling out his cell.

"We have a friend, Monsignor Joseph, a priest," Sarah said. "It'll probably be best if you stay with him for the time being. You can call him and anyone you like from the car."

With Bailey leading, they headed for the door. He opened it and was about to step outside when the barrel of an automatic was shoved in his face.

Two men stood on Bailey's doorstep. The man holding the gun was Mr. B. Grinning broadly, he gestured with the weapon for the trio to move back into the house. A burly man stood beside Mr. B., arms hanging loosely at his side. Shocked into silence, Bailey stepped back into the house so quickly that he dropped his cell phone and bumped into Sarah. She let out an involuntary shriek of surprise as he came down hard on her toe.

"Well, well, well—what do we have here?" said Mr. B as he snatched the tube from Bailey's hands. "Take it, Mitch," he said, passing the tube behind him without taking his eyes off the quaking man. Bailey, relieved of his parcel, threw his hands in the air.

Mitch unscrewed the tube's lid, checked its contents and grunted. The grinning man with the gun smiled to himself. "At last, the Scroll is ours," he said hoarsely.

"Look! You've got what you came for," pleaded Bailey, "Now just take it and go! We promise we won't phone the cops. Just leave!"

Mr. B. simply pushed further in to the room, pressing the gun barrel against Bailey's sweating forehead. Sarah and Stephen, wide-eyed, backed up in tandem with Bailey. Helpless and terrified, they remained silent. He gestured with the gun for the trio to sit as the hulking Mitch shut the door and stood close behind his boss.

"Find something to tie them!" he barked.

Mitch disappeared into the back of the house. Soon they heard the sound of shredding cloth. Mitch returned with strips from a tablecloth and proceeded to tie their hands behind them.

"You will never succeed!" snapped Stephen.

"Oh yeah? How do you figure that one?" smirked Mr. B. "We've managed to get the Scroll, I would have thought that *you*, rather, have failed."

"God never fails. This is only a temporary set back. You will never be able to use the Scroll," Stephen spat back.

"What are you going to do with us?" Sarah wailed.

"You're coming with us. You're the bonus, the frosting on the cake so to speak." He and Mitch simultaneously burst into laughter. It was a bitter, nasty sound that quickly evaporated into a sneer.

"Come on, let's go." Still gripping his weapon, Mr. B. gestured for the trio to move toward the front door. Mitch led the way as they moved in single file to the front of the house. Mr. B. cruelly jabbed Stephen in the back of the neck as he took up the rear of the line.

When they got to the door, Mitch opened it and walked to the utility van parked across the vacant street. Surveying the sidewalks, and seeing that there were no pedestrians in sight, he slid open the van's windowless rear door and signaled his boss to escort the trio outside.

Stephen whirled toward Mr. B. in protest, but he found himself staring down a gun barrel. "Keep movin'," hissed the little man, "or I'll blow your brains out and her's too." Glaring, Stephen forced himself to turn back and scramble behind Bailey and Sarah toward the van.

Before Mitch could slam the van's door, everyone turned to the sound of an approaching car. The car slowed and came to a stop just across the street from the van, its engine running. The driver appeared to examine a sheet of paper, oblivious to the van and the five people staring at him. He peered at the house address. When he turned his head. Stephen glimpsed the clerical collar beneath a dark jacket and knew instantly that it was Bishop McCarthy.

In a split second, before Mr. B. could stop him, Stephen reacted. He exploded from the van, and scrambled toward the car, yelling at the top of his voice for the Bishop drive away. Momentarily taken off guard, Mr. B. quickly gained his composure and swung his gun to follow Stephen's desperate trajectory.

Bishop McCarthy took one look Stephen lunging towards him, shouting with hands tied behind him, saw the gun pointed in his direction, and instantly pounded the gas pedal. Wheels screeching, the car lurched forward as two shots rang out, sending McCarthy's car into a horrifying spiral. McCarthy seemed to gain control of the wildly careening sedan as it screamed around the next corner and disappeared.

Mitch grabbed Stephen and lifted him bodily into the van, still kicking and shouting. Slamming the door, he vaulted into the driver's seat. Mr. B., already inside, held his gun on the trio as he shouted for

Mitch to floor it. The van's tires squealed as it sprang from the curb and sped away in the opposite direction.

※

"Anybody home?" Jackson, Andy beside him, stood outside the door. As he knocked, the door swung ajar.

"Get back in the car and put your head down," Jackson snarled as he unfastened his holster clasp and drew his gun. Andy moved reluctantly to the squad car as the lieutenant cautiously pressed the door open fully and quietly stepped into the house. Walking with his back to the walls, gun outstretched, he moved warily into the house, pausing occasionally to listen for sounds. Finding the house empty, he gestured for Andy to join him.

"There's no one here," he said, holstering his weapon.

"I wonder where they all could have gone?" Andy said.

"They said they were coming here, didn't they? You got the right address, didn't you son?"

"That is what they said…and look! That's my mom's purse." Andy's face flushed with emotion. Quickly his attention was diverted to something on the floor.

"Hey! What's this?" Andy bent down and picked up some strips of the cloth littering the hallway. Jackson took them from Andy and then let them drop onto the floor.

"They were here," he said with a tone of resignation.

"Who? My mom, Stephen—the guy who lives here?"

"Yeah—and so were the bad guys." He held Bailey's discarded phone. Looking up at the stricken Andy, he swore. "Damn! We're too late," hissed Jackson.

"What'd ya mean!?" Andy's face visibly paled and his voice quavered. "How do you know we're too late? *Too late for what?*" he cried.

"The strips of cloth were used to tie someone up—all of them I guess—"

Wailing sirens interrupted Jackson's reply. They raced out of the house to see a commotion a short distance away. Emergency vehicles screamed around the corner at the end of the street and then the sirens abruptly stopped. "Come on, let's go." Jackson raced for the corner and the crowd already gathering. Andy was close on his heels.

Rounding the corner, they could see a car perched eerily on the sidewalk against a lamppost with other cars scattered at odd angles to it on the street.

"Accident," said Jackson said over his shoulder. He caught sight of Andy's face, which was still a ghastly white. He mouthed the obvious, aware that the young man might be about to face his worst fears. "Could be them," Jackson said, and then turned to push his way through the crowd, holding his badge in the air. Andy followed courageously in his wake, terrified of what he would see, but compelled to lurch toward the truth. Jackson stopped and Andy stood shaking by his shoulder as firefighters and EMS crews extracted a bloodied and mangled body from the driver's side of the car.

"My God, it's the Bishop!" Andy shouted.

"Yeah, and he's still alive," Jackson said as the paramedics fitted a collar around the Bishop's neck, and then lowered the crumpled body onto a body board. The man's splintered glasses fell to the pavement; he glanced wildly around him, as Jackson shouted, "Bishop McCarthy, can you talk to me?" A paramedic frowned at the lieutenant until he spotted the gold badge, then moved aside as Jackson drew next to the gurney.

"Sir, we gotta move this man immediately. He's lost a lot of blood."

Jackson persisted, following the rolling gurney to the ambulance's back door. "Bishop, can you tell me what happened?"

McCarthy's face contorted with pain. His voice came in soft gurgling gasps. "When I got here...saw them taking them away...shot me as I tried to get away," he moaned.

"Who?"

"Don't know...two men." McCarthy coughed and collapsed into unconsciousness.

༄

"How is he, doctor?" Jackson stood by McCarthy's bed in intensive care. Life support tubes and wires protruded from every part of the bishop's body.

"He's stable. Good chance he'll make it. Lucky EMS showed up when they did," said the doctor.

"Is he able to talk?"

"Yeah. Should be able to as soon as he wakes up. But don't overdo it; he's lost a lot of blood."

"Sure. Can he be moved to a private room? We need to set up high security around this guy, Doc. Have to be able to screen anyone who wants to see him. I want staff clearances, too. Only people we know entering his room." Sensing some resistance coming, Jackson was quick to add, "Look, it's for his safety as well as your staff's. The Bishop witnessed a kidnapping—which is the reason for the attempt on his life. If the perps who tried to kill him learn he's still alive, they may try again. You staff could be an unintentional target."

"No problem," said the doctor, immediately comprehending the danger. "We'll cooperate fully." He paused, and then looked at Jackson squarely. "I'll get him healed—you keep him—and my staff—from harm."

"Thanks, Doc. I've already stationed two of my men outside his door and another at the elevators. I'll need a list and photos of the attending personnel," said Jackson.

"Right, I'm on it." The doctor abruptly left Jackson alone as he scurried to the main monitoring station.

Jackson drew a deep breath and glanced at the prone body of the Bishop. He wished he felt as confident as he sounded. This wasn't going to be easy, he told himself. Things were getting out of hand—going terribly wrong—and fast.

CHAPTER 45

New York City, December 3, 2000

Jackson sat across from Andy and the Monsignor.

"Any news about Sarah and Stephen?" said the Monsignor.

"No, nothing." Jackson's voice sounded more clipped than he'd intended. Andy sighed involuntarily.

"Do you have any idea where they may have taken them?" Andy asked weakly, still in shock.

"No, not yet. I'm sorry, son."

The lieutenant rose from his chair and began striding back and forth in front of the Monsignor's desk. "I hope you don't mind me pacing—helps me think." As soon as he'd spoken, he halted and said to no one in particular, "There's one thing that puzzles me."

"What's that?" Andy said.

"How is it that the kidnappers got to Michael Bailey's house almost at the same time as Stephen and Sarah did?"

"What are you suggesting?" asked the Monsignor.

"Maybe they were followed," Andy offered.

"True, they could have been followed. But even if Stephen and Sarah had been followed to Michael Bailey's house, how would their abductors have known that they were being led to the house of the person who possessed the Scroll?"

"I see what you mean. You believe that the kidnappers knew about Michael Bailey?" said the Monsignor.

"Yes. That's the only plausible explanation. Stephen and Sarah have been working for months trying to discover the identity of this person. They never had any indication that they were being followed anywhere they went. Then they discover Bailey's identity and all of a sudden, someone follows them to a house which just happens to be that of the man who possesses the Scroll."

"I see what you mean. It's too much of a coincidence," said the Monsignor pensively.

"Yeah, it is. But my question is this: did they learn about the discovery at the same time that you did?"

"Lets go over the facts and see if we can make sense of it," said the Monsignor. "I received a call from Stephen and Sarah. They wanted me to go to Mr. Bailey's house. I suggested that it would be preferable if they went to Michael Bailey's house with Bishop McCarthy. I called McCarthy to let him know that the person who had the Scroll had been located," the Monsignor said. "He left his office immediately."

"I also got a call from them. They left a message providing me with the name and address for Michael Bailey. Andy went home and found their note and then contacted me," said Jackson.

"Oh my God—the phones," Andy said.

"Exactly, our phones and offices have been bugged. That's how they knew," said Jackson.

"You mean they could be listening to us now?" said Andy.

"They could," said Jackson. "I'll have our offices and the phones checked for bugs later."

"We've got to find another place to meet. Come. I know just the place," said the Monsignor pushing back his chair and heading for the door. With Monsignor Joseph leading, the trio made their way to a small grotto on the church grounds.

"I take it that you're now convinced that finding the murderer of Gerald Woodward and finding the Scroll are inextricably linked," said the Monsignor.

"Yeah, I am now. But I don't think the only people we should be concerned about are members of the cult," said Jackson.

"You mean the Watchers?" Andy said.

"Right,"

"Give us your perspective," said the Monsignor.

"I've been doing a lot of thinking lately, and I'm inclined to believe that there's another group interested in the Scroll."

"Why do you say that?" said the Monsignor.

"Max Silver, the man who was at Gerald Woodward's house the night that he was murdered, was murdered himself, later, in hospital. I don't think the cult members were responsible."

"Why?"

"It doesn't seem to fit their mode of operating."

"If Gerald Woodward was killed by a member of the cult, and Max Silver saw all of it," said Andy, "Doesn't it seem logical that they killed Max to prevent him from identifying whoever killed Woodward and exposing them?"

"That is possible, logical even, but unlikely. You see, Max Silver was rendered blind and mute—something Sarah told me that the Watcher has the power to do. So the Watchers really had nothing to fear from Max Silver and nothing to gain by his murder."

"I see what you mean," said the Monsignor.

"When we saw Max in the hospital, he said that Gerald Woodward had asked him to meet him at his home. I don't think he was telling us the truth. Gerald Woodward met a woman earlier that evening and took her home around the time that Max Silver arrived. It's unlikely that he would've asked Max to meet him there at the same time. I think a person—or persons—interested in the Scroll asked Max to follow Woodward in hopes of locating it. Later, this same person or persons murdered Max in the hospital in order to keep his or her identity a secret."

"By Heavens! I think you're right," said the Monsignor.

"So now you have two murders to solve," said Andy.

"Looks like it."

"What are we going to do about Sarah and Stephen?" said the Monsignor.

"I'll see if the Bishop can give me a description of the kidnappers."

"It doesn't look good, does it?" said Andy dejectedly.

"I won't lie to you kid. No it doesn't."

◈

A knock rattled Mr. J's door. He rose and glanced through the peephole. Mr. Smith stood motionless and expressionless on the other side. Mr. J hurriedly fumbled with the locks and swung the door open wide.

"Mr. Smith. Come in."

"I'll be brief," said the man looking directly at Mr. J.

"Did you get the Scroll?"

"Yes. That's why I am here."

"When can I have it?"

"The boss wants to meet with you to hand it over personally."

"When?"

"Next week. Friday."

"Good. What time?"

"Seven—in the evening. We'll pick you up."

"I'll be ready."

Mr. Smith turned and began walking away, then stopped and turned. "Oh, by the way, the boss would like the Cardinal to be present."

"The who?" Mr. J's face grew ashen. He desperately tried to conceal his surprise.

"The Cardinal. The boss would like him to be present."

"Which Cardinal?" Mr. J asked, trying to bluff.

"The one who you've been working for, of course." Smith smirked at the now sweating man. "Fool," he thought to himself.

The confusion on Mr. J's face dissolved into self-righteous indignation. "But why should the Cardinal be present? You said you would give me the Scroll if I helped you."

"True, but we've known all along that you are working for the Cardinal, so the boss wants him to be present. You would've given it to him anyway wouldn't you?"

Mr. J. fell silent.

"Now, now don't tell me you wanted the Scroll all to yourself," he chided mockingly.

"No...no! I don't." Mr. J. managed to stutter.

"Good. So we'll have a nice little handing over ceremony. My people will hand over the Scroll to you *and* the Cardinal—just so we know it's in safe hands. Moreover, we need some assurances that the information that you and the Cardinal have managed to obtain about us will not be used against us. So you see," said Mr. Smith, a sly smile creasing his face, "he *has* to be present."

"What...ah...what if his duties prevent him from coming?" Mr. J. scrambled for an excuse, any excuse.

"Then we will not hand over the Scroll." Mr. Smith, said simply as he turned on his heel and marched down the stairs.

Mr. J. thought he heard the man cackle. He shivered. It was an ungodly sound.

CHAPTER 46

New York City, December 5, 1999
"Your Eminence?" Mr. J. spoke nervously into the phone.
"What is it? Have there been any new developments?" asked the Cardinal.
"I have good news, Your Eminence. The Scroll has been recovered by some associates of mine and I expect to receive it soon."
"Excellent! And just who are these associates?"
"Members of the organization of which we spoke the last time."
"Good. Let me know when you have it in your possession."
"I expect that will be soon—most likely next week."
"Very good. We must make arrangements for you to bring it to me here. When exactly will you have it?"
"I'm not sure."
There was a pause at the other end of he phone. Mr. J. heard deep breathing at the other end of the line; clearly the Cardinal wasn't happy but he'd chosen to hide his impatience.
"When you *do* know," he said slowly as if speaking to a child, "contact me and I'll given you directions as to how it must be couriered."
It was Mr. J's turn to be silent. He was cornered and he knew it. His heart raced as he thought how to confess the exact nature of Mr. Smith's demands. In the end, he blurted out, "They will not give it to me unless you are present, Your Eminence."
"Why would they want *me* there? How did they find out about *me*? I believe I made it clear to you that my name should be left out of any discussions and negotiations!"
"I believe I may have told them that I was working for a Cardinal of the Church just to enlist their help in the beginning. They want to make sure they are giving it to the right person," Mr. J. said weakly.
"This is all very irregular. You know the rules. Our relationship has always been anonymous. That is how it has always been. You should never have mentioned my involvement to them," he retorted angrily.

"My sincere apologies, Your Eminence, but I had little choice."

The line was silent for what seemed like an eternity. Mr. J's upper lip glistened with sweat; he could hear the Cardinal's heavy breathing and imagined the clergyman's scarlet face.

"Tell them I'll be there!"

Seething with rage, the Cardinal slammed down the phone. He clasped his hands together to keep them from shaking and placed them on his desk. Inhaling deeply to steady and calm himself, he stared at the wall. He hadn't expected things to turn out this way. Who were the people who wanted him to be present when the Scroll was handed over? Moreover, why did they want him there?

He'd intended all along to remain invisible in obtaining the Scroll. Now, however, not only had his identity been compromised, the years of work for the Opus Dei was also in jeopardy. Things were getting out of control, getting messy. He didn't like this turn of events. Not one bit. The cardinal concentrated on breathing. Remain calm, he told himself, regain control.

He had no doubt that if the Opus Dei was implicated in some of the events surrounding the search for the Scroll, including the shooting of McCarthy, the organization would be harmed. He couldn't let that happen. It *must not* happen!

Slowly a plan began to evolve in his mind. There was only one way to eliminate the risk and that was to eliminate the weak link in the chain—the man known as Mr. J. Without him, there would be no connection to him or to Opus Dei.

"Father, forgive me," he intoned. Abruptly he stopped in mid-prayer and picked up his private phone.

*

The Vatican, December 6, 1999

"Good morning Your Eminence."

Cardinal Folino, startled, raised his head from his work to see Nicholas Fraccaro standing before his desk. Although he permitted Nicholas Fraccaro to come into his office at any time to convey vital information, he was always unnerved by Fraccaro's habit of suddenly appearing like a ghost in a bad dream. Quickly the Cardinal regained his composure, but not before Fraccaro noticed the unsettling effect he'd had on the portly prelate.

"Good morning, Nicholas," said Folino, recovering from his momentary shock. He continued, trying to keep the annoyance out of his voice; for all Fraccaro's idiosyncrasies, the man was, for now, still extremely useful. "What can I do for you?"

"I have some news that may be of some importance."

"Please sit, Nicholas." Folino placed his pen on the blotter and gestured to a chair. "Please sit, Nicholas." Better to humor Fraccaro than risk losing his confidante.

Fraccaro lounged into a chair. "There's something you should know. I've learned that an anonymous gunman in New York has shot Bishop McCarthy. It would appear that he was attacked during the course of an assignment he was on for Cardinal Lombardi." A thin smile played on the man's oily face.

"Oh? Do you know the nature of this assignment?" Instantly Folino became guarded. Silence, he knew, would draw out his informant. It was a skill he'd perfected and it had served the Cardinal well.

"Yes. It would appear that the Bishop was trying to recover the Scroll. You'll remember that I advised you that it had been discovered." Fraccaro seemed to be taking some pleasure in parsing out the information in small bundles. The Cardinal noticed a tick beginning to work in the man's face. He could hardly wait for the day when he would be rid of this rat-faced man. Soon, he thought, soon.

"I see. Do you know if the Bishop was able to obtain this Scroll?"

"Not as yet Your Eminence. I shall try to determine that and shall inform you—immediately, of course." The tick increased in tempo.

"Thank you very much, Nicholas. Once again you have provided me with very valuable, ah, insights. I shall not forget your assistance to me."

"Thank you Your Eminence." Fraccaro rose from his seat and strode towards the door. As he reached for the doorknob, he stopped and turned around. "Excuse me Your Eminence, I do not know if I have told you this, but—about the Scroll that the Bishop was trying to recover—my sources tell me that it's reputed to be the Scroll of Miriam of Magdala." Fraccaro turned around and left the office as silently as he had entered, the tiny smile still playing across his face.

Thrilled by Fraccaro's news, the Cardinal rose from his chair with a euphoric bounce, he paused for a few minutes, and then headed straight for the corridor. He breezed by his secretary so fast that the poor man lurched back in his chair, mouth open. Fraccaro waved aside his secretary's fist full of messages with a curt, "Later!" and disappeared into the hallway. He couldn't remember the last time that he'd felt such elation. The time had come to confront his archenemy, Cardinal Lombardi.

When he got to Lombardi's suite he chuckled to see the office door shut. He knew that the Cardinal always closed his door when he wanted to nap. Eyes on the target, he stormed past the secretary in the outer office, raising his hand in dismissal to the man's weak protests. He charged ahead, a man possessed, driven by one thought alone: today was the beginning of the end for Lombardi. Today he'd lay his cards on the table. He reached the door and paused for a delicious second.

"This will wake him up!" Cardinal Folino thought as he pounded more loudly than necessary. Behind the door he heard movements and the scraping of a chair. "That's right, you old bugger—get on your feet!" he said under his breath. He walked in, not waiting for an invitation to enter.

Cardinal Lombardi looked up from the book on his desk and stared in surprise at a very flushed Cardinal Folino. Quickly he gained his composure, cleared his throat from the effects of his nap and said cheerily, "Good afternoon, my dear Cardinal. What brings you here?"

"I'm not the bearer of good news, my brother."

"Please sit down. What is it?"

Folino eased himself into a chair, a smug expression on his face.

"I'm afraid I have some information that is quite distressing to me, as it will be for you, brother. This information, if made public, could have grave consequences for our Mother the Church."

"I see. Can I help in any way?" Lombardi was used to Folino's blustering rhetoric. Better to play him out, humor him with grace, hear the latest catastrophe, and then send him on his way. This was a tiring and oft-repeated scenario, but a necessary dance with an obstreperous and annoying colleague. Why the Holy Father tolerated this man, this bully, only God knew.

"Well," Folino paused, desiring what he was about to say to have maximum effect, "This is a grave situation! Scandalous! Nefarious!" Folino stared at Lombardi, eyes bulging in his round face, expecting some sort of reaction from him. Not receiving any, he scowled and continued. "I have just learned that Bishop McCarthy has been shot and is in critical condition in a New York hospital! And—*dear brother*—you are implicated in this despicable affair!" His eyes narrowed as he sank into the chair opposite Lombardi.

"Good heavens! When did this happen?" Lombardi sounded genuinely shaken. Folino had struck a blow.

"Some time yesterday, I believe," Folino said, self-satisfied.

"I see. But why do you say it involves me? You're not suggesting I had something to do with him being shot are you?"

"Oh no. No. No! At least...not directly," Cardinal Folino sneered. "But I understand that he was working on an assignment for you, and during the course of completing this assignment, he was brutally attacked. You wouldn't want to tell me what this secret assignment is, would you?"

"I'm afraid I can't..." Cardinal Lombardi shifted uncomfortably in his seat and seemed lost for words. Momentarily stunned, he shook his head and stared at his folded hands before looking again at the gloating Folino. "But still I don't see how you think I'm involved in this tragic event," he continued.

"Oh *you are*!" Folino leaned forward in the chair, face contorted. "This is the way I see things. You sent a Bishop of the Church on a secret assignment—an assignment to recover an ancient scroll," Folino paused and stared at Lombardi, letting his words sink in. "I see the look of surprise on your face, you did not think I was aware of your activities, did you? Well, I believe that this is an assignment of which the School of Cardinals and the Holy Father should have been made aware. Now a Bishop of the Church has been shot because of your clandestine operations. What do you say to *that*?" Cardinal Folino nearly spat the last word, then glared with secret delight at Lombardi.

Cardinal Lombardi fumed silently, but gracefully retained his composure in the face of Cardinal Folino's insinuations. Less said, the better, he thought. Folino could be bluffing.

"Just as I thought!" Folino stepped up the rant, triumph in his voice. "You have no answer...no possible justification for such an outrageous indiscretion." He rose to his feet and peered down at Lombardi, playing on the height advantage. "I'll leave you to decide on the best way to break the news to the School of Cardinals *and* the Holy Father."

"What news? There's nothing to report." It was Lombardi's turn to inveigle. Under his cassock he felt a cold rivulet of sweat trickle down his spine.

"Oh, *yes*, there is!" Folino lunged forward and leaned on the desk with both knuckles, face flushed. Tiny flecks of spittle settled in the corners of his mouth. "First, you can divulge the nature of this secret assignment—the recovery of this Scroll of Miriam of Magdala—then you'll naturally have to bring up the news of the shooting of a Bishop of the Church who was on a clandestine assignment for you, and finally, the news of your decision to resign as Prefect of the CDF, because when all this comes out, you *will* be asked to resign."

Cardinal Folino rapped the desk with his knuckles and drew himself up to his full height. "I'll give you seventy-two hours before I break the news myself!" Having delivered his ultimatum, Folino whiled on his heels and marched out of the office with the pompous gait of one who knew he held all the aces.

At last the office of the head of the CDF would be his. Soon. He could almost taste it. He made up his mind to book a flight to New York as soon as possible to start his own investigation regarding the Scroll and possibly procure it. He, Folino, would be the one to personally return it to Rome. Lombardi would be history by the time he returned. A shiver rippled through his obese body; his face glowed, radiant with victory.

❧

Shaken, Cardinal Lombardi remained in his seat, staring at the wall for nearly fifteen minutes after Folino left. He tried to steady his pulse as he willed himself not to panic. He ran over in his mind the substance of Folino's rant. His gut churned as he processed the facts. McCarthy had been shot in the process of recovering the Scroll. This confirmed that the Scroll was an important document, one that must be recovered and protected by the Church. The Scroll of Mary of Magdala. He squeezed his eyes shut. Obviously this story was true—he had no doubt that Folino, for all his bluster, was telling the truth—but he had to get all the facts. Fast. Ahead of Folino.

Lombardi knew that Cardinal Folino was more than an irritation; he was a threat. He had known for a long time that the man had coveted his position as Prefect of the Congregation for the Doctrine of the Faith. The Cardinal had given subtle and not so subtle indications on many occasions that he, Folino, as the spiritual head of the Opus Dei, was the person who should head the CDF. Clearly Folino had long plotted to depose him. He didn't fear losing his position as much as he was afraid what the scandal could do to the Church.

Cardinal Lombardi believed in the Church as much as he believed that the continued success and very existence of the Mother Church pointed to her role in the Divine Plan. Folino's scandal could spell doom for the Church. He believed that such power brokers had no place in the modern Church. He'd always believed that, but now was the time for action. He had to do whatever he could to stop Folino.

Lombardi picked up the phone; his secretary answered promptly. Waving aside his secretary's apologies for the Cardinal's impromptu visit to the Cardinal's office, he quietly issued a succinct directive.

"Get me on the first flight to New York City and then issue a memo to the members of the Standing Committee of the CDF to say where I'm going. Write that I shall convene a special meeting when I return."

CHAPTER 47

New York City, December 7, 2000

The Messenger rose from behind the antique writing desk. Glancing at the table that held the cardboard tube containing the Scroll, excitement shivered through her limbs. The Scroll was now in her possession. Now all that remained was to open it at the appointed time. Then, and only then, all of its secrets would be revealed.

Her elation, however, was tempered. Although two of her rivals for the Scroll had been intercepted and detained, the Messenger knew that it was still a long way to the cusp of the Millennium when she could open the Scroll. Anything could happen between now and then. She was certain that attempts would be made to liberate the trio in her custody and recover the Scroll. She knew that she had to be vigilant—ensure that her minions were also vigilant. She could not afford to let all she'd gain slip from her grasp.

The phone rang. The Messenger reached for it with long elegant fingers.

"It is I, Master," said the man on the other end. She detected a trace of anxiety in the caller's voice.

"Good morning. You have done well in finding the Scroll and bringing me the people who were so close to snatching it from our grasp. You were right to bring Bailey along with them. You shall be amply rewarded," said the Messenger magnanimously.

"Thank you, Master," came the obsequious voice, "but I am afraid this time I do not bring good news."

"Oh?" said the Messenger.

"The Bishop is still alive. The police managed to get him to the hospital. He's in intensive care."

The Messenger fumed silently for a few seconds, squeezing her eyes shut as if the pain that suddenly crossed her forehead could be intercepted with the reflex. Why, she thought to herself, was she continually surrounded by such incompetence?

"What exactly is the Bishop's condition?" she snapped, trying to restrain her anger.

"He's in critical condition—on life support," said the man.

"Where?"

"General Hospital."

"The Bishop must be eliminated at all costs. He cannot be allowed to live. He could identify you."

"Fool!" her brain screamed as rage rose in her breast.

"It shall be done, Master," came the hushed response.

"No!" she snarled in distain. "Do nothing. I shall attend to it myself." The Messenger slammed down the receiver.

New York City, December 8, 1999

The tall nun carried a modest bouquet as she walked to hospital reception. "Good morning friend, I'm here to see His Grace, Bishop McCarthy. Can you direct me to his room?" She flashed a benevolent smile to the woman behind the desk.

The woman smiled back. "Yes, of course, sister," she replied in a strong Scottish brogue. "He's in intensive care. That's fourth floor, South Wing."

"Thank you."

"Terrible what happened to him. I've been praying to the Blessed Virgin for his recovery since he was admitted," offered the receptionist.

"You are a Catholic?" said the nun.

"Yes, I am."

"Well, you must continue your prayers and take good care of him; he's a good man."

"I will, Sister."

The nun gave the woman another beatific smile, bowed her head slightly and turned in the direction of the elevators. When she got to the elevators, she quickly glanced around, pushed the button with a gloved finger and entered the empty car. Exiting on the fourth floor, she followed signs to the intensive care unit. Within seconds, she saw the policeman sitting in the corridor and deduced that he must be watching the Bishop.

The nun strode confidently toward the room, and when she drew close, the cop raised his head and stood. She flashed a pious grin.

"Good afternoon officer." To increase the effect, she tilted her head to the side.

"Good afternoon, ma'am...er...Sister." said the officer tipping his hat.

"I'm here to pray for the Bishop. May I?"

"Well, I have orders not to let anyone who is not a doctor or attending staff into the room, Ma'am...I mean, Sister."

"Well, I guess that excludes me. Although, after this horrible tragedy, I understand the need for such security. But, officer, surely you're not afraid of a nun are you?" She batted her eyelashes.

"No Sister," the policeman smiled warily at the black habit and the gentle face surrounded by the starched white cowl. Memories of his own parochial school days were interrupted by her next question.

"Do you want to search me?" The nun, a mischievous look on her face, stretched out her arms.

The policeman, apparently scandalized, waved his palms in front of his face and shook his head, "Oh, no, Sister. It's just that I have my orders."

"Do you believe in prayer, officer?" asked the nun softly, lowering her hands, and again tilting her head.

"Why yes, Sister. As a matter of fact. Yes I do."

"Then you would not want to deny the Bishop a prayer in his time of need...would you?" The cop looked at his shoes and began shaking his head. "Look," she rushed to add, "I'll compromise with you. Why don't you come in with me, that way I can pray for him and you can watch over me."

"I guess I...well, that is,..." stammered the policeman. Uncertainty furrowed his brow.

"Well, of course you can," she finished for him. "Now I couldn't possibly do any harm with you there, could I?"

"I guess not."

"I mean with your big gun and all," the nun winked.

"I guess...ah...I guess that's OK."

"OK. Let's go." She shoved the flowers into his hands and stepped past him.

Hastily, the policeman fumbled to hold the door open for the nun. He followed her into the Bishop's room.

✠

Around the same time that the nun entered McCarthy's room, Jackson walked into the lobby of the hospital's south wing and headed for the elevators. He pushed the button and stared impatiently at the illuminated numbers above the doors. The elevator took what appeared to be an eternity to descend from one floor to the next. When the doors opened, he entered and pushed the button for the fourth floor.

As the elevator ascended, Jackson's gut spasmed. His instinct, honed by years of police work, told him that something was wrong. But what was it? He hurried off the elevator and quickly headed along the hallway to ICU. Just inside the unit's doors, he saw the empty seat outside the slightly ajar door to McCarthy's room. His heart sank. There should have been a cop outside the door.

"Damn!" With his heart hammering against his chest, Jackson drew his gun and broke into a run. Where was the uniform? Had something happened to the Bishop? He prayed that he wasn't too late.

❦

McCarthy, still connected by a variety of tubes, slept, his breathing rhythmic.

The nun retrieved the bouquet from the officer's hands, placed it on a table beside the bed and proceeded to rearrange the flowers, apparently in no hurry to pray. When she was done, she reached into her pocket, removed a rosary and small black book, and sank into a chair beside McCarthy's bed. Over her shoulder, she flashed the policeman a smile, then turned toward the Bishop, crossed herself and started reciting the rosary, lips moving silently.

The policeman removed his hat, stood with his back to the door and started fidgeting with the brim. After about a minute he leaned forward and whispered over the nun's shoulder.

"Sister? How long're you going to be?"

She turned her head and glanced earnestly into his face. "Well, I'm saying the whole rosary, so, maybe half an hour?"

"I guess it would be OK to leave you—after all, you're just praying."

The nun smiled, touched his arm with an affectionate squeeze, and returned to her rosary. He turned his back and softly headed toward the door. A second before he reached the threshold, the policeman heard something shuffle behind him.

"Officer?"

As the policeman turned, he nearly collided with the nun. In a split second his mind filled with terror. How had she come so close to him so quickly? And why? Who was this woman? Something was definitely wrong with this picture; he knew he had to act fast.

Instinctively his hand went to his weapon, but he was too late. In one fluid movement, the nun lunged at him, yanked him forcibly towards her by his collar. Her strength seemed superhuman. Her breath, hot on his face, smelled of sulfur. He never saw the syringe that she plunged into the right side of his neck. He had no time to cry out. One last question filled his mind with horror. How could a nun be so strong? His gaping mouth released no sound. He felt his body go limp as he slipped out of her grip, onto the ground and into darkness. By the time his head hit the floor his heart had already stopped.

Stepping back from the cop, she swiftly moved to McCarthy's bedside. In a single movement, she swung her hand through the numerous wires and tubes that connected McCarthy, disabling them in an instant. McCarthy jolted in the bed, but he remained unconscious. From within a flowing sleeve, she produced another syringe, flushed the needle with a squirt into the air, and then advanced on the prone figure.

With a crash, the door to the private room slammed open.

The nun whirled to face Jackson, his gun drawn, standing at the door. He was as shocked to see her as she was to see him. For a brief moment, only the sound of Jackson's panting filled the room. Down the hall, the sound of rushing feet and alarms swept into the room.

Instantly, with the swiftness of a panther, she dropped the syringe, leapt over the body of the dead officer, and charged Jackson. Her agility and speed left him no time to react as her body powerfully connected with his, hurtling him heavily against the wall. Momentarily dazed, the wind knocked out of his chest, he sank to the floor, watching helplessly and dumbfounded as she streaked past him and out of the room.

As nurses rushed for the Bishop's room, she walked briskly in the opposite direction and darted into a fire exit. Scuttling down the staircase and into the next floor's corridor, she stopped in front of a janitor's closet, pushed open the door and quietly closed it behind her. The hallway had been vacant; for the moment she was well concealed. She pressed her back against the door and in the dark consciously slowed her heart and waited for the sound of her own normal breath to resume.

Feeling in the dark for the lock, she slipped the bolt, and then began to disrobe. The cowl and flowing robe slipped from her pale naked body. She crammed the garments into a garbage bag. Slipping into dark blue coveralls she'd found inside, she stuffed her long hair under a cap, pulled on thick glasses, picked up a mop and pail and exited the room. Near the front door, she parked the janitorial paraphernalia and walked calmly to the hospital parking lot.

She'd been in the hospital less than twenty minutes.

Scowling, The Messenger slipped into the silver sedan's driver's seat. She sat still for a moment, then flipped the glasses and the cap onto the passenger seat. Firing the engine, she waited a moment. Rage coursed through her body as the extent of her failure became apparent. Violently, she banged the steering wheel with open palms, let go a torrent of obscenities, and then gunned the car out of the parking lot. Her vehicle quickly disappeared into traffic.

Meanwhile, Jackson, still stunned by the force of the blow that had sent him into the wall, rose on unsteady feet. The medical staff, alerted by monitor alarms, had shoved past him, barely noticing the dead cop on the floor. Within seconds they'd reconnected essential tubes and wires to their patient.

Two nurses, having ascertained the policeman was dead, worked around him, not wishing to disturb what was clearly a crime scene.

One of the nurses recognized Jackson. "You OK, Lieutenant?"

"Yeah. I think. Yeah, I'm fine. Just got the wind knocked outa me. You see the woman who left the room?" He holstered his weapon and reached for the phone.

"Not really. Looked like a nun or something. She was just walking away from the room, but our first priority is our patient—we didn't follow her."

"So you didn't see where she went."

"Nope. Lieutenant, you really should have that head checked out—looks like a nasty bump."

"Right." Jackson dialed for backup.

After securing the scene and briefing the officers that flooded onto the floor, Jackson was finally alone. Moving to a nearby waiting room, he dropped into a chair. His breathing grew labored; his head throbbed. Neither the physical exertion nor the injuries he'd suffered could explain what he was feeling. Fear rocked his very core as the awareness came over him that he'd barely escaped being killed by the Messenger. Angry resolve quickly replace the fear, for Jackson knew that despite the disguise, he would never forget the nun's face—it was none other than Marianne Waters.

She was the Messenger, just as he'd always suspected. Now he had all the confirmation that he needed to arrest Marianne Waters on sight.

CHAPTER 48

New York City, December 10, 1999

Jackson sighed as he walked towards Bishop McCarthy's private hospital room. His eyes ringed with dark circles, Jackson's fatigue was compounded by his frustration over his inability to locate Stephen and Sarah. There was no clue as to their whereabouts or the mysterious Mr. Bailey. Dead ends seemed to multiply everywhere he turned.

He'd been baffled by the findings of the department's surveillance techs who'd swept the various offices for listening devices. None were found in his own offices, but they had discovered bugs in Bishop McCarthy's office and suites. Jackson was surprised about that since no one knew McCarthy was also involved in locating the Scroll except himself, Monsignor, Stephen, Sarah and Andy. Anyone interested in recovering the Scroll knew that the Monsignor and his friends were actively seeking the Scroll, yet their phones and rooms weren't bugged either.

Logically only someone close to Bishop McCarthy would have known that he was actively seeking the Scroll. That meant someone close to the Bishop had planted the listening devices. Jackson had no doubt in his mind that it was this same person who had alerted the kidnappers about the Scroll's discovery. More questions flooded his mind.

Was this person connected in any way with the Messenger? That was a possibility, but Jackson wasn't sure. Clearly, if he found this person, he would find Stephen and Sarah.

Jackson arrived at the Bishop's room. Outside, two uniformed officers drew to attention and smartly saluted him.

"Morning lieutenant," said a burly officer.

Jackson nodded. "How is he?"

"Getting better, sir…I think. At least that's what I gather from the staff. I think he's awake, sir."

Jackson gently pushed open the door and peered around it.

The Bishop was resting, but raised his head when the door opened. "Good morning, Lieutenant. Come in." Jackson sat beside his bed. "Here to ask more questions?"

"Yeah. Good to see you awake, Bishop. Feel up to a little chat?"

"I think so."

"I need you to tell me as much as you remember about the day you were shot."

"I'm happy to co-operate, lieutenant, though my memory seems to be pretty sketchy."

"Well, let's just get started and perhaps you'll recall some extra details as we go. Do you remember how many kidnappers there were?"

"Two, I think."

"Male? Female?"

"They were both men." McCarthy began to wheeze and clutched at his chest. The spasm quickly left his body. He reached for a water cup, drew deeply on the straw, and then sank again into his pillow.

"You all right? Can we continue?"

McCarthy nodded. "Just a cramp."

"Can you describe these men?"

"Not really. All I can say is that one of them was very tall, muscular. He was the one who pointed the gun at me. He looked like a basketball player. I didn't get too good a view of the second man, but I think he was shorter—chunky."

"Any special characteristics or facial features?"

"No. Sorry. It all happened so fast. I saw the gun, heard the shot, and then...well you know the rest."

"Bishop McCarthy, how many people close to you knew that you were trying to recover the Scroll?"

"Just Bishop Case, the bishop of New Jersey, Reverend Boyle, the pastor of the Manhattan parish, and Cardinal Lombardi at the Vatican."

"I see." Jackson took a moment writing down the names in his notebook.

"Why do you ask? Surely you don't think any one of these clergymen had anything to do with the shooting?"

"Can't say. I need to know about everyone who was aware of your interest in the Scroll—which seems to be the common denominator here. I do know, however, that your office and phone were bugged. Unless there's some other reason why someone would want to bug your office and home, we can assume that someone was eavesdropping on conversations regarding the progress of your investigation.

"I see. Of course," he said wearily.

"And only someone close to you would have known that you were working on trying to recover the Scroll."

"That's true." The Bishop looked distressed and began to wheeze again. A nurse appeared at his door with medication. She cast a disapproving glance at the lieutenant.

"Thanks, Bishop McCarthy. I think that's enough for today. If you think of anything, let the officers outside know and they'll contact me."

McCarthy nodded. "Is it true that someone tried to kill me in the hospital?" he said weakly.

Jackson nodded. "It won't happen again, I promise."

New York City, December 11, 1999

The Alitalia flight touched down on JFK's runway number 7E at precisely 10:00 a.m. and arrived at terminal 44 fifteen minutes later.

Cardinal Lombardi, followed by a somber Nicholas Fraccaro, emerged from the aircraft and was ushered by an attendant past immigration and customs to the diplomatic lounge where Reverend Boyle and Bishop Case waited for them.

"Good morning Your Eminence." Bishop Case stepped forward and shook the Cardinal's hand. "This is Reverend Boyle, pastor of the Manhattan parish."

"Greetings. This is my assistant, Nicholas Fraccaro." The four men exchanged handshakes. "Can we leave directly for the hospital? I'd like to see Bishop McCarthy as soon as possible," said Lombardi.

"Certainly, Your Eminence. One of our staff has already retrieved your baggage and is loading it into the limousine. Please follow me," said the Bishop.

With Case leading the way, the men exited the terminal into the parking lot. The Cardinal's luggage, Fracarro's suitcase, and a small shoulder bag, had been stowed in the waiting limo. Within moments, the car blended into traffic and headed into the city.

"How is he?" asked Cardinal Lombardi. Accompanied by Bishop Case, the Cardinal stood before Dr. Philip Howe, Chief of Surgery.

"He's doing well considering his age and where he was wounded. He'll be delighted to see you. I was just about to leave to check in on him myself so I'll take you to his room," offered Howe.

The clerics followed Howe along the maze of hospital corridors and soon arrived at McCarthy's room where two uniformed policeman stood in front of the door.

"You'll have to be searched before you enter," explained Howe. "A necessary precaution. As you may have heard by now, a woman dressed as a nun attempted to kill the Bishop. She failed in her mission, but unfortunately she succeeded in killing a police officer guarding him. Since then, we have police surveillance 24—7. Only police and select hospital staff have access."

"Of course, Dr. Howe. We understand," murmured the Bishop. Lombardi nodded assent.

Howe turned to the officer. "Sir, here are the personal identification documents for Bishop Case and Cardinal Lombardi."

One policeman peered at the documents, glancing at the photo ID and scrutinizing their faces. Taking his time, he reviewed a list of pre-approved visitors, then put down his clipboard and instructed the men to step forward individually, arms extended. The second cop stood firm, hand resting on his weapon. As he watched, his partner patted down each man. Next he scanned each priest with a portable metal detector. The detector beeped as it passed over the Cardinal's crucifix. The cop asked the Cardinal to remove it. The detector's next sweep produced only silence. Satisfied, the cop motioned the men to follow Howe into the room.

Awake, Bishop McCarthy moved to sit up when he saw his surgeon and the Bishop.

"Good morning Jeffery, you have a visitor," said Bishop Case, stepping aside to reveal the Cardinal. McCarthy forced a smile as the two walked toward his bed.

"Your Eminence. This is a surprise," McCarthy whispered.

"I had to come, and see for myself how you are doing. After all, I'm partly to blame for your being in this position," said Cardinal Lombardi kindly. "How are you?"

"Much better, I gather, from what everyone is telling me. Thanks be to God." He cast a questioning eye at Howe, who merely nodded and smiled.

"Good. We have much to discuss." Cardinal Lombardi turned to Howe. "Do you know when our good Bishop's going to be discharged?"

"Perhaps in a couple of days, but," Howe shifted his gaze to McCarthy, "You'll have to take it easy for some time; even though we were able to move you out of ICU, you're still in early recovery. There's going to be some physio and you're not entirely out of the woods yet with regard to that wound. Your body's suffered severe trauma. We had to do a lot of reconstruction, you remember." Everyone, including McCarthy, nodded.

Cardinal Lombardi smiled at McCarthy and gave him an affectionate pat on the arm. "We've got plenty of time to talk. You remain in our prayers. For now, though, it's good to see you on the mend." Lombardi looked deeply into McCarthy's eyes. "I think it's important that we leave you to catch some rest. We'll talk in a couple of days."

As Lombardi and Case left the room, McCarthy let out an almost inaudible sigh of relief. He closed his eyes and sank back into his pillow. Howe checked his chart, jotted a few notes, and then noticing the Bishop's closed eyes, quietly left the room.

There was going to be hell to pay, McCarthy thought to himself as he slipped into a fitful sleep.

CHAPTER 49

New York City, December 12, 1999

Jackson entered McCarthy's office where Bishop Case had arranged for him to meet the Cardinal. Why, he wondered, do all church offices look alike—dark woods and somber details—and have the faint, though not unpleasant mixture of incense and beeswax?

The Bishop and a very distinguished cleric stood as he entered the room. Jackson figured from the way they were dressed that the latter must be the Cardinal. Momentarily, he caught sight of another priest, a swarthy man, lurking in the shadows. Instantly the man averted his eyes and turned away, but not before the perceptive lieutenant noted the wild tic animating the side of the man's face. "He oughta get that fixed," thought Jackson to himself. "Makes him look guilty as hell about something. Jackson's attention was pulled back by the Bishop's voice.

"Lieutenant Jackson, I'd like you to meet Cardinal Lombardi. Prefect of the Congregation of the Doctrine of the Faith—the principal theologian of the Catholic Church," he explained. "And this is Father Fraccaro, also from the Vatican."

"Morning. Nice to meet you." Jackson extended a hand to the Cardinal. He noticed that Fraccaro moved away from the trio in obvious deference to Lombardi and Case. At least, that's what he assumed.

"Good morning, Lieutenant. How good of you to meet with us. Bishop McCarthy has kindly arranged for me to stay in his rooms here in the City." Jackson looked toward the back of the room. The other priest, obviously an assistant of some kind, took a seat in the corner and was quickly preoccupied with writing in a leather notebook. Jackson returned his focus on the other two men.

Case got right down to business.

"Lieutenant Jackson, His Eminence is on a fact-finding mission. He's eager to learn about the progress of your investigation—and particularly to glean any information that you may have about the Scroll."

"Sure, but first, pardon my ignorance, you said the Cardinal was the head of what exactly?"

"The Congregation of the Doctrine of the Faith," repeated Bishop Case.

"Perhaps I should explain," said the Cardinal patiently.

Case nodded and sat back in his chair.

"The Catholic Church all over the world is run from the Vatican, which you know is a sovereign entity, separate from the country of Italy. There are a number of offices within the Vatican that make policy for the Catholic Church all over the world. One of these is the Congregation of the Doctrine of the Faith. The CDF, as we call it, is responsible for everything that concerns the teachings or the doctrine of the Church."

"You mean that it lays down rules that govern all the Catholics around the world?"

"You could say that?"

"That makes you a very powerful man," said Jackson. The priest in the back of the room shot a glance of distain at the cop. Jackson ignored him.

"I prefer to see it as having a lot of responsibilities rather than power." said Cardinal Lombardi.

"I see."

"Can you tell the Cardinal anything you've learned so far about the shooting and the kidnappers who took the Scroll?" said McCarthy.

"Sure." Jackson settled in and stared directly at the Cardinal. "Well, with the exception of the theory that the members of a satanic cult are at the bottom of the kidnapping, we haven't been able to identify the person or persons responsible."

"I see. May I ask, how close are you to making an arrest in Bishop McCarthy's shooting?"

"Quite close. You know that there was an attempt on Bishop McCarthy's life after he was admitted to hospital. I was able to positively identify the woman who tried to kill him. She's been a wanted fugitive for quite sometime time now. It is only a matter of time before we apprehend her. I believe that if we bring her in, we'll also find the men who shot Bishop McCarthy and kidnapped the others."

"And these are the men who have the Scroll?"

"Either that or they may know who has it, "said Case.

"There is one more twist in the whole scenario that I should bring to your attention," said Jackson, ignoring the officious Case.

"What's that?" said Cardinal Lombardi.

"When the Monsignor's friends identified the man who initially had the Scroll, they called both the Bishop and me, leaving messages for us concerning the address of this Bailey person. The kidnappers followed him to Mr. Bailey's home. I think that the only way the kidnappers could have found the location almost at the same time as we learned about it is if they had first-hand knowledge about the discovery of Bailey's identity. They needed instant access to the information—which led me to believe that our phones must have been bugged."

"Really?" said Case.

"I had all our phones and our offices checked for bugs. The only bugs that we uncovered were in Bishop McCarthy's office and residence—right here."

"Someone bugged *these* phones and *this* office? How could that be!?" Bishop Case sounded incredulous.

"Affirmative. I believe that it was done by someone close to the bishop, someone who knew that you were searching for the Scroll," said Jackson. He glanced at Case. The third man in the room, Jackson noticed, shifted uncomfortably in his chair.

"That's a serious allegation, Lieutenant. There are only a few people who know about the Scroll," said Cardinal Lombardi.

"Just McCarthy, Reverend Boyle, Bishop Case and Cardinal Lombardi."

"There's no other explanation?"

"So you're saying it could be any of us," said the Cardinal calmly.

"Excluding the Cardinal, of course," interjected Case, nervously, "Why, he wasn't in the country, so he can't be the implicated!"

"Maybe."

"I beg your pardon! What do you mean, *maybe*?" challenged Case.

"He may not have been here, but he could've got someone to do it." The lieutenant's gaze never left the Cardinal's face. Lombardi didn't react.

He paused, then added, "I'm not saying he did, but that's a possibility I can't overlook."

"This is all very distressing," said Cardinal Lombardi.

"I think this person, the one who planted the bugs in the Bishop's office, alerted the kidnappers after the discovery of the identity and address of our man Mr. Bailey. The man who had the Scroll. I believe that if we find this person, we'll also be led to the kidnappers and the Scroll." Jackson's eyes wandered to Fracarro and this time the rodent-faced priest ignored the cop's gaze.

"Is this place still bugged?" Case fretfully cast his eyes around the office.

"No, it's clean."

"How do you propose to find this person?" said Cardinal Lombardi.

"I'm not sure...yet. But, rest assured, my staff is working on it."

The meeting concluded a few minutes later. Jackson made a mental note to find out more about this man, Fraccaro.

CHAPTER 50

New York City, December 15, 1999
"Lieutenant...?"
"Yeah, John?"
Jackson raised his gaze from the file before him to see one of his staff at his office door. Beside him was a woman carrying a parcel.
"Lady's here to see you. She asked specifically for you."
"Please come in ma'am." Jackson rose, shook hands with the woman and gestured for her to take a seat.
The woman sank into the chair with a sigh as if the parcel she carried weighed a great deal. She appeared to have been crying and dabbed her eyes with a bunched tissue.
"Can I get you anything—some coffee, water?"
The woman shook her head. "I'll be fine," she said softly.
"What can I do for you?"
"My name is Nancy Marshall. I work for Mr. Bellamy," she sniffed, lowered her eyes, then added, "the private investigator."
"Oh—Rudy. I know Rudy. Real sorry about his death. Heard he had a heart attack at the airport. You're his assistant?"
The woman nodded.
"That's why I've come. You see," her voice lowered to almost a whisper, "I don't think he really had a heart attack."
"You don't? What gave you that idea?" he prodded gently.
"Maybe...I mean...I'm not making sense. What I mean is the heart attack wasn't natural...or...whatever. I...I think he has murdered," she stammered. She raised her head and looked pleadingly at Jackson, tears welling.
"Why do you think that?" Jackson asked gently, leaning forward on his elbows.
"Well, ah, we have a lot of clients you see, and...uh...some of them like to remain anonymous—you know what I mean?"
"Yeah, I do. That's kinda common in Rudy's line of work—mine too for that matter."

"Well, we have this wealthy client, we only know him as Mr. J. He occasionally gives us work and then he pays us. He pays very good money. We don't ask any questions about his identity. And," she hastened to add, "he's never asked us to do anything illegal."

Jackson nodded. This was going to take time, but his gut told him it was important. He watched her carefully, trying not to intimidate the woman who was obviously struggling to get out the whole story. Something told him it was a story he needed to hear.

"Well, some weeks back, this Mr. J. called and wanted Rudy to find out some information about a property in the city. He wanted to know who lived there. Well, Rudy started work on it and then...I noticed he became very...ah, uncomfortable...with the assignment. He told me once that he had a bad feeling about the job. Well, he finished the work..."she paused, "and then he mailed all the information about the person who lived on the property to this Mr. J." Jackson nodded for her to continue.

"Shortly after that Rudy became very withdrawn. Like...he rarely spoke at work and he stopped joking around like he used to. Of course, I didn't think much of it at the time. Then on the same day that he got the heart attack at the airport...earlier, like...he called me and told me he was going away for about a month. He'd never done anything like that before...just go like that, I mean. I remember thinking that he seemed really jumpy about something—and it kinda scared me too because he wouldn't tell me what it was.

"But what really scared me was..." she gulped, and looked directly at Jackson, "he asked me to keep the duplicates of the information he had gathered this last time for Mr. J. He asked me to put it in his safety deposit box...I've got the key...and it really weirded me out because he said I should give this file to the police if he didn't return in about a month—or—if something *unusual* happened to him."

The woman dropped her eyes and stared at her hands resting on the package on her lap. Jackson thought he detected a shiver rattle through her slim frame.

"Be cool," he thought to himself. "This gal's really frightened." Something in his stomach churned again.

"I see. That's what brought you here," he gently prompted.

"First, I thought he had died naturally," she wailed, "but then it all seemed too convenient—him getting a heart attack just before he got away...like, got away from whoever was scaring him."

"I see. You think someone scared him."

"Yeah…I mean, yes sir. That was when I decided to bring the documents to you."

"OK. Let's have a look at them."

Nancy Marshall quickly handed the package over to Jackson seemingly relieved that she'd rid herself of an onerous duty. She watched anxiously as Jackson put on latex gloves and carefully opened the package. Page by page he scanned the documents.

"Did he discuss the case with anyone else?" he asked as he continued to leaf through the pages.

"Not really…I mean I don't think…oh yeah! Craig. Craig Emond. He helped Rudy get some IRS documents that told us about the person who owned the property."

"Do you have any idea what this person, Mr. J, was looking for?"

"No. We were just asked to find the name of the person who lived at the address."

"47 Dovercourt Avenue?"

"Yeah…I mean, yes, sir."

"I see from this that a corporation's listed as the owner."

"That's right. That's why Rudy went to see Craig Emond. He thought the IRS returns for the corporation would show the names of the people running the corporation."

"I see. It looks like I may have to speak to this Craig Emond. You say he's at the IRS?"

"Yeah. The Manhattan Office."

"OK. I'll look into this Ms. Marshall. Thank you for bringing it to us. You did the right thing. Here's my card. Phone me if there's anything else that you recall later about this file or Mr. J. or Rudy. Right? Don't hesitate to call me."

She stood to leave, breathed in deeply and looked gratefully at the card then at Jackson. "Thank you," she whispered, visibly relieved and composed.

Jackson escorted her to the exit, shook her hand, and returned to his office.

Jackson placed the documents on a table and carefully read each page. They all related to a company called Tricom Limited and, at face value, seemed quite innocuous. There was nothing in them that pointed to anything sinister or seemed to implicate the death of Rudy Bellamy. From years of experience, however, Jackson had learned not to disregard things that appeared obvious. Jackson believed that there was a connection between the death of Rudy Bellamy and Rudy's prior investigation into Tricom Limited. He trusted his instincts.

Jackson also knew not to believe in coincidences. Coincidences, as he always said, were nothing more than providence pointing in the direction that he needed to look. Jackson didn't believe that it was merely coincidental Rudy Bellamy's death was suspicious—at least according to Nancy Marshall—and that this emerged at the time he was investigating the murder of Gerald Woodward, the kidnapping of Stephen and Sarah, and the attempted murder of Bishop McCarthy. Intuitively he knew that they were all linked in some way. He didn't know how, but he intended to find out.

Jackson rose stuffed the bundle of documents back into the envelope and headed for the door. He needed to speak Mr. Craig Emond...fast.

⚜

"Hello, Master. We may have a problem."

"What is it?" The Messenger sounded exasperated. She'd grown increasingly agitated and frustrated at the ineptitude of her minions. The hospital incident had left her rattled; she'd come too close to being discovered. If they had done their work well, she wouldn't have had to place herself in such jeopardy. A stream of obscenities filled her head and she glared at the emissary cowering in front of her desk.

"Well?"

"Master, I have just learned from our police contact that a bundle of documents concerning Tricom Limited and 47 Dovercourt Avenue were delivered there this afternoon."

"Who delivered the documents?"

"It would appear that the deceased private investigator kept a copy to be handed to the police in the event that anything happened to him. They were delivered to the police by his assistant—to Lieutenant Jackson."

"Damn!" The Messenger slammed her fist onto the desk and plunged into silence, fuming within.

After several minutes, the man said, "I await your instructions, Master."

"Who else knows about the information contained in the documents delivered to Jackson?" she snapped.

"Apart from him, the man called Mr. J., Craig Emond, an employee of the Internal Revenue Service, and a Ms. Marshall, the private investigator's assistant." The man counted the three people on his fingers as he named them.

"Forget the assistant and Emond. The only loose ends are the police and Mr. J. Now that we've recovered the Scroll, our mission must not be placed in jeopardy. Mr. J. and the policeman in charge of the investigation must be eliminated—the cop immediately. I have my own plan for Mr. J."

"It shall be done, Master."

꘎

"Craig Emond?"

"Yes." Emond glanced up from his paperwork.

"Lieutenant Jackson, NYPD. Got time for a little chat?"

Emond's face flushed. "Sure. What about?"

"Rudy Bellamy. I understand he came to see you regarding one of his recent investigations."

"Am I in any kind of trouble?" He dropped his pen on the paper and held his head in one hand. "I knew helping him would get me in trouble," said Emond.

"Look. You're not in any trouble, I just need to know something about a certain investigation—the one where he asked for your help."

"Right. OK. He came to me and wanted to know the owners of some property in the City, very expensive property. He said he'd found that the owner was an offshore corporation registered—in Guernsey, I think—and since he couldn't go to Guernsey, he figured that I'd have some information in our tax files."

"Like?"

"Like who wrote the checks to pay the property taxes, that sort of thing. A name or a local address."

"So what did you find?"

"Nothing really."

"Nothing?"

"Yeah. I knew that we wouldn't find anything even before I searched the files. I told him so. And I was right. There's no one listed in the tax records, the taxes are paid directly by wire transfer from a Swiss Bank. Corporations like that are registered offshore—usually because they want their affairs kept secret."

"I see. Did you discuss any other matter?"

"No, just that. Can I ask a question?"

"Sure."

"Why all the questions if I'm not in any kind of trouble?"

"Let's put it this way. Questions have been raised about the circumstances surrounding his death and I am making a few inquiries."

"Really. I see."

"Is there anything else that you think I should know?"

"Like what?" Emond was hesitant, defensive.

"Anything else that you may have discussed. For example, did he express any doubts or fears about his investigation?"

"Not really. Nothing I can put my finger on..." Emond paused, brow furrowed. "Wait a minute. Yeah, he did. Just before he left, I mean just before he was about to catch a flight, he mentioned something that seemed a little strange. I mean, I didn't think so at the time, but now that you're here..."

"What did he say?"

"He called me from the airport. Told me that he was going to lie low for a while. Said his investigation had ruffled a few feathers. He suggested that I should also consider lying low for a while. Scared me at the time, but I didn't think about it much after a day or so. That was just before he had the heart attack, I think. I just thought he was being paranoid or dramatic or something. You know? I just didn't take it too seriously after I thought about it some. Wasn't until a week or so later I heard he'd had a heart attack. Figured—too bad—I had nothin' to worry about. I didn't see a connection or anything..."

"I see."

"Oh my God, I get it! You don't think he really died of a heart attack, do you?" Emond's voice faltered' he looked scared. Jackson saw a thin film of sweat break out on the man's upper lip.

Emond gulped; his voice came out with a small squeaking sound. "You think he was murdered don't you?"

"Like I said, some questions have been raised about his death and I'm making a routine inquiry."

"Oh God, do you think I'm in any danger!" Agitated, Emond half rose from his seat.

"I can't say, Mr. Emond. Anyway, you've been very helpful. If there's anything more you remember, give me a call." Jackson handed Emond his business card and headed for the door.

"Wait! There's one more thing—I'm sorry—it just came to me." Emond lurched around from behind the desk and stood in front of Jackson.

"What is it?"

"We also found out that the corporation, Tricom Limited operates a charity called 'The Brotherhood of the Ram.' It's in the tax records."

Jackson pondered this last bit of information. "Do the tax records say what this charity does? How it operates?"

"No. I never heard of it before this."

"Well, thanks. Let me know if anything else comes to mind. Take care." Jackson walked out of the office, leaving a pale and clearly shaken Emond.

Two men chatted in the hallway outside Emond's office. Jackson nodded to them as he walked by and headed for the elevators, so preoccupied he didn't notice that their eyes followed him until he entered the elevator.

Jackson exited the elevator into the underground garage, his head filled with questions. After the talk with Craig Emond, it was clear that Rudy Bellamy had been afraid for his life—just as Nancy Marshall had suggested. It didn't take a rocket scientist to connect the dots. Rudy's investigation had unearthed a secret, something that had more than ruffled a few feathers. Rudy had most likely been killed to silence him—but from telling what? And what did this Brotherhood of the Ram have to do with anything? He'd better check that out with the Monsignor.

Jackson got into his car and rested his head against the headrest. Questions flooded his brain. What was the secret Rudy had stumbled upon? Did the answer lie within 47 Dovercourt Avenue? Had Rudy been killed to preserve some secret about the owners? Were Stephen, Sarah and Bailey being held at 47 Dovercourt Avenue property? That was a huge leap, but somehow it didn't seem like it at the moment. And what about this Brotherhood of the Ram? Did it have anything to do with the satanic cult Stephen and Sarah had gone on about? Jackson figured there were links between the answers to these questions—but what was the common factor? Jackson sighed. He'd find out soon, he told himself.

Jackson inserted the key into the ignition and turned it. There was a whirring sound and the engine coughed but wouldn't catch.

"Damn," Jackson hissed as he pumped the gas pedal and cranked the key again. Nothing.

Suddenly Jackson's years of experience took over. The hair on the back on his neck rose and his heart pounded against his chest. He threw open his door, tumbled out and raced away from the vehicle.

A second later, the car exploded into a billowing fireball. Deafened by the blast, and scorched by the intense heat, Jackson was hurled six feet into the air and slammed against the concrete. His hands flew to cover the back of his neck. Dust and debris rained down on his prone body. He crawled a few more feet away from the inferno. A secondary explosion from another car next to his sent him sprawling in front of the elevator doors. He dodged into a stairwell and sank to the floor behind the steel door. Sirens began to sound throughout the building.

After his nerves steadied and his hearing returned, he stood and looked through the door's reinforced window. Emergency vehicles and a fire crew had come on the scene. Foam engulfed the burning bits of metal and rubber that used to be his car. The damaged cars on either side of his smoldered—blackened shells.

Jackson knew that his hunch about Rudy's death and how it connected to this case had just been elevated into fact. This was all the confirmation he needed. Someone wanted him dead.

That could only mean one thing: he was on the right track.

CHAPTER 51

New York City, December 19, 1999

When the phone rang Mr. J. dropped the book on the seat beside him and swiftly reached for the receiver. He'd been expecting the call and paused momentarily to steady his nerves.

"Hello?"

"Hello. I'm at the Sheraton, 790, 7th Avenue at 51st Street. Everything ready?"

"Yes. I'm supposed to call when we're ready to meet with them."

"What is the number that you are supposed to call?"

"716-444-7659."

"Good. Call and advise them that we're ready to meet this evening. I'll let them know where later. Meet me in the hotel lobby in one hour."

"How will I know you, Your Eminence?"

"You shall be contacted."

"I shall be there, Your Eminence."

"One more thing, Mr. J." the voice paused, "I'll dress informally—no cassock or clerical."

About an hour later at The Sheraton Mr. J. emerged from a taxi wearing a dark jacket over a tan shirt and pants. He paid the driver and then walked into the lobby. He stopped and surveyed the busy scene. Excitement rippled through his body. Finally he was going to meet the man he knew only as "the Cardinal." Nervously he clenched and unclenched his clammy hands then wiped them on his cords. He inhaled deeply to calm himself and headed towards a bank of couches surrounding a glass coffee table with an over-sized silk floral arrangement. Several people had already clustered there. As he sank into the couch furthest from the other people, he made eye contact with the men who appeared to be on their own and flashed a nervous smile just in case any of them could be the Cardinal. The men all looked away and he settled in to wait for his client.

Mr. J. shifted nervously in his seat. Soon, he'd never have to be uncomfortable again. Soon, he'd have his hands on the most powerful document in the world. Power. Wealth. Feeling himself becoming giddy with anticipation, Mr. J. consciously stopped his speculations and focused on one sobering thought. After delivering the Cardinal and obtaining the Scroll, he'd have to dispose of the Cardinal. His brow furrowed; justifications flooded his mind. "Had to be done," he reasoned to himself, practicing the rationale. His pulse quickened as images of spectacular wealth and power once again flooded his mind.

"Excuse me sir." Mr. J. glanced up at the concierge standing before him. The man, balding and dressed in a navy suit and tie leaned close to Mr. J. and said softly, "Sir, I've been asked to escort you upstairs. The Cardinal is waiting." The man smiled, but his black button eyes remained impassive. Light glinted on his gold nametag with engraved letters next to the Sheraton logo. There was something vaguely familiar about the man, but Mr. J. couldn't quite put his finger on what it was.

"Oh. Thank you." Mr. J rose and followed the uniformed man to the elevators. The concierge pushed the button and stood slightly in front of him as they watched the illuminated numbers over the doors descend. Shortly, the doors opened and they entered. Just as the elevator was about to close a woman scuttled towards it. The concierge politely but firmly blocked her entry.

"Sorry madam, this car is going to the penthouse. Please use the next elevator to our right." The doors silently slid closed on her astonished face. Mr. J. swallowed hard. Too late to turn back now. This is what he'd been waiting for. He chided himself for having a case of nerves.

The concierge inserted a card into a slot and pushed a button. The elevator responded instantly. Mr. J. glanced at the numbers on the panel and noticed that there were no letters signifying the penthouse.

"There's a penthouse?" Mr. J. turned to the concierge.

"Oh yes."

"It's just that I noticed that there isn't a button for the penthouse on the elevator panel."

"That's right. Our penthouse doesn't have a separate floor like some other hotels. The third floor in this hotel is the topmost floor and one of the rooms is designated the penthouse," the concierge smiled.

Mr. J. noticed the man's shoes were brown and didn't match the quality of his suit.

"I see." Mr. J. turned and stared at his face in the elevator's reflective doors. As the elevator ascended, Mr. J. grew uneasy. Something was wrong. He glanced at the man's reflection. Standing slightly behind him, the concierge's facial features, contorted by the uneven surface of the elevator door, stared back at him. A facial tic contorted the image even more. Something was terribly wrong.

And then he knew.

It was the voice—the voice of the man Mr. J. knew as "the Cardinal."

Without warning Mr. J. saw the concierge lunge at him, arms held like a great bird over his head. Instantly he felt a thin wire bite into his throat and pull him backwards. Gurgling sounds clogged around his thickening tongue as he clawed at the sides of his neck. His feet kicked and bucked in a desperate attempt to free himself, but all to no avail. The man's grip was like a vise and the pain was excruciating. Soon he felt himself weakening and the light in the elevator began to fade. Then darkness and silence flooded his brain.

In one swift motion, the concierge towered over the dead body of Mr. J. and removed the wire from his victim's neck. He slowly coiled the wire around the wooden handles and slipped the weapon into his pocket. He pushed the *STOP* button on the elevator panel. With a jerk, the elevator came to an abrupt stop at the second floor. The concierge, the same man Mr. J. knew as "the Cardinal," stepped out of the elevator, pulled down a fire alarm toggle, and disappeared into the closest emergency exit as alarms began to sound.

Outside the Hotel, the man pocketed the brass nameplate. Purposefully he punched numbers into his cell phone as he strode away from the hotel. Approaching sirens filled the air as he flagged a taxi and slipped inside. He barked an address to the cabbie; the number he'd dialed answered.

"Hello this is the Cardinal." He paused. "You wanted to meet with me. I have the money for the Scroll."

"What about Mr. J.?"

"Unfortunately, he is indisposed and will not be able to make it," said the man.

CHAPTER 52

New York City, December 20, 1999

The air was crisp and the sky a pearly overcast. The bench on the grounds of the Parish of Manhattan wasn't the most comfortable meeting place in the City—but it was, for the moment, the most secure. Jackson and Andy flanked the Monsignor.

"Thanks, guys, for coming," said Jackson.

"Any developments, Lieutenant? I'm afraid my young friend is getting quite discouraged," said the Monsignor.

"Actually, yes. I may know where Stephen, Sarah and Michael Bailey are being held."

Andy's head shot up and he leaned toward Jackson. "Really!?" he said.

"Yeah. A few days ago a woman came to my office with documents she had been asked to deliver to me in the event that her boss, a private investigator, met with an untimely death. The investigator had been instructed by an anonymous client, a man known only as Mr. J., to identify the property owners here in New York. It appears that during the course of the investigation this investigator uncovered some sensitive information and created a few unwanted ripples.

"The private investigator decided to lie low for a while. But not before asking his assistant to make copies of the file and bring them to me if something happened to him—which did—he's dead. Well, when I got the file, I made a few inquiries. It turns out that the owners of the property operate a charity called the Brotherhood of the Ram."

"*The Watchers*," said the Monsignor definitively.

"So that's who they are! That was my next question. Monsignor, your answer just made a few more pieces drop into place. The address of the property is 47 Dovercourt Avenue—big mansion. Mean anything to either of you?"

"Is that where Mom and the others are being held?" asked Andy anxiously.

"Yeah kid, I think so. Everything points to it."

"The address means nothing to me. So what are you going to do?" said the Monsignor, his sightless eyes scanning the air between himself and Jackson. His agitation was subtle, but evident.

"I intend to obtain a warrant and organize a night raid on the premises using a select group of officers. You must keep this information between yourselves. I don't want anyone tipping them off if that is where they're based. May take me a day or two to get the warrant; meantime, I've assigned a surveillance team to keep watch on the property."

"Certainly," said the Monsignor.

"Have any idea who this Mr. J. is?" Andy said.

"Not yet."

"There is one thing of which you should be aware before you conduct this raid," cautioned the Monsignor.

"What's that?" said Jackson.

"If the address is the location from which the Messenger operates, it will not be easy getting in or out."

"It's OK, Monsignor, My men are trained in this sort of thing," said Jackson.

"I am not referring to your expertise to conduct the raid. Although you and your men may be experienced policemen, you will be entering the domain of a demon. The evil one. A supernatural creature. The perils that you will encounter will be very different from anything you've ever experienced."

"We'll be well armed and..."

"Don't you understand? Your weapons will be useless should you come face to face with the Messenger," interrupted the Monsignor.

"What do you suggest?" said Jackson, frustration creeping into his voice.

"Take this along with you." The Monsignor delved into his pocket and brought out a palm-sized silver crucifix.

"What am I supposed to do, point it at her when she approaches?" Jackson snorted. "Doubt if it'll be of much use. It's not as if we're hunting some vampire," he laughed.

"Do not make light of this, Lieutenant. And do not scorn my advice or enter that place on your own power and understanding—or you will fail. Take this. You will know what to do when the time comes. I also suggest that you take Andy with you. He may not be a policeman, but he may be the only one who will know how to save you should you come face to face with the Messenger."

"I don't know, Monsignor. It could be dangerous." Jackson cast an uncertain glance at Andy.

"I've been in more dangerous situations, Lieutenant Jackson."

Jackson was surprised by the sudden stillness in the boy. A wave of maturity seemed to suddenly replace the anxiety that had been etched on his face moments earlier. The transformation startled Jackson. He was silent for a minute, then quietly spoke.

"Well, under normal circumstances I wouldn't allow a civilian to go in with us, but I agree this isn't exactly a typical situation. OK I'll take you along, Andy, on one condition—that you stay close to me and avoid any heroics. This isn't a Hollywood movie. These are real bad guys and there's certain danger. If we find your Mom and the others, you'll let us do the rescuing, right?"

"Sure, I understand," said Andy. "I think I can help you, though. I've been through this kind of a situation against The Watchers before. I know what to expect in ways that you might not."

"Right. I'll let you know when we're going in and then you can come."

Jackson slipped the crucifix in his pocket, took his leave of the Monsignor and Andy, and headed for his car.

Although Jackson believed that the Scroll was linked to Woodward's murder, he still had a hard time believing in this mumbo jumbo about the supernatural. In his mind, there were more earthly matters to attend to. The crucifix weighed heavily in his coat pocket. His fingers played over its smooth cool surfaces. "What the hell," he thought, "may as well cover all the bases."

He assured himself he'd taken the crucifix and agreed to take Andy along only because he didn't want to hurt the Monsignor's feelings. This supernatural angle just wasn't playing with him; but he'd humor the guy. The kid, well, he'd have to think about actually letting him into the premises when he and his guys went in. More than likely he'd keep Andy outside the perimeter with the rescue unit where he'd be safe.

Still, Jackson couldn't totally dismiss the Monsignor's warnings. He wasn't going to take any unnecessary risks and he wasn't going to kid himself about how dangerous this operation was going to be. He'd already come face-to-face with the Messenger in Bishop McCarthy's hospital room.

"*The Messenger*, yeah right," he growled. Jackson had met her all right—and he knew she was none other than Marianne Waters. He still didn't believe that she possessed any demonic powers—despite the Monsignor's passionate conviction. She was agile, a fit woman who had surprised him in the hospital room. Sure she'd caught him off guard, off balance. Yeah, she escaped. But she was an ordinary human, a criminal, and a murderer, not a supernatural power. Of that—he was certain.

Last time, she'd eluded him, but this time, he would be ready for her.

CHAPTER 53

New York City, December 21, 1999

Three dark figures crouched close to the wall that circled 47 Dovercourt Avenue. Several blocks away, in a police situation van, Andy reluctantly waited. Jackson had read him the riot act; he'd be arrested if he tried to follow the SWAT team. Jackson had deployed the team around the house and instructed them to hold down until he gave the order. Ambulances surrounded by police units waited in the dark, ominously silent, their emergency lights extinguished.

Surveillance teams hadn't detected traffic into or out of the grounds for the last twenty-four hours. Jackson had finally convinced a judge that there was probable cause to believe hostages were inside. It'd been an excruciating process that had taken days, but the lack of activity at the mansion had finally pushed the judge to sign the documents and the recovery mission had swung into full operation. He hoped they weren't too late.

Jackson and his team, Joe Lang and Fred Nichols wore night vision goggles, Kevlar vests, and shoulder holsters for their Glock automatics. Each man spoke into a headset monitored by the control center. Their voices, hardly audible, were clearly transmitted into their earpieces. Jackson signaled them to advance to the side of the mansion.

With gloved hands, Jackson clutched a rope coil with a grappling iron at the end. He walked a short distance away from the other two, whirled the grappling iron around his head a few times, then flung it over the wall. There was a muffled thud as the grappling iron hit dirt on the other side. Slowly, he drew it up the wall until its prongs firmly engaged and the rope became taut. He signaled Fred and Joe. They clambered up the rope and over the wall with ease. Jackson followed.

Dropping silently to the ground, they found themselves concealed behind a hedge that ran along the wall. Parting the hedge, they peered at the side of the architecturally impressive structure. A hundred and fifty feet from where they stood it loomed darkly. It was huge—just as the aerial surveillance photos had revealed. In the night, however, it was an eerie, gloomy island, submerged in the total darkness of the landscaped lawns.

There were no lights coming from the windows. Two coach lamps on either side of the front door illuminated the front of the house. Two other low voltage security lights glowed on the northern and southern corners of the house. With the exception of these lights, there was no other light on the grounds. A deathly quiet cast a pall over the entire scene. The only movement was a filmy mist that floated and undulated close to the earth, stirred by an almost imperceptible breath of wind.

A shiver iced down Jackson's spine. He signaled to the others and placed his index finger over his mouth. Through night vision lenses, he surveyed the grounds, looking for security devices. He presumed that an organization that went to such an extent to keep its affairs a secret would have some form of security system in place: guards, guard dogs, cameras or infra red sensors. But, there was nothing—which was precisely what the surveillance had revealed. That worried Jackson. He would have preferred knowing what they were up against.

Having satisfied himself that they were safe to precede, Jackson pulled down the grappling iron, re-coiled the rope and put the apparatus back into his knapsack. He slid the pack onto his back and then crept towards the other two.

"OK, let's move, one at a time—head for the bushes clustered on the southern side of the house. I'll go first, then Joe, and Fred you follow. Any trouble, we signal, right? We'll make our way around to the back, OK?" said Jackson.

The men nodded.

"Right. Let's go."

Each man ran for the bushes, crouched close to the ground behind the shielding tangle of bare branches.

Jackson peered around. The grounds were still quiet. No evidence they'd been detected. He signaled to Joe and Fred to make a run for shadows cast by a tree on the southern side of the house. He brought up the rear. So far, so good. Then with Jackson in the lead, weapons drawn, and with their backs to the wall, they crept towards the back door.

The men soon came upon an extensive garden surrounded by well-placed exquisitely pruned evergreens. A short flight of tiled stairs led from the lawn to a pair of French doors illuminated by a single low voltage lamp. Jackson raised his hand and the other two stopped in their tracks.

He scanned the garden for any sign of activity or security devices. Not hearing or seeing anything, they advanced further into the garden and concealed themselves where they could still have a clear view of the doors. The house interior was inky black and eerily silent.

"Looks empty to me," said Joe.

"Too quiet if you ask me. The place's spooky," Fred whispered.

"Sure there's anyone here?" asked Joe. "Looks pretty vacant."

"That's what were here to find out," said Jackson. Silently he prayed that they hadn't arrived too late.

"We going in by the doors?" said Joe.

"Not my first choice, but I don't see any other way in, do you?" said Jackson.

"What about the other side of the house—a basement window or something," said Fred.

"OK. Joe. You scout the other side—see if there's another way in. Fred and I'll wait here."

"Sure," said Joe as he disappeared into the mist. His voice came through their earpieces a few minutes later.

"There's a ground floor window on this side of the house."

"Let's go," said Jackson.

The two men made their way around the corner to Joe. The single pane window was tall and its sill was close to the ground.

"There's a latch on the other side." Fred.

Jackson slipped the knapsack off his back and removed a small circular glasscutter that employed a suction system. He placed the cutter on the glass and depressed the knob on the handle to fasten the instrument to the window's surface. He rotated another knob to engage the circular cutting blade. When he finished, there was a neat hole in the window.

Jackson inserted his hand into the hole and turned the latch. The window slid open noiselessly. The three men climbed into the dark room. Using night vision glasses, they looked around them.

"Looks like a large laundry room," whispered Joe.

Jackson gestured to the others to follow him through the door. Weapons drawn, they moved forward cautiously, each secretly dreading what they might find on the other side. Reaching the door, Jackson leaned gently on it, twisted the knob and pulled the door slowly open. A thin sliver of light appeared in the crack between the edge of the door and the doorframe. Jackson placed his ear against the crack and listened. Nothing. He slowly continued pulling on the door. As the space widened, they saw what appeared to be a short hallway beside a flight of stairs. It led to a larger room, probably a living room.

Jackson gestured for the others to wait. He crept through the doorway and crouched into the space beneath the stairs. Listening intently, he still could hear no sounds and could see no one. Inside, the house wasn't much warmer than the exterior. He assumed that there was no one home, but was his presumption correct? Too early to tell.

He beckoned to the others, rose from beneath the staircase and made his way carefully into the shadowy silence of the room. The others followed warily, snapping on their flashlights and holding the torches next to their outstretched weapons.

Their light beams raked across an expensively furnished living room with three large matching leather sofas and antique oriental rugs scattered across the hardwood floor.

Jackson walked over to the unlit fireplace. No ashes. The fireplace was clean; the grate was cold.

"What do you think?" Joe whispered.

"Don't know," said Jackson.

"Doesn't look like there's anyone on the main," said Fred.

"Maybe. Why don't we check some of the rooms and see what we find," said Jackson. "Joe, you look around down here. Fred, check to see if there's a basement. I'll take the upstairs."

Jackson ascended the darkened oak stairs. Reaching the landing his light revealed only two doors, one at the end of the hallway and the second about fifteen feet from the top of the stairs. Either the rooms behind these doors were enormous, he thought, or there were more hallways beyond them.

Jackson stopped and listened for sound. Instinctively, he sniffed the air for any indication of flesh decay, that acrid sweet horror. The house was still. He crept towards the first of the two doors. A sliver of pale light played from beneath the door. He placed his ear against the wood. Not hearing anything, he grasped the doorknob and rapidly opened the door. A small desk lamp partially illuminated an extensive library. The room was empty.

He shut the door quietly, and his back to the wall, moved stealthily towards the next door. A few feet from it, a floorboard under Jackson's foot squeaked, shattering the dark silence of the house. Jackson froze. For what seemed like an eternity, he remained where he stood, listening for any noises to suggest that he'd given himself away.

No other sound ensued. No one appeared. He continued, treading warily, towards the second door. Jackson once again pressed his ear against the door. It wasn't fully closed. After a few seconds, he slowly pushed it open.

He found himself in a large boardroom. Heavy drapes immersed the room in total darkness, but with the night goggles he could see a large boardroom table surrounded by matching ornate oak chairs. He stood in the doorway looking around the apparently vacant room.

Suddenly his attention was drawn to a chair at the head of the table farthest away from him. His heart began to pound as adrenalin coursed through his body. The chair had been turned around so that the back of the chair faced the table. What looked like human arms dangled from both of the chair's arm rests. Immediately, he crouched in firing position.

"Police! Place your hands on your head, and turn around, slowly," he called out.

The room remained eerily silent. The arms didn't move. In his earpiece he could hear the sound of Joe and Fred breathing hard as they rushed upstairs. Jackson advanced and stopped four feet to the side of the chair.

His flashlight revealed the motionless form of a man with his head drooped on a bloody chest. Jackson moved closer and played the beam over motionless figure's face. His fingers moved to the man's throat as he checked for vital signs. Nothing. The man's lifeless head fell to the side; coagulated blood drew a thin line from the corner of his mouth to the end of his jaw. A large circle of blood stained his shoulder where the shirt had soaked up the dripping blood.

Just then Fred and Joe burst into the room.

"Hit the lights. This guy's the only person in the house unless you two found something else.

"Nope," said Fred.

"Clear," echoed Joe as he reached for the light switch.

The three men circled the victim's chair.

"Jesus!" Jackson exclaimed, "Just like Woodward!"

The man's black cassock had been torn open at the chest. The massive bloody wound glistened with ripped fleshy edges. Bits of shredded lungs hung within the cavity like torn curtains. Where the heart should have been was a velvety dark space.

Joe gasped. "Shit! What the fu..." He didn't finish the word.

Fred turned away quickly, his shoes slipping on the sticky pool of blood under the victim's feet. "Geeze...how the hell..."

"Who is he?" Joe asked.

"Not sure, but he looks like the Cardinal's assistant—that Fraccaro dude. Funny thing is, he's dressed up just like the Cardinal. Even got the little red beanie."

"What! What would the Cardinal's assistant be doing here?"

"Your guess is as good as mine. This case gets more twisted every minute. I just hope our three hostages haven't met the same fate as this poor son-of-a-bitch."

Jackson's attention was suddenly averted to a large paper Scroll on the table behind Fraccaro's mutilated body. He nudged open the coiled end.

The Scroll was blank, except for two words scrawled in large letters: *Greed! Imposter!*

CHAPTER 54

New York City, December 31, 1999

    Marianne hung the chain attached to the ceremonial dagger around her neck and zipped up a small bag. Her heart seemed to be slamming against her ribs; this was it. Although she known for some time this day would come, fear dogged her excitement. She knew what she had to do, but she didn't know what to expect.

    Her fingers traced over her forehead; the dark burn mark was still there. She sighed, pulled on her coat and walked out of the abandoned house and into the street. Spotting a police cruiser, she immediately bent down and pretended to read the headlines in a nearby newspaper box. When the cruiser passed, she straightened and hailed a taxi. She gave the driver directions. How well she knew the place—she'd been there several times, always waking to find blood on her hands. She shivered at the memory. It would be different after tonight, she reassured herself. The cab pulled away from the curb and merged into traffic. Marianne rested her head on the back of the seat and shut her eyes.

    When the taxi stopped, she opened her eyes, looked at the fare counter, and reached into her purse for some bills. As she handed the man the cash, she leaned forward.

    "Can you get the police on your radio?" Marianne said, keeping her voice neutral. The cabbie glanced at her questioningly.

    "Yeah lady, sure I can. You thinkin' maybe you need to call the cops?" He laughed, obviously not taking the question seriously.

    "OK, this is what I want you to do, and it's very important. When I get out of the cab and you pull away, I want you to call the police, ask for Lieutenant Jackson, OK?"

    "What? You serious? What am I supposed to say to this Lieutenant Jackson," the man challenged. "Look, if he's your boyfriend or somethin'..." irritation dripped in his voice.

    "Tell him that you brought me to this address. My name is Marianne Waters. Remember that: *Marianne...Waters...*," she repeated slowly.

Hey, lady, I ain't no message service. I'm a busy man...got lots to..."

Marianne, voice level, interrupted his rant.

"Look. I'm wanted for murder. Tell him that I am ready to give myself up. Tell him that if he wants to bring me in and stop the killings, he has to be here by nine tonight or it will be too late. Got that?"

Stunned the man twisted in his seat, astonishment robbing him of further protest. He stared open-mouthed.

Marianne reached for the door handle. As she did, her coat opened revealing the ceremonial dagger around her neck.

The driver flinched; his mouth worked wordlessly until he found the words.

"Yeah, yeah! Lady, I'll do what you say—I'll call the police and tell them! Just...please don't hurt me, I got a wife and two kids," the man wailed.

"I'm not going to hurt you. Just call the police and tell Lieutenant Jackson to be here at nine tonight. Thanks."

Marianne had barely closed the passenger door when the driver gunned it and sped away on squealing tires.

⚜

Jackson and Andy were on their way to the station when the police radio crackled. Jackson reached for it.

"Jackson here."

"Hello, Lieutenant," said a female voice. "We just got a call from a cab driver. He sounded pretty frightened. Says he drove a woman to the Park. His passenger said she's going to kill some people and that you're to get there by 9:00 tonight."

"Another prank?"

"Don't think so boss."

"Well, send a couple of cruisers over there. We're following a lead on the psychic and her missing friends."

"You may want to get to the Park yourself, Lieutenant."

"Why's that?"

"Well, the driver said the woman specifically asked him to call you. She gave him your name and said to tell you her name's Marianne Waters."

"Shit!" said Jackson. "OK. Send a couple of cruisers to the Park. Tell them to wait for me. I'll meet them there."

"Right."

"Hold on young man, change of plans." Jackson hit the lights and siren as he stomped on the gas. "Looks like your mum's friend is up to her tricks again. This time I'm going to bring her in—if it is the last thing I do."

CHAPTER 55

New York City, December 31, 1999

The van rolled to a stop in the shadows. Under cover of darkness, two men nudged Sarah, Stephen and Bailey into the cold night. With hands tied in front of their bodies, herded by their captors, the trio lurched awkwardly into a large clump of trees. Behind them, the vehicle sped away.

"Know where we are?" Stephen whispered.

"No. Looks like a park, but I lost my sense of direction while they had us on the van floor. Could be any one of a dozen parks; nothing looks familiar at night," Sarah sighed.

"What's going to happen to us?" Bailey said hoarsely.

"Don't know, we just have to…" Sarah said.

"Quiet," the man with the gun hissed as he butted Sarah's back with the side of his weapon. She stumbled, but kept walking. Bailey, she noticed, began shaking uncontrollably.

As they marched further into the woods, the eerie silence gave way to a hum of voices that grew in intensity as they approached. Soon they emerged from the trees into a large clearing. There an animated collection of people clustered on the perimeter, all dressed in long, shapeless hooded gowns.

As Sarah, Stephen and Bailey were urged forward, a hush fell over the gathering as everyone turned to look at them. The trio were ushered to the side of the gathering and led to a large tree where they were secured with long ropes. The rough bark chaffed their backs as they stood shoulder-to-shoulder facing the clearing. Ropes were wound around their torsos, securing them to the tree. When they were secure, a sprinkle of excited conversations resumed among the cloaked spectators. Tones emanating from their blackened hoods reached the bound victims. There wasn't enough light to see their faces and their words were indistinct. The sounds exposed a controlled fervor, sinister and dangerous.

"We're going to be killed, aren't we?" said Bailey. Fear had drained the color from his face.

"They won't succeed," Sarah said determinedly. "Just try to keep calm. Focus!"

"You have a plan?" Bailey said, hopefully.

"No."

"What are we going to do?" Bailey's voice trembled.

"Just pray, Mr. Bailey. If you know a good prayer, now would be the time to use it," Stephen said.

Sarah shut her eyes and began to pray silently, willing the fear to leave her throat and diaphragm so that she could breathe more easily.

Half an hour later, when the moon was nearly full, a gong sounded somewhere in the distance, and, except for the slight rustling of wind in the conifers, a deathly silence fell over the gathering. Another gong sounded from another place, and the gathering, as a group, turned to their left and bowed in the direction in which the second sound had echoed through the trees.

Sarah, Stephen and Bailey looked in unison to the place the throng faced. Then, they saw her.

The Watcher wore a long flowing white silk gown that, in the light of the moon gave her an ethereal presence. In the moonlight it glowed transparently, revealing that she was naked underneath. She seemed to float toward the gathering with a slow and majestic pace. Her countenance was regal, commanding, filled with tremendous authority. Her blatant sexuality was aggressive, sensual: the image of raw power.

As the Watcher drew close to the gathering, Sarah felt a tingling sensation course down her body and she was filled with an overpowering sense of fear. She knew that despite the angelic beauty of this woman, they were in the presence of a supernatural evil personified.

The Watcher reached the edge of the gathering; the crowd parted as she walked through them to the clearing. At the front of the gathering two men approached her with heads bowed. They draped a black shimmering gown over her head. As the fabric fell to the ground, the scaly texture of the garment slithered around her elegant form. Then she turned to face the gathering. For the first time, Sarah clearly saw her face and let out an audible gasp.

"What's wrong?" Stephen said.

"It's her! Oh My God! It's her," Sarah gasped.

"Who?"

"Marianne! It's her! I saw her face as she turned."

"Are you sure?"

"Yes I am. Oh my God! How could I have been so wrong?" Sarah agonized.

"So she *was* the Watcher after all," Stephen said resignedly.

"How can this be? How could she do this...to us?" Sarah choked back a sob.

The Watcher addressed her followers. Her voice was gentle, yet filled with triumph. She began speaking slowly, but as she continued, her voice increased in tempo and intensity until she was shouting.

"My brethren. It has been a long journey. The time has come. The day for which we have all been waiting is finally here. Today, we reclaim our inheritance. Behold, I hold in my hand the secrets of the power over life and death!"

The Watcher extended the Scroll over her head to loud shouts of approval and applause from the gathering.

She allowed their adulation to wash over her and then signalled for silence. Immediately a hush fell over the gathering. She whirled and pointed to Sarah, Stephen and Bailey.

"Bring me the man who possessed the Scroll," she demanded venomously.

The two guards who had accompanied the trio untied the ropes that bound Bailey and pushed him to the front of the crowd. Bailey struggled and shouted, but to no avail. In the center of the clearing a circle of robed men and women stepped aside to reveal a stone slab. Bailey's shirt was ripped open, exposing his bare chest. He was forced to lie face-up, spread-eagle, his limbs secured to the four corners on the massive rock. A cloth quickly stuffed into his mouth stifled his screams. Wild-eyed, he rocked his head from side to side until a woman stepped forward and dug her fingers into his hair, painfully preventing his head from moving.

As if on cue, the gathering began an atonal chant as they swayed to its rhythmic monotonous phrasing. The Watcher glided forward until she was two feet away from the prone form of Bailey. His chest rose and fell rapidly as the terrified man struggled for breath. His body, rigid with fear, arched above the stone. The Watcher knelt down on one knee beside him and slowly stretched her right hand high above her head. Her arm seemed disproportionately long and muscular. As it reached its fullest extension, the crowd stopped their chanting. An expectant hush fell over them.

Suddenly, the silence was shattered by Jackson's loud voice. All heads whirled to see a powerful light beam of light slice through the thick darkness and envelop the Watcher's kneeling form. Jackson, his gun levelled at the Watcher, stood a short distance away to the side of the gathering.

"Police! Get up slowly and move away from the man with your hands up," he bellowed. Shock undulated through the crowd. The Watcher remained motionless, her hand still clawing the darkness above her.

In the commotion created by Jackson's appearance, Sarah and Stephen's guards rushed toward The Watcher as if to protect her. Andy, who'd concealed himself in the bushes behind Jackson, ran to his mother and Stephen. He began untying their restraints. Once freed, they concealed themselves in the shrubs and watched the unfolding drama.

"One more time, Ms. Waters! Move away from Mr. Bailey! I will not ask again. I am prepared to use force. Now—move!"

To their startled relief, Stephen, Sarah and Andy saw the Watcher move away from Bailey. She rose, both arms now in the air. Sarah chilled when she noticed the woman's features twist into an evil grin.

Then, without the slightest warning, the Watcher violently flung her arms sideways. Jackson's gun and torch flew out of his hands as if struck by some unseen lightening bolt. The Watcher seemed to grow in height and weight before their very eyes. Her left hand extended toward the lieutenant. Jackson, unable to resist the supernatural force emanating from her, was bodily propelled towards the Watcher. When his body came near, she lunged forward, and with a low growl, gripped Jackson by the throat. Effortlessly she raised him off the ground with one hand. Helpless, he dangled in front of her, his feet and arms thrashing, connecting with only air. With a sudden dismissive gesture, the Watcher hurled Jackson by his throat into a tree at the edge of the clearing where he collapsed to the ground with a bone-breaking thud.

Sarah, Stephen and Andy watched in horror as the Watcher's facial features began transforming, morphing into forms unrecognizable as either human or animal. The sounds radiating from her mouth were unrecognizable as anything natural. The meaning, however, was clear: she, or it, was enraged. As soon as the transformation had taken place, it subsided, revealing once again the finely-featured woman. She breathed deeply and smoothed the scales on her robe. They gleamed beneath the caress of her fingers.

Immediately following Jackson's collapse, a powerful wind rattled through the bare branches and swirled in the clearing. The Watcher's head snapped upward in full alert. A powerful voice sliced through the roar of the wind.

I am the Alpha and the Omega, the First and the Last, the Beginning and the end, who is, and who was and who is to come, the Almighty.

As the disembodied voice repeated the phrase, the crowd of Satanists cowered and some covered their heads with their arms. Within seconds they caught sight of a figure at the end of the clearing and turned in unison toward it. There a woman stood alone, dressed in a copper-colored silk gown tied at the waist with a silver rope. A large silver crucifix was suspended around her neck on a gleaming chain.

"Who *is* that?" Stephen whispered from his hiding place.

"I don't know," replied Sarah as she crouched beside him, her arm around her son.

As the trio watched, the woman walked forward. She passed the gathering—no one moved to intercept her—and stood about ten feet from the Watcher.

"You have taken something that belongs to me," she said looking directly at the other woman.

"Who are you?"

"I am what you will never be."

"So, *you* are the one," said the Watcher.

"Yes I am," said the woman. "I demand that you return the Scroll to me."

"You demand? *You demand!*" The Watcher let out a high-pitched snarl. "How dare you. Do you know who I am?"

"Yes I do. I know also that you would have no power unless it was given you by God."

"Silence! And what if I don't give you the Scroll? Do you really think you can take it from me?"

"Yes. I am here to take it from you. And then you shall face the wrath of the Almighty."

A hush fell over the gathering. The hooded assembly looked from one woman to the other. They began to cower and some slipped away, melting noiselessly into the woods.

For a brief moment the Watcher turned away from the copper-clad woman and clenched her fists. When she turned around again to face the woman and the crowd, her face once again transformed—beautifully chiselled human features shrivelled into a demonic face and burning yellow eyes. Beneath the wide openings of her sleeves, her fingers grew into long talons. The crowd gasped; the woman in the copper gown held her ground.

Swiftly the Watcher strode toward the woman and struck her across the face; the force sent her crashing to the ground. Slowly, the Watcher advanced on the dazed woman. As the Watcher drew menacingly closer, two shots rang out and hit the Watcher squarely in the chest. Momentarily she stopped her in her tracks. The bullets had ripped into her chest, tearing at the scaly robe, but no blood issued forth, and the creature seemed only mildly stunned. Jackson stood some distance away, weapon outstretched.

The Watcher reeled in the direction from where the shots had been fired and hurled herself at Jackson. He fired another round but missed. The Watcher landed a short distance in front of Jackson. With an animal-like shriek of rage, she struck him. Jackson screamed in pain as the Watcher's claw-like fingers sliced through his jacked and cut deep gouges on his chest. He collapsed to the ground. The Watcher stood over Jackson for a few seconds as he writhed on the ground. Then she turned and again strode toward the woman who had struggled to her feet.

Suddenly the Watcher hesitated. She saw that the other woman was enveloped from head to foot in an ethereal glow. Her garment glowed like bronze armor.

Ignoring her opponent's changed appearance, the Watcher snorted and continued to advance. Within reach of the woman, the Watcher lunged, simultaneously striking out with her talons. But as the Watcher's hand came into contact with the light surrounding the woman, her arm was propelled backwards by some impenetrable force. She howled in pain. Repeatedly, with increasing intensity, she struck at the woman, but the result was the same: the woman remained untouched, protected by an enveloping radiance.

Having failed in its attempt, the Watcher spun around, and catching a glimpse of Sarah, Stephen and Andy hiding in the bushes, rapidly advanced on them. Having witnessed the failure to harm her opponent, the trio intuitively sought safety with the woman surrounded by supernatural light. They scrambled toward her beckoning arms.

"Stay behind me," the woman shouted.

Sarah suddenly froze. She peered at the woman. Andy caught her hand and pulled his mother toward the woman. Sarah's other hand flew to her mouth in disbelief.

"It's..." she said, shocked into inertia.

"Mom! It's Marianne," yelled Andy. "Come on, keep running, Mom!" Andy pulled on her hand, nearly dislocating her arm. Behind them, the Watcher bellowed in rage.

"It's who?" Stephen shouted, pulling up next to Sarah.

"Marianne!.... It's Marianne...but...how? Wha..."

"MOM! Now!"

The trio began running again and were soon enveloped in the woman's radiant umbrella. Marianne grasped her friend's shoulder and firmly moved Sarah behind her. Stephen and Andy followed suit.

"Later." Marianne shouted as she glanced at Sarah. She turned to see that the Watcher had changed directions and was moving towards them.

"Now all of you must stay behind me. Whatever happens just stay behind me!"

Stephen, Andy and Sarah stood transfixed in terror as the Watcher, with fangs barred and talons spread, advanced slowly and menacingly towards them like a predator stalking prey.

When the Watcher got close, they saw Marianne remove a large dagger shaped like a crucifix from around her neck. Her voice rose clearly in a declaration of her own power.

Yea, though I walk through the valley of the shadow of death, I will fear no evil.

And in one swift movement, she raised the crucifix dagger and stabbed herself in the thigh. Simultaneously the Watcher staggered and shrieked in a combination of pain and fury. She stared in disbelief at the blood flowing from her thigh. An enraged snarl escaped her terrible lips. She took a step towards Marianne, but paused as if reassessing her strategies.

"Ha! Very Clever. How many times can you do *that*?" the Watcher sneered.

"As many times as it takes to kill you," Marianne paused, sucking in air as she too winced in pain. She raised her head and stared at The Watcher.

"I am prepared to die for I know that I shall be raised. Are you?"

With a single jerk, Marianne pulled the dagger from her thigh and once again plunged it into that same thigh. She nearly fainted from the pain. Sarah broke into tears as blood gushed from the wound. The Watcher howled again in pain, fell on one knee and glared at Marianne.

Again Marianne pulled the dagger out of her thigh and held it high above her head.

Unexpectedly, without the slightest warning, the Watcher turned on her heels and rushed to the stone slab and snatched the Scroll.

Holding it close to herself, she ran out of the clearing and disappeared into the woods.

"Quickly, we must follow her! We must recover the Scroll," shouted Marianne. She gasped in pain as she began limping in the direction the Watcher had fled.

Jackson, still bleeding from deep scratches across his chest ran to Marianne, and then stopped short. "I...I...thought she was you...I mean...I get it now, but..."

"It's OK, Lieutenant. There's too much to explain now. We have to get the Scroll!"

"Go ahead, I'll follow. I've called backup to apprehend all these people. Got a chopper on the way. They'll use their searchlight—light this place up like the Fourth!"

Jackson's radio sputtered to life and he barked more commands. Sarah and Andy rushed to Marianne's side. They put their arms around her waist, then, with Stephen in the lead, they supported the limping Marianne and hurried out of the moonlit clearing into the woods. Within seconds, the sound of the chopper blades washed down on them and its powerful searchlight illuminated their path through the trees.

"How will we find her?" Stephen shouted above the roar of the chopper over his head.

"She's here, not far. I can feel her—we'll find her. She'll most likely be making her way back to the parking—she'll try to get away by disappearing into traffic," said Marianne. "She's wounded, so she can't easily morph into other forms. You'll see. She's close by."

"Are you OK, Marianne? Are you sure you can go on like this?" Sarah slowed to a stop and stared at the wound on Marianne's thigh. "My God, your gown is drenched in blood! She looked at Andy. "We've got to do something to stop the bleeding," pleaded Sarah.

"Stephen, wait," Andy called.

Stephen, who was ahead of the others, slowed and rushed back to them.

"We've got to do something about Marianne's bleeding," Sarah repeated.

"She's getting weaker. We've got to make a tourniquet—stop the bleeding until we can get her to a hospital." Stephen took off his jacket, then ripped a sleeve from his shirt. With two long strips of cloth he bound Marianne's thigh.

"That's good, that's good," Marianne said. "Don't worry about me—let's get on with it! No time to lose!" She reached for Andy and Sarah and they hobbled onward.

"Look, I know this isn't the time for long explanations, but Marianne, I just have to ask: why didn't you tell me you had a sister?" Sarah said.

"I didn't know until a few weeks ago. I just knew I wasn't crazy and so I had to find an explanation for the dreams. The only explanation that I could come up with was that someone else was pulling me into these dreams. It had to be a shared consciousness. So, on a hunch, I checked the birth records to see if I had a sister—lo and behold, I did. A twin!"

"You never knew?" Sarah said breathlessly.

"No. I don't even think my adoptive mother knew. She'd have told me. The records showed that we were both given up for adoption at birth. Separate families..."

Stephen suddenly stopped on the trail ahead of them. "Sshh," he said, glancing over his shoulder.

"What is it?" Sarah said.

"Voices. I think that we're close to the edge of the park. I can hear cars too," Stephen said.

"She's close," Marianne said. "Look—blood!"

Just as they emerged from the trees, Stephen heard a rustling and saw a movement out of the corner of his eye. He turned as the Watcher hurled herself at them from out of the darkness. Stephen dove quickly to the side, but the Watcher struck Sarah and Marianne and sent them sprawling. In one fluid movement she caught Andy in a chokehold.

"Let him go!" commanded Marianne. "You don't want him—it's me you're after!" Marianne rose and started towards the Watcher.

"One more step and I'll break his neck!" she hissed. "Who says I need you? I have all I want here." The Watcher shook the Scroll in her raised hand.

"Herein are the secrets of life and death. Do you know what that means? Absolute power! I become not *as* God, but God *Himself*! Can you imagine what that means? How it will feel, to be able to rise from the dead? This is my inheritance. *I* was the chosen one. *The Son of the Morning* they called me. And it was all taken away from me—*fallen from Heaven* they said. Ha! Do you know how long I've waited for this?" The Watcher's face and body contorted with fury.

"You must stop. You don't know what you are doing, The Scroll is more powerful than you can imagine," Marianne said evenly, not taking her eyes from the Watcher.

"Yes, yes! I *do* know its power. And soon that power will be mine to wield. No one can stop me now," she shrieked.

The Watcher slammed Andy to the ground and placed a foot on the youth's neck. Stunned and terrified, Andy remained passive. Hurriedly she began opening the Scroll.

Marianne stretched her hands toward the Watcher. "Stop! I warn you. Don't open the Scroll—you cannot possess it—it is not for you!"

The Watcher sneered, then concentrated on the Scroll. There was no stopping her. In her hands the Scroll unfurled. Time seemed to stand still. Helplessly they looked on as the Watcher's face filled with awe and wonder. The trees around them seemed to vanish and they were immersed in a velvety darkness, separated from the rest of the world, isolated from the rest of humanity.

Almost immediately, a small glow materialized between the Scroll and the Watcher, increasing in size until it encompassed the whole Scroll and the hands and face of the Watcher.

"Andy! Shut your eyes! Turn your face away!" Marianne shouted.

Just as Marianne screamed, the face of the Watcher changed from one of awe and wonder to one of sheer terror. Her hands began to tremor, then shook with uncontrollable spasms. There was an explosion of light and the Watcher screamed, staggered backwards, and dropped the Scroll. Simultaneously her hands and face ignited in furious flames. Instantly, she released her hold on Andy as she tried extinguishing the flames licking at her body.

The scroll snapped back into a compact roll and Andy quickly snatched it from the ground and ran towards the others.

The flames on the Watcher disappeared leaving shreds of blackened skin peeling from her bloodied face and hands. She reached for Andy, but he dodged behind Marianne.

"It's mine! Give me the Scroll!" Her fury was etched with hysteria.

Protectively Marianne shoved Stephen, Andy, and Sarah behind her. "You shall not have the Scroll," Marianne shouted as she pulled a small bottle of water from her pocket and held it high above her head.

"I command thee in the Name of He who created thee, and of His Son, the Christ, to depart and return from whence you came."

Marianne hurled the bottle's contents at the Watcher striking her in the chest.

The Watcher writhed in pain as if the water had scalded her entire body.

Marianne and the others stepped back and witnessed the Watcher raise her hands, throw her head back, and let out an ear splitting roar. Before their eyes, the feminine features of the Watcher underwent a horrendous metamorphosis. She became totally demonic. The beast laughed, walked a few steps toward them and stopped.

"You think some holy water is enough to stop me?" it growled. "*I am* the Messenger. *I am* one with the Master. You cannot stop me!"

Again it advanced on them, but as it moved, two shots rang out. A bullet hit the beast squarely in the chest, but nothing stopped it.

Marianne shrank back, extending her arms behind her back, corralling her friends. She shouted for Jackson, who had fired the shots, to quickly join the group.

"Form a circle around me, quickly," Marianne cried. "Whatever happens—don't break the circle."

Sarah, Stephen, Andy and Jackson quickly obeyed and circled around Marianne as the Watcher approached.

"What do we do now?" Stephen pleaded.

"Pray," Marianne said calmly but firmly.

"What?" said Jackson.

"Pray!" Sarah barked and began reciting the twenty-third Psalm. The others, including Jackson, joined in. The Watcher continued to advance. Marianne stood fearlessly in the centre of the circle, her eyes shut in deep prayer.

Suddenly a golden glow emanated from Marianne's head like a fountain and blanketed them all. Simultaneously, the Watcher rushed forward, murder in its eyes, but it rebounded as if it had struck an invisible wall around the little group. Jackson unwittingly flinched at the sight of the demon bearing down on them and momentarily broke his hold. Andy reached out and gripped him firmly. Again the Watcher charged and was hurled back by the force of the protective light shield.

Then as Sarah, Stephen, Andy and Jackson continued to pray and watch, they lifted their eyes to see Marianne raise the dagger above her head.

"No! Marianne, no!" Sarah shouted, broke her hold and tried to reach out to stop Marianne.

The Watcher turned its attention to Marianne and the dagger held above her. It retreated a short distance away from the group and its countenance shifted again to the figure of a woman. A tiny voice pleaded to Marianne.

"Don't do this Marianne, we are sisters—remember?—twins. We were cast from the same womb." The Watcher's voice became submissive, beseeching.

"You can change me, Marianne, if you want to. It doesn't have to end this way. You mustn't do this Marianne, sister. You'll die, too, Marianne, you know that." The voice became childlike, imploring.

For a second, from the centre of the circle Marianne stared at the pitiful woman. The dagger in her hands never wavered. Tears coursed down face and her body shuddered with a sob.

"Don't cry, Marianne...sister." The Watcher advanced slowly, hands stretched in a gesture of reconciliation.

"Stay where you are. You are the great liar, master of deception. I renounce you!" Marianne screamed.

The Watcher halted in her tracks; a smile crossed her destroyed face and her little-girl voice assumed a mocking tone. "You can't kill me, you know. You'll only send me away for a period of time, and then I'll be back again. I'll be back!"

"This has to end. This is the only way."

With great authority Marianne said in a loud voice, "He that believeth in me, even though he shall die, even shall he live!"

All of a sudden, the Watcher charged the group, and Marianne plunged the dagger into her own chest and collapsed on to the ground. A few feet before reaching the circle, the Watcher buckled into a formless heap, all life extinguished.

"No!" Sarah screamed as she broke the circle and hovered over Marianne's crumpled and bleeding body. Silence encased the group. Paralyzed by all that had happened, the men stood around the sobbing Sarah as she cradled Marianne in her arms. Helpless, they stood in silence.

Before they could move, they heard the sound of wind moving the boughs behind them. They turned to see a section of the woods bathed in white light. Jackson and Stephen looked up to see if the police chopper was above them, but there was no chopper, only the wind. And the light.

Then, they heard the sound of a horse's hooves. Looking again into the forest, they saw a rider clad completely in white emerge from the light. He rode a white horse and held a lance in his right hand. Two men, also clad in white, appeared from either side of rider, approached the Watcher, picked her up, and returned to the light. The man on the horse stared at the prone form of Marianne, turned his horse around, and vanished into a brilliant orb.

"Help, someone! Someone call 911!" Sarah shouted to a small group of people who had gathered at a distance to see what had happened. "She's got a pulse—Marianne's alive!"

Jackson, though wounded, launched into action and radioed for help.

"Let's get her closer to the park perimeter where it'll be easier for the paramedics to reach us. Why don't you and Andy see if you can find someone with a cell to direct the paramedics," he shouted.

As Andy and Sarah ran for help, Stephen gathered Marianne in his arms and with Jackson leading the way, headed for the park's edge. When they reached it, Stephen placed the unconscious Marianne on a bench, removed his jacket, and bundled it up beneath her head.

"Here," Jackson said, "Use my shirt to compress the wound. She could bleed to death before the paramedics get here," Stephen faltered and then held his hands tightly over the gash in Marianne's chest. Blood squeezed through his fingers. He sobbed, but held this hands firmly over the wound.

"Easy, Stephen. Look, I don't think she's going to make it. May have got her heart," Jackson said.

"You could be right," Stephen said, "but I'm not quitting. Marianne! Marianne, can you hear me? Don't go. Stay with me, Marianne!"

Marianne, partly conscious, heard the voice as if it were at the end of a long tunnel.

"Marianne, Marianne."

She tried to rise, but there was a sharp pain in her chest. She raised her hand, touched her gown and felt the saturated cloth. It was sticky. She knew she was bleeding; she could taste blood in her mouth. As she drifted into unconsciousness again, she heard the faint sound of the sirens.

"Marianne, Marianne."

The voice, again. No, it was a different voice; it sounded urgent. She knew it was Sarah. She tried to respond to let Sarah know where she was, but the pain dimmed her eyes and nausea swept through her body.

She began to wonder if this was going to be the end. Through the veil clouding her consciousness, she saw the faces of the people that circled around—they appeared misshapen, staring at her. She saw a man leave the crowd and come to her side.

"Be still, Marianne, we've called an ambulance." His words didn't seem to match his mouth movements. The man's voice was familiar.

"Miriam, Miriam." She heard the voice, again. This time it didn't sound like Sarah's voice. It was different, authoritative. It was a man's voice—and the man had called her *Miriam*. It was a voice and name she recognized. It was her name. It was his voice.

Marianne looked at the man standing beside her. His face was blank. Marianne knew that he was not the one who had called her Miriam—this man hadn't heard the voice that had called her Miriam.

Marianne forced her eyes open. She cast her gaze around the faces of the people standing around her, trying to make out the face of the man who had called her Miriam. But she could not see the man.

Marianne began drifting into unconsciousness when she heard the voice once more. "Miriam. Rise Miriam. Your faith has healed thee."

She opened her eyes again and surveyed the anxious faces—and then she saw him—not a man, but a child in his mother's arms. His little arm extended toward her. Their eyes met and Marianne knew that it was Him, her Master. Healing began to course through her body.

His child's eyes, so innocent and gentle and yet so wise, held her gaze, bore into her, filled her with energy, and willed her to rise.

She pushed herself up on the bench, using her weak arms as levers, until she was sitting.

"You've must lie still," said the man who stood beside her. She could see him clearly now; it was Stephen.

"I want to get up. I must rise, or I'll die," Marianne muttered through the pain. The crowd around her, retreated, giving her room. Jackson was speechless. No one in her condition should be able to move like that. Behind Marianne, he spotted Sarah and Andy running toward them. Cardinal Lombardi and Bailey followed close behind.

Standing on her own, Marianne held the bench for balance. Just as she stood upright, she heard more voices.

"Marianne! Marianne!" Sarah pushed her way through the crowd and rushed to her friend's side.

Instinctively, Sarah threw her arms around Marianne. Marianne winced.

"Oh! Sorry. Can I help? Don't you want to sit down?" Sarah released her hold on Marianne. "Please, Marianne, you shouldn't be standing."

"I'm going to be fine. I saw Him. He asked me to rise. He gave me strength," Marianne said weakly. "I feel stronger already, really."

"Who did you see?" said Stephen.

"The Master," Andy interjected. The group turned to him, looking for explanation.

"Who?" Jackson repeated.

"The Christ. She's seen the Christ," Andy said calmly, a glow spreading across his smiling face.

"Where? Where is He?" Sarah turned quickly and scanned the crowd.

Marianne turned with a grimace and pointed. "Over there, the child with his mother." She indicated the place where the mother and the child had been. "They're gone now. They were there, but they're gone." She smiled.

"Where? I was right here. I didn't see Him," Jackson moaned.

"Jackson, you saw Him but you didn't know Him," Andy said quietly.

Andy's remark hung in the surrounding silence. Stephen and Sarah put their arms around Andy and quietly began praying. The Cardinal crossed himself and sank to his knees. Jackson stared at the spot where Marianne had pointed, then slowly lowered himself onto the bench.

Marianne, exhausted but no longer in pain, no longer bleeding, spoke to the crowd.

"Open your hearts, and one day, He shall reveal Himself to you all." She stood—steady, joyful.

CHAPTER 56

New York City, January 1, 2000

"We found the body of your assistant, Fraccaro, in the home of the Messenger," Jackson said, staring in the direction of Cardinal Lombardi. He let himself fall into the chair beside Marianne's hospital bed. He was bandaged and sore and still looked shaken by the previous night's supernatural encounter.

"My assistant, Fraccaro?" the Cardinal said with obvious astonishment. "What was he doing there?"

Jackson shrugged. "Your guess is as good as mine".

"Did you find out who bugged my offices," McCarthy said.

"I still don't know that. I guess its one of those things that will remain unsolved."

The group had gathered in Marianne's hospital room. She sat up in bed, surrounded by her husband Peter, and her friends Andy, Sarah and Stephen. Lieutenant Jackson, Bailey and Cardinal Lombardi sat in a circle at the end of her bed. The night had taken its toll on all of them, but miraculously, Marianne's wounds appeared superficial and were healing at an unprecedented rate. The Monsignor had joined them and sat contentedly in a corner where he could hear everyone.

"The Scroll! What happened to my Scroll?" Bailey asked. Still shaken from the night's drama, his voice was hoarse.

"I have it here," Andy said softly as he handed it to Marianne.

"Can I have it back?" Bailey's question echoed in the room. He sat back in his chair, chastened by everyone's silence. They all looked at Marianne.

"Before I answer that question, I'm sure you'd all like to know what it says. You all deserve to know after all we've been through."

"Can you read it? Isn't it in Aramaic or some other ancient language?" Bailey inquired.

"Yes. It is in Aramaic."

"Marianne, I didn't know you read Aramaic," Sarah said.

"I didn't know myself until a few weeks ago. I'll give my best translation." Marianne proceeded to unfurl the beginning of the Scroll and began to read.

"I, Miriam of Magdala, beloved disciple of our Master Yeshua, give to the world the secrets entrusted to me by my Master. Let all who have ears hear and know these teachings.

Marianne read the story of Christ's life and death. She continued for some time. The room's occupants remained still as they absorbed a familiar story told in greater detail than ever before. Marianne continued, gently unrolling the scroll as she read. She came to the Resurrection.

I went into the Master's tomb and wept, for they had taken His body away. Then the angels of the Lord came to me and said, "Fear not for He is risen as He said."

I left the tomb in sorrow and fell on the ground in tears.

Then I heard a voice say, Miriam, why do you weep? Whom are you seeking? Do you not rejoice that I have risen?

I raised my head and beheld the Master. I turned to Him with joy, but the Master said, "Cling not to me, for I am yet to go to my Father. But do not weep, Miriam, for as I have risen, so shall you and all who believe in me rise. I go to prepare a place at the side of my Father so that all who believe may have a place at the side of my Father after the resurrection. And upon my return I shall take all who believe with me to the Kingdom of my Father. Go to my brethren and tell them this is so.

Then I said to the Master, "Yeshua, Rabboni. Teach me of life and death and of the resurrection of the body after death of which you speak."

The Master said, "I shall teach you these truths, but you shall keep these truths secret until the coming of the time of the divine in man and not before.

Then the Master Yeshua spoke these words. "There is no death, but death of the body and no resurrection, but resurrection of the divine, the hope and glory of the living."

Then I asked the Master, "Yeshua, but how can this be, for did not Lazarus, whom you raised from the dead, die?"

Then the Master Yeshua said, "The death of the body that we see is but a door that we do not see to the divine: the hope and glory of the living. Death opens the door that the living do not see to the resurrection of the divine. For the death of the body and the resurrection of the divine are one."

Then I asked the Master, "Yeshua, what of your return? How shall we know of your coming so that we may prepare for your return?"

"You cannot know of the day or time of my return, for it is written that even the angels do not know the day or time of my return, only my Father knows the day and time of my return. But know ye this, it shall come to pass in those

days when brother shall war against brother and sister shall be pitted against sister, the sound shall go forth calling for the return of the Christos, the Anointed one. And at the hour when the wheel of time has run its course and a new age shall dawn as night gives way to day, and the Christos returns to walk the face of the earth, then shall I also return. But fear not, for I shall send forth the Counsellor to be with you till my return and He shall comfort you".

Then I asked the Master, "who is this Christos of whom you speak?"

Then the Master spoke these words, "the Christos and my Father are one, as I and the Christos are one."

Then I asked, "how are we to know you, Rabboni?"

The Master said, "the Christos shall neither appear to the King of Kings, nor to the High Priests in the holy temples. For even as a child shall he appear to those whose heart is pure, and with a pure heart and mind strive to see him. To them shall be revealed the glorious face of the Christos in the secret place of the Most High. Ponder on these words I have spoken, for in these words are revealed the secrets of life and death and of my return."

The Master then said "Go now and tell the others that I have risen as I said I would, but do not tell them of these truths that I have revealed to you, but keep them secret until the time of the coming of the divine in man.

"So there is more to the resurrection story than we are told in the Bible. Miriam of Magdala had a lengthy conversation with the risen Jesus," Sarah said.

"Yes, but she did not disclose this to the disciples because Jesus had asked her not to," Marianne said.

"Wow," Stephen said softly.

"So you see, Mr. Bailey, the Scroll is too important to be entrusted to you. Its secrets must be made known to the whole world. But," she paused, "not at this time. The time has not come for its secrets to be revealed."

Bailey nodded. "I understand," he said reverently.

"I agree. Can you imagine what would happen if this knowledge was widely known? I don't think humanity's ready for that yet," Sarah said quietly.

The Cardinal stood and joined the group around Marianne. He outstretched his hands and she placed hers in his.

"So, my dear, from what we've heard you read in this scroll, Mary Magdalene is *the beloved Disciple*—the one John records as *the disciple whom Jesus loved*," said Cardinal Lombardi.

"Yes," Marianne said.

"What does he mean?" Sarah asked.

"One of the questions that have plagued theologians is the identity of the disciple who is referred to as *the disciple whom Jesus loved* in the Gospel of John. Some scholars throughout the ages have maintained that this refers to Mary Magdalene and not John, son of Zebedee, who authored the fourth gospel."

"So the Gospel of John was not authored by John, but by Mary Magdalene?" Stephen said.

"I can't say that for sure, for John was certainly a disciple and he wrote other books of the Bible," Marianne said, "but I believe she is the same person who is also referred to in various places in the Fourth Gospel as *the beloved disciple*."

"But how can that be?" Cardinal Lombardi asked gently. "If you remember, in the account of the crucifixion in the Gospel of John, the beloved disciple along with other women including Mary Magdalene are at the foot of the cross. How could Mary Magdalene and the beloved disciple be one and the same if they are both at the foot of the cross?"

"Well, the Nag Hammadi texts, specifically, the Gospel of Phillip and the Gospel of Mary consistently identify Mary Magdalene, as the disciple whom Jesus loved. I don't think it is mere coincidence that these two texts refer to Mary Magdalene as the beloved disciple in much the same way as the Fourth Gospel refers to the anonymous disciple," Marianne said.

"Well, if the beloved disciple is so historically important that he or she could not be left out of the story, then maybe whoever wrote the Fourth Gospel had a reason for keeping the identity of the beloved disciple a secret," said Sarah.

"Precisely," Marianne said.

"What would be the reason for wanting to keep her identity a secret?" Stephen asked.

"Because the beloved disciple is a woman. Remember that Mary Magdalene was the one who is the first witness of the resurrected Christ. She was instructed by Jesus to go to the disciples to tell them that He is risen. Thus, it is Mary Magdalene—and not Paul, the one who had a vision on the road to Damascus—who is the founder of the Christian church. Christianity was born out of the spiritual communication between the risen Christ and Mary Magdalene. This is the testimony of Mary Magdalene."

Marianne touched the Scroll in her lap. "Such an idea was definitely not welcome at the time—in a patriarchal society. Women had little or no status. In Luke's Gospel, he plays down Mary Magdalene's role and describes Peter as the first one who goes to the tomb to actually verify that Christ indeed has risen. Then he reports that Simon saw the risen Lord."

"So Christianity was born out of the testimony of a woman," Sarah said.

"Yes," said Marianne.

"Well, I'll be..." Jackson said.

"The question is: what do we do with this knowledge?" Marianne asked.

"I could have the text transcribed and then published for all to know the truth," Bailey offered.

"Eventually, I'd like that very much—but for now I don't think the world is ready for this revelation," Marianne said. "Look at all that has happened because of the Scroll. People have been murdered—all in the name of truth. We in this room have seen natural and supernatural worlds collide with devastating results."

"Yes. There has been much havoc and too much blood spilled," Stephen said.

"So what do you intend to do with the Scroll?" Jackson asked.

"I believe that the best solution is to send the Scroll to the Roman Catholic Church—with certain conditions."

"What would those conditions be?" Cardinal Lombardi asked.

"First, that the Catholic Church begin the process of correcting its history and assign Mary Magdalene her rightful place in the Church's History and second, that the Church re-examine its teachings in the light of what is in this Scroll." Marianne stared at Cardinal Lombardi. "Cardinal, you have the authority to convene a meeting with the Pontiff. At that time we can hand over the Scroll and make these requests."

"I believe this could be arranged," said Lombardi, smiling.

Jackson turned to Marianne. "This is all way over my head. I still have one question that hasn't been answered. I'm still wondering about your identity. I know who you are not. You aren't the murderer—though heaven only knows how I'll be able to convince the D.A. of what I witnessed here tonight. I have to ask, *who are you*, really, Ms. Waters?"

"She's Miriam of Magdala," said Andy brightly.

"You don't mean...?" gasped Bailey.

"Who?" said Jackson, thoroughly confused.

"You heard him correctly the first time," said Sarah.

EPILOGUE

Between 1963-1965, fragments of 14 manuscript scrolls were found at the remains of the fortress of Masada, the last stronghold of the Jewish zealots after the insurrection of 70 AD, that had fallen to the Romans in 73 AD. The fragmented scrolls contained parts of the Old Testament, and certain Aprocryphal texts. In 1964, one Donovan Joyce, who had tried to gain access to the excavations at Masada and had been denied permission, was approached by one Max Grosset, who allegedly had gained access to the excavations and had obtained a well preserved scroll purported to have been authored by Jesus, or at the behest of Jesus, maybe by Mary Magdalene. Max Grosset tried to get Donovan Joyce to smuggle the scroll out of Israel. Donovan Joyce refused. The scroll did eventually make its way out of Israel, but it mysteriously disappeared. This scroll purported to have been authored by Jesus or, by Mary Magdalene at the behest of Jesus, has not been found to this day. It is rumored to be in the possession of the Vatican.

In January 2003, Pope John Paul II, recognizing that Mary Magdalene was the first to proclaim the Resurrection of Christ, honoured her with the title *apostola apostolorum*, which means, *Apostle to the Apostles*.

Made in the USA

598450